Erotica

New *X Rated* titles from *X Libris*:

The *X Libris* series:

Erotica Omnibus One

Dark Secret
Marina Anderson

Sisters Under the Skin
Vanessa Davies

Educating Eleanor
Nina Sheridan

LIBRIS

An *X Libris* Book

This omnibus edition first published by X Libris in 1997
This edition published in 2001

Dark Secret copyright © Marina Anderson 1995
Sisters Under the Skin copyright © Vanessa Davies 1996
Educating Eleanor copyright © Nina Sheridan 1997

The moral right of the authors has been asserted.

A CIP catalogue record for this book
is available from the British Library.

ISBN 0 7515 3178 2

Typeset by
Derek Doyle & Associates, Liverpool
Printed and bound in Great Britain by
Clays Ltd, St Ives plc

X Libris
A Division of
Little, Brown and Company (UK)
Brettenham House
Lancaster Place
London WC2E 7EN

www.littlebrown.co.uk

Erotica Omnibus One

Dark Secret

Marina Anderson

Chapter One

'HARRIET, WHERE'S YOUR ring?' asked Ella, her RADA trained voice carrying to every corner of the wine bar.

Harriet blushed and removed her left hand from the top of the table, sliding it out of sight beneath the tablecloth. 'Keep your voice down,' she muttered.

'But where is it?' persisted Ella. 'Surely the ever-efficient Miss Radcliffe hasn't mislaid her impeccably tasteful and priceless engagement ring? What on earth will James say?' she added.

'James won't be worried. I've given it back to him,' said Harriet.

Ella stared at her friend in astonishment and then drained her glass. It was her usual reaction to any kind of shock. 'You mean, you're not going to marry James after all?'

Harriet nodded. 'That's what I mean.'

'But why? You were the perfect couple, and with you at his side James would have gone right to the top. God, I wish I could find a merchant banker to marry me, I can tell you.'

Despite her depression, Harriet laughed. 'Ella, you could never marry anyone like James. You'd die of boredom on your honeymoon.'

'Really?' Ella leant forward eagerly. 'You mean you're finally going to confess the secrets of your sex life together? Wasn't he any good in bed?'

Harriet shrugged. 'He was all right. I mean, he was always very considerate and made sure I was satisfied, it was just that there was never any . . . I don't know, excitement really. I suppose he loved me, but he lacked real passion. I was in bed with him last Saturday and when he turned on his side and his hand went straight to the same place as it always did I suddenly thought, I can't stand this any more; if he touches me there one more time I shall scream. Well, he touched me and I did.'

'You screamed?' Ella was stunned.

Harriet laughed. 'Yes! I actually screamed "*Don't do that*" at him. I felt terrible afterwards. He was so hurt, and kept saying "but I thought you liked it", which I did the first few times. Anyway, that was it really. He said I must be having a breakdown and needed a rest. I said it wasn't that at all; it was simply that I'd finally come to my senses and realised he wasn't the man for me. Then I gave him back his ring and he left. End of story.'

'But the wedding!' exclaimed Ella. 'All those guests, and the presents you've already had.'

Harriet nodded. 'I know. Luckily since my parents are still abroad and weren't even coming they won't kick up a fuss. It's poor James who'll have to cope with his family's wrath.'

'Have you told them at work?' asked Ella.

'There wasn't any need. I went in to work on

the Monday and handed in my notice.'

'Get another bottle of wine,' said Ella. 'This is too much to cope with sober. I mean to say, Harriet, we've known each other for over ten years and in all that time you've never done anything unexpected. You passed all your exams easily, got a wonderful job in the City as PA to a top company director, became engaged to a handsome, wealthy merchant banker and were just about to marry him and produce the requisite son and daughter – in the correct order no doubt – and then you decide to go totally off the rails. That's *my* prerogative. I'm the actress, I'm the one who does outrageous things and you always listen and give me good advice that I ignore. How come our roles have been reversed?'

Harriet's hands twisted together in her lap. 'I don't know. Like I say, it just happened out of the blue. I mean, there has to be more to life, Ella, doesn't there?'

'More what?' enquired Ella, pouring herself a glass of wine from the second bottle. 'Money? Sex? Career? Which particular rejected aspect of your wonderful life were you hoping to improve on?'

'All of them,' confessed Harriet.

Ella looked at her friend. At twenty-three she was a tall, slim, leggy brunette with grey eyes and a cool air of self-possession. This evening, as always, she was dressed impeccably, in a suit with a long-line jacket that ended three inches above the hem of her skirt and a knotted cream silk scarf at her throat. Her appearance suited her life, or the life she'd led until now. Suddenly Ella wondered what hidden depths there were to her friend.

'Right then,' she said briskly. 'If you want to improve them all, where do you intend to start?'

'I want an interesting job; something really different,' declared Harriet.

'Any ideas?'

Harriet pulled a face. 'That's the trouble, I can't think what I want to do, I only know that it has to be exciting and different.'

'Try being an actress,' suggested Ella. 'There's plenty of excitement there. Will I be working this time next week or not!'

Harriet sighed. 'I know I've probably been stupid but I simply couldn't stop myself. It was as though a voice in my head was telling me that this was my last chance. If I didn't stop now, change direction quickly, it would be too late.'

'Stupid or not, you've done it,' said Ella. 'Have you looked for a job yet?'

'I glanced through some adverts in the evening paper, but there wasn't anything that appealed to me. There are several jobs like the one that I had, but there's no point in that.'

Ella dived into the large canvas bag that she always carried around with her. 'Let's see what I've got here. *The Stage* – well that's no good to you, you haven't got an Equity card! *Evening Standard* – you've seen that; *The Times* – let's try that.'

'That won't have anything exciting,' protested Harriet, but Ella was already scanning the situations vacant column, muttering to herself as her eyes raced over the words.

'Hey, this looks promising,' she exclaimed suddenly. 'Listen Harriet. "American actress on six-month stay in England needs PA of sociable

4

disposition who is willing to work unusual hours. CV and photograph essential.'' Then there's a box number for replies. What do you think?'

'It's a PA job again,' said Harriet doubtfully.

'Hardly the same as working in the City,' Ella pointed out. 'It might be Meryl Streep or Sharon Stone. How fantastic to see them at close quarters!'

'Don't be silly,' aid Harriet. 'They wouldn't need to put an advert in *The Times*. Besides, why do I have to send a photograph?'

'I don't know. Perhaps the actress has a fragile ego and doesn't want any competition. You could be too good-looking for the job.'

Harriet laughed. 'I doubt it. If anyone was likely to put a film star's nose out of joint it would be you, not me.'

Ella studied her friend and silently disagreed. She knew that she was attractive, and with make-up could look beautiful, but there was something special about Harriet, something that had always made people look twice. She was so immaculate, so apparently assured and yet in her eyes, and her body language, there was quite often the suggestion that beneath this surface there lay something more. A vulnerability certainly, but also the very quality that Harriet herself had said James lacked – passion. An untapped passion, as Ella knew very well, was an irresistible aphrodisiac to a lot of men.

'I think you should answer the advert,' she said decisively. 'You've nothing to lose.'

Harriet felt her stomach move with nervous excitement. It would be exciting, and different, but she also sensed something more from the

5

wording of the advertisement. Somehow she knew that if she sent off a photograph and was given an interview her whole life would change, and she hesitated because if that happened there would be no going back.

'Well?' demanded Ella impatiently.

Harriet hesitated for only a second. 'You've convinced me,' she agreed with a nervous laugh. 'I'll send off a photo and my CV tomorrow.'

'No, tonight,' said Ella firmly. 'We'll go back to your place and I'll help you choose the best picture, then we'll make sure it goes first post tomorrow.'

That night, as Harriet prepared for bed, she thought for a moment about the letter, now lying in a pillar box awaiting the postman in the morning. Would anything come of it? she thought to herself. Had her meeting with Ella and the fact that she'd had a copy of *The Times* with her been part of some predestined plan? Or would she hear nothing more and spend the next few months wondering if she'd been right to give up James and her job in the space of three days? She rather suspected it would be the latter, but couldn't help nurturing a hope that at least she'd manage to get an interview, if only in order to find out who the actress in question was.

Two days later she returned from visiting a friend to find her telephone ringing. She ran to answer it.

'Miss Radcliffe?' asked an icily detached female voice at the other end.

'Yes,' replied Harriet, somewhat mystified as to who the called could be.

'You replied to an advertisement in *The Times* recently.'

Harriet's stomach lurched. 'Yes, yes I did.'

'Your CV and photograph were satisfactory. Would you be free to attend an interview tomorrow morning at eleven?' asked the voice.

Harriet felt flustered. 'Tomorrow? Let me see, I . . .'

'Tomorrow is the only time that our client has free.'

'I'm sure it will be fine. I'll just check my diary,' replied Harriet, determined not to let the caller know that at this particular moment she had nothing planned for the rest of her life. She waited a couple of minutes and then returned to the phone. 'Yes, I can manage that,' she said, hoping she sounded as indifferent as the other woman.

'Excellent, I'll give you the address. Do you have a pen and paper to hand?'

She must think I'm six years old, thought Harriet to herself, but she kept the annoyance out of her voice and scribbled down the address and directions as to how to get there. It was only when she replaced the receiver that her legs went weak and she had to sit on the sofa to recover.

It was all so quick, she thought in astonishment. An advertisement like that must have attracted masses of applications, and yet she'd been called by phone in less than forty-eight hours. The speed of the response made her nervous and later that evening she rang Ella.

'Why are you worrying?' Ella demanded. 'You should be grateful. Where do you have to go?'

'Regent's Park. I've looked it up on the map – I think it's one of those large houses that overlook the park.'

'Fantastic! You'll probably have your own suite of rooms and use of a swimming pool – when the star isn't keeping in trim, of course. Did they say who she was?'

'No, but no doubt I'll find out early on in the interview.'

'Make sure you let me know,' said Ella. 'I'm consumed with curiosity.'

'So am I,' responded Harriet.

By the time she actually arrived at the house the following morning she was consumed by nerves as well. She drove herself there in her blue BMW which had to stop at the huge padlocked wrought-iron gates while a gateman came out, took her name and phoned through to the house. Then he opened them with apparent reluctance and when she waved and smiled at him as she drove in he simply stared blankly at her. 'Let's hope the rest of the household are more friendly,' she muttered to herself.

The house was large and imposing. It was built of Portland stone and stood well back in what Harriet estimated to be about two to three acres of parkland. When she halted her car outside the front door she looked down across an immaculate lawn with green conifers and bushes on either side extended right back to the gates. As far as she could see, the garden at the side was less well tended and comprised more shrubs than lawn, but the entire perimeter of the area was protected by tall trees which successfully shut out the rest of the world.

A butler opened the front door to her, and she stepped into a long entrance hall, at the far end of which she could see a modern open-plan winding staircase. The carpet was a deep coral colour, the walls and ceiling a textured white and on either side of the hall there were numerous china and porcelain ornaments ranging from a life-size greyhound sitting to attention to an exquisitely delicate ballerina which was little more than six inches in height and stood on an ornate glass table. The ornaments had no apparent connection with each other and none of them matched in colour or design but Harriet suspected that every one of them was priceless.

'If you would wait here, Miss Radcliffe,' said the butler politely, ushering her into a tiny ante-room. 'Miss Farmer will be with you in a moment.'

Harriet sat down on the nearest chair and wondered if she could possibly have heard him right. If Miss Farmer was her possible future employer then there was only one person it could be. Rowena Farmer, who had shot to fame in two huge box office successes as a sexy private investigator, becoming at the same time one of the greatest sex symbols since Marilyn Monroe. Harriet's heart began to beat more rapidly, but then she told herself firmly that Miss Farmer was probably a secretary whose job it was to weed out unsuitable applicants. It was hardly likely that someone like Rowena Farmer would do her own interviewing.

Just as she'd calmed her nerves the door opened and Rowena Farmer made her entrance.

There was no other expression that applied, thought Harriet to herself, as the petite titian-haired beauty stood framed in the doorway. Dressed in a canary yellow cropped top and a bronze organdie skirt with a pale green sleeveless overtop that reached to her ankles she stood directly in the light from the opposite window, her hair gleaming and her immaculately made-up face glowing with health, and smiled a brilliant, professional smile at Harriet.

'I'm so sorry to have kept you waiting, Miss Radcliffe,' she murmured in the famous low husky voice that Harriet recognised from her films. 'There's so much to do at the moment. We only arrived three days ago and . . . well, you can imagine what it's like, I'm sure.'

Again she smiled, but Harriet knew that the smile wasn't really for her. It was an automatic response to another person's presence, and as such meaningless, but at least she was being polite. Somehow Harriet had expected her to be spoilt and petulant in private. Then she reminded herself that this wasn't in private. Rowena Farmer was performing for a possible employee. The real Miss Farmer was unlikely to emerge until you were actually in her employment.

'Come this way,' continued the film star, gliding smoothly out into the hall, and Harriet followed her to the far end and then through a heavy oak door into a drawing-room.

The carpet here was pure white, while the walls were white with the faintest suggestion of apple green, a tone that was complimented by the low green sofa and two winged chairs. In the middle of the room a large glass table top was supported by four green chinese dragons whose images were repeated in the draped and tied curtains that had been fastened in such a way as to allow in only a very little light.

Rowena Farmer sank into one of the chairs and indicated that Harriet should sit on the sofa. It was lower than normal and she wished that she'd worn a longer skirt as hers rose above her thighs and left her sitting with her knees tightly together and angled to her left. She still had the suspicion that Rowena Farmer must be able to see right up her skirt if she wanted to, but the film star's eyes never left Harriet's face until she picked up the application and read it through as though to remind herself of its contents.

At the far end of the drawing-room, directly opposite Harriet, was an ornate mirror that took up half the wall. She smiled to herself. Probably film stars liked mirrors everywhere, and certainly Rowena Farmer had every cause to be proud of her beauty, which was as spectacular in the flesh as on the screen.

While Harriet tried to sit still and Rowena read her CV, a man sitting concealed behind the mirror glanced down at the written notes on the table in front of him. His long fingers picked up a pen and he began to scribble comments in the margins of the pages, and all the time he watched the unsuspecting Harriet through the two-way mirror. Beneath heavy dark brows his brown eyes gleamed with appreciation.

After what seemed to be a very long time, Rowena put the letter of application to one side and turned her attention to Harriet. 'Why did you leave your last job?' she enquired.

11

Harriet had already decided to be completely honest. 'I was bored,' she confessed. 'The work was interesting at first but it quickly became routine. The money was good and so were the working conditions, but I needed a change. I wanted to do something where every day would be slightly different. I was doing a lot of figure work you see, and I really prefer people.' She smiled at Rowena, but the film star didn't smile back. Her eyes were quite blank, as though she didn't understand what Harriet was saying.

Harriet felt she had to explain further, because she wanted this job very badly. The thought of actually working for someone as famous as Rowena Farmer was irresistible. 'I was engaged until recently, but I realised that the engagement was rather like my job, agreeable but unexciting. I was afraid that if I didn't change, didn't try something different – broaden my horizons more – I'd end up regretting it.'

'You want to broaden your horizons?' queried Rowena with sudden interest.

'Yes!' said Harriet eagerly. 'I'm twenty-three now; soon it will be too late.'

'Twenty-three is young,' murmured the film star regretfully.

'But it's so easy to settle for too little,' said Harriet, warming to her theme. 'Ever since I was young I've thought that it was being safe that mattered. Everything I did was carefully thought out, and if there was ever any risk, any chance of something going wrong, I discarded that option. Now I think I was wrong, and I want to do something different with my life while I still can.'

'You're looking for danger?'

Behind the mirror the man leant forward slightly, his chin resting on his hands. This was going far better than he could ever have anticipated. So far she was perfect.

Harriet smiled. 'Not danger in the way of climbing rock faces or sailing round the world in a yacht, but I'd like to take a chance or two before I settle down.'

Rowena nodded. 'And at the moment do you have any emotional attachments?'

The hidden man almost stopped breathing as he waited for Harriet's answer. If she said yes then she would be of no use to them, and he desperately wanted her to join their household.

Harriet shook her head. 'There's no one. I'm not in a hurry to replace James. In fact, I'm enjoying the feeling of freedom!'

Rowena laughed, but again Harriet had the disconcerting impression that it was a professional laugh. This woman wasn't amused, and in a way she hardly seemed interested enough in what Harriet was saying. She put the questions, but then her attention seemed to wander and she would stare over Harriet's shoulder and out of the window rather than at her face.

'The thing is Harriet – I may call you Harriet, I hope?' Harriet nodded. 'Good. The thing is that I'm here to make a very special film, and it's vital that no word of this gets out until everything is settled. You know – script, cast, contracts signed, all those boring things that have to be done before you can be sure a project is underway.'

'I'm afraid I don't know anything about the way the film industry works,' confessed Harriet.

Rowena shrugged dismissively. 'That doesn't

matter, you'd soon learn. No, what I need is a discreet, efficient English secretary. They're famous for their discretion and efficiency, you know. Unfortunately, in order to fit in with my rather demanding schedule it would be necessary for the successful applicant to live in for the length of my stay here.'

'Live in?' said Harriet in astonishment.

'It's the time difference, darling,' explained Rowena, longing to light up a cigarette but aware that Lewis, watching from behind the mirror, would disapprove. 'You'd get telephone calls at all hours. Also, I suffer from insomnia – sometimes I'd want to dictate letters in the middle of the night if I couldn't sleep.'

Harriet stared at the other woman. She'd have thought that a fax machine would have taken care of night-time calls, and as for insomnia, everyone knew that film stars lived on sleeping pills, but she wasn't going to argue. It was a beautiful house and the job was only for six months. She had no objection to living in. She could easily go back to her own flat now and again, during her time off, and make sure everything there was secure. Just the same, it was a strange request.

'I'd pay double your previous salary,' said Rowena suddenly.

Harriet tried not to let her astonishment show. She'd been very well paid in her previous job; doubling it when she was going to live in was extraordinary.

'To make up for the inconvenience of losing your social life for six months,' explained Rowena. 'I doubt if you'll have much free time. I'm afraid I'm very demanding!' Again the practised laugh.

'But I would have time off?' queried Harriet.

'Of course, although not necessarily set days. It's so difficult in this business to know when you'll need someone and when you won't. You do understand?'

'Yes, of course. It's just all rather strange to me, I'm afraid.'

Rowena curled her legs under her in the chair, looking frail and kittenish. 'But surely that's what you wanted, Harriet? A change. Something that would broaden your horizons. I can certainly promise you that.'

Go for it, said a voice in Harriet's head. You wanted a chance to experience new things and this is it. Why are you hanging back? She gave herself a mental shake. 'It sounds very exciting,' she said with a laugh.

Rowena seemed to relax suddenly, and let out her breath with an audible sigh. 'That's great, Harriet. Naturally there are one or two points I have to check up on. References, that kind of thing, but I'm sure we won't come across any problems there. With any luck I can let you know definitely by the end of tomorrow.'

As Harriet rose to her feet and let Rowena usher her out of the room she wondered briefly who the 'we' was. She had no idea if Rowena was married or not, and decided that if she got the job she must ring Ella and find out all she could about the woman she'd be working for.

As they reached the front door the butler materialised, but Rowena waved him away and opened the door herself. She then extended a small, perfectly manicured hand to Harriet. 'I'm

15

sure you'd fit in very well here, Harriet,' she said with the warmest smile she'd managed during the entire interview. 'I do so admire cool English women. I'm afraid we're rather more upfront in the States.'

'Maybe you're just more friendly,' suggested Harriet.

'I trust that if you do join us you won't find our way of life too overwhelming,' responded Rowena. 'Not that it will matter. As you said, you wanted a change.'

Harriet smiled and made her way to her car. She had a sneaking suspicion that instead of cool, Rowena Farmer had actually meant boring or inhibited, but it didn't bother her. She wanted the job, and she couldn't imagine a similar opportunity ever coming her way again. She just hoped that the film star thought she was suitable.

The film star in question watched the BMW draw away from the house and leant against the wall, totally drained by her own performance. She'd woken that morning exhausted and sated by a night of love-making, her head throbbing from an excess of champagne, and she'd completely forgotten about Harriet until twenty minutes before she arrived. Even then it was only fear of her husband's fury that had driven her to leave her bed and she'd then bullied and cajoled her dresser into getting her ready on time.

Slowly she returned to the drawing-room where the interview had taken place. Lewis was already there, lounging in the second armchair, his long legs stretched out in front of him. She stood on the threshold of the room and studied him carefully. At thirty-nine he was even more attractive now than when she'd met him four years earlier and she thought how unfair it was that men improved with the years while women didn't – at least not film stars who built their reputations on looks and glamour.

Lewis was going to change all that though. This new film, his brainchild and as such a guaranteed box office success, would show people that she was more than a sex symbol. That she could show depth and passion, and she was willing to bare her soul in order to regain her place in the hall of fame. She was scared, but Lewis would help her.

He turned his head. 'You did well,' he said slowly.

Rowena sat down in her chair and with trembling hands reached for the cigarettes in her handbag. She heard him sigh but ignored him. There were times, moments like this, when the danger of what they were doing overwhelmed her and she had to have help. He'd weaned her off her drugs, restricted her drinking but had so far failed to get her to give up smoking. Sometimes his almost puritanical approach to certain aspects of life irritated her, but she knew that it made him what he was and was responsible for his incredible success.

'She's the one, isn't she?' commented Rowena, drawing on the cigarette.

'She could have stepped straight from the pages of the script,' agreed Lewis. 'It's incredible. Those long legs, that fantastic air of self-contained reserve with the suggestion of so much more beneath. And those eyes! Did you see them? They reveal everything she tries to conceal. I can't wait to begin.'

Rowena couldn't remember when she'd last seen her husband so enthusiastic. 'What about Chris?' she asked.

He raised his eyebrows. 'Chris will go along with our decision. I bore his preferences in mind when I made out my list of essential requirements.'

'I'm not sure she'll stay, even if she takes the job,' said Rowena.

'She'll stay.' Lewis sounded supremely confident and it annoyed his wife.

'When she said she wanted to broaden her horizons I'm not sure she meant them to expand quite as far as you intend.'

'It will all be done very slowly,' Lewis reminded her. 'By the time she realises what's happening she'll be too involved to leave. Trust me, Rowena. If there's one thing I do know about, apart from making films, it's women.'

Rowena knew this was true. She'd had a lot of men herself, but never anyone like Lewis. He was everything she could ever have asked for, totally uninhibited and unashamed, prepared to go to any lengths to satisfy her needs and desires. Yet even that wasn't enough, she thought bitterly. Even Lewis with his intelligence, good looks and sexual skill had been unable to help her. Which was why they were here, and why they needed Harriet.

'Ring her tomorrow at six o'clock,' said Lewis, getting out of his chair and taking the half-smoked cigarette from between his wife's fingers. 'By then she'll be worrying that you're not going to call and should accept straight away. Now get back to bed, you look exhausted. And do stop smoking these things. They don't help your skin or your nerves and I loathe the smell.'

'Just because all your films are moral crusades, do you have to carry it over into your private life?' enquired Rowena irritably.

Lewis smiled. 'You more than anyone should know that I'm not quite what people think!'

'Sometimes I'm not sure I know you at all,' retorted Rowena.

Lewis reached forward and stroked her left cheek softly with the middle finger of his right hand. 'You know all you need to know,' he murmured. 'Now go and rest. I have to work on the script.'

'Is it all right if I show her photograph to Chris?' asked Rowena.

'No,' said Lewis sharply. 'I don't want him to set eyes on her until she's actually living in this house.'

They both knew that Rowena wouldn't disobey him, because if she did then the delicate balance of the script would be changed, and the script was entirely Lewis's responsibility.

At five past six the following evening the telephone rang in Harriet's apartment. She had been pacing back and forth in front of it for the past half hour and almost snatched it off the rest in her haste. 'Hello?'

'Miss Radcliffe?' asked the husky voice of Rowena Farmer.

'Yes,' said Harriet, eagerly.

'I'm delighted to say that all your references checked out satisfactorily and I'd like to offer you

19

the job,' said Rowena.

Harriet felt almost light-headed with excitement. The few things that had been troubling her, any doubts as to the wisdom of such a change, vanished in the wave of relief that the job was hers, just as Lewis had anticipated.

'Are you still interested?' Rowena sounded anxious, and Harriet realised that she hadn't said a word yet.

'Yes, yes of course!' she exclaimed. 'I'm really pleased.'

'So are we,' responded Rowena, and again Harriet wondered about her use of the word *we*. 'I was wondering if you could start next week? I didn't bring my secretary with me and the correspondence is already beginning to pile up.'

'Of course,' said Harriet swiftly. 'I have to make a few arrangements about the flat, but I could certainly start next Monday.'

'And you'll bring all you need then?'

'Well, yes.'

'I realised I didn't show you your rooms,' said Rowena, sounding embarrassed by her own error. 'If you wanted to come and have a look before Monday that could easily be arranged. You'll have your own bedroom, bathroom and living-room on the first floor. The rooms are all large here; I'm sure you'll find them acceptable.'

Remembering what she'd seen of the house so far, Harriet couldn't imagine otherwise. 'I'm sure they'll be perfect,' she assured Rowena. 'Honestly, I don't need to come and look.'

'Well, if there's anything you don't like we can always have it changed,' responded the film star. In the short pause that followed Harriet heard another voice, a man's deep and soft, almost like a whisper. 'Oh, yes!' exclaimed Rowena. 'There is one little thing I forgot. I'm afraid you won't be able to have visitors here. It's the film, you see. Everything is at such a delicate stage that I don't want any word to escape and if . . .'

'It's all right,' Harriet assured her. 'I can always go out to see my friends. Really, there's no problem.'

'I'm so glad you understand.' The relief in Rowena's voice was clear and for a moment Harriet felt sorry for her, although she couldn't imagine why. 'We'll see you on Monday morning then, let's say at eleven-thirty. The household should be awake at that time!'

'Fine,' said Harriet. 'And thank you.'

'I should be thanking you,' said Rowena softly, and then she hung up.

As Harriet started to dial Ella's number, Rowena turned to Lewis, who had been standing at her elbow throughout the call. 'There, it's settled,' she said triumphantly.

He nuzzled the nape of her neck while his arms wound themselves round her body and his hands caressed her breasts through the flimsy material of her blouse. 'Well done,' he murmured. 'Now we can begin.'

They sank on to the carpet together and as his cool, clever fingers played over her warm flesh her last coherent thought was to wonder what Chris would think of their choice.

Chapter Two

ON THE MONDAY morning, as Harriet packed the last of her belongings into suitcases, Rowena stirred sleepily in her four-poster bed. Lewis had awoken earlier, she'd heard him dress and leave, and remembering that today was an important one for them all Rowena decided that perhaps she should join him for a cup of coffee and some fruit juice before dressing.

She opened her eyes, but not a glimmer of light penetrated the room. Still half-asleep she turned her head towards the window, and realised with a shiver of excitement that she was wearing a blindfold. Instinctively she tried to move her hands, to test exactly what had been used to cover her eyes, but immediately a pair of wiry hands gripped her wrists, pinning them to her pillow.

'Chris, stop it!' she protested half-heartedly. 'I have to get up this morning. Harriet will be here soon.'

'I want to know about Harriet,' he whispered in her ear, his breath warm against her skin. 'Tell me what she looks like. Is she beautiful? Will I want her enough for the plot to work?'

'I can't tell you,' she explained, twisting her body in her efforts to free herself. Chris grasped her legs and pushed them roughly upwards so that her knees were bent against her ample breasts and then she felt him move over her until her ankles were on his shoulders and his erection was resting against her. She knew that she was already moist, already wanting him, and knew that Chris was aware of it too because he laughed softly deep in his throat.

'Tell me,' he taunted her, letting the tip of his penis brush lightly up and down her slowly parting outer sex-lips. 'Tell me about Harriet and then you can have me.'

'I can't! repeated Rowena, wishing that she could just so that she could feel him hard and urgent inside her.

Chris rotated his hips slightly and she felt the soft tip of his penis caressing the sensitive nerve endings around her clitoris. Immediately she tried to arch herself upwards to increase the stimulation but her movements were restricted by the position he'd chosen and she whimpered with frustration.

Suddenly he withdrew from between her legs, pressed her legs down flat on the bed, then lay on top of her, his hands going to her breasts. Still unable to see, Rowena's breathing increased as she waited for his next move. She could feel her body trembling with need, a need mixed with the glorious fear that Chris always aroused in her. A fear that she had grown to need, to rely on for her greatest moments of pleasure.

Very softly his fingers closed round her right breast. They skimmed lightly over the surface and Rowena's lips parted as she waited for what was to come. Very gradually, with tantalising slowness, his fingers moved across the surface of the rounded breast until it reached the aureola. Then the finger nails scratched lightly at the most sensitive part of the film star's breasts and as her nipple rose with her increased excitement Chris lowered his head and sucked it into his mouth.

The pressure combined with the insistent scratching meant that Rowena's hips twisted on the bed as she sought some kind of contact against the lower half of her body, but Chris moved to the side of her, denying her stimulation of any kind.

'Tell me what Harriet looks like,' he repeated and she could have cried because when he spoke he released her imprisoned nipple from his mouth.

'No!' She made her voice firmer, aware that no matter what he did this time he wasn't going to have his way and he might as well know it now.

'Why do you let him do this to us?' whispered Chris, and to her amazement and gratitude she felt one of his hands straying between her thighs, idly caressing the soft, damp, swollen flesh. 'We're not social misfits, or politicians. He should stick to his dramatised documentaries, not use us to launch him into fiction.'

'It isn't fiction,' Rowena said softly. 'It's faction. That's why we're so necessary, and I need this film, Chris. I need it badly. I'm thirty now, I can't rely on my looks any more. I have to show that I can act.'

'This isn't acting,' exclaimed Chris, and behind the darkness of the blindfold, Rowena was startled by the sudden insertion into her vagina of a gently rounded vibrator that Chris immediately switched on to the higher setting.

As its pulsations spread through her, as her outer nerve endings were stimulated by the strength of the movements within her, Rowena's body began to climb to orgasm. She felt her nipples standing erect, felt the hot melting sensation deep within the core of her and when Chris's spare hand gripped her right breast, her head began to move almost imperceptibly on the pillow and she heard herself moaning.

'Do you want me instead of this toy?' he asked, his own voice trembling with excitement.

'Yes! Yes, please Chris, now! Quickly!' Rowena was frantic to feel him inside her, to know that he was there when she finally toppled into orgasm.

'Then tell me about Harriet,' he demanded.

Rowena's stomach was rigid with sexual tension and her thighs began to shake as the orgasm drew closer. 'Please, Chris, I can't. Just take me, take me now.'

'Bitch!' he muttered, and to her horror the vibrator was withdrawn, her breast released and the blissful sparks began to die away. Without thinking Rowena's own hand moved between her thighs, to finish what Chris had so abruptly ended, but his hands stopped her and he kept her imprisoned flat on the bed, still unable to see because of the blindfold, and only released her when her body had finally returned to its former unaroused state. Then he pulled off the dark scarf and stared down at her.

'You shouldn't have done that!' cried Rowena. 'It wasn't fair.'

'You and Lewis shouldn't have chosen Harriet without asking my opinion.'

'He's my husband and the director of the film, whereas you're—'

'Just a small-part actor?' he queried.

'No, of course not, but he has to run this his way. He wants it to be as accurate as possible, that's why we need Harriet. He chose the characters and he wants to see how they really react to the situation his film characters will face. Don't you see how real it will make it? No one will be able to say "that's not how people behave" because we'll already have behaved like it. We *are* his film.'

'He's trying to get rid of me,' said Chris.

Rowena reached up to brush his fair curly hair out of his eyes. 'He could never do that, Chris,' she assured him. 'I couldn't live without you, you know that and Lewis knows it too.'

Chris leant over her and kissed her deeply, his tongue thrusting into her mouth just as she'd wanted his erection to thrust a few minutes earlier. Her arms went round his neck and she arched up so that her nipples brushed the soft down on his chest. 'Please, let's do it now,' she begged him.

'No,' said Chris curtly, and he pushed her off the bed. 'Get dressed. Your husband's probably waiting for you.'

'Sometimes I hate you,' said Rowena, refusing to let herself cry because it would ruin her looks for the rest of the morning.

Chris laughed. 'It didn't look that way earlier.'

'What's wrong with us?' demanded Rowena. 'Why can't we be . . .'

'Normal?' enquired Chris. He smiled his most boyish smile. 'I've no idea. Perhaps Lewis will discover the answer as the plot unravels.'

Harriet was surprised when Rowena Farmer opened the front door to her in person. Now that she'd accepted the job she hadn't expected the film star to bother to be even professionally friendly. Ella had made it quite clear over the telephone that this star in particular was one who took her position as a sex goddess very seriously.

'She wants to be known as an "actress" too,' Ella had informed her friend. 'That's probably why she's here. The Americans think that the best serious films are made in England. Incidentally,' Ella had added, 'Ms Farmer just happens to be married to the hottest director in the States at the moment, and I mean hot. He's the new Oliver Stone and incredibly handsome. I saw him once on a clip of film showing them together and one glimpse made my knees go weak!'

'I don't suppose I'll see much of him,' Harriet had responded, and then thought very little more about it.

Now though, as Rowena motioned for a waiting maid to take Harriet's suitcases and then led her through to the drawing-room she remembered Ella's words, because Rowena was talking about her husband.

'You must meet Lewis before I show you your rooms,' she said gaily. 'He's usually locked away in his study working on the script or talking on the telephone, but I've told him that when you're not busy with my work he can borrow you – I didn't think you'd mind – so he's taken time out to meet you.'

Harriet had the feeling that Rowena felt this was a great honour, but she found it hard to feel overwhelmed. It was after all only courtesy to say hello to someone who was going to type your letters and probably be a general dogsbody.

She followed Rowena into the room and immediately the man sitting in the chair opposite the door rose to his feet. He was tall, an inch or so over six feet, Harriet thought, and his hair was thick and jet black, swept off his face, accentuating the unusually strong bone structure with its high cheekbones and straight nose. Beneath dark and heavy brows his eyes were a deep brown, thickly lashed and intelligent-looking while his mouth was wide with a full lower lip. He held out a hand in greeting, and the leather strap of his watch stood out against his golden brown skin. Harriet remembered Ella mentioning mixed parentage – a Portuguese mother or something similar. It showed in his colouring, but although Harriet didn't know it his height and breadth came from a Texan father. The combination was, as Ella had said, quite breathtaking.

'Nice to meet you, Harriet,' he said warmly, and his fingers closed around hers for a moment in a gesture that was almost a caress. Startled she raised her eyes to his and saw that he was watching her closely. She quickly withdrew her hand and without realising it took a step away from him. Lewis's mouth curved in a smile.

'Rowena and I hope you'll be happy here,' he continued smoothly. 'I'm afraid life can be a bit

28

chaotic, but she tells me you're tired of routine work so that shouldn't worry you.'

'It will certainly be different,' responded Harriet, wishing that she wasn't quite so aware of his physical presence. She was busy admiring the breadth of his shoulders compared to his slim hips, and that wasn't the way she usually responded to men. What made it worse was that he seemed to know because he hardly took his gaze off her.

'Is Chris around, darling?' asked Lewis, draping an arm casually around Rowena's shoulders.

Rowena smiled up at him. 'I think I saw him coming back from the pool.'

'Give him a call, then Harriet will know the three most important people in the house!' He laughed, but softly, as though at some private joke.

Rowena left the room for a moment and Harriet decided that she wasn't going to stand around feeling like an awkward schoolgirl, so she sat down on the low sofa and immediately watched her hemline rise to her thighs again.

Lewis glanced briefly at her legs and then away. Harriet wondered if he was simply so used to seeing women's legs that they no longer interested him, or if Rowena's were far better than hers. For some ridiculous reason she hoped it wasn't the latter. She'd always thought her legs were one of her best points.

'I hope you and Rowena get along all right,' said Lewis quietly. 'She's going through a difficult time at the moment. The film we're getting ready is going to test her like she's never been tested before. She needs a lot of understanding and support. Sometimes she can seem difficult, but it's insecurity. You find most actors and actresses are basically insecure.'

'I'd be insecure if my work depended on my appearance,' said Harriet.

Lewis looked directly at her. 'I don't think you'd have any reason for your insecurity.'

Harriet went warm at the unexpected compliment and couldn't think how to respond. 'I think Rowena's beautiful,' she said eventually.

'She was beautiful, but at thirty the camera can be very unkind.'

'Is she thirty? She doesn't look it!' exclaimed Harriet.

Lewis raised an eyebrow. 'You're learning fast. That's exactly the kind of thing she needs to hear.'

'But it's true,' protested Harriet.

'Having you here won't help her believe that,' he remarked.

'Well, she chose me. It isn't my fault I'm only twenty-three.'

'Of course not,' said Lewis reassuringly, knowing that it was he and not Rowena who'd chosen Harriet, and his choice had been a very careful one. He needed to stoke Rowena's insecurity, to trigger off some form of jealousy if the plan was to work. It was the only way he could think of to help her.

An awkward silence fell, but then the door opened and Rowena returned with a slim, blond-haired, blue-eyed young man behind her. His complexion was fresh and at first glance he looked little more than a boy, but on closer inspection Harriet thought he was probably in his late twenties.

'Chris, this is Harriet Radcliffe,' said Rowena proudly. 'Harriet, I'd like you to meet Chris Falkener, my half-brother.'

Harriet sat forward on the sofa and shook hands with the young man who was staring at her quite openly. 'You're a knock-out!' he exclaimed in apparent surprise. 'Whatever were you thinking of, Rowena, letting a beautiful young lady like this loose in the house?'

To Harriet's dismay Rowena flushed and in the light from the window it looked as though there were tears in her eyes, although when she spoke her voice was quite steady. 'Don't be silly, Chris, you'll embarrass Harriet. Besides, why shouldn't I have an attractive personal assistant for a change? You know I like beautiful things around me.'

'Things yeah, but not women. Well, you're the nicest surprise I've had since Christmas, Harriet. Welcome to our little family.'

Harriet smiled politely, but her first impression of him wasn't favourable. He seemed spoilt and ill-mannered, and it was difficult to believe he was Rowena's half-brother.

After the introductions a maid was summoned to take Harriet to her rooms. 'If there's anything you don't like, let me know,' said Rowena with a smile. 'We want you to feel really at home here. Part of the family unit.'

'Thank you,' said Harriet politely, privately thinking that as a personal assistant she was unlikely to be involved in their domestic life, and in any case it was hardly a family. A husband, wife and half-brother didn't seem to her to symbolise a close-knit unit, exclusion from which would be devastating. She decided it was just a typical exaggeration by an actress.

Her rooms astonished her. She had expected them to be large, but not particularly plush. In fact the bedroom, decorated in varying shades of blue, looked large enough for two couples rather than a single female. The deep blue carpet flecked with white was wool, its pile thick and luxurious beneath her feet, and was beautifully complemented by the blue curtains patterned with tiny white flowers. As for the bed, Harriet could hardly believe her eyes at the sight of it.

It was enormous, the largest bed she'd ever seen, and at each corner an ornate gold column rose up at least five feet towards the ceiling, while at the foot of the bed the gold theme was continued with a twisted rope pattern that led from each of the side poles to meet in the middle in a two-feet-tall figure of two lovers embracing. The blue and white padded headboard was unusually high and surrounded by a design that matched the entwined gold rope at the opposite end.

The en suite bathroom was a total contrast. The floor was covered in white rugs and the bath was white enamel set in a solid wood surround and shaped to fit the body, broad at one end, then narrowing at the end where the taps were. It was also unexpectedly deep, and Harriet wondered if there was enough hot water for everyone in the house to fill similar baths.

On the walls were tiny pen and ink etchings, all framed in wood that matched the bath surround. On closer inspection Harriet could see that each etching showed a couple engaged in some form of love-making, most of them the kind of positions that made her ache at the very prospect.

At her bedside table was a telephone, and on a sudden impulse she picked it up and dialled Ella's number. For once it wasn't the answerphone and Ella was clearly delighted to hear from her.

As soon as Harriet lifted her receiver a light flashed on the phone in Lewis's study and he carefully picked up his own handset, then sat listening with interest to Harriet's conversation.

'Ella, you were right!' she said dramatically.

'About what?' asked Ella, intrigued by Harriet's unusual enthusiasm.

'Rowena's husband. He is incredibly handsome, and there's something about him I can't explain it but it just makes you feel weird all over when he looks at you.'

'Nice weird?'

'Of course! I know now that I was right to leave James. I never once lusted after him in all the years I knew him!'

'You mean you lust after Lewis James? Harriet, he's a respectable married man!' laughed Ella.

'I know, disgraceful isn't it? I can't help it, Ella. I'd give anything to know what it was like to have a man like that make love to me. Still, I'll settle for living in the same house.'

'I wouldn't,' said Ella bluntly, and in his study Lewis smiled. 'You should go for it,' continued Ella. 'It could be difficult though, he's not what you'd call a ladies' man. As far as I know from the gossip columns he's been faithful to Rowena Farmer since they married, and word has it that even she comes second to his work.'

'Sounds quite a challenge,' said Harriet.

'Let me know if you make any progress!' laughed Ella. 'What are your rooms like?'

'I've only seen my bedroom and bathroom, and they're out of this world. I'm sure the living-room will be just as grand.'

'Better than working for Mr Grant, I take it?' queried Ella.

'No comparison!' agreed Harriet. 'I'd better go now. Oh yes, one thing. Did you know Rowena Farmer had a half-brother called Chris?'

Ella hesitated. 'Now you come to mention it I did read something about him once. I think he only gets to act in her films, you know – a kind of hanger-on. Why, is he there too?'

'Yes, but he doesn't look anything like her. In fact, I wasn't that struck on him.'

'That's because you only had eyes for Lewis,' laughed Ella. 'I'll have to go now. I'm auditioning in half an hour, but keep me up to date, won't you?'

'I certainly will,' Harriet assured her and when she replaced the receiver she failed to notice the faint click as Lewis did the same.

Her living-room was equally luxurious, the colour theme an unusual burnt orange with cream furniture, including an antique chaise longue and the largest armchair Harriet had ever seen.

When she went back into her bedroom the maid was unpacking her clothes and hanging them in the cupboards. 'Miss Farmer would like to see you downstairs in the conservatory when you're ready,' she informed Harriet.

'I'll go now,' Harriet said quickly. 'Where is it?'

'Just past the bottom of the staircase, first door on your left.'

When Harriet entered Rowena was sitting

slumped in a wicker chair, her head back and her face drained of its usual colour. Harriet cleared her throat and at once the film star's head came up and a professional sparkle returned to her features.

'Was everything all right, Harriet?' she asked sweetly.

'The rooms are incredible; I shall get thoroughly spoilt here.'

'I hope so,' said Rowena vaguely. 'You must help me get this room straight. It needs lots of potted plants, spice ropes – that kind of thing. Would you see to it for me?'

Harriet, though she thought the clean unclut-tered lines of the room very attractive, agreed. If Rowena wanted plants, plants it should be.

Harriet stood by the large glass windows of the conservatory and stared out across the grass that gently sloped away from the back of the house.

'I hadn't realised quite how beautiful you were,' said Rowena suddenly.

Harriet turned to look at her. 'I'm sorry?'

'You're young as well.'

'I'm twenty-three,' said Harriet, wondering why Rowena should suddenly start talking about her PA's appearance.

'Unfortunately I'm not. I hadn't expected Chris to find you so attractive.' Harriet, uncertain as to what she should say, kept silent. 'Did you find him attractive?' continued Rowena.

Harriet gave a small smile, embarrassed by the question. 'I really don't know – I hardly saw him – but not especially. He isn't my type.'

'Then what is your "type", as you so quaintly put it?' queried Rowena.

Now Harriet realised that she was in trouble. 'I prefer dark men,' she said slowly.

'Then presumably you find my husband attractive, if not my half-brother?'

Harriet wished Rowena would change the subject. If she kept on like this it was going to be impossible not to antagonise her, and her voice already had an edge to it, as though she was annoyed by something Harriet had done.

'He's very handsome,' she replied diplomatically.

'Handsome! Yes, of course he's handsome, but so are thousands of men. Isn't he attractive to you?'

'I hadn't thought about it,' lied Harriet.

Rowena sat up straight in her chair. 'That's a lie. I saw the way you looked at him. You felt it, the same as all women do. You wanted him, didn't you? Even then, in those first moments, you were wondering what it would be like to go to bed with him.'

'I most certainly was not!' said Harriet, trying her best to sound offended. 'I'm sorry, Rowena, but I'm not sure where this is leading. Have I done something wrong? Would you like me to leave, is that it?'

Rowena leant across the table towards her. 'I think perhaps there's something you should know,' she said slowly.

'And what could that be?' asked Lewis, strolling into the room and pouring himself a mug of coffee from the percolator on the table.

Rowena turned her head towards him. 'I didn't hear you coming, darling.'

He smiled at her, and absentmindedly ran the

fingers of his left hand down her bare arm. Rowena stretched and made a small sound of pleasure. His arm slid up to her shoulder and pushed the mass of red-gold hair behind her ear so that he could softly stroke the side of her neck. 'What did you want Harriet to know?' he repeated.

'I can't remember now, you've distracted me!' laughed Rowena. 'It wasn't important, only something about my fan mail.'

Lewis looked over at Harriet. 'My wife gets a lot of fan mail. You'll spend a great deal of time answering it, I'm afraid. She has ten standard letters of reply on the computer, all designed to appear personal. You just have to be careful to check that the person you're replying to hasn't written before. If they have then the letter's on a separate disk and you choose from ten follow-up replies. "How wonderful to hear from you again", that kind of thing.'

'Do people write more than once?' asked Harriet.

'Darling, sometimes they write every week,' laughed Rowena. 'The only difference then is that we call them cranks, not fans, and bin the letters.'

'Haven't you ever had a crush on a film star?' asked Lewis.

Harriet shook her head. 'I'm not very well up on films, or plays for that matter. I like museums, art galleries and antique shops, but not acting.'

'You'll be good for us then. We're usually surrounded by people bitten by the acting bug.' He looked thoughtfully at her. 'I imagine you're too sensible to let your heart get the better of your head in any situation.'

He made the remark sound like an insult. 'I prefer to keep my emotions hidden,' said Harriet coolly. 'Now, perhaps there are some things I could do for you, Miss Farmer.'

'Please, not Miss Farmer,' laughed Rowena, suddenly relaxed and friendly again. 'You must always call me Rowena. I'm sure we're going to be friends.'

Harriet wasn't sure about anything any more, except for the fact that watching Lewis's hands stray over Rowena's arm and neck had been highly unsettling and left her face feeling hot. 'I'm sorry, Rowena it is. What would you like me to do?'

'The fan mail then, if you're desperate to start earning your keep. Lewis, be an angel and show her the room where she'll be working. I simply must have another cup of coffee.'

'Sure.' Lewis put his own mug down and led Harriet up the open staircase and through a door on the first floor. 'We've earmarked this for your office. The computer, telephone and fax machine are all in place, but although we've got the filing cabinets in I'm afraid none of Rowena's correspondence has been put away. We thought you'd like to use your own system.'

Harriet stared about the room. It was light and airy, the furniture all solid mahogany and the walls covered in heavy patterned wallpaper. 'It's certainly big enough!' she said with a smile.

'All the rooms are large. This seemed the best because Rowena has a room through the adjoining door there where she goes to learn her lines, try on clothes, experiment with make-up – that kind of thing. It means you'll be near when she might need you.'

'Fine. So where are the fan letters?' asked Harriet, standing facing the desk and looking over the piles of papers set out on it.

Lewis came up behind her and she felt his body brush against her back as he reached over her shoulder. 'I think they're there,' he said quietly.

Harriet straightened slightly and her buttocks and thighs pressed up against him. She half-turned in order to move away but her arm caught the pile of papers at the end of the desk and it went flying. As she bent down to pick them up, Lewis bent as well and their hands met as they reached in unison for one of the letters.

Again, just as at their first meeting, Lewis's fingers seemed to linger on hers. This time the pads of his fingertips brushed along the tops of her fingers and she shivered suddenly. Slowly her stood up, letting his hand trail up her arm and over her shoulder before removing it.

'I'll leave you to sort them out then,' he said calmly.

Harriet nodded, her mouth so dry she wasn't sure she'd be able to speak. It had been deliberate, she was certain of that; his touch, the way his body had moved against hers had indicated that. Yet in his eyes and voice there was no sign of interest or desire. Perhaps he was just very tactile, she told herself as he left the room.

After leaving Harriet, Lewis went in search of Rowena. He found her sitting on the tiles by the side of the large, heated indoor pool, her arms wrapped round her knees. For a moment he looked down at her thoughtfully, well aware of the kind of thoughts that must be going through her head at the moment, then he pulled one of the loungers forward and sat down on it.

'As I thought, she's perfect,' he said casually.

Rowena turned to look at him. 'I didn't expect Chris to be so impressed,' she said miserably.

'Of course he was impressed. I knew he would be; that was one of the main considerations in choosing her. That and her youth,' he added thoughtfully.

Rowena flushed. 'Chris is older than I am.' Her tone was defensive.

'Only by eighteen months! In any case, the older men get, the younger the women they desire.'

'Stop doing this!' shouted Rowena, standing up and glaring down at him. 'You of all people know how much I worry about my age. I expect Chris to be cruel, but not you.'

'Then why do you love Chris more?' asked Lewis softly.

The anger faded from Rowena's eyes and a look of despair filled them. 'I don't know! I wish I did. I wish I could tear myself away from him, but I can't. He's like a drug. Even when I think I'm getting free he draws me back.'

'Which is precisely why we're making this film, remember?'

'I don't think I can go through with it.'

Lewis frowned. 'Nonsense. In any case, you have no choice. No one else is anxious to put you in a film. I'm your only hope.'

'But why this film, this story?'

He sighed. They'd been over it so many times and still she seemed unable, or unwilling, to understand. 'Rowena, I've never done fiction before. My films have all had social messages, or exposed corruption. When this idea was put to me I didn't want to do it either. I was afraid, just as you're afraid now. But then I realised how perfect it was for us. A film about a brother and sister whose sexual relationship began when they were in their teens and refused to die. A man who marries the sister, knowing all about the relationship but thinking he can take her away from her brother, only to find that he can't. It's *our* story, it isn't fiction; it's our problem and if it's our problem it's other people's problem too. No one knows because it isn't something people talk about. AIDS yes, or drug addiction or alcoholism, but not sibling incest. This might help people, but more importantly it might help us.'

She stared at him. 'There was no other woman in that original idea you were sent.'

Lewis smiled. 'But it needed a catalyst. Someone who would force all the others to reassess their lives, make decisions instead of letting the situation drift. Once I'd thought of that I knew it could be a special film; all I needed to do was see the drama played out for real first, to make sure that I got it right. That's why the scriptwriters are here in England. I'll have regular meetings with them, tell them what direction the story takes every step of the way. We *are* the film, Rowena, and then when it's over you'll star in the screen version and you'll have all your emotional recall to use. Believe me, with the film done this way you could end up with an Oscar.'

As he'd known it would the very word made Rowena's eyes brighten, but then she frowned again. 'What if I don't like the ending?'

He tried hard to keep any hint of irritation out of his voice. 'It doesn't matter if you like it or not; it will be truthful, and that's what I want, a truthful film about a forbidden subject.'

Rowena ran her hands through her hair, sweeping it back behind her ears, and turned towards the pool again, revealing her famously perfect profile. 'You're using me,' she said sullenly. 'I don't believe you love me or you wouldn't do this.'

'If you loved me, you'd leave your half-brother,' Lewis's voice was soft, but she could hear the annoyance beneath.

'Perhaps if I'd felt safer with you I would have left him,' she responded.

Lewis stood up, unable to control his temper any longer. 'If you remember, Rowena, it was you who came to me in hysterical tears begging me to help you. I've never interfered, never tried to come between you and Chris. I knew about him when we married and I accepted him. All the dramas, all the weeping and wailing have come from you. And not only do you claim you want to be rid of him, you also want "to be a proper actress". Well, for your information real acting hurts. You have to put yourself through a hell of a lot of emotional pain if you're going to pull off a part like this. I warned you before we began, but you said it was what you wanted. I'm afraid there's too much money involved for you to pull out now.'

Rowena turned and pressed herself against her husband's body. 'Make love to me,' she whispered.

'No,' said Lewis, gently removing her arms

42

from around his neck.

Startled she took a step backward. 'Why not?'

'I haven't time right now.'

'You've always had time before.'

He kissed her gently on the mouth. 'Then perhaps I just don't want to,' he murmured, and to her dismay he walked away, back into the house.

Chapter Three

HARRIET HAD BEEN working for Rowena for a week now and she still didn't understand her. Sometimes she was charm itself, smiling, making jokes and sharing female confidences with Harriet as though they were friends. At other times she was sullen and withdrawn, criticising everything Harriet did and impossible to please.

It didn't worry Harriet. She accepted it as part of Rowena's artistic temperament, and even if it had worried her, being near Lewis would have been ample compensation. With every day that passed she found herself more and more obsessed by him. She was sure that he was interested in her. Whenever Rowena had been particularly difficult he would go out of his way to be extra warm towards Harriet, as though he knew exactly the kind of day she'd had. He was always watching her too, yet he still was clearly in love with his wife, forever touching or stroking her as he passed.

Once Harriet had come upon them embracing passionately on the stairs. Lewis's back had been to the wall and Rowena's legs were straddling his right thigh as she pressed her body against his. Although Harriet had retreated as quietly as possible the image had stayed with her and seemed to return almost every night when she was trying to get to sleep.

On this particular day she'd been working on the word processor nearly non-stop for the entire morning and when she straightened up for lunch her neck and shoulders were rigid with tension. Rowena came in to sign the fan mail and looked at her sympathetically.

'You've spent too long hunched over that machine. Why don't you have a massage? My masseur's in the house somewhere – you're welcome to use her.'

Harriet couldn't think of anything nicer. 'That would be great. Are you having lunch today?' she added. Rowena's eating habits were unpredictable.

Rowena shook her head. 'Tell Lewis I'm going over something with Chris, would you? There's a script he's been sent to look at. He needs my advice.'

'Of course,' agreed Harriet. Privately she thought it highly unlikely that Chris would ever be anything like the kind of star his half-sister was, but she'd already come to realise that in Rowena's eyes Chris was perfect.

They always had lunch in the spacious conservatory, although it was no longer quite so spacious since Harriet had obeyed Rowena's instructions and half-filled it with exotic green plants, which the film star herself attended to every day, claiming it was therapeutic for her.

Lewis looked up when Harriet entered. 'No Rowena?'

'She and Chris have a script to go through.'

He looked surprised. 'Really? I'm surprised she didn't mention it to me. Did it come through the post today?'

'If it did, I didn't open it,' replied Harriet. 'Do you know where Rowena's masseur is?' she added. 'My shoulders are stiff and she said I could use her.'

'She's gone I'm afraid, but I'm very good at reflexology. Would that help?' Harriet assumed he was joking and smiled politely. 'I'm serious,' he continued. 'Rowena finds it very helpful. Why not try it?'

Harriet's heart seemed to jump in her chest as she thought about Lewis using his hands on her, letting his long slim fingers massage her feet. She longed for it, but for some reason the words of acceptance refused to pass he rlips.

'Come along,' said Lewis briskly. 'Sit in the basket chair by the window and I'll do it before we eat.'

He sounded so matter-of-fact that some of her awkwardness faded. Even if her thoughts were running along sexual lines it didn't seem as if his were, and this chastening realisation made it easier for her to do as he said.

She sat in the chair and slipped off her high heeled shoes. 'What about your stockings?' he asked with a smile.

'I wear tights,' said Harriet, realising this was hardly a sexy admission.

Lewis pulled a face. 'How dull! Well, I can't massage your feet through tights; you'll have to slip them off.'

Harriet went to go into another room but he blocked her way. 'For heaven's sake, Harriet, I've seen more actresses changing clothes than you've typed letters!'

'Sorry,' she mumbled and her hands slid up beneath her thankfully full skirt and she tugged her tights down in what she was aware was a decidedly unerotic display of stripping.

'Now sit down and relax,' Lewis commanded her, but Harriet's shoulders felt worse than when she'd finished working for Rowena. She watched as Lewis took a bottle of olive oil from the work top then sat on the wooden floor at her feet, his legs tucked sideways. He drew her right foot on to the top of his thighs, poured some of the oil into the palm of one hand, rubbed his hands together and slowly, with firm but gentle kneading movements, worked his way from the centre of the her foot towards the sides. He began at the heel and in a leisurely fashion moved towards the toes. When he reached the soft padded part of the sole behind the toes themselves he pushed his thumb down hard and rotated it in tiny circles.

As he worked Harriet could feel her whole body responding. Her shoulders and neck muscles did relax but the rest of her didn't. She could feel her breathing quickening and her nipples brushing against her silk camisole top.

It was as much as she could do stop herself from wriggling around on the seat of the cushioned wicker chair, and when Lewis glanced up at her face she felt sure that he must know from her face exactly the effect he was having on her.

Lewis did. He reached for the oil again and

dipped a forefinger into it before softly pushing his slippery digit in and out between each of Harriet's toes in turn, twisting it from side to side as he went. The sexual implication behind the movement, coupled with the marvellously erotic sensation, made Harriet feel as though she was turning into liquid and she knew she was becoming moist between her thighs.

When he'd finished with her right foot he put it tenderly to the floor and proceeded to repeat the whole process with her left. It was almost more than she could bear; the tender, sensual caresses that soothed and yet aroused at the same time made her whole body long for his touch. If he could have this much effect on her by touching her feet she wondered what would happen if he moved on to more intimate places.

As he reached her toes for the second time and his silken finger slipped insinuatingly between them she suddenly felt her thighs begin to tremble and the whole of her lower body tightened. To her shock and horror she realised that if he didn't stop she was going to have an orgasm, and she tried to draw her foot away.

'Keep still,' he whispered. 'Let yourself relax. Enjoy it, that's the whole idea.'

'No, really I'm fine now I . . .'

It was too late and before she could finish her sentence Harriet's body was shaken by a tiny tremor and her toes curled upwards with the pleasure. She was mortified, but if Lewis knew what had happened he gave no sign of it. He merely ran his hands over the arch of her foot in one final tender caress and then took her foot off his thigh.

48

'Better?' he asked politely.

Harriet, her face flushed and her pupils dilated, managed to nod and mutter a strangled, 'Yes, much better thank you.'

'Then you'd better put your tights back on, unless you prefer to be without them? It's a shame to cover your legs. I like long, bare, tanned legs – very sexy indeed.'

Still in a daze, Harriet muttered something about tanning easily and stumbled to her seat at the table. Lewis sat opposite her and broke off a piece of French bread then passed her Parma ham and cheese.

Her hands still trembling slightly, Harriet began to eat. When Lewis poured her a glass of wine without asking she didn't comment, although normally she never drank at lunch-time because it made her too sleepy to work in the afternoon. Today she felt she needed it.

'How are you enjoying working here?' he enquired casually.

'Very much; it's certainly not boring.'

'No, I imagine not. But what about your social life? You haven't had a day off yet. When were you planning on taking some time for yourself?'

'I thought I'd probably go and spend the weekend at my flat if I'm not needed,' said Harriet. 'Rowena said you were entertaining on Saturday night, so I thought I'd be better out of the way and in any case I've promised to meet a friend soon.'

'A male friend?' asked Lewis, his eyes smiling at her in what was very definitely an intimate manner.

Harriet shook her head. 'No, a girlfriend.'

'Tell me, what was your last lover like?' he asked politely.

The wine she was drinking went down the wrong way, and Harriet was shaken by a coughing fit. He was obviously trying to shock her, she thought to herself as she began to recover. Well, he wasn't going to succeed. He might be handsome and sensual but she wasn't prepared to let him make a fool of her.

'Adequate,' she said levelly when she could speak again.

'Adequate!' What a very good description. I can almost picture him from that one word. And the one before him?'

'Inadequate. I'm afraid there's only one before that, and he was even worse so this conversation isn't going to be very interesting,' said Harriet.

'At least they've got progressively better,' he laughed.

'Perhaps it's just that I've improved,' said Harriet, astonished at her own boldness.

'There's always that possibility, of course, but the right partner can make a very big difference.'

Considering that he'd just brought her to a climax by massaging her feet, this was scarcely news to Harriet. She couldn't help thinking about the number of times she'd laboured for what seemed an eternity in order to achieve any kind of satisfaction with James.

'I'd like to make love to you,' he said softly.

'I'm sure you say that to every woman you meet,' responded a startled Harriet.

'No, I don't. In fact, I'm very fussy.'

'Then I'm flattered.'

He reached across the table and gripped her by

both wrists. 'You want me too, don't you?'

The way her flesh was responding now, let alone earlier, it would have been stupid to say no, thought Harriet, but she still had enough control of herself to remember why she was in this house in the first place.

'Even if I do, you're married to Rowena,' she reminded him.

He let his fingers stroke the exquisitely soft flesh of her inner wrists. 'We have a very open marriage. Believe me, Rowena wouldn't mind in the least.'

'Perhaps I mind.'

He moved one hand to stroke the side of her face. 'That would be rather a waste, don't you think?'

Harriet swallowed hard. The wine had dulled her brain, and his insistent touching of her, although only on her wrists and face, was proving irresistible. 'Please, don't do this,' she said quietly. 'I like my work. It will make things too awkward. I'd have to go and—'

Lewis stood up and moved swiftly round the table to stand next to her. Then he drew her to her feet and tipped her chin up so that she was looking directly into his eyes. 'I promise you, your work won't be affected. Trust me, I know what I'm doing. I don't want you to leave any more than you do. That won't be a problem.'

All the time he was speaking he was touching her. His hands were moving through her hair, smoothing her forehead, gentling her until she was leaning against him, her head on his chest, and she could feel his arousal clearly through his linen trousers.

51

'Take this afternoon off,' he whispered in her ear. 'Rowena's busy, you've worked all the morning, no one will mind. I want to make love to all of you, not just your feet. I want to touch you everywhere, to drive you mad with pleasure. Please, Harriet, let me do that.'

Every word, every touch inflamed Harriet's already clamouring senses until she knew that she was going to give in. It was what she'd wanted ever since she set eyes on him, and whatever the result she knew it would be worth it.

'I'd like that,' she said huskily.

Without another word Lewis took her hand and led her up two flights of stairs to the second floor, where she'd never been before. There he drew her into his bedroom, closing and locking the bedroom door behind him to ensure total privacy.

For a moment, as she saw the enormous bed, the piles of pillows and his discarded clothes scattered around the room, Harriet hesitated. This was a man more experienced than she could ever hope to be, a man who'd had countless women and would probably expect far more from her than she'd be able to give.

'What is it? What's the matter?' he murmured, sensing her fear.

'I'm afraid I'll disappoint you,' she said quietly.

'You couldn't,' he assured her. 'We'll be perfect together, as long as you trust me. You do trust me, don't you?'

Harriet nodded.

Watching from the adjoining room through a cleverly concealed peephole, Chris gave a smothered laugh and turned to his half-sister. 'She trusts Lewis!' he exclaimed. 'Talk about an innocent. Aren't you going to watch?'

Rowena, who had a comfortable seat by another spyhole, nodded. 'Of course, but I can't be bothered with his chat-up lines. Tell me when the action starts.'

'It's starting,' murmured Chris. 'He's about to undress her.'

Totally unaware of the hidden watchers, Harriet felt Lewis's hands unfastening the waistband of her skirt and as it fell to the floor she stepped out of it, grateful for the fact that she hadn't, in the end, bothered to replace her tights earlier. She knew that her long legs were shown to advantage by the angled cut-away tops of her cream-coloured french knickers but was less certain as to how he would respond to the rest of her body.

With infinite slowness, Lewis unbuttoned her blouse, peeling it back to expose the cream-coloured camisole top beneath. She wasn't wearing a bra and he drew one of the thin silken straps off her left shoulder, but to her surprise did not remove the garment.

'Keep it on,' he murmured, 'I prefer you like that.'

All the time he was undressing her his hands had moved up and down her legs, back and stomach and now, as he lowered her carefully on to the bed, he sat at her feet and nibbled lightly at her calves and the sensitive skin behind her knees.

Under his expert manipulation Harriet was encouraged to stretch out and give her body over to him. He didn't seem to expect anything from her except acceptance. She saw him reach across to his bedside table and pour something from a bottle into one hand, and the next moment he was massaging jasmine-scented lotion into her abdomen with the palm of his hand.

Harriet closed her eyes as the wonderful sensations swept over her.

'No,' he said firmly. 'Look at me, I want to watch your expressions change. I need to see what you like and what you don't.'

She felt ridiculously shy letting him watch her; she'd always closed her eyes with James, it had felt safer that way. Lewis's words made it impossible for her to pretend she was alone, which was what she'd always done before. He was forcing her to be more involved and this added a new dimension of excitement.

The lotion was spread over her legs, including her inner thighs, but when he came to her sex-lips he simply brushed lightly over them, ignoring her sudden upward-thrusting movement.

Next he worked his way over her rib cage, moving the delicate lace camisole top back as he went until it was rucked up over the top of her breasts, which were now rapidly swelling, the blue veins becoming more obvious as her excitement grew. Once more he ignored this erogenous zone and merely let the tips of his fingers dance across the surface before spreading the lotion over her shoulders and down the insides of her arms.

Every nerve in Harriet's body seemed to be alive now. She was trembling with excitement and frantic for more intimate touches but when she reached for his hand to try and move it where she wanted he shook his head. 'It's better to wait,' he assured her.

In the adjoining room Chris felt his own breathing quicken. Lewis was playing her with consummate skill, and her restlessly moving legs and upthrusting young breasts were testimony to her arousal. He himself was hard, and longed to be allowed to join in, to take the girl in the ways that he liked, the ways that kept Rowena enthralled. He was surprised by his reaction. Normally he would simply have wanted Rowena more than ever, but he knew that he was going to have to have Harriet before too long.

At last Lewis took pity on Harriet and lightly kneaded some of the lotion into each of her breasts in turn. He heard her breath catch in her throat and her eyes were grateful. Then, to Harriet's surprise, he moved himself up the bed so that he was straddling her body above the waist and, grasping his penis, he used the tip to trace a line around each nipple. The sensation was so glorious that Harriet reached up to increase the pressure on her nipples but again he restrained her, insisting on dictating the pace himself.

When she began to whimper softly with rising excitement he moved his body to the side of her and turned himself around so that he could spread the lotion on to her swelling vulva.

Harriet gasped at the first touch of his fingers on the delicate tissue, her hips moved without her knowledge and tight cords of sexual excitement seemed to connect her nipples to the core of her, where he was caressing her now, so that she couldn't tell where her pleasure was coming from. She only knew that her whole body was screaming with desire for release from the tight, mounting tension.

At last, when she was going frantic with desire, he let one of his fingers move slowly and delicately to the clitoris itself and massaged the side of the tiny swollen bud until her whimpers turned to moans and he could see her belly tightening and expanding as her whole pelvic area engorged with blood.

'Please,' whispered Harriet.

'Please what?' he teased, inserting two fingers inside her and rotating them just inside where he knew she would be most sensitive.

'Take me now,' she begged, and behind the peephole Chris fought almost as hard as Harriet to control himself while Rowena watched not the unfolding scene but her half-brother's face.

'Not yet,' he responded, feeling around the opening of her vagina for the tiny little bump that would show him where her G-spot was, while at the same time he continued to caress around her clitoris. 'And you mustn't come yet either.'

Harriet couldn't believe what he was saying. Her body was screaming for release, building towards what she felt certain would be the biggest orgasm she'd ever had and he was telling her not to come.

'I must,' she moaned. 'I can't help it.'

'Don't disappoint me, Harriet,' he murmured. 'It's better to delay the final moment.'

'Then stop touching me like that!' she cried, 'I can't bear it.'

'Of course you can. You can do anything I say,'

he assured her, and his fingers kept up their skilful manipulations as Harriet's body seemed to swell and bunch in its frantic climb to the peak of ecstasy.

She bit on her lower lip, tried to think of other things, to ignore what his fingers were doing, but it was impossible. Her whole body was damp and hot with need and there was an ache above her pubic bone that was increasing every time he touched her.

Suddenly Lewis found the elusive G-spot. He flicked his finger back and forth across it while the hand that was on her vulva grasped the hard damp clitoris between two fingers and squeezed with almost imperceptible pressure.

He knew it would finish her, but still murmured, 'Not yet.'

Harriet heard the words but her body took over. With a scream that was almost one of pain so intense were the feelings, she gave herself up to the forbidden pleasure and her back arched up off the bed as the glorious rippling contractions tore through her in what seemed like an endless spasm of bliss until at last she was finished and fell back limply on to the bed.

'That was nearly very good,' said Lewis tenderly.

Harriet couldn't imagine how it could get any better. She looked at him through half-closed eyes and saw that his erection was enormous, far larger than that of any of her previous lovers, and the purple glans had a glistening drop of clear liquid at the end. His obvious need for her acted as an aphrodisiac and she reached out for him.

'Turn over,' he murmured. 'Put your face down

on the pillow and bend your legs up from the knees.' She obeyed without question, knowing that whatever he decided to do, however he took her, it would be wonderful.

Once she was in position, Lewis knelt upright between her knees and his large hands reached beneath her so that he could caress her lower stomach while his penis nudged the cheeks of her bottom apart.

Then, as his fingers caressed her increasingly slippery clitoris his erection slid along her equally damp channel and came to a halt at the entrance to her vagina. The sensations his fingers were causing had already started Harriet's body on another climb towards orgasm and when she felt the soft velvet of his flesh against her opening she thrust backwards to try and hurry him into her. She wanted the sensation of fullness, needed to feel him deep within her, taking as well as giving pleasure.

Lewis drew back a little, aware that sometimes he was too large for his partner's comfort unless she was thoroughly aroused but when Harriet continued to move restlessly against him he slowly let himself slide into her.

For Harriet there was a moment of discomfort as her body stretched to accommodate him, but then one of his fingers tapped lightly at the base of her clitoris and incredible sensations of melting pleasure spread through her lower body and with them came increased lubrication that made his movements within her easier.

Lewis was finding his own rhythm now, different from the one that he used on Rowena, who liked him to thrust hard and fast. This time he moved slowly, sliding in and out at a leisurely pace, pausing now and again to rotate his hips so that Harriet could feel him touching her vaginal walls in what was almost a massaging motion.

The tingling darts that preceded her orgasms began in earnest now, shooting up through her belly, and her breasts ached with need so that she wriggled on the bed, stimulating her nipples herself. She could hear her own soft cries of mounting excitement and the way Lewis's breathing was also quickening.

All at once he changed pace and thrust fiercely forward, hitting the front of her vaginal wall exactly on her G-spot so that at the same time as his fingers teased her pulsating bud of pleasure on the outside, he was stimulating the crucial place within her.

The result was a sudden rush of sexual arousal that seemed to flood upwards from her feet and suffuse every nerve ending in her body with sensation. Her heart pounded and her belly tightened as she reached the brink of orgasm.

Lewis knew that he couldn't hold back any longer. The sight of her bent submissively in front of him, her slender long legs pressed against his, her smooth back and shoulders twisting in excitement all drove him to a fever pitch. When he felt the onset of his own release he moved his right hand and let the fingers dig softly into the flesh just above Harriet's pubic bone.

She climaxed seconds before him, and the rippling contractions of her inner walls around him were the trigger for his release too. He groaned and finally thrust as hard as he did with Rowena, determined to get the maximum pleasure from this moment.

Harriet could feel him shuddering above her but she was more aware of her own body and the incredible relief from the long, slow build-up of tension he had given her. No previous lover had ever given her such pleasure and she was startled by the realisation of her body's possible potential.

When Lewis was finally spent he gently straightened Harriet's legs and lay down next to her, turning her so that they could look into each other's eyes. He smiled and she smiled back at him, clearly as sated as he'd hoped.

'I told you it would be good,' he murmured, letting his hands run through her hair and noticing the difference in texture from Rowena's. Where hers was thick and curly, Harriet's was straight and much finer, but he liked the softness of it and the lack of hair lacquer which Rowena always used to excess.

'I'm sure everyone tells you this, but you really are beautiful,' he said with a smile, tracing a line down her nose and across the middle of her mouth.

'No one's ever told me that,' she replied with total honesty. 'Attractive yes, but never beautiful.'

'Well I think you're beautiful, and the camera would too.'

'Camera?' She felt a momentary stirring of unease.

'I'm a film director, remember? I always look at bone structure and profiles. I try and see what the camera would see. It would adore you.'

'It adores Rowena,' Harriet pointed out.

'Everyone adores Rowena. She has a particular kind of beauty. Yours is different, but it's still beauty.'

'You don't have to say that, you know,' remarked Harriet, letting her hands wander down the golden brown skin of his muscular chest.

'I wouldn't, if it weren't true. You're also very good at sex!' he added with a laugh.

'You made me feel good,' said Harriet with tenderness, and in the next room Chris nearly laughed aloud. He had to hand it to Lewis. He knew how to handle women, especially in the early stages of an affair, although he hadn't expected him to sound quite so enthusiastic.

Next to him Rowena turned away from the scene. 'He really likes her,' she said shortly, and walked out of the room.

When Harriet entered the dining-room at eight that evening and saw Lewis standing by the fireplace with his arm round Rowena she felt an immediate surge of jealousy. Only a few hours earlier his arms had been round her, in the most passionate sexual encounter of her life so far. Now, in front of her eyes, he was engaged in an open display of affection with another woman, and it hurt. The fact that this woman was his wife and Harriet the interloper didn't make it any easier.

Rowena smiled at her, but to Harriet's over-active imagination the smile seemed strained. 'You're looking very well tonight, Harriet. Taking the afternoon off obviously agreed with you.'

'I told Rowena you'd taken off for a few hours,' said Lewis smoothly. 'She'd got so used to your efficiency she'd quite forgotten you'd been working non-stop for a week.'

'Where did you go?' asked Chris, sitting down at table with a large glass of whisky in his hand.

61

'I went shopping,' said Harriet, caught unawares.

'How nice. What did you buy?' enquired Rowena.

'Nothing, I just window-shopped.'

'I wish Rowena exercised such self-control!' laughed Lewis.

'Anyone can tell Harriet knows a lot about self-control,' said Chris softly. 'Do you ever let yourself go, Harriet?'

This apparently innocent question brought a blush to Harriet's cheeks as she remembered how abandoned she'd been with Lewis. 'Not in public,' she said shortly.

'Then we must get together in private,' responded Chris.

Rowena frowned at him and turned to Lewis. 'Shall we eat? I'm exhausted and need an early night.'

He rang the small bell set in the middle of the table. The maid responded promptly, as she always did, and Harriet was extremely thankful when the food was served. She knew it was ridiculous to worry, that Rowena couldn't possibly know that had happened between her and Lewis that afternoon, but there was a distinctly strained atmosphere in the room and all she wanted to do was get away from the three of them.

The meal began with asparagus soup, followed by prawns and salmon in a delicious mayonnaise sauce served with a green salad and new potatoes. After that they all had slices of the cook's superb *tarte citronne*, then finally cheese and biscuits and coffee.

As usual Lewis ate well, while Rowena merely picked at the main course, pushed her dessert aside after one mouthful and ignored the cheese and biscuits.

'No appetite?' asked Chris, smiling at his half-sister as though at some private joke.

'I've put on three pounds. I need to be careful,' responded Rowena, glaring at him.

Lewis looked surprised. 'I didn't think you'd put on weight, in fact quite the reverse.'

'I'm flattered you've had time to notice,' retorted Rowena sharply.

'That's not fair,' said Chris. 'You know how important this project is to Lewis. He's been working hard on it all day, haven't you, Lew?'

His brother-in-law looked directly at him, his eyes cool. 'What do you mean by that?'

'Just that you've been busy!'

'No busier than you, I imagine. Harriet told me you were going over a script with Rowena. Was it good?'

Chris shrugged. 'Not really. We've binned it.'

'Do let me look before it gets thrown away. I might know someone who could use it.'

'I shredded it,' said Rowena.

'Goodness, it must have been bad!' laughed Lewis.

Harriet kept her eyes on her plate. She knew now that she wasn't mistaken. The other three were definitely sniping at each other beneath the cover of normal conversation and her own guilty conscience made the situation even worse.

'What shops did you wander round?' demanded Rowena abruptly.

Harriet swallowed her last fragment of cheese.

'I . . . Bond Street.'

'You mean there's a shop called Bond Street? I must go there.'

'No, of course there isn't a shop. I meant I wandered up and down Bond Street.'

'Was it busy?'

'Bond Street's always busy,' said Harriet calmly, but her stomach was churning as Rowena's questions continued.

'I think Harriet's private life is her own affair, Rowena,' said Lewis suddenly. 'If you're really tired, darling, do you want to go up to bed now?'

Rowena nodded. 'I think I will. I'll take a pill and go straight to sleep. Perhaps you wouldn't mind sleeping in your own room tonight.'

Lewis nodded. 'As you like. I've got a lot to do before I go up, so that way I won't have to worry about disturbing you.'

Rowena stood up. She looked at Harriet and opened her mouth to speak. 'Good night, Rowena,' said Lewis sharply. At the sound of his voice she turned her head towards him, met his warning glance and quickly left the room.

'Not a good day for her, I'm afraid,' said Chris with an apologetic look at Harriet. 'She found a grey hair this morning, that's enough to ruin her week!'

'She doesn't have to worry, she's still beautiful,' said Harriet. 'A friend of mine is an actress and she was saying that she'd never seen anyone with such a magical presence as Rowena in her first film.'

'Yes, but that was a few years ago now. She was only your age then; it's harder to maintain that glowing illusion as the years pass.'

'She was twenty-three when she made *A Lady Calls*?'

'That's right, isn't it, Lewis?'

'Something like that,' he agreed, leaning across the table to refill Harriet's wine glass and running his thumb over the top of her fingers as he did so. She swallowed hard, hoping that Chris hadn't noticed.

After a few minutes Chris yawned and pushed back his chair. 'I think I'll go up too. I'll probably sleep off the meal and then do a few laps of the pool. According to Rowena I don't get enough exercise.

'Don't drown,' murmured Lewis.

Chris smiled sweetly at him. 'I'll try not to give you that pleasure. Good night, Harriet. Sleep well.'

'What did he mean?' asked Harriet as the door closed behind him. 'Why would his death give you pleasure?'

'He thinks I disapprove of him because he lives off Rowena,' said Lewis shortly. 'The truth is, I scarcely think about him at all.'

'Rowena was in a bad mood tonight. She can't have guessed, can she?' asked Harriet anxiously.

'Not unless you told her! Don't feel so guilty, Harriet. You are entitled to some pleasure in life.'

'But not with her husband,' protested Harriet.

'Don't tell me you're going to say we can't do it again.'

'It's awkward. When I see you with Rowena I feel terrible.'

Lewis looked annoyed. 'You seem to have some very middle-class hang-ups about sex.'

'Unlike you I'm not artistic, which seems to be a

blanket term for lack of morals,' retorted Harriet, sounding more annoyed than she was because she wanted nothing more than to have Lewis make love to her again.

'If you think my morals are bad then perhaps I'd better show you something that will take away your guilt,' he said slowly.

'Show me what?'

Lewis caught hold of her wrist and pulled her roughly to her feet. 'Come with me, Harriet. I'll show you something that will make our little entertainment this afternoon seem like a Sunday school outing.'

Harriet tried to pull away from him. 'Let me go, I don't want to see anything.'

'I think you'll want to see this,' he assured her, and despite her protests he drew her out of the room and up the winding staircase, back to the second floor.

Chapter Four

WHEN LEWIS LED Harriet into a tiny room two doors down the landing from his bedroom she thought first that she was in a cupboard, but as her eyes grew accustomed to the darkness she realised that it had originally been intended as a dressing room, although the adjoining door had now been filled in. There was little furniture there, only a high backed chair and a two-seater settee in front of a square window, which let in no light at all.

She turned to Lewis in bewilderment. 'What is this room?'

'Sit here next to me on the sofa and look carefully at the window,' he said softly.

Puzzled, she stared at the glass, and after a few seconds realised that she was looking into a distinctly feminine bedroom lavishly decorated in various shades of lilac. As she watched, a figure crossed her line of vision, and she saw Rowena walking totally naked from her adjoining bathroom back to her bed.

Harriet ducked down and Lewis laughed. 'She

can't see you, it's a two-way mirror.'

'You mean, anyone can sit here and watch her without her knowing?'

'Yes. It's surprising what you get to see as well.'

A knot of excitement formed in Harriet's chest as Rowena turned so that she was facing the hidden spectators. Her figure was superb, her breasts high and full with large nipples and her waist tiny, curving out into softly rounded hips which gave her the traditional hour-glass figure of the sex symbol. Only her legs were less than perfect. They were shorter than Harriet had expected from her films, and the calves of her legs clearly defined.

'Can she hear us?' whispered Harriet.

'Only if we crash about. She can't hear us talking, but unfortunately we can't hear her talking either.'

Harriet couldn't think why this mattered since Rowena was only getting ready for bed, but almost as soon as Lewis had finished speaking a second figure entered Rowena's bedroom and Harriet's eyes grew wide with astonishment as the film star made no attempt to cover herself when Chris strode across the carpet towards her.

In the bedroom, totally unaware of what Lewis was doing, Rowena looked at her half-brother with a mixture of fear and longing. 'Not tonight, Chris,' she said softly. 'I really am tired and . . .'

'You're not tired, you're afraid,' said Chris. 'Now that Lewis's little piece of *cinéma vérité* is underway you don't like it, do you?'

'How would you like seeing your wife making love to another man?' demanded Rowena.

'A stupid question since I don't have a wife and

never intend to take one. I only need you, and you only need me, but you were too stupid to realise it. Perhaps this game of Lewis's will show you that at last.'

'I love Lewis,' protested Rowena.

'No, you love me,' said Chris fiercely. 'Lewis gives you respectability, and you think he's going to save your career, but you don't love him. He can't give you what I can, what you need, can he?'

'Leave it, Chris,' said Rowena, turning away. 'I need to sleep.'

'I need you,' he muttered and before she realised what was happening he'd grabbed her by the shoulders, pulled her arms behind her and tied them with a silk cord. She backed away towards the bed, already aroused, already longing for whatever he was going to do to her. 'I meant it,' she protested, 'I don't want you.'

Chris flicked at one of her erect nipples. 'This tells me a different story. I want you to wear the Japanese belt tonight.'

'No!' protested Rowena.

'You love it. Why deny yourself the pleasure?'

'Because you make it too intense.'

He smiled. 'Which is what you want, and why you need me so badly.' He reached into a drawer next to her bed and withdrew the slim rounded cord that fastened with a metal clip within which was a tiny spring. Very slowly Rowena moved towards him and when he fastened it around her she moistened her suddenly dry lips with the tip of her tongue. On the settee next to Harriet Lewis drew in his breath sharply at the look of naked sexuality on his wife's face.

'Now for the cloth,' murmured Chris.

69

Rowena stood at the foot of her bed, her hands still bound behind her as Chris fetched the long piece of silk material that went with the belt. He fastened it into the special openings in the belt at the back of her then drew it teasingly between her slightly opened thighs and up the front of her abdomen until he could fasten the other end in the front openings.

The cloth was now hanging loosely behind her thighs, but when Chris pressed on the side fastening of the belt the cloth was drawn upwards and he kept his finger there until it was brushing lightly against her vulva. He then released the spring. 'I think it's best to start with it loose, don't you?' he said reflectively.

Rowena shivered and he bent his head to tongue softly at the undersides of her famous breasts. 'I think I'll bind these too,' he whispered.

'No, please don't. Not both at the same time,' begged Rowena, but her words were all part of their game and Chris knew it. It was a game that had begun many years ago, when they'd first become aware of their bodies, and it had escalated out of control until now it sometimes didn't seem like a game to Rowena, but a contest of wills.

He licked and sucked at the still hardening nipples and when they were fully erect bound a silk scarf tightly round them, so that they could be seen straining against the cloth.

'Wonderful!' he enthused. 'Now we can begin.'

He guided Rowena backwards until she came to rest against the large chair on which she had earlier thrown her clothes. Sweeping these to the floor he lowered her on to it and then reclined the back. With her arms fastened behind her and her upper torso set at an angle this meant that her tightly bound breasts were even more prominent, and he pulled her lower in the chair until the cheeks of her bottom were balanced on the edge of the seat.

Unable to tear her eyes away from the scene that was unfolding in front of her, Harriet felt a stirring of sexual excitement in her own breasts and belly. She knew that she shouldn't be watching, that by doing so she was invading a very private and forbidden moment for Rowena, but even if Lewis hadn't had a restraining hand on her arm she knew that she wouldn't have left. She had to see what was to follow.

'Are you comfortable?' asked Chris.

Rowena nodded, wondering what his next move would be and quivering with excited anticipation. It was always like this when they were together. Her body became alive in a way it never did for anyone else, not even Lewis no matter how skilfully he played with her body.

'I think I'd prefer you a little less comfortable,' mused Chris aloud, and reaching into his pocket he withdrew an object that Rowena knew only too well. It was a small vibrator with a bulbous head. She shook her head and pressed her bottom more firmly into the chair but Chris's hands easily lifted her and then he started to ease it into her back passage.

In the next room Harriet gasped and Lewis glanced at her. 'Haven't you ever tried that?'

She shook her head, wondering how Rowena could bear to take the object into such a tender part of her body.

Rowena was wondering the same thing, but as the walls of her rectum struggled to accommodate the vibrator, Chris crouched in front of her and lazily drew the tip of his tongue along the centre of the silk material covering her vulva. The feel of the warm dampness through the silk, the way the material then clung to her more tightly and her swelling clitoris all combined to make her twist her lower body with excitement and the twisting movement assisted Chris in his task until the head of the vibrator was finally drawn into her rectum and she felt it filling her until her bowels cramped with the pressure.

As soon as it was fully inserted Chris turned it on at the lowest setting, then pressed her into the seat so that she was left to endure the constant stimulation of her most sensitive nerve endings.

She writhed in an ecstasy of dark excitement and watched as he went across to the drinks cabinet and refrigerator that was always kept fully stocked in her bedroom. From the fridge he took ice-cubes, put them into the silver ice bucket and carried them over to Rowena.

She was making small whimpering sounds of excitement and he smiled as he carefully picked up one of the cubes with the tongs and then drew it in a straight line across both her breasts, making sure that her nipples and areolae received plenty of attention. He loved to see the dark outlines of the area appearing through the thin white material, and loved to watch Rowena's eyes as she was forced to wait for him to provide further stimulation. Without him she was helpless to gain her satisfaction, and he loved the feeling of power that this gave him, just as she adored the sensation of domination.

When her nipples were like two rigid peaks poking through the binding he nibbled at them with his teeth and she screamed with pleasure. 'Naughty!' he reproved her. 'You're going too fast.'

Rowena couldn't help it, her body's responses to him were shaming but uncontrollable.

'I'll have to punish you a little,' he said quietly, and pressed the button at the side of the Japanese belt. At once the material between her legs was drawn upwards and this time he didn't release the catch until it was tight against her sex-lips.

In her back passage the plug was still vibrating continuously and as the silky material pressed against her throbbing vulva the plug's pressure too was increased. Rowena's body trembled more violently and a tiny spasm of pleasure swept through her.

She gazed at Chris who gazed back at her, his eyes suddenly cold. 'Did you come then?' he asked his half-sister.

Rowena nodded.

'Tell me,' he ordered her.

'Yes, I came.' Her voice was dark with shame.

'You're losing control far too easily these days.' His tone was severe, and he reached beneath her to increase the speed of the vibrator. Once that was done he watched the titian-haired figure shuddering beneath the stimulation and smiled to himself before taking a fresh cube of ice from the bucket and with deliberately tantalising slowness drew it down the middle of her silk-covered sex-lips.

The ice-cold dampness against her over-heated

flesh made Rowena groan. When the ice-cube was removed Chris scratched delicately against the material with his finger nails, and whenever he scratched over the clitoris Rowena's belly jerked and her legs trembled violently.

He continued to alternate the ice-cubes and his fingers and mouth on both her breasts and her vulva, and every time she came he would tighten the material between her legs until finally it was drawn up so hard against her that it slipped between her outer sex-lips and clung to the sticky inner lips, inexhorably stimulating the entire area.

Rowena began to scream at her half-brother, pleading with him to take her, to satisfy her properly, but he ignored her. Instead he dipped his tongue into her navel and swirled it around there, arousing yet more of her screaming nerve endings and causing another violent contraction of her internal muscles.

Harriet had lost count of the number of times the film star had been brought to orgasm by her own half-brother. She watched with rising excitement as the woman writhed, sobbed and threw her head around in what seemed to be a world of total pleasure, but a dark, forbidden pleasure that Harriet had never imagined existing. Next to her, Lewis put a hand on her knee and squeezed softly. 'Arousing, don't you think?'

'But they're related!' she exclaimed.

'They share the same father, yes.'

'Don't you mind?' she asked in astonishment.

'I find it very interesting,' was all he said.

Back in the bedroom, Chris decided the game had gone on long enough. Putting his hands round Rowena's waist he pulled her to her feet, pushed her head down and then withdrew the plughead from between her curved buttocks. He heard her sharp intake of breath as the bulbous head was finally removed and felt his own erection harden still more.

'Bend over the end of the bed,' he said hoarsely, and as she obeyed him he let his trousers drop to the floor, drew the damp, clinging material out of her sex-lips, pushed it to one side then thrust into her back passage himself.

As he drove into her, Rowena frantically caressed her own nipples by writhing on the bedspread while Chris used his fingers to stimulate her clitoris, at last giving it the firmer pressure that it had been screaming for throughout the game.

Rowena struggled to keep her final cresting orgasm at bay, knowing that in this game Chris always had to come first during the final session. To her horror he seemed to be lasting longer than ever before and she could feel her body swelling and the burning darts of pleasure streaked through her at an increasing rate until finally she reached the point of no return and with a despairing scream she toppled over the edge and let the climax tear through her.

Her resulting spasms were reflected in the walls of her rectum and as they tightened around Chris he lost his self-control and felt his seed rising upwards in a flood until with a shuddering gasp he was releasing himself into her still twitching body.

The moment he'd finished he withdrew, his face dark with anger. 'You came first!' he said accusingly.

Rowena struggled to turn over and looked up at him apologetically. 'I couldn't help it, Chris. You'd done everything too well, I just lost control.'

'Then I'll make you lose control again.'

'No, I've had enough. I can't,' she begged, but Chris was beyond stopping. Covering the fingers of his right hand in lubricating jelly he began to massage it into her exhausted tissue, spreading it around the sides and base of her clitoris until she was squirming once more.

'Let me see you come again,' he demanded.

Rowena closed her eyes and gave herself over to his touch, but her flesh was tired and she couldn't reach the peak he was asking of her. Infuriated, Chris knelt down and then she felt his tongue licking round the entrance to her vagina and the heat of an orgasm began to spread through her belly.

'Yes! Yes!' she whimpered.

His tongue snaked inside her, swirled around with the lightest of touches and slowly she felt herself melting into a pool of liquid. The heat increased, spread upwards through her entire body and her head went back hard into the mattress. 'I'm coming now!' she gasped.

Chris withdrew his tongue and stood up. 'I've changed my mind,' he said coldly. 'I think you were right, you'd had enough already.' With that he turned and left the room, leaving Rowena with her hands still tied behind her, lying on the bed screaming at him to come back and finish what he'd begun.

Harriet watched the internationally renowned screen goddess struggling fruitlessly to free her hands and turned to Lewis, sitting silently beside her. 'Will Chris come back?' she whispered.

'He won't need to. Rowena's very resourceful. I'm sure she'll manage on her own. She has the additional incentive of knowing that she can't afford to let her maid discover her like that in the morning.'

Harriet was shocked by his casual acceptance of what they'd seen. Rowena was his wife, and even an open marriage didn't usually include letting your wife have sex with her half-brother. She decided he was simply good at hiding his emotions, and that this was the only way he could cope with the situation.

She was wrong. Lewis was drawn to Rowena sexually; like most men he admired her body and found her sexual magnetism alluring, but emotionally he was untouched by her. Their marriage had suited him as much as it suited her. The joining together of his analytical, much-admired director's brain and her renowned sexuality and beauty had attracted almost as much attention in Hollywood as Marilyn Monroe's marriage to Arthur Miller.

Looking into the bedroom again, Harriet realised that Rowena's first priority didn't seem to be freedom from her bonds so much as freedom from her frustration, for once she failed to loosen her wrists she got to her feet and stood in front of one of the bed-posts. She pressed herself against it, thrusting her pelvis forward so that her silk-encased vulva rubbed against the rounded, patterned wood and as she found her rhythm her head went back and her red-gold hair streamed down the gentle curve of her back.

Neither Harriet nor Lewis could hear anything, but they could both imagine the sounds she would be making as the tension mounted in her rounded body until with a long shudder she finally reached the summit of pleasure and her muscles went rigid before gradually dissolving into relaxed softness once her body was calm again.

For a few minutes Rowena stayed leaning against the bed-post, her eyes half-closed and her breathing ragged, but then, still totally unaware of the onlookers, she set her mind to the problem of her bound wrists. Glancing round the room she saw the sharp edges of her drinks cabinet. The silk cords were slim and it only took a few minutes of rubbing against one of the edges before they broke and she was finally free.

She massaged each of the red marks lightly, taking perverse pleasure from the stinging pain as the blood-flow was restored. She was annoyed with Chris, but not as annoyed as she was with Lewis. That afternoon, when he'd been making love to Harriet, he'd done it with a tenderness and enthusiasm she hadn't expected and it had unsettled her.

Until now she'd taken Lewis for granted. She knew he wasn't in love with her but he liked being married to her and she liked having him as a husband. His love-making was excellent, and his detached, calm temperament was the perfect foil for all her insecurities.

If only she'd been able to give up Chris then none of this would be happening, she mused as she slipped into a satin nightdress and began to brush her hair. She had been certain that after a time Lewis would make Chris unnecessary to her, but it hadn't happened. Chris knew her body better than any other man, and Lewis either couldn't or wouldn't do the things that Chris did for her.

As Lewis became more successful and his work took him away from her for weeks at a time she'd turned increasingly to Chris, and had felt her marriage slipping away. When Lewis had suggested the film, explaining that through it the two of them would resolve their situation, she'd been as enthusiastic as him. Certainly watching him with Harriet had aroused unexpected feelings of jealousy, but tonight when Chris had almost forced himself on her she'd known that her need for Chris had been increased by what they'd witnessed earlier that day. It should have had the opposite effect, she should have wanted Lewis more and Chris less, but Chris was her comfort. He was always there, always able to stimulate and ultimately soothe her. There was another reason as well; Chris liked Harriet.

Rowena knew that Lewis had chosen Harriet because he'd been attracted to her – the plot could scarcely work if the second woman wasn't one that he fancied – but she hadn't for a moment considered the possibility that Chris would like her too.

Tonight, as her half-brother had tantalised and tormented her to higher and higher peaks of delight, she'd had the terrible feeling that at the back of his mind he was picturing Harriet in her place. She didn't know if it was just paranoia or her usually reliable sixth sense, but right now, at the very start of Lewis's story when the plot was only just starting to unfold, Rowena found herself horribly afraid.

Before she slid beneath the sheets she glanced at herself in the full-length mirror. She still looked stunning and sexy, she told herself, and it was true, in which case she shouldn't be worrying. Harriet was there to push Rowena into making a choice between the men, not as a threat to her relationship with them both. The sooner she remembered that and used her considerable assets the more certain she could feel that the outcome would suit her and not Harriet.

After all, she told herself as she drifted off to sleep, Harriet was nothing special. Young and attractive, yes, but hardly in the same league as an international sex symbol. The thought comforted her, although not as much as she'd hoped.

Lewis and Harriet remained in their seats until Rowena's head was on her pillow, her eyes closed in readiness for sleep, then Lewis rose to his feet. 'There, perhaps now you won't feel so guilty about our affair.'

'How long has it been going on?' asked a stunned Harriet.

'The affair with Chris? Ever since they were teenagers. Their father was married to Chris's mother when he got Rowena's mother pregnant. There are only twelve months between them. When Chris was three their father left his family and went to live with Rowena and her mother. When Chris was ten his mother died and he joined his father's second family. Obviously the two children became close. I don't think either of the adults had much time for the pair of them and they relied on each other for everything. Once their bodies started to mature the inevitable happened.'

'But once they were old enough to know it was wrong, why didn't they stop?' asked Harriet.

Lewis smiled to himself in the darkness. 'We all have special needs, Harriet. Dark, hidden desires that we don't feel we can reveal to the world. Chris and Rowena have no fear of each other; their relationship is totally open. Family genes seem to have meant that their needs are remarkably similar, they complement each other perfectly. Why should they have stopped?'

By this time he and Harriet were standing on the landing and he put both his hands on her shoulders, feeling her quivering beneath his touch. She'd been aroused by what they'd seen, just as he had, but for tonight she would have to wait. Their love-making, when it happened, would be all the sweeter for the delay.

'Because it's wrong!' exclaimed Harriet.

'That isn't a view that I subscribe to,' said Lewis. 'The only thing I insist on is that I take precedence. In sexual matters a husband should come before a half-brother, don't you agree?'

Harriet moved away from him, suddenly wanting nothing more to do with this dark, sexually magnetic man who seemed totally untroubled by moral scruples. 'You must be very broad-minded indeed to be able to make jokes about it,' she said shortly. 'Either that or you don't care about Rowena.'

'Perhaps I don't.'

Harriet hesitated at the top of the stairs. 'Did you ever?' she asked curiously.

'I really can't remember,' said Lewis.

The next morning as Rowena dictated numerous letters to Harriet, Lewis was closeted in his study with Mark, his scriptwriter for *Dark Secret*.

'Okay,' said Mark, lighting up one of his cigars. 'So we've had the sex scene between the husband and the secretary. What happens next?'

'Next I think the wife and her brother will make passionate love.'

Mark shook his head. 'No, it doesn't ring true. If the wife and the brother had been watching the husband and the secretary then the wife would be jealous. She'd start trying to think of ways to get the husband into her bed, not roll around with her brother.'

'I think you're wrong.'

'Why?' asked Mark.

Lewis thought for a moment. 'Perhaps because she's always turned to her brother when she's been troubled. Or looking at it from another point of view, perhaps the brother's turned on by what he's been watching and he forces himself on his only slightly reluctant sister. Yes, that's the way it should go.'

'You mean the brother fancies the secretary too?'

'Not necessarily, he might just have been aroused by the sex itself.'

'So the brother doesn't fancy the second woman?'

Lewis grinned. 'He might in time, I'm not sure yet.'

Mark sighed. 'It's bloody difficult writing it this way. If I had more of an idea of how the whole thing was going to develop I could slant the dialogue that way. You know, give subtle pointers to the audience.'

'I don't want the plot to be signposted. I want it to unfold slowly, giving up its secrets a little at a time; rather like a woman when you think about it.'

'You're the boss,' muttered Mark, clearly unhappy with the way things were going. 'So, what kind of a sex scene is this one?'

Lewis pretended to think about the question for a moment or two. 'Mild bondage, pseudo-force, that kind of thing.'

'Who gets tied up?'

'The woman,' said Lewis with a sigh. 'Didn't I say at the beginning that this was the way her brother kept her tied to him.'

Mark laughed. 'You meant literally!'

Lewis's face went cold. 'If you don't want the job, Mark, there are plenty of other equally good scriptwriters I could use.'

Mark quickly stopped laughing. 'Hey, Lewis, it was a joke. You know I want the job. It's weird, but it's sure as hell different.'

'Good. Bring it over to me when you've finished the scene. By then I should know what direction I want it to take after that.'

'And Rowena's really going to star in this?' asked Mark.

'She can't wait,' Lewis assured him. 'Don't forget the dinner party on Saturday, will you.'

In the front room Rowena heard the door slam and saw Mark walking towards his car. She bit on her lower lip, wondering what Lewis had said to him and how different the plot would have been if he'd seen her and Chris last night.

She felt guilty about that. Not about what they'd done together but about the fact that she hadn't told Lewis. How could his film be truthful if he didn't know everything? For a moment she thought about admitting it all, but changed her mind again. It wasn't as though she'd wanted it to happen, it had been at Chris's instigation and she'd just given in. Lewis was only interested in Rowena's reactions.

'Anything else?' asked Harriet politely.

Rowena looked blankly at her.

'You were in the middle of a letter. You'd just said . . .'

'Leave that one. You've plenty of others to type,' said Rowena, suddenly anxious to see her husband. 'I'll sign them after lunch.'

Harriet stood up, closing her notebook and giving her employer a quick smile. Rowena noticed that Harriet's skirt was far shorter than the ones she'd been wearing, and that her silk top clung to her breasts in a distinctly provocative way.

'You look different today,' she said abruptly.

Harriet, who felt different, tried not to blush. 'I thought this outfit would be more comfortable. It's much warmer today.'

'That explains why you've left your tights off,' murmured Rowena. 'If you want to top up your tan you can always use the sunbed. It's in a cubicle off the swimming pool.' Harriet thanked her and went away to start typing.

Rowena checked her appearance in the mirror above the fireplace, then went along to Lewis's study. He was sitting at his desk writing in longhand, and when she came into the room he pushed the papers into a folder. 'I thought you were busy this morning, darling.'

Rowena perched on the edge of his desk and bent slightly forward, giving him an excellent view of her perfect cleavage. 'I've finished dictating now. I thought perhaps we could talk about the film.'

'There's nothing to talk about. You saw what happened yesterday afternoon. That's the only scene I've got so far.'

'Did you enjoy making love to her?' asked Rowena.

Lewis stared into her bright blue eyes. 'Yes, very much. She was gratifyingly responsive.'

'More responsive than I am?'

'I didn't say that.'

'Make love to me now,' said Rowena, sliding off the desk and moving round so that she could sit on his lap.

'I have to spend my time with Harriet,' Lewis reminded her. 'If the next part of our plan is to succeed then it's vital that for the next few days I concentrate on pleasuring her. Her body must get used to me. When I stop visiting her, her body has to be left screaming for satisfaction. It's the only way we'll get her to go along with us.'

Rowena had heard all this many months earlier, but it hadn't mattered then because at that time the second woman hadn't been chosen. It was different now that Harriet was in the house.

'You've never been a once-a-day man,' she whispered to Lewis, pulling his swivel chair round so that he was facing her and sitting on his thighs, her legs hanging down on either side of him. 'Surely you've still got some energy left for me?'

Lewis eyed her curiously. Her black and red Lycra dress clung to every curve and the self-tie halter top was too tempting to be ignored. It was plain to him that she'd intended to have him from the moment she got up that morning, otherwise she would have been wearing her normal work-type clothes of designer jeans and cropped top.

Slowly his arms went round her and his hands slid up her back so that he could unfasten the dress. His fingers were quick and deft and within seconds he was peeling the top forward, revealing her rounded breasts, their nipples already partly erect.

Rowena gave a sigh of satisfaction and pulled his head down. She wanted to feel his long tongue against her, needed the gentle grazing of his teeth against her straining nipples. Lewis let her have her way. He moved his head from side to side so that his tongue could harden each of the rosy peaks in turn and then he drew her right nipple carefully into his mouth and sucked lightly until he felt her squirming against his thighs.

Her dress rode up her legs and he realised that she hadn't bothered to put on any underwear except stockings. His excitement increased and he felt himself hardening. Suddenly he wanted to take her quickly and violently right now, without any further preliminaries, and his right hand went to his zip to free his imprisoned erection.

Rowena made a soft sound of pleasure and lifted her hips to accommodate him, at the same time pressing her breasts more firmly against his face. Lewis slid into her and his hands grasped her by the hips in order to move her at the pace he wanted.

Rowena's eyes closed and she reached a hand down between their bodies to stimulate her clitoris as Lewis continued to move her up and down in an increasingly rapid rhythm.

At the touch of her own fingers on the slowly swelling bud, Rowena began to shiver and tiny tendrils of excitement started to snake their way up through her stomach. Lewis nibbled gently on the nipple in his mouth and this extra sensation gave Rowena the stimulation her climax seemed to need.

She felt it throbbing between her thighs like a pulse beating beneath the paper-thin skin of her perineum, and knew that she was about to come. Lewis was aware of it too and he let the fingers of his hands dig firmly into her hips.

'Yes, yes!' she shouted and her body began to arch away from him so that he had to tighten his grip on her hips in order to keep her in position.

At that moment there was a light tap on the study door and Harriet walked in. 'Lewis, have you seen Rowena? I can't find her anywhere and she's wanted on the telephone.'

Chapter Five

LEWIS STARED AT Harriet, hiding his anger behind a mask of indifference. Inwardly he was raging, not only at the fact that she had come into the room uninvited but also at his own stupidity in allowing Rowena to persuade him to make love to her at a time when he should have been concentrating solely on Harriet.

'Rowena will be with you in a moment,' he said smoothly, his arousal dissipating at great speed.

Harriet's eyes were wide and she stared at her employer as Rowena, ignoring the younger woman's presence, continued to move herself up and down on Lewis until with a cry of pleasure her body gave itself over to the warm flooding joy of orgasm.

Harriet knew that she should leave the room but her legs seemed unable to move. She stayed rooted to the spot watching Rowena's total abandonment to her sexuality. She felt almost consumed by envy, having spent most of her waking hours imagining what her next sexual encounter with Lewis would be like. Now she was forced to face the fact that he was pleasuring his wife at the same time, despite what he had seen her doing the previous night.

For a moment she wavered, thought of leaving the house and turning her back on all of them. Their way of life and lack of what she considered morality were so alien to her she didn't now how she could stay. But then she looked at Lewis, still watching her over his wife's head and she knew that she couldn't go. She wanted this man more than she'd ever wanted anyone and if possible she intended to take him away from Rowena.

This revelation was a shock to Harriet. She knew that it was illogical, that so far he'd only made love to her once and that he probably anticipated losing interest in her once the novelty had worn off, but watching him with Rowena, seeing those golden hands caressing her body, she decided that regardless of how impossible it seemed she would have her way. She would be very careful how she went about it though, since Lewis must think he was the hunter.

Lewis saw Harriet's eyes changing, and wondered what was going through her head. He hoped she wasn't planning to leave them, not just when everything was going so well. Cursing the fact that Rowena had wound her arms round his neck and was nestling against his chest like a small child, probably in order to remind Harriet that this was her husband, he raised his eyebrows apologetically at the silent girl.

'I'll ask the caller to ring back,' said Harriet, delighted to find that her voice sounded rock steady.

'That would be helpful,' said Lewis politely. He

wondered if Harriet felt as ridiculous as he did carrying out such a banal conversation considering the scene she'd just witnessed.

'I'm sorry I interrupted,' Harriet added. 'I thought you called for me to come in. Obviously I was wrong.'

'Has she gone?' demanded Rowena when she heard the door close.

Lewis sighed. 'Yes, I only hope she doesn't decide to go for good.'

Rowena laughed and sat back on his lap, her eyes bright and her cheeks flushed. 'Surely you didn't tell her we never slept together? Even Harriet wouldn't fall for an old cliché like that!'

'Of course I didn't, but this shouldn't have happened.'

Rowena stretched voluptuously and kissed him on the side of his neck. 'I'm very glad it did; it was delicious. I wonder who this call was from?'

Lewis, frustrated both sexually and by the turn of events, couldn't have cared less. 'You'd better go and find out,' he said shortly. 'And for God's sake don't go talking about this to Harriet. Keep a dignified silence. The pair of you aren't meant to talk about anything intimate at this stage in the plot.'

'Don't worry, I've got the outline safely in my head.'

'If you let me down over this, Rowena, I'll never forgive you,' said Lewis seriously. 'It has to be done properly, otherwise it will be just another film. I want it to be a true story.'

'I was just having a little rehearsal for one of the scenes,' laughed his wife, sliding from his lap. 'Will you be at lunch or are you planning another afternoon session with my PA?'

'After this I'll be lucky to get into her room tonight,' he said gloomily.

When Rowena returned to Harriet's office she found her typing efficiently, but when she lifted her head to speak to Rowena the grey eyes held a look that troubled the film star. It wasn't anger, which she'd half-expected, and nor was it envy; it was almost a sympathetic look.

'Who rang?' demanded Rowena abruptly.

'They didn't say, but it was an American man.'

'An American? Perhaps it was my agent. Why didn't you . . .?'

'I tried to tell you it was important, but you were very busy,' said Harriet calmly.

It was Rowena's turn to change colour and she had to go to her room and sit quietly trying to visualise a peaceful summer scene, as her personal physician had suggested, before she could calm herself. If it had been her agent he might have work for her, work that would be less emotionally demanding than this venture of Lewis's. But then again, it wasn't likely to carry the chance of an Oscar, and an Oscar was something Rowena yearned for.

Lewis stayed in his study for the rest of the day, only leaving it once to go for a walk in the grounds. Harriet saw him from her office window, strolling across the grass with his hands in his pockets and his head bent in thought.

Even the way he moved aroused her. His long, smooth stride and the tightness of his buttocks beneath his trousers reminded her of the way he looked naked. His bronze-coloured body, his dark hair and eyes made her stomach flutter with

91

excitement. She wondered why it was that he had this effect on her.

Dinner that night consisted of roast chicken cooked with lemon and tarragon followed by a passion fruit sorbet. This time Rowena ate hungrily and it was Harriet who picked at her food, her appetite dulled by her sexual hunger for Lewis.

Chris watched Harriet with interest. He knew as well as Rowena did the way the plot was meant to unravel and could hardly wait for the moment when he was able to take her himself. She would be so different from Rowena, hopefully reluctant to accept the ways he used to pleasure his women. The prospect of her reluctance and the knowledge that in the end she would almost certainly submit caused him to harden, and he decided that if Lewis was going to have her again that night then he would watch. This time he wouldn't take Rowena with him either.

'You're quiet, Chris,' said Rowena suddenly.

'I went down to the gym this afternoon and worked out for a couple of hours; I'm exhausted,' he said with a grin.

Lewis glanced at him. 'Which gym?'

'Luigi's.'

'That's funny; when I spoke to him on the phone earlier he didn't mention seeing you, and it would have been something of an event, don't you agree?'

'Well I was there,' lied Chris, who'd really been round all the sex shops he could find, buying additional equipment for his collection.

'More wine, Harriet?' asked Lewis.

She nodded. It dulled the fear that he wasn't

going to make love to her again unless she made a move, and at the moment she didn't know what kind of a move to make. As he filled her glass his head moved close to hers. I'll come to your room at eleven,' he whispered.

Harriet didn't take in much of the conversation that followed his promise. Her hand trembled when she raised the wine glass to her lips and she found it hard to stop herself watching Lewis all the time. Across the table from her, Chris continued to study Harriet. He'd seen Lewis murmur something and noted the effect of his words. Despite her cool, controlled exterior he already knew that she was a deeply sexual person; now it seemed that her emotions were involved as well. He was starting to enjoy Lewis's plot more with every moment that passed.

Dinner ended at nine-thirty. While the other three took coffee in the drawing-room, Harriet excused herself and went up to her bedroom. There she had a long bath, using the expensive bath oil and body lotion that had been left for her. Then she washed her hair with a jasmine-scented shampoo and conditioner before blow-drying it, using her fingers as a comb so that instead of falling in a sleek curtain to her shoulders it looked tousled and casual.

Finally she dabbed some Worth perfume, a present from James the previous Christmas, behind her ears, beneath her breasts and at the back of her knees before pulling on an ankle-length jade silk peignoir over a matching nightdress.

By the time she'd finished another hour had passed but she still had thirty minutes to kill. She spent them working out ways in which she could give Lewis pleasure as well as letting him give it to her.

When he finally tapped on the door she was in a state of intense anticipation. The bath, the massaging of her own body with the lotion and the feel of the silk against her warm flesh had all heightened her senses. She longed for him with a hunger so intense it actually hurt her physically.

Lewis eyed her appreciatively and then kissed her on the temples. 'You smell delicious,' he murmured. 'Good enough to eat, I think.'

As he slipped the peignoir off her shoulders, Harriet started to unfasten the buttons of his shirt and he stood compliantly, letting her undress him while his hands continually touched and stroked her body.

When he was finally naked she put her hands on his chest and pushed him towards the bed. He looked slightly surprised but obeyed, then stretched out on his back. 'I take it you've got something special in mind?' he said with a smile.

'I want to make you as happy as you make me,' she whispered.

Lewis was intrigued by this turn of events. It hadn't entered his mind that she would start to take the initiative so early, but the very fact that she had excited him, and he felt his penis swelling rapidly until it was fully erect.

Harriet slid the shoulder straps of her nightdress off and let them fall teasingly down her arms. From the bed Lewis watched, his eyes growing dark with desire. Then she wriggled her hips and the garment fell to the floor leaving her as naked as he was.

Now she joined him on the bed and lay on top of him with her head on his stomach. Since his penis was straining upwards this put her in the perfect position to take it in her mouth and she heard his swift intake of breath as her tongue swept round the circumference of his glans while her lips applied gentle suction.

The surprise of what she was doing, coupled with the sensations her mouth was causing him, made self-control difficult for Lewis. He knew that if their love-making was to last he must distract himself slightly, without stopping Harriet doing what she wanted to do.

His hands caressed the rounded cheeks of her bottom, so tantalisingly displayed for him, and moved up over her hips then round to her belly. Her skin rippled beneath his touch and when he let his fingers brush fleetingly against her vulva he could feel that her outer lips had opened up and she was damp with desire.

He moistened a finger in her liquid excitement and as she began to move her head up and down along the shaft of his penis he very slowly inserted the tip of the finger into the tiny puckered opening between the pale globes in front of him.

For a moment Harriet froze. No one had ever touched her there, and she wasn't certain that she wanted Lewis to, but then the gentle pressure sent a new and different kind of pleasure through her and as her body tightened all the nerve endings around her clitoris were indirectly stimulated so that the excitement was doubled.

After her slight hesitation Lewis felt Harriet relax again, and he continued this form of stimulation for her while his penis began to strain under the continuous pleasuring, until he knew that if he left it a moment longer he would lose control. Putting his hands on her waist he pulled softly. 'That's enough, Harriet. I don't want the evening to end yet, you know.'

She felt a thrill of excitement at this proof of her power over him and reluctantly slid her mouth along the saliva-dampened shaft one final time as she released him. He felt her tongue dip into the tiny slit at the tip as she lapped at the droplet of pre-ejaculatory fluid gathered there, and that small touch nearly finished him.

The well trained muscles of his abdomen fought to subdue his increasing need to climax and he pulled Harriet off him before she could torment him further with her mouth.

'Now it's my turn,' he whispered in her ear, and her body seemed to swell at the words. Turning her on to her belly he pushed two pillows beneath it. This meant that her buttocks were thrust high into the air and he then pulled her legs wider apart until she was totally open to him. Harriet wriggled with delicious excitement.

'Keep still,' he said, his voice thick with sexual hunger. 'Only move when I say you can.'

The very command added to her need to move. Lying still seemed an impossibility and yet she did as he said because she knew that it would add an extra dimension to her final satisfaction.

Taking a slim vibrator from the bedside drawer, Lewis put it on the lowest setting and then very softly let it massage Harriet's perineum. As she felt the soft tingling sensation in the skin between her front and back passages Harriet thrust her buttocks still higher, only to feel a slight burning sensation as Lewis flicked her with his fingers. 'I said keep still,' he reminded her.

Startled by the stinging flick she immediately lay motionless, and it was then that Lewis increased the vibrator's speed and let it roam around her clitoris, avoiding the hard little knot of nerve endings itself but concentrating on the sensitive tissue surrounding it.

Harriet longed to move, her hips seemed to have taken on a life of their own, and as the nerve endings sent thrilling messages of pleasure to her brain she had to fight to still her movements. It was agony, but exquisite agony, and lack of movement meant that she was even more aware of the incredible sensations that were engulfing her.

Lewis watched her carefully, admiring the way she kept her hips still and her acceptance of this new sexual game, so clearly not a part of her previous experience.

Her breathing was audible and ragged as the pressure within her increased and her tight stomach was further stimulated by the pillows beneath it, pillows that positively invited her to press deep into them and gain further satisfaction, an invitation she knew Lewis would not expect her to accept.

When she was fully in control of herself, enjoying the glorious streaks of ecstasy and the mounting heaviness deep within her core, Lewis decided to add more stimulation. Slowly he slid the head of the vibrator down her damp, slippery channel and into the hungry opening of her vagina. At the same time he lowered his head and let his tongue take over from the vibrator around her clitoris.

Harriet felt like screaming at the new sensation. Lewis started to vary the speeds of the vibrator. When he slowed it down he slowed the movement of his tongue, quickening them both in unison as soon as her body had adjusted to the more rapid touch. As the stimulation continued she lost all sense of what was happening to her, all she could concentrate on were the mounting waves of excitement and the increasingly rapid pulse beating behind the clitoris itself.

Her stomach ached it was so tight and tense, and she heard herself pleading with Lewis to allow her to move but he flicked his fingers against her inner thighs and she knew the burning stinging sensation was his answer. Suddenly all the sparks of sensation, all the sharp darts and tendrils of arousal, began to join together and Lewis saw the cheeks of her bottom tighten as her orgasm approached.

'Keep still a moment longer,' he whispered to the straining Harriet, and then he withdrew the vibrator and with one abrupt thrusting movement allowed his rampant erection to slide into her, taking care to keep up the stimulation of her clitoris with his fingers instead of his tongue.

Harriet felt that she was going to explode. Her body was being racked by liquid fire and then the incessant drumming of the pulse between her legs changed to a startlingly intense tingling that felt hot and rushed upwards through her with terrifying speed.

She shouted out loud, knowing that she could no longer keep her body still even to please this man who meant so much to her.

At the sound Lewis moved his fingers to the side of her clitoris and rubbed the slippery tissue with tiny circular motions as he moved in and out of her, his own body straining for relief from the continuous sexual tension as much as Harriet's.

It was Harriet who came first and as her body went taut with the first fierce contractions of her orgasm her vaginal walls contracted tightly around Lewis so that she felt as though she was milking him. She heard him groan and then he was thrusting without thought for her, thrusting solely to give himself the satisfaction that he knew Harriet was about to get.

Harriet's climax, having been delayed so long, built to a crescendo and then stopped, keeping her body tight and balanced on the edge of release for so long that she wondered how it was possible to bear such pleasure. Then it flooded through her and she felt the resulting explosion in every part of her, even her fingers and toes tingling with the final orgasmic convulsion.

Beads of sweat covered Lewis's forehead and upper lip and for a moment he looked down at Harriet's supine body with an expression of surprise on his face. Even for him it had been an unusually intense orgasm and he wondered why it had been so good.

Harriet, unable to see his face since her head was still buried in the duvet, longed for him to say something loving, something to show that it had been special for him, but all he did was lie down next to her and draw her to him, soothing and petting her with his large hands.

Through the peephole, Chris continued his

silent vigil. His own excitement was so great that he could scarcely control it, but he had no intention of going to Rowena tonight. He wanted to lie in his bed and think about Harriet. She'd been wonderful with Lewis, obeying his every command and showing depths of passion that were amazing, but it wasn't the same as it would be when Chris finally got to have her.

Then the instructions would be orders, and disobedience would be punished by more than a gentle flick of the fingers. He wondered how she would respond to that kind of sexual game. As for Lewis, his behaviour had been intriguing. Chris had seen his brother-in-law making love to Rowena in all kinds of ways but he'd never seen him so involved. The man had always appeared detached, taking his sexual pleasure in much the same way as through food or drink. Tonight he had let himself lose control, and the final soothing of the post-orgasmic Harriet showed far more concern for her as a person than Chris would have expected. All in all he thought it was a very interesting situation.

Half an hour later Lewis left Harriet asleep in her bed and went downstairs to his study. From there he telephoned Mark, who answered the phone sounding sleepy and irritable.

'I want you over here now,' said Lewis.

'Bloody hell, Lew, do you know what time it is?'

'Since you scarcely work in the day at the moment I don't think that matters. Get here and make it fast.'

*

'What's the urgency?' demanded Mark twenty minutes later after Lewis had let him in to the silent house.

'I've had this idea and I want to sound it out on you.'

'You're the boss.'

'That's right,' said Lewis with a smile that didn't reach his eyes. 'I am. Now, let's say that after making love to her brother our heroine decides that she wants to seduce her husband.'

'She doesn't have to seduce him, they're married,' objected Mark.

'Yes, but this *is* a seduction. She could go to his office and make love to him there, something like that.'

'On the desk top you mean? That always looks a bit tacky.'

'Okay,' agreed Lewis, smiling to himself. 'Not the desk then, let's say she just lifts her dress and sits on his lap while he's sitting in his chair.'

'Sounds good to me.'

'Fine, then at the vital moment, when they're both approaching the point of no return, the secretary walks in.'

'Why?' asked Mark. 'Surely she'd knock first?'

'Right, so we'll make her knock but she takes the sounds of passion coming from inside as permission to enter.'

Mark grinned. 'I like it! Then what?'

'This is a bit difficult, but I think she'll stay and watch.'

'Miss Super Secretary doesn't turn tail and run?' exclaimed Mark.

'No, she might like to, in fact we'd better make her show she'd like to, but the eroticism of the scene stops her from moving.'

'And how does the wife react?' queried Mark.

Lewis smiled. 'I think the wife would feel rather pleased with herself. After all, this girl is a threat and she knows it. How better to reduce the threat than to show the intruder that her husband can still be so overwhelmed with lust for his wife that he can't wait for the privacy of their bedroom?'

'But won't the next meeting between the two women be awkward?'

'Of course it will. The wife naturally expects the secretary to be miserable, but I don't want that to happen. I want the secretary to unsettle the wife.'

'How?'

Lewis sighed. 'That's the trouble, I'm not sure. By accepting it all, I suppose. She can carry on as though nothing's happened – that would make the wife feel uncomfortable. If someone doesn't behave in the way you've anticipated it's always unsettling.'

'You think Miss Super Secretary is capable of handling it like that this early on?'

Lewis nodded. 'Yes, I do. In fact, to underline that nothing's changed, she and the husband can have another passionate encounter that very night.'

Mark grinned. 'So the husband's a bit of a superman!'

'No, he's just highly sexed. Besides, isn't it every man's fantasy to have two women in his house, both of them anxious for his sexual favours?'

'It wouldn't be mine,' said Mark, scribbling down notes. 'In my experience women have a habit of coming off best in any situation, even one like this.'

'That's not the ending I've got in mind,' said Lewis shortly.

'You mean you know how it's going to end? I thought you were working this out a step at a time.'

'I am.' Lewis's voice was irritable now. 'That doesn't mean I don't have a final objective in view, but you're right, the plot might not develop the way I think.'

Mark stared at the director for a moment, wondering exactly what was going on in this house, but it wasn't his place to ask questions and already he had the gut feeling that the film was going to be something really special. 'What time's dinner on Saturday?' he asked as he put his notes away.

'Eight-thirty for nine. Don't bring anyone; we've got a spare woman coming.'

'I hope she's good-looking.'

'She's probably hoping the same about you!' laughed Lewis, and as he showed Mark out he made a mental note to himself to invite Harriet to join them. He wanted Mark to see her, if only to discover whether or not Mark guessed how Lewis was working on his plot. Closing the front door quietly, Lewis finally went up to his room to sleep.

In the morning Rowena was in a foul mood. She didn't appear until the others had finished breakfast, then when she finally joined them there were dark shadows beneath her eyes and her face looked puffy.

'Bad night?' asked Lewis after one quick glance.

'Yes, I couldn't sleep. Even the pills didn't work.'

'You'd better have a facial.'

Rowena glared at her husband. 'I know I look bad, you don't have to rub it in.'

'I didn't say that. Facials always relax you. Do you need me for anything this morning, only I'd planned to go out for a couple of hours. People to see, papers to sign, that kind of thing. And this afternoon I'll need to borrow Harriet.'

'I'm sure Harriet won't mind, will you?' responded Rowena.

Harriet smiled at Lewis. 'I'd be delighted.'

The smile irritated Rowena even more. 'Unless you intend to work your way through another pot of coffee perhaps you could go through some of those letters from agents representing authors who want to do my authorised biography,' she said curtly. 'Weed out anyone who hasn't already done at least two, and check the names against my hate list.'

'Hate list?' Harriet was bewildered.

'My beloved sister keeps a list of all the people she's offended along her climb to stardom. She's terrified one of them will come back and wreak vengeance one day,' explained Chris.

'Do you think you can manage that?' demanded Rowena.

Harriet nodded, turned to leave and bumped into Lewis, who had turned to go at the same time. His hands caught her arm and for a moment his grip tightened into intimacy, which set her blood racing. 'Sorry!' he apologised, and then with a wink he was gone.

Rowena missed the byplay, but her half-brother didn't. Once the pair of them were alone he considered mentioning it, then decided there was no point. He hated it when Rowena got in a bad mood and always tried to bring her out of it.

'What are you staring at?' Rowena demanded.

Chris smiled his lazy smile. 'I was admiring your outfit.'

Rowena was wearing a short, figure-hugging black skirt, a lace trimmed black bra and a pure white linen overshirt that reached to her hips and was unbuttoned far enough to show the black bra peeping through. Once it would have been an unthinkable way of dressing, but Rowena was careful to keep up with new fashions and this look was very popular at the moment. It was also, as she appreciated very well, sexy.

'Where were you last night?' she muttered. 'I needed you.'

'I was asleep.'

'Liar! I rang your room and you didn't answer.'

'I don't answer the phone in my sleep.'

'Didn't you guess I was expecting you? I don't like what's happening; I don't know how to react or even what I really want. I've got to be able to depend on you still. We're always there for each other, you promised that wouldn't change.'

Chris tipped his chair back. 'I thought you wanted it to change. The whole idea of this film is to get you away from me, isn't it?'

'Just less dependent.' Rowena's voice was soft now, almost caressing as she started to play him like a fish. Her body lusted for him, for his urgent, harsh love-making, but she knew that he liked to hear how much he was wanted.

'It wouldn't appear to be working.'

'I know one thing,' said Rowena with total honesty. 'I hate having Harriet in the house. It's ridiculous, she was meant to be jealous of me and

I'm becoming jealous of her.'

'It's a competition – of course you're jealous, but you hold all the cards. Harriet's only a secondary player.'

'I hope she knows that,' said Rowena fiercely. She looked at Chris lounging back in his chair, his blond curls unbrushed and his light blue eyes continually flicking to her cleavage. 'Let's do it now, Chris,' she whispered.

'In here?'

'Why not? Harriet's busy, Lewis has gone out and I don't think I can wait until tonight. Please, Chris.'

He could never resist her. Their dependency was mutual and yet as he worked out how best to satisfy her in the confines of the breakfast room he found that he was imagining doing it with Harriet watching them. This idea added to his excitement and he felt himself growing hard.

'Crouch on the kitchen chair,' he said shortly. 'Put your feet on the seat and grip the back with your hands. If you thrust backwards I'll be able to stand on the floor and take you from behind.'

Rowena's mouth went dry. This was what she craved from him; swift, urgent couplings spiced with the risk of discovery were almost as satisfying to her as their long dark sessions where she allowed him to dominate her totally.

As she squatted on the chair, her feet as far apart as the seat would allow, her skirt rose up and Chris realised with a thrill of excitement that she was wearing crotchless panties. He put his hands on her waist and without any preliminaries at all thrust roughly into her.

As he thrust he put his mouth close to her ear

and each time she was pushed forward by the force of him Rowena heard him whispering, 'You're mine, mine, do you hear?'

The words increased her excitement and she slid her right hand beneath the hem of her skirt so that she could stimulate herself but it was hardly necessary. Already her excitement was mounting and when Chris moved his hands upwards and cupped her breasts through the linen shirt she contracted the muscles of her pelvic floor with the result that her pre-orgasmic tremors intensified. As her half-brother muttered, 'I'll never let you go, never,' her body exploded in a dizzying mass of pleasure until she slumped forward with her head resting against the rounded top of the kitchen chair.

Chris leant against her back, his breathing gradually calming. When his erection had subsided he slid out of her and with one final tweak of her nipples stepped away, adjusting his clothing.

When he left her, when her body was physically separated from his, Rowena felt a shiver of fear. Suddenly she wanted him back inside her, not for the sex – she was sated now – but to reassure herself that they were still close.

Chris saw her tremble. 'What's the matter?'

'I don't know. I'm so afraid all the time.'

'It isn't your heart that's going to be broken, it's Harriet's. She's falling in love with Lewis.'

Rowena climbed down off the chair and pulled her skirt back into place. 'Don't be stupid, she doesn't know him except physically. Anyway, Harriet doesn't look to me like the kind of girl who falls in love. She's much too sensible – an admirable English virtue.'

'I think you're wrong, but it needn't worry you.'

'It would worry me if it were true,' responded Rowena, running a hand through Chris's hair in a proprietory manner. 'Men are susceptible to women who fall in love with them. It flatters their ego.'

'Lewis doesn't have an ego problem.'

Rowena smiled. 'All men have an ego problem. I'd better go and see how Harriet's getting on. I was a bit short with her earlier.'

'She won't have minded. She expects you to be temperamental; it goes with the territory, as they say.'

Chris was right. Rowena's bad mood hadn't perturbed Harriet, particularly after Lewis had managed to touch her, however briefly. She wasn't foolish enough to imagine that he was in love with her, but she did think that he liked her as a person as well as a sexual partner.

His emotional detachment from Rowena was starting to show itself to her. Given his continuing lack of jealousy over his wife's extraordinary relationship with her half-brother this was beginning to seem the most logical explanation, and if his emotions weren't engaged anywhere else then so much the better for her.

At the same time as Harriet was working out a strategy to get the man she wanted, Lewis was finalising his plan for drawing Harriet deeper into the web they were all spinning around her. Her sexual response to him was gratifying, and with a body so clearly made for sex it should be easy to train it to expect constant satisfaction. Once that was done, once she was used to a full and satisfying sex-life, then he would leave her for a time.

It would be harder than he'd imagined because he enjoyed giving her pleasure but his enjoyment was of secondary importance to the film, and the film's plot meant that Harriet had to be persuaded to go a step further into the world inhabited by all who lived in the house in Regent's Park.

Probably the only member of the household without any worries at this time was Chris. He was thoroughly enjoying himself. Rowena was turning to him more, not less as he'd feared, while Harriet fascinated him as no woman apart from his half-sister had ever done. He knew that in time he'd be allowed to use her, because the film called for Rowena to watch and assist him in this.

Anticipation of that moment, coupled with Rowena's urgent need, meant that for the first time in his life he was totally content. He was also amused because he had the feeling that Lewis's plan, so cleverly contrived to remove Chris and drive Rowena into her husband's arms, was going to misfire, and what he wanted more than anything else in the world was to see Lewis fail at something.

Chapter Six

THAT EVENING CHRIS and Rowena went to the opera. Lewis hated opera. 'Good music spoilt by bad acting,' was his opinion and nothing he saw ever made him change his mind. After they'd gone he went in search of Harriet and found her reading a book in the comfort of the drawing-room.

'We've got the house to ourselves,' he said with a smile. 'How would you like a nice bath? We can use the tub in Rowena's bathroom – it's meant for two.'

Harriet lifted her eyes from the page. 'I had a shower this morning, thanks.'

For a moment Lewis couldn't believe he'd heard her correctly. 'You don't have to be dirty,' he said with a laugh. 'It's meant to be a sensual pleasure.'

Harriet smiled in an absent-minded way. 'I'm sure it would be, but I'm a bit tired tonight.'

Since nothing in his imaginary script had prepared Lewis for this he was totally at a loss. 'I'd like it,' he said slowly. 'Doesn't that matter to you?'

With a soft sigh Harriet put the book to one side. 'Of course it does, Lewis, but I'm sure I'm not the only woman in London who'd be willing to give you a bath.'

'You're the only one I want to give me a bath,' he replied, frantically trying to work out how to handle this.

'Then you'll have to settle for a shower,' she said gently.

Lewis stared at her. 'What's all this about, Harriet? I thought you were enjoying our affair as much as I am.'

'I am, but I'm not in the mood tonight.'

He cursed silently. The whole plot hinged on the fact that she found him irresistible, that her need for him was total and when he left her she had to be devastated. This cool woman sitting looking at him with a half-smile on her face seemed to have suddenly stepped out character.

Much to Lewis's amazement it dawned on him that he wasn't only put out because of this divergence from the plot. He was also disappointed for himself. Their times together had been good, and his enjoyment had probably equalled hers. To be rejected wasn't something that happened to him very often and neither was it usual for any rejection to matter.

Harriet watched the way Lewis hovered in the doorway. He seemed unable to accept her words and leave, but at the same time she sensed that it was almost beyond him to press any harder. His personal pride would be offended at the thought that he'd had to beg for sex from any woman.

After careful thought Lewis went and sat on the arm of Harriet's chair, then he tenderly stroked

111

her hair and the side of her face. 'You're not ill, are you?'

She laughed. 'Do I have to be ill before I say no?'

'Of course not. I had the apparently incorrect idea that what we had was special for both of us. It's difficult for me to have my hopes for a wonderful evening dashed, that's all.'

It was hard for Harriet to maintain her attitude of indifference when he was touching her so tenderly, his hand massaging her scalp in slow easy movements before travelling in a lingering caress down her neck. Despite herself she began to tremble.

Lewis felt her reaction. 'Please, Harriet,' he said huskily. 'I don't know what your real reason is for refusing, but I do know that it isn't because you don't want me. If it's Rowena, forget it. For all I know she and Chris haven't even gone to the opera, they may be at some party together. It doesn't matter to me, and this wouldn't matter to her.'

'It isn't Rowena,' Harriet assured him. 'After James I'm not very keen on getting involved with anyone on a regular basis.'

'But we're good together,' he protested, deciding that whatever else happened he wasn't going to pass this scene on to Mark; it was too humiliating ever to repeat aloud.

Harriet decided that she'd kept him waiting long enough, and he was certainly sufficiently unsettled to think twice before he took her compliance for granted again. 'Well, perhaps a bath would be nice,' she conceded. 'Usually I take showers.'

112

Lewis was amazed by the wave of relief that washed over him. His heart was beating rapidly and it took all of his self-control not to simply take Harriet there and then on the floor of the drawing-room.

Instead, pausing only to collect a bottle of chilled Chardonnay and two glasses, he led her upstairs to Rowena's bathroom and there filled the tub with water, adding plenty of erotic Japanese sandalwood oil which engulfed the room with its subtly arousing fragrance.

Slowly he undressed Harriet, then let her undress him, and all the time he kept touching and kissing her, whispering in her ear exactly what he proposed to do during their time together.

He sat her between his outspread legs with her back to him and the warm water came up to her breasts. Tenderly he soaped her along her spine using long featherlight strokes. Harriet felt herself dissolving beneath his touch and when he laid her back in the water so that her head was against his chest she expected him to move on to her breasts, which were tight and aching, but instead he washed her arms, ending with the hands which he lingered over, teasing every finger until the rest of her body was screaming for attention.

It seemed an eternity before his hands picked up the soap and he lathered it over her stomach, causing the muscles to leap and jump in a dance of their own. Once he brushed her breasts, but it was such a faint caress that she could almost have imagined it and it served only to increase the aching sensation behind each nipple.

After that he got her to move so that she was on

all fours with her head at the tap end of the bath. Then she had to raise her buttocks high above the water. He proceeded to cover the cheeks of her bottom with the suds before lightly running a finger between them. The slight tickling of the bubbles was incredibly arousing, and when he washed them off with bathwater she wanted to ask him to do it again, but Lewis had other plans.

He turned her over again and this time crouched above her, straddling her body in the water until at last his hands were washing each of her breasts in turn, taking particular care over the nipples, which he covered in suds until they vanished from sight.

Again the bubbles burst, tickling the tender flesh and causing her breasts to harden and the veins to become visible. Lewis smiled at her, then took a sponge and held it high above her before squeezing the contents out in a steady stream over her nipples.

Harriet gave a gasp of pleasure and Lewis repeated the procedure, this time holding the sponge above the soapy breasts for even longer until she was begging him to let the water cascade down.

He had intended letting her wash him, but their love play had aroused him more than he'd anticipated and he didn't want to wait any longer before possessing her.

Pushing her soapy hands gently off him he climbed out of the bath. 'I'll take my turn another time,' he promised. He then wrapped her in a warm towel, picked her up and carried her out of the bathroom, through Rowena's room and into his own. Once he'd laid her on his bed he went back to the bathroom for the wine and together they drank from opposite sides of the same glass, stopping now and again to exchange kisses and let the crisp refreshing liquid pass from one mouth to the other.

They were both frantic for each other now, but Harriet had already discovered the joys of delaying the ultimate pleasure and it was she who got Lewis to lie on his stomach so that she could pour some of the wine on to the top of his spine.

His body jerked at the unexpected coldness, then as it trickled across each vertebra he felt her soft warm tongue licking at it. Her tongue and the wine were an incredible contrast to each other. This time he was the one to writhe against the duvet, and Harriet watched his movements with fascination.

'Keep still,' she told him, remembering her own struggles to control her body, and beneath her Lewis stiffened, then forced himself to obey, fascinated by this change in the balance of power.

After working down his spine with her tongue, Harriet dipped her middle finger in the wine and then eased it between the cheeks of his bottom, stopping every time he gave an involuntary jerk.

For Lewis it was the most delicious torment as he tried to quell his excitement sufficiently for her finger to reach its ultimate goal. She refused to let him hurry her, or to move except when he was still, but eventually the tip of the finger touched his prostate gland and he felt his already hard erection swell. The pressure in his tightly drawn up testicles seemed unbearable.

When her finger caressed the gland again he had to move to stop himself from coming.

115

'Harriet, stop! I can't take any more,' he murmured, and she felt a surge of triumph as she withdrew her teasing digit and let him roll onto his back.

Lewis saw Harriet looking down at him and for the first time since their affair had begun he reached his hands up, pulled her face down and kissed her long and deeply on the mouth. His tongue teased the insides of her soft lips and then flicked round her teeth before easing its way between them. Her own tongue responded, and she licked the corners of his mouth before the tempo of the kiss increased and he started to thrust his tongue deeper into her mouth, duplicating the urgent thrusting of his erection.

They were lying locked together now, Harriet on top of him, revelling in the feel of his muscular body beneath her, and when he rolled her on to her side so that they were face-to-face she stared deeply into his eyes, trying to read something from their expression.

Lewis stared back. His breathing was still rapid and his hands unable to leave her alone as they moved down her side, over her hipbone and down the slender flank. His penis strained against her lower abdomen and he moved down the bed so that he could use it to caress her clitoris with tiny teasing movements, then watched as her eyes darkened and the pupils enlarged with her growing excitement.

Harriet began to wriggle with impatience, suddenly no longer concerned with whether or not she could see any true emotion in his eyes. All she wanted was to have him inside her, to be filled yet again in order to satisfy the craving that he had aroused in her.

Lewis was lying on his left side and he raised Harriet's left leg over his waist then slid deep into her, his hands clasped round her buttocks. For a moment they both stayed motionless, each of them savouring their body's sensations, and then Lewis moved.

He withdrew to the entrance of her vagina, tantalised her frantic flesh for a few seconds, then pulled hard on her buttocks so that she was propelled on to him and he re-entered her in a rush.

The angle of penetration was perfect for Harriet because every time he withdrew and then pulled her back to him all the nerve endings around her clitoris were stimulated and the tense tightness that she'd come to associate with their love-making filled her pelvic area, spreading slowly upwards in darting streaks.

When the tempo of his thrusting increased, Harriet lost all control of herself. Her only thought was for the pleasure he brought her and she gave herself over to it utterly. Her tiny cries and whimpers stimulated Lewis more than any wild thrashing would have done and when she finally took up the rhythm he'd started for herself, moving her own body against his at the pace they both wanted, he let one of his hands move between the cheeks of her bottom and inserted a finger into her rear.

He moved it very slowly, just sufficiently to allow him to press firmly against the walls of her rectum and as Harriet's body gathered itself together for the final explosion of excitement the delicate nerve endings deep within her were stimulated and the pressure travelled through to her front so that all sensations were doubled.

Lewis felt her body arching against him, heard her moan of delight and then she was twisting and turning, almost jerking away from him in the mindless spasms of her climax. Aroused to incredible heights himself he caught hold of her body and roughly pulled her back against him, his penis now so tight and swollen that he could feel the sides of her vaginal walls pulsating around him and with a shout he spilled himself into her warm velvet softness.

As Harriet's body started to recover from her orgasm she realised that there was still a soft but undeniable pulse beating between her thighs. She tried to keep still, ashamed to think that her body might be demanding yet more satisfaction.

Lewis lay quietly, his erection subsiding within her, but watching her closely he knew from the expression in her eyes and the almost imperceptible movements of her hips that she was capable of more.

He was pleased. This was what he'd hoped for. A woman who would become more and more capable of sexual arousal. A woman whose body would take over from her mind so that in the end she would do anything for the satisfaction he had taught her to need.

'You'd like more, wouldn't you?' he whispered.

Harriet shook her head, still denying her own sexuality.

'There's no reason to be ashamed,' he assured her. 'It's a compliment to me.'

'But I've never been like this,' protested Harriet, remembering how relieved she always was when James had finished.

'This is a new life. You can be quite different here,' he murmured and with relief she felt one of his hands pressing against her lower belly just above the pubic bone, exactly where she always ached when need for release started to build in her.

His hand moved in circles, the pressure increasing as Harriet's body responded. Suddenly she felt a new sensation, a strange heaviness buried so deep inside her it was impossible to be sure where it began, and sharp sensations like currents of electricity speared through her from below her clitoris up to where his hand was moving relentlessly.

Lewis knew exactly what was happening. He was arousing not only the nerve endings from the clitoris but also those leading from the bladder and the combination lead, for some women, to their most intense orgasms.

Harriet seemed likely to be one of those women because she began to cry out, and her eyes were enormous as she looked up at him. 'Don't stop!' she begged when his hand was briefly still. 'It feels incredible.'

'You like it?'

Harriet bit on her lip as his hand dug deeper and the hot, tingling pressure intensified. 'Yes,' she assured him, although now the sensation was so intense that she wasn't quite sure it could be pleasure.

Her body knew better than she did, and began to swell until the skin of her abdomen felt too tight. Moaning she tried to move, to slow down the mounting sensations that threatened to overwhelm her. Lewis simply let the fingers of his hand part the top of her outer lips, and while he continued to press firmly against her lower belly he also teased the sides of her pulsating bud, never staying in one place for more than a few seconds but all the time moving so that her flesh jumped and the throbbing between her legs seemed to be echoed by the sound of her pulse drumming in her ears.

Lewis's own erection had now subsided but at the sight of Harriet being aroused to new and only dimly understood heights, he felt himself start to stir again.

As the startling feelings continued to grow, Harriet's breasts began to ache and after only a slight hesitation she reached up, drawing Lewis's head down towards her.

'Tell me what you want,' he murmured.

'My breasts,' she moaned, thrusting them up towards his mouth. 'They ache.'

'And what do you want me to do about it?' he teased.

Harriet didn't know if she could tell him, but the insistent clamouring of her needy flesh won over her deeply ingrained reticence at vocalising her desires. 'Suck them for me, Lewis, please.'

'Hard or soft?' he asked, his hand still continuing its pressing movements and his finger drawing up the clitoral hood as he worked so that he could brush lightly across the top of the exposed nub.

'Hard!' she begged, her body now nothing but a pressurised aching need for the final stimuation that would allow her another crescendo of pleasure.

He smiled and then his mouth closed around one of her hard nipples and he was sucking steadily. The pressure grew, just as the pressure on her clitoris and the over-excited nerves from her bladder grew and with this final touch the flashes and the streaks of bliss that were searing through her at last came together and she was wracked by almost painfully fierce muscular contractions that seemed to turn her whole body into hot liquid as it tumbled into total satisfaction.

Somewhere in the distance Harriet heard a strange keening sound, little realising that it was her own cry of ecstasy, and as her back arched and her upper torso twisted and turned Lewis let his teeth graze the very tip of the nipple in his mouth and he continued stimulating her clitoris until the final tiny muscular tremors had died away and she was at last still.

For Harriet, covered in a thin sheen of perspiration, her limbs almost weightless, it had been the best moment yet and she closed her eyes to try and recall exactly how it had felt at the final moment when her orgasm swept over her. She could remember the earlier sensations, the strange sharp pressure, the aching nipple and the feeling of Lewis's mouth covering it, but those last glorious moments eluded her. They were impossible to recreate by memory.

When she opened her eyes Lewis was propped up on one elbow, watching her with an expression of tenderness. 'Do you want any more?' he asked with a smile.

Harriet shook her head. 'That was out of this world. I never thought . . . I wouldn't have believed it possible to feel so much.'

'Believe me there's still plenty more for you to discover, but not tonight, I think!' He kissed her gently on the forehead, his hands stroking the sides of her neck. 'I really should go and do some work. Will you be all right on your own?'

'I can't stay here,' said Harriet quickly. 'I must get back to my own room.'

'Nonsense,' said Lewis easily. 'Rowena won't look in here tonight, and you'll be up long before her in the morning. Besides, when I do come to bed I want you to be here for me. I'd like to spend the night next to you.'

Unexpectedly touched, Harriet sighed voluptuously and gave in. He must know what he was doing, and anyway she felt too tired to go down to the first floor. The prospect of a cold bed was distinctly unappealing as well. 'All right,' she conceded and with a final kiss Lewis left her.

'Why do I have to keep coming out at night?' asked Mark irritably.

'My best ideas come to me then,' replied Lewis smoothly.

'I haven't finished the last part you gave me yet.'

'As long as it's out of my head and into yours that's all that interests me. I've decided to add a complication.'

'You mean the film isn't complex enough?' asked Mark incredulously.

'The idea is, but the relationships were too cut and dried. I want the hero to start feeling something for the secretary.'

'Love?'

Lewis shook his head. 'No, not love, but

122

something more than he'd intended. She has to matter as a person, not just as a catalyst. He brought her in to try and get his wife back, now he finds himself feeling tenderness or compassion towards her.'

'Why?' asked Mark, wondering who was going to play the hero. Good looks and virility were easy enough; deeper emotions often eluded the stars who were best at the surface charm.

'Because she's special. She's got to have something that draws him to her. It can't be beauty – after all the heroine has that in abundance. Let's say a certain unpredictability, plus intelligence.'

'You mean she's moody?'

Lewis struggled to keep his temper in check. 'No, moody women are not enchanting in life or on film. I thought she might start being a little remote, succumb less easily to the hero's seductions. When he has to work harder he finds her more interesting.'

Mark sighed and started to scribble notes.

'Why the sighing?' asked Lewis.

'You know what they say about film treatments – you should be able to sum up the basic idea in one sentence. I'd like to see you do that with this story.'

'None of my films have conformed, but it hasn't stopped them succeeding.'

'I'm not saying this won't be a great film, just that you're breaking all the rules.'

'I certainly am,' retorted Lewis.

At that moment Rowena put her head round the door. 'Heavens, still working, Lewis? And what are you doing here at this hour, Mark?'

'I called him over. How was *Rigoletto*?'

123

'It was *Attila* and it was great. For once the acting was good too.'

'I'll take your word for it.'

'Will you be long?' asked Rowena, and Lewis knew by the look in her eyes what she meant.

'I'm not sure,' he said carefully, but he made sure he gave her a warm smile before turning his attention back to Mark.

'Try not to be,' murmured Rowena, closing the door softly behind her.

Mark, who still thought Rowena was the sexiest woman he'd ever met, glanced at Lewis. 'Do you want to leave it there?'

'Just read it back to me,' said Lewis. 'I want to be sure you've got it right.' As Mark read back his notes, Lewis tried to picture what was going on upstairs.

Rowena, encouraged by her husband's warm glance and feeling aroused after the excitement of the opera and a long, lingering meal with Chris, had decided that she'd wait for Lewis in his room. Chris would be expecting her, but tonight she wanted Lewis. She wanted to be in control, to play the sex goddess. It was never like that with Chris. He'd known her for too long and understood her too well for it to be possible.

She didn't bother to change her clothes. Lewis enjoyed undressing her and frequently chose to leave some of her underwear on while he took her, finding the sight of the soft silks and satins with their hand-made lace edging against her skin arousing.

Walking along the top landing she opened the door into his bedroom and was halfway towards the bed before she realised that it was already

124

occupied. With a quickly smothered sound of surprise she stood looking at the sleeping Harriet.

Exhausted, Harriet had fallen asleep on her back, totally naked, and was lying with her limbs sprawled out over the duvet. Her normally smooth hair was rumpled and her skin shone with what Rowena recognised as the glow of total sexual satisfaction.

For a long time the film star stood there, studying the naked woman, realising that while she and Chris had been dining together, exciting each other with tales of what they would do with Harriet when she'd been drawn into their sexual games, Lewis had yet again been making love to her.

Remembering how the younger woman had looked the first time she'd been to bed with Lewis, Rowena wondered what she looked like now. She wondered if her body was more adventurous, if she played a more active role, and as her thoughts took off in that direction she found herself becoming even more aroused.

She was so lost in her thoughts that she never heard Lewis come in – it was only when he put a hand over her mouth from behind that she realised he was there. 'What were you thinking?' he whispered softly.

'I was wondering what she'd been like tonight?' Rowena whispered back.

'Magnificent. Do you want to touch her?'

She frowned. 'Surely she'd never let me.'

'She won't know,' Lewis promised her, keeping his voice low. Rowena watched him draw a black velvet mask from his pocket, then he sat on the bed beside the sleeping Harriet and carefully slipped it over her head until her eyes were covered. Exhausted, Harriet slumbered on.

'Touch her,' breathed Lewis against Rowena's ear. 'Touch her breasts, they're very responsive. If she wakes, I'll speak.'

'She'll know it isn't you.' Rowena's protest was only half-hearted. The prospect of touching the unknowing girl, of stirring her senses back to life, was deliciously exciting.

'She's very tired,' Lewis assured her. 'Her mind won't function that well, and she certainly won't be expecting it to be anyone but me touching her.

Rowena licked the tip of her right forefinger and then crept close to the bed. As Lewis sat at Harriet's head, Rowena sat halfway down the bed and then leant over the prone figure to draw a damp teasing circle round Harriet's right nipple. Harriet made a small sound of pleasure in her sleep and the nipple began to swell. Rowena glanced at her husband but he was watching Harriet's reaction. Encouraged, Rowena slid her fingertip round the areola and watched the ring of flesh expand.

In her dreams Harriet was lying on a grassy bank and Lewis was touching her breast which was exposed to the warm summer air. She moved a little, trying to get him to touch the other breast and to her delight he did. This time the touch was firmer, and then suddenly her nipple was pinched very lightly between his fingertips and this increase in sensation began to draw her out of her sleep.

Rowena smiled at the sight of the recently pinched nipple standing so proudly erect. She let her hand trace a delicate pattern round the circumference of the breast and then at a sign from Lewis bent her head and caressed it with her lips.

Harriet's eyes opened slowly. She was aware now that it wasn't a dream, that Lewis really was touching her breasts, but to her shock she couldn't see anything and she struggled to sit up.

Rowena quickly drew back, anxious not to betray her presence, while Lewis wrapped his arms round Harriet's shoulders. 'It's all right,' he soothed her. 'I've put a mask on you; it increases the intensity of the sensation.'

'I'm tired,' Harriet murmured.

'Then let me do all the work,' said Lewis, laying her back against the pillows.

Harriet waited. Her breasts felt cool now that the saliva was evaporating but suddenly she felt something warm being spread across her belly and inner thighs. It felt like a lotion, and was too thick for oil.

'What's that?' she demanded.

'Something very special,' said Lewis, watching his titian-haired wife spreading the gel over his mistress's body. 'You'll love it.' She did like it, liked the tingling warmth of it, the way her blood began to course more quickly through her veins, and she felt herself moistening between her thighs.

Lewis was careful not to keep his arms round Harriet while Rowena worked, knowing that even in her half-sleeping state she could realise that there were too many hands on her. When Rowena started to blow on the gel he pressed his hands on Harriet's shoulders, aware that what followed would have her twisting and turning and afraid of contact between the two women.

Rowena had often used the gel before, and she too knew how the soft warmth of its application increased to a fiery glow almost more than the body could take, and she watched the way Harriet's belly began to tighten and heard with amusement the low guttural sound deep in her throat.

For Harriet the stimulation was unexpected and not entirely to her liking. She twisted her lower body around on the bed, hoping for some relief from the strange burning that was permeating her flesh but movement only increased the effect of the gel and she began to make protesting sounds.

'Wait,' said Lewis. 'It gets better.'

He released Harriet who sat upright but stayed on the bed because of the mask. Rowena went into the bathroom and soaked a hand towel in cold water. She returned and Lewis told Harriet to lie down again, promising that now she'd start to enjoy what he was doing to her.

Harriet trusted him, their tender lovemaking of earlier in the evening had increased the depth of her feelings for him and the last thing she wanted to do now was give him any hint that she might not appreciate his more sophisticated games and so she went along with what he wanted.

The shock of the ice-cold towel being laid across her overheated belly made her cry out despite herself and then the towel was wrapped tightly beneath her sides. Lewis did this, knowing that the size of his hands would be felt, which should reassure her if any reassurance was needed.

Rowena waited until the cold towel was in place, and then as Harriet's nerve endings started to spark with the contrast of hot and cold, the film star slid her finger, still covered with some of the heat-inducing gel, inside the other woman's vagina.

Lewis reached out to stop her, but he was too late and suddenly Harriet was writhing uncontrollably, her legs jerking and her hips twisting as the stimulating gel spread warmth through her delicate internal tissue.

She was literally on fire for him now. Aroused beyond bearing by what Rowena had done, Harriet's body couldn't keep still and she heard herself crying out for Lewis to help her, to bring her to the climax that the gel had initiated but was unable to satisfy.

Rowena watched her PA as she begged Lewis to do something to help her climax, to touch her on her aching needy clitoris, and her own heart raced at the eroticism of the scene and the knowledge that she had been responsible for bringing Harriet to this state of abandonment.

Lewis watched Harriet's straining body and knew that she would need something special to assuage the burning desire Rowena had aroused in her. Murmuring reassurances to his mistress he slipped out of his clothes and his eyes flicked towards the massage oil standing on his dressing table. Rowena understood what he meant and tiptoed to fetch it. Pouring it into her right hand she lavishly oiled his belly and thighs before letting her hands slide over his straining penis and testicles.

She oiled him cleverly, easing the lubrication around the rim of the glans, a movement which she knew he loved and which caused the glans to

129

turn an even deeper shade of purple as his excitement grew.

Harriet was still moaning, calling Lewis's name and trying to reach for him. Lewis had to turn away from his wife's ministrations before she caused him to ejaculate. Rowena felt a pang of disappointment when he moved but consoled herself with the thought that she would be able to watch him attempting to satisfy the desperate Harriet.

As Lewis turned Harriet on to her face she struggled against him. 'I just want you inside me!' she protested. 'I don't need any more stimulation.' He ignored her, and when he slid the oiled lower half of his body backwards and forwards across her thighs and buttocks she caught her breath in surprise.

It was a wonderful sensation. His hard smooth body slipped to and fro in a gentle flowing movement and the stimulation was delicate yet intense. When he moved low on her his penis slipped between her parted legs and she felt it brush against her hungry sex.

At last he penetrated her, but so slowly that at first she couldn't believe that was what he was doing. Then she realised that each penetration coincided with an upward glide of his body and all the time his hand was massaging her shoulders and the back of her neck.

Each liquid penetration eased the dreadful sensation of fiery need that had filled her and instead it was as though she was melting with the bliss of the contact.

When he turned her on to her back again she didn't make any protest because she was now lost in the exquisite gliding movements of their dance of love. Gently he pressed her knees towards her breasts, at the same time sliding his oiled penis back into her.

Harriet's body felt ripe and lush to her, as though her whole being was changing because of what he was doing. She wanted it to go on forever.

Lewis started to rock his pelvis in slow rhythmic movements which aroused every nerve ending within her, and those nerve endings – already brought to fever pitch by Rowena's gel – sent frantic messages to her brain that made her muscles coil and ripple, then start to tense as her climax began to approach. She could feel it building higher and higher and thrust against Lewis in an attempt to hurry the final explosion along, but he slowed her with hands and soft whispers. When she continued to move, he stopped and only began again once she was still.

From the end of the bed Rowena watched in trembling excitement. She'd never imagined Harriet capable of such passion. The sight of the other woman's swollen straining body, of seeing her own husband glide over another woman in practised movements, all made her long for a climax of her own and without realising it she slipped her hand inside her blouse and started to fondle her breasts, pinching the already tight nipples between her fingers.

Finally Harriet's body could wait no longer. Despite her own lack of movement, despite Lewis urging her to delay just a little longer, the pleasure started on its final upward spiral and her head moved restlessly against the pillows while a delicate pink flush of arousal suffused her neck and breasts.

Finally Lewis allowed his pace to increase and his hips moved faster. Harriet stared into the midnight blackness caused by the mask and felt her entire body gather in on itself before seeming to shatter into a thousand pieces. Bright lights exploded behind her eyelids as her body was finally allowed to come.

'There, wasn't that good?' whispered Lewis against her ear.

Exhausted, Harriet could only murmur something unintelligible and then she fell back to sleep, a sleep from which Lewis and Rowena had already aroused her once that night.

When he was certain she was asleep. Lewis left Harriet and walked across to his wife. He removed her hands from inside her blouse and smiled into her feverishly bright eyes. 'Perhaps you'd better pay Chris a visit,' he suggested. 'I'm sure he was expecting you anyway.'

'I want you,' said Rowena, winding herself around him like a cat.

He pushed her firmly away. 'Not tonight, Rowena. Tonight belongs to Harriet. Be grateful you were allowed to watch. It wasn't meant to happen yet.'

'She'll never know. Take me here!' urged Rowena, but Lewis refused and drew her out of his bedroom. He was well satisfied with the night's events.

Chapter Seven

FOR THE NEXT two nights Lewis spent hours in either Harriet's or his own room, bringing her time and again to the heights of ecstasy she had come to expect from him, and every time she climaxed, every time he taught her something new, she was bound more closely to him. The fact that he was slowly being bound more closely to her was something Lewis chose to ignore. Then, on the Saturday, everything changed.

Harriet had been surprised to be invited to the dinner party, and had cancelled her planned evening with Ella because she didn't want to miss the chance of a genuine film star's party. Ella green with envy, had understood but demanded a full report in exchange for being let down.

'I want to hear all about what Rowena wore, ate, drank and how she behaved,' she told Harriet.

'Of course. I'll tell you about Lewis too.'

'I'm sure you will,' said Ella, who already had her suspicions about Harriet and the star's husband.

When they finally sat down to dinner, Harriet found that she was seated next to a man called Mark who told her he was a scriptwriter.

'Have you worked on any big films?' asked Harriet politely, keeping a careful eye on Lewis who was deep in animated conversation with a beautiful Eurasian girl.

'Both of Lewis's Oscar-winning hits. Not that they were the same kind of film as his next one, but the script was important. You can't always rely on images to tell the whole story for you.'

'I suppose not,' said Harriet vaguely.

'What do you do?' enquired Mark, who thought she was a most unlikely dinner guest for Lewis and Rowena. She was very attractive, but didn't seem to have any idea about the film industry.

'I'm Rowena's personal assistant,' said Harriet. 'She's hired me for the time she's over here. Sometimes I do work for Lewis as well.'

Mark stared at Harriet with a new found interest. 'You mean, Rowena's really taken on an attractive secretary?'

Harriet laughed. 'I'm certainly a secretary! Why the surprise?'

Mark struggled to regain his composure. He couldn't believe that he was thinking along the right lines. Surely even Lewis wouldn't go to such extreme lengths in order to get the film right, but then again Lewis was known as a man who'd do anything for his art.

'I supposed I expected her to have someone middle-aged and frumpy. Fragile ego, that sort of thing, you know how film stars are!' he said lightly.

'Actually I don't,' responded Harriet. 'I've never had anything to do with films before, but I do admire Lewis a lot. He's so well balanced.' She glanced down the table at him as she spoke, and Mark could tell by the stiffening of her body that Lewis's clear interest in the Eurasian girl upset her.

'Are you engaged, married or fancy free?' he asked casually, trying to find a way of confirming his growing suspicion about Harriet's real role in the household, while at the same time hoping for her sake that he was wrong.

She laughed. 'Entirely fancy free! I was engaged, but ended it just before I came to work here. This has been a new start for me.'

'And you like it?' queried Mark.

Harriet couldn't help another fleeting look at Lewis. 'Yes, it's the best job I've ever had.'

'You don't find Rowena too demanding?'

'Actually she's been very kind. Quite often she's busy helping Chris go through scripts and things like that, so once I've finished her work I type out letters for Lewis. If he hasn't anything for me then I'm free to do what I like.'

At the memory of what that frequently entailed, Harriet's cheeks were stained a delicate pink and Mark knew then with absolute certainty that he was right. Incredible as it seemed, Lewis was actually playing out his film in his own home. This explained the strange changes in script direction, the sudden alterations in the balance of power. It wasn't that Lewis was having midnight brain storms, the man was simply telling Mark things that had happened.

The scriptwriter stared at Harriet through new

eyes. If she was really having an affair with Lewis then Rowena must know about it. Not only that but as far as he could remember there had been a time when Harriet must have caught Rowena and Lewis making love in his study. Looking at her it was hard to believe she would allow herself to be caught up in any kind of sexual triangle, but as he was well aware looks could be deceptive.

For a moment he felt like warning Harriet. She was clearly in love with Lewis, not simply having a good time with him, and although she thought she was in competition with Rowena there was no way she could ever guess the true complexity of the game she was so innocently playing.

'Harriet,' he said tentatively.

She smiled at him. 'Yes?'

'Do you think this is really the right job for you?' he blurted out.

Stunned, Harriet stared at him in silence, trying to understand what he was saying.

'They're very sophisticated people,' Mark blundered on. 'If you ever want to get away, to . . .'

'I'm not a prisoner,' protested Harriet, her voice rising with indignation. 'I'm free to leave whenever I like.'

Lewis couldn't hear Harriet's words but he could hear her voice and knew by the tone that something Mark had said had made her anxious. He looked down the table at his scriptwriter and his eyes were dark. 'Something wrong?' he asked politely.

Mark shook his head. 'Of course not.'

'Harriet?'

She smiled at Lewis. 'No, nothing's wrong.

Mark was just warning me about the perils of working for people like you!'

'If he thinks it's that perilous he'd better find himself a new employer,' said Lewis. He kept his voice light but Mark felt a chill run through him. Lewis was ruthless, and if he thought for one moment that Mark was endangering his work then he would instantly have him removed and sent back to the States. The two previous Oscars, their years of collaboration, would count for nothing.

'Luckily Harriet's far too sensible to listen to me,' Mark retorted. 'I was only trying to prise her away so that she could work for me. I'm in desperate need of a good secretary myself.'

'Harriet's far more than a secreatary,' said Rowena, breaking off her conversation with one of the film's financial backers. 'Why, she's really one of the family now – isn't that right, Harriet?'

Out of the blue Harriet remembered the feel of hands on her body a few nights earlier. Hands that had given her such pleasure when she'd been half-asleep and masked. She looked at Rowena's hands, wondering why she should think of that at this moment when Rowena hadn't even been there. Guilt, she supposed.

'Harriet?' repeated Rowena.

She managed a warm smile. 'It's very kind of you to say so, Rowena.'

Rowena's best professional bubbly laugh sounded round the room. 'So modest – it's a wonderful English virtue, I find! Why, Harriet's charmed us all. My husband, my brother Chris, and me too of course. None of us can imagine how things were before she joined us, isn't that true, Lew?'

Lewis, realising that his wife had probably had too much to drink, attempted to change the direction of the conversation. 'Quite true, darling. I've never seen your filing in such good order! The tomato and olive tart was superb – you must congratulate the cook.'

'I think Harriet should do some work for me,' said Chris suddenly.

Harriet turned her head towards him. 'I'd be glad to, as long as I wasn't needed by Rowena or Lewis.'

Chris, his face flushed by wine, laughed heartily. 'You could spare her occasionally, couldn't you, Rowena?'

Rowena's lips tightened. 'I hardly think you need a secretary to read scripts for you, Chris, and you certainly don't have fan mail to deal with.'

All round the table people fell silent. It was common knowledge that Rowena and Chris were devoted to each other, so this sudden sharpness and the deliberate put-down were totally unexpected.

Chris didn't look taken aback though, he merely smiled his most charming smile. 'Perhaps that would change if I wasn't forever living in your shadow, Rowena. Now that your days as a sex goddess are over it might be my turn to carry on the family tradition. I'd love to play a handsome seducer.'

'Rowena's days as a sex goddess are only "over", as you put it, because she wants to be taken seriously as an actress,' said Lewis quickly. 'I'm sure we can all see tonight that the choice must have been hers.'

'Absolutely,' said Mark, quick to pick up a cue.

Rowena smiled at both men, ignoring her half-brother. 'How sweet of you, Lewis, and you too, Mark. Goodness, is that the time? Does anyone want any more cheese or shall we ladies withdraw?'

The tiny goats' cheeses wrapped in vine leaves had been delicious, as had the strawberry sorbet before them, but Harriet had tasted very little, and it was with some relief that she went with the other women into the drawing-room. Despite her denial, Mark's words had unsettled her, and so had Lewis's admiration of his companion at the dinner table.

Although her fame had come through her ability to portray great sexual magnetism on the screen, Rowena was unusual in so far as she had always been able to gain the admiration of women as well. Tonight, laughing and chatting with the other female guests, she wove her spell over them all and Harriet noticed the way even the Eurasian girl's beauty and youth seemed to dim in Rowena's presence.

Briefly she wondered how she could ever hope to capture Lewis's heart, but then she told herself that whatever her hold over him, Rowena certainly didn't have his heart, in which case Harriet had as much chance as anyone of winning it.

Later the men joined them and the conversation became noisier while the air grew thick with cigar smoke. After a time Harriet felt she'd suffocate if she didn't get any air and she made her way outside.

She went to the walled garden at the bottom of the sloping lawn and sat down on the carved wooden seat, drawing in deep breaths of the mild summer night air.

When she heard someone approaching her heart began to beat faster. She was sure that it was Lewis, that he'd followed her outside to make arrangements for when the guests had gone, and her body tingled with excited anticipation. 'I thought I saw you leave,' said a voice, but it didn't belong to Lewis, it belonged to Chris.

'It was stuffy in there,' explained Harriet, struggling to keep the disappointment out of her voice. 'I hope Rowena won't think me rude.'

'She won't notice you've gone!' laughed Chris. 'When Rowena's centre stage she doesn't keep a head count of the admiring audience. As long as there are plenty of people she's satisfied.'

'I think you're being unfair to her,' retorted Harriet. 'She isn't nearly as vain as I'd expected her to be.'

'And you're far more beautiful than I'd expected you to be,' murmured Chris, sitting down next to her.

Harriet moved her legs slightly so that her knees weren't touching his. She didn't like his intimate tone, and she couldn't help remembering how she'd seen him behaving with Rowena in the film star's bedroom. The strange sick excitement she'd felt then was still stirred at the memory, but it made her want Lewis, not Chris.

'Have you always been beautiful?' Chris asked, resting an arm along the back of the seat.

Harriet felt like laughing, but there was something about him that made the idea seem a dangerous one so she attempted to brush the remark aside in another way. 'Yes, from the moment I was born. Nurses swooned away and one of the doctors asked my mother if he could come and ask for my hand eighteen years on.'

'You really are beautiful,' said Chris. 'Surely you know that?'

'I think you've drunk too much wine,' said Harriet. 'Rowena's beautiful, I'm attractive. There's a big difference.'

He put a hand on her knee and she froze into stillness. 'Rowena's a witch,' he confided. 'She traps people with her beauty and then they can't get free. You wouldn't do that, would you?'

'I've no idea. I haven't managed to trap anyone yet.'

'It's no joke, being trapped,' he continued, his voice verging on self-pity. 'You end up despising yourself for your weakness, but it doesn't make any difference.'

Harriet knew she had to pretend that she wasn't aware of Chris's intimate reltionship with Rowena. 'You're only her half-brother!' she protested. 'If you got married, made a life for yourself, you'd be free straight away. Why hang around here if she makes you miserable?'

'Because I need her,' he said fiercely. 'We need each other. Sometimes I think we'll only be free when one of us is dead.'

His hand tightened on her knee and she edged further away from him. At once the arm along the back of the seat grabbed her round her shoulders. 'Don't you know what an obsession's like?' he demanded. 'Haven't you ever been consumed with need for someone?'

Yes, thought Harriet, I'm consumed with need for Lewis right now but even if he wants to come and see me he can't because you're sitting here preventing him. 'No,' she said calmly.

'I think that's a lie,' said Chris softly, and then she felt the hand on her left shoulder start to edge up the side of her neck in an undeniably intimate gesture.

Harriet jumped to her feet. 'I'd better go back now.'

'Why?' he asked sulkily.

'I feel better, that's why.'

'Lewis won't have missed you; he's busy with Marita. She's stunning, don't you think? And Lewis's type as well.'

'Really?'

'Oh yes, Lewis likes women like that. She's quite without emotion you see. All Marita wants is to get on in films, and she's beautiful enough to manage it. You can still sleep your way to a reasonable amount of success, but Lewis will sleep with her and not use her in any film. He dislikes emotional commitment, you see.'

'He married Rowena,' Harriet pointed out, longing to get back to the house and see if what Chris was saying was true.

'He married her and he scares her but he sure as hell isn't in love with her,' snarled Chris. 'If he was he'd try to satisfy her more.'

'I don't think you should be talking to me like this,' protested Harriet.

Chris stood up and grabbed her by an arm, twisting her round to face him. 'Why not? You're being screwed by Lewis, aren't you? Surely that puts you on an equal footing with Rowena, and I

142

often discuss Lewis's failings as a husband with her.'

'If you don't let go of me,' said Harriet fiercely, 'I shall slap your face and shout for help.'

For a moment Chris hesitated, but then his hand dropped to his side and he sank back on the seat again. 'Run back to Lewis,' he jeered, 'but don't blame me when you find he's no longer interested. He has the attention span of a two-year-old where women are concerned. No doubt he had a great time with you, but that time's over now.'

'You're drunk and I don't want to hear another word,' snapped Harriet, and then she was running away from him, back up the lawn towards the crowded house.

While she'd been gone some of the dinner guests had paired off and were engaged in acts of varying intimacy in the hall, the drawing-room and even on the stairs. Rowena was sitting in the conservatory drinking coffee and talking to another woman but there was no sign of Lewis, or the Eurasian girl, Marita.

'I'm off to bed,' Harriet told Rowena. 'It was a lovely evening.'

Rowena peered at her through the smoke of one of her rare cigarettes. 'Did you enjoy it? You don't look very happy.'

'I'm just tired. I'm not used to such late hours!'

'Have you seen my brother?'

'Chris went into the garden,' Harriet told her.

Rowena smiled. 'He's drunk too much. I'll say goodnight to Lewis for you; he's busy right now.'

The woman with her laughed. 'He certainly is. Marita keeps most men busy. She nearly killed my husband last year!' Rowena's laughter joined her friend's and Harriet fled upstairs, certain that they were secretly mocking her.

She lay awake until six in the morning but Lewis didn't join her, and she guessed then that the story must have been true and Marita had kept him busy. At first she wept, but then she told herself that crying was useless. A man like that was bound to be used to casual affairs – what she had to do was make herself indispensable to him, no matter what was necessary to achieve it.

As Harriet finally fell asleep, Lewis disengaged himself from the smooth golden limbs of his companion and lay on his back wondering why it was that despite Marita's athleticism and incredible skill at fellatio she had failed to hold his attention. Once or twice he'd found himself thinking about Harriet, picturing her in the Eurasian girl's place. It was all very unsettling and most unlike him.

In the end he woke Marita, handed her her clothes and sent her home in his car. He didn't want any more to do with her, and knew by the expression on her face that she wouldn't want anything to do with him again. It was of no importance. It had only ever been intended as a moment's pleasure and a spur to what was intended to be Harriet's increasing need for him now that he was going to leave her alone for a time. The realisation that he wouldn't be sleeping with her for nearly a week hurt. She was meant to miss him but he hadn't anticipated missing her as well.

No one appeared downstairs in the house the following morning until twelve o' clock, and even then it was only Harriet. She made herself toast and coffee then took it into the sun-drenched conservatory. She wanted to see Lewis, to speak to him, and her body ached for his skilled touch but she wasn't sure what she was going to say when he did come down.

He and Rowena eventually joined her a little after two in the afternoon, and much to her surprise the pair of them seemed thoroughly absorbed in each other. Just as he had when Harriet first arrived at the house, Lewis kept touching his wife. His hands would caress her back and shoulders, or he would touch her on the arm to emphasise a point in his conversation. They both looked cheerful and were friendly towards Harriet but she felt herself being subtly excluded as they exchanged quick smiles or laughed at private jokes.

Harriet couldn't understand it. Lewis hadn't appeared to be tiring of her. Their last session together had been the best ever, and yet now it looked as though it was all over.

Later, Lewis left the house and then Chris joined the two women. He barely spoke to Harriet, managing a brief greeting but refusing to meet her eye. With Rowena though he was so intimate that once again Harriet felt like an interloper. He touched her as intimately as Lewis had touched her, and once he bent his head and kissed the top of her spine where the vertebrae were exposed by the scoop neck of the blouse she was wearing. The sight of the kiss on the tender flesh sent a shiver through Harriet. She didn't want Chris, bu she longed for Lewis to kiss her in the same way.

Confused and frustrated she passed the day as best she could on her own, swimming in the pool, using the sunbed and later walking in the garden. By this time Lewis had returned. He stood next to his wife and together they watched the tall, slim figure wandering along the path at the side of the house.

'She's missing you already,' said Rowena.

'Good; that means she'll miss me even more by the end of the week. You and Chris have kept Friday night free?' His wife nodded, and her belly stirred at the prospect of what lay ahead for them all.

That night, despite what had happened in the day, Harriet still lay awake hoping that Lewis would come to her, but he didn't. She waited until two in the morning and then slept fitfully, her body – so well tutored in recent days – reluctant to rest without the sensual pleasures it was used to.

The next night Harriet used her hands to pleasure herself but although she gained physical release it wasn't the same and afterwards she cried into her pillow. She'd tried to pretend her hands belonged to Lewis, had conjured up an image of him as her fingers teased her clitoris, but it hadn't worked. The price of satisfaction was too high and she vowed not to attempt it again.

With every night that passed, Harriet became more and more short-tempered. Rowena, aware of what the younger woman was going through, pretended not to notice and was kindness itself. Lewis kept out of Harriet's way, even taking his meals in his study under the pretext of work.

By the Friday night Harriet didn't know what to

do. It seemed that Chris had been right in saying that Lewis never stayed constant to any woman for more than a short period, yet she was still certain that their intimacy had been more than physical. She longed for the courage to speak to him, to ask what had gone wrong, but on the few occasions that she'd had the chance her nerve always deserted her.

When she retired to bed she had a shower, then put her night light on and began to read a novel. Even the feel of the satin sheets against her skin worked as a reminder of her thwarted sensuality. Wriggling between them she recalled the way Lewis had dried her in a towel and then covered her in massage oil, and her toes curled at the memory.

When a light tap came at her door she decided she must have misheard. She'd ceased to expect Lewis any more. The tap was repeated, and this time the sound was unmistakable. 'Who is it?' she asked nervously.

'Who do you think!'

At the familiar sound of Lewis's voice Harriet was out of bed and opening the door in seconds, shamed by her own eagerness but unable to control it. She did at least manage to look surprised as she let him in. 'What do you want, stranger?' she queried lightly.

Lewis smiled down at her. 'I haven't come to read you a bedtime story!'

'I'm reading to myself,' she said, gesturing towards the open book on the bed.

'Can't you think of anything you'd rather do?'

She wished she had the strength of character to send him away, to say that he couldn't play these games with her, ignoring her for days at a time and then turning up as though nothing had happened, but her body needed him so badly that she rejected the thought at once. Besides, if she was to gain any kind of place in his affections then she knew instinctively that whining and complaining wouldn't do it.

'May I finish my chapter first?' she asked sweetly.

If it hadn't been for the rapid movements of the swell of her breasts, clearly visible above the lace of her nightdress, Lewis would have been inclined to believe her casual tone. As it was he admired her attitude, and felt a rush of affection for her. 'As long as you take off your nightdress, sit cross-legged on the bed as you read and I'm allowed to watch you,' he retorted.

'You can watch,' conceded Harriet, 'but until I've finished you can't touch.'

Realising she was serious Lewis had to sit at the foot of her bed and for the next five minutes endured the kind of physical frustration he'd forced on her for a week. He found that he didn't like it at all. Finally Harriet closed the book and smiled sweetly at him. 'I do like a good mystery! Now then, tell me what you had in mind.'

'I want you to put these on,' said Lewis, placing a cardboard box on Harriet's bed. She opened it, pushed aside the layers of tissue paper and drew out a white suspender belt, white stockings and a flimsy white camisole top with holes for her nipples. 'I like to see women partially clothed at first,' he said by way of explanation. 'It's much sexier, don't you think?'

Harriet was beyond thinking at all. She wanted

his hands on her as soon as possible, but she knew that he liked to extend lovemaking, that it was always prolonged and varied with him. Although she'd never worn a suspender belt before she found once the outfit was on and she'd paraded in front of her bedroom mirror that he was right, it did look extremely erotic.

Lewis stripped off all his clothes and then brought in the wooden chair from Harriet's bathroom. He placed it in the middle of the floor and sat down on the padded seat, his erection already pointing upwards. 'Come and sit on my lap,' he murmured. 'Face the mirror and lean back against me, that way we can watch ourselves at the same time.'

Obediently Harriet lowered herself across his thighs and she felt the silk stockings rubbing against his bare flesh. One of his hands glided over the the area of skin between her stocking top and hip bone while the other went round her upper body and spread itself over her left breast.

'Look in the mirror,' he urged her.

Harriet looked, and was startled by the expression of sensual abandon in her eyes as she pressed her back against his chest and spread her legs wide over him. Her naked vulva was damp with desire and when he began to massage her breast she started to tremble from head to toe at the blissful familiarity of his movements.

Her body, starved of attention for too long, leapt into life and Lewis knew that it was going to be difficult to do what he had to do unless he was very careful. Already Harriet was squirming against his legs and the flush of arousal stained her neck and chest. 'Keep still,' he whispered.

'We've plenty of time.'

Harriet didn't want to play the delaying game this time. Her body felt ready to burst with suppressed need and she had no intention of doing as Lewis said. She allowed the excitement to build and the exhilarating pre-orgasmic tingles darted through her vulva and lower belly so that she gave a groan of gratitude.

Lewis slid his right hand between her thighs and brushed his fingers over the tips of her curly pubic hair, allowing her only the faintest pressure. Harriet jerked upwards, desperate for greater stimulation but he moved his hand away again and the tendrils of desire that had begun to throb behind her pubic bone flickered briefly and then started to fade.

'Lewis, hurry up!' she begged him.

'Look at yourself,' he urged her. 'Have you ever seen anything so wanton?'

Glancing in the mirror she saw that she looked totally different. Her cheeks were flushed, her eyes huge and she was wriggling and rubbing against Lewis in a way that would have been unimaginable in her days with James, but she didn't care. This was what she liked, what her body adored and this man was the one she knew she had to keep with her for ever.

'Touch yourself,' said Lewis, moving his right hand upwards in order to stimulate her breasts but leaving her lower body alone. Frantically Harriet obeyed, knowing that if her clitoris didn't soon receive the stimulation it was screaming for, she'd go mad. Her fingers slid down the channel between her outer lips until they located the hard little button and as soon as contact was made her

150

legs began to stiffen.

Lewis felt her body tense and he kissed the side of her neck while his hands massaged her breasts through the camisole in a soft kneading motion, sometimes drifting down the sides and beneath her armpits to tantalise the highly sensitive flesh there.

Harriet was moaning now, but she wanted it to be Lewis who triggered her climax and so as her outer lips opened wide and wetness flooded her tissue she reached upwards for one of his hands.

He knew that she was right on the edge, that she needed only one more delicate brushing movement across the clitoris, one rotation of his hand on her lower belly and she would be there but this was the very thing she couldn't have, not if the plan was to work.

To Harriet's astonishment he caught her hand and held it tight, then his left hand grabbed her left wrist and he stood up so unexpectedly that she would have fallen forward if he hadn't kept a tight hold on her wrists.

Shocked she stared at them both in the mirror. He tall and suddenly stern-looking, she struggling against what was happening while her aroused flesh screamed for relief.

'What are you doing?' she asked in bewilderment. 'I was about to come!'

He smiled at her in the mirror. 'Wouldn't you like to share your pleasure?'

'Share it?' she asked stupidly.

'Why don't we let Rowena and Chris watch?' he suggested softly, his lips warm against the nape of her neck.

Harriet tried to wrench herself free. 'No!' she

protested vehemently. 'I just want you.'

He sighed. 'Then we'll have to take a break and start again a little later.

'Why?'

'Because I'd been looking forward to letting them see us together. If we're not going to, I might have some trouble satisfying you just yet.'

Harriet was bewildered. She could tell how excited he was by the rock hard erection nudging against her. That was proof enough of his desire – he couldn't possibly need a rest.

'Don't do this, Lewis,' she begged him, attempting to turn and press her aching flesh against his naked body. 'Please, I need you now.'

He let his mouth continue kissing the top of her spine but at the same time drew her hands behind her back and then imprisoned her wrists in one of his large hands. The movement meant that her breasts, so swollen and hard from his touch, were jutted forward yet more proudly and she could see her nipples standing out through the holes in the camisole.

'Let's join them,' he whispered again as she shivered beneath the teasing lightness of his mouth aginst her vertebrae. 'Think how Rowena will envy you. Besides, it will be a new experience for you. I thought you wanted new experiences.'

Harriet tried to think straight, but it was difficult when her body was throbbing and tight with its own needs, and after being deprived of Lewis for several days all she could think about was the totally consuming pleasure he would bring her.

'I don't know,' she said hesitantly.

In the mirror she saw him lift his head and

frown. 'You could have stayed safely with your fiancé, or secure in your old job if you hadn't wanted to expand your horizons,' he pointed out. Then he dropped his voice. 'I want them to see us,' he said persuasively. 'Rowena will be stunned when she sees us together.'

It was this which convinced Harriet, together with the incessant urging of her body. She wanted Rowena to witness her and Lewis making love. The prospect of his wife being forced to witness the way their bodies responded to each other was unbearably exciting and to Lewis's relief she finally nodded. 'Yes,' she said softly. 'I want them to see us too.'

She expected him to suggest they changed rooms but instead he simply went to the door and opened it. Rowena and Chris walked in. At that moment Harriet realised that the idea hadn't been a sudden one, but a carefully plotted plan and that he had always known she would accede to his wishes.

Rowena smiled at the younger woman. She was wearing a short shocking pink A-line skirt with a fitted black and pink short-sleeved top and her legs were encased in black stockings with a long seam down the back which, coupled with her black stiletto shoes, made a very sexy combination.

Chris looked as though he'd come from working out in a gym. His casual long-sleeved cotton top and tracksuit bottom seemed incongruous next to Lewis's nakedness, but almost as soon as he was in the room he stripped them off to reveal his naked chest, covered in tight fair curls, and beneath his trousers he was wearing a pair of tight-fitting black briefs.

'You look very attractive, Harriet,' said Rowena huskily. Lewis's hands tightened round Harriet so that his wife could examine her at her leisure. Harriet tensed against him. This wasn't what she'd expected. She'd thought that Rowena and Chris would simply watch, not touch her themselves.

The film star ran her hands up beneath the flimsy camisole, drawing a delicate line along each of the ribs in turn. Then she withdrew her hands and looked at the nipples now sticking out through the holes in the top. With a soft laugh she moved her head and her tongue flicked at each of them in turn, sending tiny vibrations through the other woman's breasts.

Helpless, Harriet squirmed and despite her shock she felt her arousal growing again. Rowena ran a finger beneath the top of the suspender belt and the stomach muscles contracted beneath her touch. Lifting the lower lacey edge she let her tongue dip into the quaking belly button and at this Harriet's body jerked, pushing her hips forward.

Rowena's eyes were bright. 'She's certainly very responsive,' she murmured, turning to her half-brother.

Chris, who'd been standing at a distance watching, moved to Rowena's side and they kissed each other lightly on the lips before looking back at Harriet. 'I knew she would be,' said Chris. 'I think we're all in for a very exciting night.'

Chapter Eight

'*SHALL WE LET* her have an orgasm before we begin in earnest?' asked Lewis, his arms wrapped round Harriet's upper body, pinning her arms to her sides.

Rowena looked thoughtfully at the girl. 'I think so. It should make what follows easier.'

'If I keep hold of her then you can use your skills,' said Lewis.

'I want you to do it,' protested Harriet, determined not to keep silent despite the unexpected turn of events.

'I'm afraid that tonight what you want isn't our paramount consideration,' said Rowena. 'Lewis has kept you more than satisfied in that direction. Tonight we want to see just how far you can be taken.'

'Why?' asked Harriet, shocked at the casual amusement in her employer's voice.

'Because it will be fun. Besides, Lewis seems to think you're something special. Chris and I want to see if it's true.'

Lewis's grip tightened for a moment and he

made soothing sounds to comfort Harriet but some of her fear was already dissipating. If this was a challenge, if Rowena wanted to see whether Harriet was capable of holding a man like Lewis for any length of time, then she would show her that she could.

With her upper body unable to move Harriet stared at herself in the mirror. Her nipples were still peeping through the holes in the silk camisole top and she realised that if anything her excitement was increasing with every passing second.

'Spread your legs further apart,' said Rowena. Harriet did, and watched as Rowena opened a large handbag and drew out an electric toothbrush. She glanced up at the other woman for a moment, then withdrew a tube of gel. Carefully she parted Harriet's outer sex-lips and then spread some of it over the delicate tissue.

The gel was cold and Harriet gave a tiny gasp of surprise. At once Chris stepped forward and in his hand was a tiny riding crop. He flicked it over the flesh beneath the suspender belt and immediately a thin red line appeared. Harriet screamed.

'You're meant to keep silent while Rowena works,' said Chris shortly. 'Every time you make a sound you'll feel the crop.'

The burning sensation of the blow was changing now, and thrills of arousal followed. Rowena, working between Harriet's thighs, turned to her brother. 'She liked that, she's become far more moist. Do it again.'

'No!' protested Harriet, and at once the crop fell, this time at the base of her camisole top.

'Keep silent,' Lewis urged her.

Rowena watched as Harriet's juices started to

flow more copiously and she mixed those with the gel so that soon the entire area was throughly wet. Now she picked up the toothbrush and put it on the lowest setting before letting it travel up the straining girl's inner thighs.

Harriet heard her breath quickening and tried to subdue the sound. She didn't want the crop, despite the strange burning thrill of excitement that followed each blow. The brush head was small and delicate, the touch insidiously arousing, and Harriet longed for it to touch her where the gel had been spread but Rowena refused to hurry.

She moved it into the join at the top of the inner thighs and across the skin above the line of her pubic hair but it was lower down that Harriet's body was straining for contact and despite herself she gave a low groan of need.

When the crop flicked across her nipples she slammed back into Lewis with shock. His tongue flicked into her ear, sliding round and then jabbing into the earhole in simulated intercourse. Her nipples felt on fire, but they were throbbing, the blood coursing through them as her whole body screamed for satisfaction.

'You're so near, aren't you?' whispered Rowena against Harriet's belly. Harriet nearly answered her, but was stopped by a warning squeeze from Lewis. The film star laughed. 'Well done! I think perhaps it's time now. Are you tingling here?' and her finger circled the hard nub of the clitoris.

This touch alone started the strange darting feelings that Harriet so enjoyed. They moved within her pelvis and belly as her muscles gathered themselves together and her nerve endings responded to the urgently needed touch.

'I'm sure you are,' continued Rowena, and finally she held the outer lips apart with her left hand and moved the toothbrush to the screaming tissue so wickedly tantalised already.

At first the brush was held against the opening of Harriet's vagina and then with tortuous slowness it moved in tiny circles upwards until she felt the tingles inceasing and electric sparks shot through her, while her breasts burgeoned.

Rowena watched the clitoris closely. As Harriet's excitement began to peak it started to withdraw beneath its protective hood and she quickly pulled upwards on the skin above it so that it had nowhere to hide before allowing the bristles to caress the most sensitive part of Harriet's body.

The touch of the rotating softness against her screaming nerve endings at last triggered the climax Harriet had been waiting for. Suddenly the sparks lanced right through her, her thighs tried to close and then she was lost in the throes of release as everything came together and her body doubled forward with the uncontrollable contractions of her muscles.

'There,' said Rowena to her husband. 'That should have warmed her up nicely.'

As Harriet's body calmed and her breathing returned to normal she felt a terrible sense of shame and averted her eyes from Rowena and Chris. 'Now for a change of location,' said Lewis, quietly, and she found herself being picked up in his arms and carried along the second-floor landing to his bedroom.

Unknown to Harriet this had been carefully prepared beforehand, including the installation of concealed video cameras. Lewis knew that during the ensuing excitement he wouldn't be able to remain detached, and had decided to record the entire scene so that he could play it back later and watch their various expressions and attitudes the next day. That way he hoped that he would be able to see the truth for himself, and the ending of his film might finally become clear.

The curtains had been drawn and the main light extinguished, only small wall lights were on but above the bed several bright spotlights were carefully angled around the entire room.

'Can I change her clothes?' asked Chris, his voice shaking at the prospect.

Lewis nodded and placed Harriet in the centre of his large bed. She lay looking up at him in dazzed incomprehension. He seemed to be as happy to share her as he had been to share his wife, and the realisation chastened her. She'd been so sure that she was different, that his feelings were special, that she'd never considered the possible dangers of their affair. Only now, when she was entirely at the mercy of the three of them, did she fully understand the risk she'd taken. And now was too late.

The next thing she knew, Chris's hands were unfastening her white silk stockings, peeling them slowly down her legs while his fingers stroked the smooth flesh of her legs. Then he unfastened her suspender belt, removed it and finally eased the straps of her camisole top down her arms before rolling it down across her breasts, making sure that his fingers flicked at the still aching nipples as the material was drawn away.

Naked and vulnerable she waited, her body

taut and trembling with a mixture of fear and desire as the three of them studied her nude figure. 'She'll look good in the playsuit,' said Rowena.

'Excellent idea,' replied Chris. Quickly he manhandled her to the edge of the bed and then she was being squeezed into a plunging cupless black leather playsuit. It zipped up the centre, ending between the undersides of her breasts. There was a black collar with a ring at the back, and a second zip to allow easy access between her thighs, but for the moment this was closed and she felt the pressure of the leather against her vulva.

Now her hands were drawn behind her back and fastened with soft padded handcuffs and then she was pushed in front of a mirror to look at herself. The sight of her firm creamy breasts hanging free beneath the leather collar, slightly lifted by the underwired edges of the corset part of the suit astounded her. She looked even more wanton than she had during sex with Lewis and without thinking she thrust her shoulders back further to emphasise her sexuality.

Chris laughed. 'An exhibitionist! Wonderful! I'm afraid you'll have to wait a little though. It's your turn to watch now.' He drew a fine chain through the ring at the back of her collar and fastened her to one of the bedposts. Here she was visible to one of the cameras and also free to see what was happening in the room.

Rowena watched the transformation of Harriet from cool efficient PA to a tousle haired leather-clad temptress with fascination. She wondered how well she would perform. The clothes were only the start for Chris's games of domination. A thrill ran through her as her half-brother spoke. 'Hands behind your back, Rowena. Lewis has a present for you, haven't you Lew?'

His brother-in-law nodded, and then bound his wife's hands tightly with leather cord before covering her eyes with a black silk scarf and knotting it securely at the back of her head. 'Kneel on the carpet, Rowena,' he said quietly. Rowena remained standing. Resistance always increased her pleasure, but normally Lewis wouldn't play the game the way she liked it – he never seemed to relish the power it gave him over her.

This time it was different. His hands grabbed her fiercely at the back of her neck and then he was pushing her down, forcing her on to her knees in seconds. Then he released her and she strained to hear where he was, but it was difficult as the scarf covered her ears as well.

Harriet watched and found that her mouth was dry. Her breasts began to ache and she could feel the pressure of the corset beneath them. Chris, who was watching her, casually fondled each breast in turn and she heard herself sigh voluptuously at his touch.

Lewis, who was walking round to the front of Rowena, glanced across and his eyes widened in surprise. He'd expected Harriet to be more cowed, at least initially, but she already seemed to be revelling in what was happening.

Reaching down, Lewis caught hold of Rowena's head and guided her mouth towards his straining erection. She parted her lips and teased the sensitive tip with her tongue, tasting the salty tang of him as she worked. She loved it when she was blindfolded – every other sense was so heightened that it doubled her pleasure.

Lewis's hands dug into her hair and he began to move his hips, thrusting in and out of her mouth far faster than he usually did. She struggled to accommodate him. Then, when he felt himself nearing orgasm, Lewis stopped her with his hands and withdrew.

Rowena felt bereft. She'd wanted Harriet to see Lewis ejaculate into her mouth, but Lewis had spoiled it for her and she experienced a moment's rage. His hand descended on the back of her head again and he kept pressing until her forehead was resting on the carpet. It was an awkward position and totally exposed her buttocks to the gaze of those standing behind her, including Harriet.

Now Lewis went over to Harriet. He drew a long ostrich plume from beneath his duvet and started stroking her breasts with it in such slow, teasing movements that she had a desperate desire for a hard touch, even the flick of the crop, anything to distract her from the relentless soft teasing of the plume that made her breasts ache and started the familiar throbbing beneath the zip fastener between her thighs.

In the meantime Chris had taken up his position behind Rowena. In his right hand he held the riding crop and using alternate backhand and forehand strokes he began to strike her on each of her buttocks in turn. Every blow was light but the stinging sensation it engendered was strong and Rowena couldn't help moving her buttocks in an attempt to evade the blows. Chris was too clever for her and anticipated every move so that soon the cheeks of her bottom were glowing a soft pink and her vulva began to open, the sex-lips flattening outwards in readiness for the penetration she longed for.

Harriet, still being stimulated by the unbearable delicacy of the plume, watched and her stomach, so tightly encased in leather, felt it would burst. She shivered at the touch of the leather beneath her and moved her hips to try and stimulate herself more. 'Keep still, Harriet,' said Lewis sharply, but his eyes were dark with longing for her.

Rowena was making strange mewing sounds now, her upper body swaying from side to side as she brushed the tips of her breasts over the soft pile of the carpet. Chris smiled to himself and with one final crisp flick of the wrist stepped away from her.

Now he and Lewis changed places again, and at last the incessant soft brushing on Harriet's breasts stopped and she let her head fall back against the bed-post in relief.

Lewis covered a double-headed vibrator in the gel that Rowena had used on Harriet earlier in the week and then let the heads rest against her two openings. Rowena felt the slippery hardness of them and thrust backwards towards him, straining for something to fill her aching flesh but Lewis simply tapped them softly against the rim of her rectum and the front of her vagina, and suddenly she felt the warmth of the gel as it came into contact with her skin.

Realising that once the two prongs were inside her all her delicate inner tissue would be subjected to the burning heat she froze, unable to believe that Lewis would be willing to push her to such extremes of sensation, but when his free hand pressed against her spine she knew from the size of the fingers that it was indeed him and not her half-brother.

Lewis teased her a little longer, knowing that anticipation would increase her fear of the gel, and then he slid the twin dildo in with a smooth twisting action, making certain that the sides touched the flesh of the walls of both her passages and within seconds her lower body was twitching and jerking. Ignoring this he slid the dildo back and forth, forcing yet more nerve paths to be aroused until Rowena felt she would go mad with the burning itching sensation that set her flesh leaping, while at the same time the rhythmic movements of the two prongs brought her closer and closer to orgasm.

She knew that when she climaxed the walls of both her rectum and vagina would close more tightly about the prongs and that then the glowing warmth would increase so she tried to stave off the moment. However, Lewis suddenly circled the vibrator so that her G-spot was stimulated, and when she cried out with pleasure he kept his hand motionless and concentrated on maintaining a steady pressure against the tiny place.

It was this that forced a wrenching climax from her and Harriet watched as the titian-haired star's body locked with tension and her head was thrown back while she screamed aloud as her muscles contracted and the gel was rubbed more firmly into her flesh.

With every contraction, every spasm, the warm

164

flooding sensation increased until it seemed as though a fire was rushing up through Rowena's belly and even her breasts. No sooner had her first orgasm stopped than she was wracked by a second more intense one and when that was over she collapsed on to the carpet, sobbing with satisfaction.

Harriet knew that the leather between her legs was very damp. She could feel her juices flowing and her body longed to be part of what she'd seen. Chris crouched down and carefully unzipped her, releasing her vulva to the cool air. When he let an exploratory finger enter her, he drew some of the moisture from her vagina and spread it upwards along the highly sensitive stem of her clitoris.

'How does it feel?' he asked.

Harriet couldn't explain, couldn't begin to tell him about the pulsating heat that was consuming her.

'I want to know,' he insisted.

'I'm so hot,' moaned Harriet, her body perspiring beneath its casing of leather.

Chris was prepared for this. He reached for the ice bucket that was at his feet and then very carefully slid one inside the opening between Harriet's thighs. At the feel of the freezing cube against her flesh Harriet went still with shock, but he continued to ease it into her until it was just inside her and there it slowly melted, letting the cool water mingle with her body fluids.

Harriet shivered. The contrast was incredible, and then her eyes widened as he stood up and popped an ice-cube into her mouth. 'Suck on it slowly,' he instructed her. Harriet sucked, watched by Lewis who thought he might lose control and spill his seed on the carpet at the sight of her, she looked so magnificently wild and sensual.

Finally Chris drew an ice-cube over her breasts, rubbing it in circles round the nipples until she found herself leaning towards him, pulling against her chain in an effort to obtain contact.

'Can I take her now?' Chris asked Lewis.

Harriet stared at her lover, unwilling to believe he was going to allow this man to penetrate her, but almost excited at the thought. Lewis smiled at her. 'Yes,' he murmured. 'I want to see her come for you.'

The words almost made her climax, and her eager body strained harder. Chris released her from the bed-post and laid her on the bed, then re-fastened her hands but this time spread-eagled so that her body formed an X shape. The ice-cube inside her vagina had melted completely now and as Harriet watched, Chris readied his large penis. 'I want you to remember this,' he said softly, sliding a pillow beneath her hips. He spread some lubrication across the tip before sliding it into her, his hips moving in tiny circles as he penetrated a fraction at a time until at last he was deeply inside her.

'Use the quill pen on her clitoris,' suggested Lewis, fascinated by the scene. At once Rowena climbed on to the bed and as Chris increased the tempo of his movements Harriet felt the feather of the pen teasing her throbbing bud. Without any warning an orgasm tore through her, pushing her stomach upwards and wrenching at her abdominal muscles with the sudden shocking urgency of release.

Taken by surprise Chris could only watch the perspiration gathering on Harriet's skin and saw the rapid flush of arousal spread over her breasts and neck. When she was still he withdrew, then slid back into her, his hands digging into the sides of her waist as he lifted her lower body the way he wanted it.

He was far rougher than Lewis, his movements less controlled, but Harriet's body was still aroused from the earlier stimulation and after a few minutes she felt another orgasm beginning.

'Wait for me,' said Chris, 'or you'll be punished.'

Harriet gasped and tried to quell her flesh, but then Rowena drew back the clitoral hood again and swirled the feather over the glistening nub, making self-control impossible. Harriet climaxed helplessly.

'I didn't mean to!' she protested as Chris stared down at her.

'That isn't the point,' he said coldly. 'You failed, which means that I have to punish you.'

Rowena saw the startled look on Harriet's face and smiled. 'Isn't Chris incredible? I adore his punishments.'

'I don't think I would,' moaned Harriet, struggling against her bonds.

Lewis watched the other three with interest. It was clear that Chris was fascinated by Harriet. She was the first woman he'd responded to apart from Rowena, and Lewis wondered how Rowena felt about that.

From the expression on her face he guessed that she wasn't pleased. He wished that he could see inside her head, discover how much of her jealousy was over him and how much over Chris. For a time he'd thought that the experiment was driving her towards him, and Chris was being excluded. Now he wasn't sure.

Strangely he didn't mind as much as he'd expected. He realised that he was actually more interested in Harriet, and Harriet's response to the night's adventures. In his original idea, the catalyst – at that time faceless and characterless – had been of no importance as a person. Her purpose had simply been to force Rowena into making a choice. It was different now. Harriet was flesh and blood, and very much a person in her own right. A person whose responses were beginning to be of more importance to Lewis than Rowena's, and that meant that the film wasn't going to work in the way he'd intended.

He couldn't do anything about it though. He had to accept what happened or the experiment was pointless. One possible problem of the new development was that there might need to be a change of emphasis in the casting. The heroine might not be Rowena, but Harriet. This thought did trouble him, because Rowena would never accept it. He gave a small sigh, wondering if this time his project had been too ambitious.

'Let me up,' said Harriet, having discovered that it was impossible for her to get free without help from one of the others. 'I don't want to be tied down any more.'

'Don't you understand that the choice isn't yours?' asked Rowena, running a hand caressingly round the exposed breasts and enjoying the instant response of the nipples.

'Lewis!' called Harriet beseechingly.

Drawn out of his reverie he looked over to the

bed. He was already hard with desire and the sight of Rowena playing carelessly with Harriet's body while the younger woman attempted to subdue her clearly visible response aroused him even more.

'What?' he asked huskily.

'Please untie me,' she begged him.

'Let her go,' said Lewis curtly.

'She's to be punished!' protested Chris.

'I know that, but first let her sit up. We'll all have a short break. And take that suit off her, I want everyone naked.'

'I can undress myself,' protested Harriet as her hands were freed, but she wasn't given the chance. As Rowena and Chris peeled the leather playsuit off her, their hands fondled and teased her at every opportunity until she was breathless from the sensations.

She went to get off the bed, but instead the other three joined her there, and they all sat cross-legged and naked while Rowena handed round a bowl of fruit. There were pears, soft ripe plums and slices of water melon. Harriet chose a golden pear with a delicate bloom of pink on it. When she bit into the fruit the juices ran down her chin, trickling on to her neck and breasts, but when she went to wipe it away Lewis stopped her. 'We'll clean each other up when we've finished!' he laughed.

Harriet watched Lewis bite into a slice of water melon. He leant foward to try and prevent it going down his chin and instead the watery juice splashed on to his upper thighs. He looked at Harriet, and it was as much as she could do to stop herself crawling across the bed and licking it off him there and then.

Rowena had chosen a pear as well and although she tipped her head back as she ate, the juice still spilt down over her chin and tiny fragments of soft pulpy flesh made their way slowly on to her abundant breasts.

It was Chris who broke first. He moved over to Harriet and started licking at the corners of her mouth, his tongue flicking delicately at the skin and then he nibbled his way down her neck, lapping at her from time to time like a kitten at a saucer of cream.

Lewis watched and felt his erection pulsating. For one brief moment he hated Chris. He'd wanted to do what his brother-in-law was doing, and the sight of Harriet closing her eyes and luxuriating in the touch of Chris's mouth and tongue inflamed him yet more.

Rowena glanced at her husband and was shoked by the rage in his eyes. She looked back at Chris and noticed that he was already erect again, and that he was no longer aware of anything but Harriet. A dreadful sense of loneliness gripped her. Bending her head she started to clean the water melon off Lewis's thighs.

As she worked her way inwards, letting her mouth nuzzle against the stem of his penis and inside the tender flesh of his inner thighs, Lewis wanted to catch hold of her hair and stop her. It was the wrong mouth. Despite the fact that this was what he'd wanted, that he'd intended to force Rowena to choose him over her brother, now that she was doing that he didn't want her. Realising that the story could not be allowed to resolve itself through his feelings, that it must be Rowena who decided, he made himself keep still and was about to respond by pushing Rowena on to her back and sucking the pear juice off her undeniably magnificent breasts when Harriet opened her eyes and looked at him.

For a few seconds she didn't seem certain who he was, she was so utterly lost in the sensuality of what Chris was doing to her, but then recognition dawned and she smiled at Lewis. It was an open, fearless smile; the smile of a woman confident in her sexuality and without thought he reached out a hand towards her.

Rowena caught his hand and guided it to her breasts. 'I'm still sticky, darling,' she said coolly.

'Then I must make you clean,' he laughed, but inside his stomach was churning. He knew that his feelings for Harriet were far deeper and more complex than for any women before her. The thought infuriated him, threatening as it did both his film and his peace of mind, and his response was immediate.

'In a minute Chris must decide on Harriet's punishment,' he said casually.

Harriet, who'd been watching him closely, was shocked. She'd felt sure she'd seen real affection in his eyes a moment earlier, but now his voice was cold and his gaze detached. As Chris lapped the last of the pear juice away he nuzzled her neck.

'I know just how to punish you,' he whispered. 'I shall use the brushes.'

Remembering the kind of games Chris and Rowena had played, Harriet didn't want any punishment from her employer's half-brother and she opened her mouth to protest, but Lewis covered it with his hand. 'Relax,' he whispered. 'Who knows, you might find you enjoy yourself.'

171

Before she'd had time to consider further, the other three quickly spread-eagled Harriet on the bed, and once more her wrists were fastened to the bed-posts, but this time her ankles were secured as well leaving her legs open and the area between her thighs totally unprotected.

'I think the blindfold again,' murmured Chris to Rowena, and once more Harriet was plunged into the world of darkness. She lay tensely, wondering what Chris intended to do to her, and whereabouts on her body he would start.

Lewis watched the fastened girl and his desire for her was so great that he could hardly breathe. The sight of her body, naked and totally in their power, was an even greater aphrodisiac than he'd expected, but he didn't want Chris to be the one to arouse new sensations in her. He wanted it to be him, and for the first time he disliked the role in which he'd cast himself for the duration of their experiment.

Rowena watched her husband and knew by the expression on his face that his feelings for Harriet were greater than any he'd ever had for her. No matter what happened as a result of tonight, he would never be hers in the way they'd both intended. Far from drawing them closer together, Harriet had succeeded in widening the gulf between them, and Rowena didn't like it.

She still wasn't sure which of the two men in the room she wanted to be with more, but she hadn't envisaged a situation where her choice might not be welcome. Lewis had always been the suppliant, trying to draw her away from Chris with a different kind of sexuality, a softer kind that after a time had bored her. He no longer looked like a man who would be interested. Rowena had never taken second place to another woman in her life, and the surge of jealousy that swept through her was astonishing in its power. She looked at her half-brother and felt a brief flicker of triumph. He understood her, and through him she could get her revenge.

'I'll help you,' she said softly. Chris smiled.

The hidden cameras rolled on, recording every flicker of emotion, every nuance of expression on all their faces for Lewis to view later.

For Harriet the wait seemed interminable. She could hear someone moving about, opening and shutting drawers and placing things on surfaces, and she heard Rowena's words but she still had no idea what was going to happen to her. Although tense her body had never felt more alive. Her skin was still sticky from the pear juice and her flesh seemed as ripe as the fruit itself, continually tingling with excitement even when no one was stimulating her. It was as though she was being taken over by her senses, and nothing mattered any more except sensation. Sensation and Lewis; the two were now indistinguishable in her mind.

All at once she felt Chris's arm brush against her shoulder and at once her body went taut with expectation. Her imagination had conjured up all kinds of strange things, but not once had she thought that what he would do was firmly but slowly pull a bristle hairbrush through her long locks. He was careful not to pull or tangle her hair, concentrating instead on stimulating her scalp. The sensation was both soothing and invigorating as the movement of the brush lulled her while the touch of the bristles on her scalp made the nerve endings there tingle.

She let herself relax into the sensation and her whole body became soft and pliant. Lewis watched the way her upper thighs fell further apart and her breathing became deeper.

Once Chris's rhythm was established and Harriet successfully lulled into a state of languid acceptance, Rowena took a tiny baby's hairbrush in her hand and carefully brushed it down the insides of Harriet's imprisoned arms. The caress was like a whisper, so soft as to render Harriet uncertain it was even happening at first, but then as it continued her flesh responded.

The skin there was tender and receptive. Sometimes Rowena used the brush in circles, sometimes in straight lines, but she worked ceaselessly on the same area until at last the pleasure became more of an irritation and Harriet wanted the soft caress to move to other parts of her body.

Rowena knew that this happened; Chris had done it to her often enough so it gave her immense pleasure to watch Harriet's mouth tighten in a grimace as the brushing continued.

Lewis saw Harriet's hips start to move and she twisted her upper torso as much as her bonds would permit to try and force the brush into contact with another area of skin. Only when she gave a tiny moan did Rowena move, and then she let the brush drift across the centre of the upthrust breasts until both the nipples were red and swollen. Once her object was achieved she changed the brush for a fine-pointed artist's paintbrush and after licking it swirled it around the rock hard buds making Harriet's whole body quiver with rising desire.

All the time his half-sister was working, Chris was continuing to brush carefully at Harriet's hair. Her whole scalp had now been massaged for over ten minutes and she didn't think she could stand it any longer. She tried to pull away from him, but escape was impossible and she heard him laugh to himself.

Her breasts were aching as Rowena continued to amuse herself with the engorged nipples, and when the brushing of her hair finally ceased Harriet didn't stop to wonder what would happen next, she was simply grateful for the respite.

Lewis studied Rowena and Chris. They were both totally absorbed in what they were doing, and worked like a well-established team on the hapless body squirming beneath them. He swallowed hard, trying to dampen down his ferocious need for Harriet that was causing him physical pain. He watched Chris's next move with interest, wondering how Harriet would respond.

Harriet, lying beneath the cruelly teasing touch of the slim, brush-point, couldn't make up her mind whether she was in heaven or hell. The sensations were exquisite, but although the result was a steady building of pressure within her, the touch of the brush alone wasn't enough to allow the build-up to progress beyond a certain point. As a result her whole body was tight and aching with need and there was nothing she could do to push her responses beyond the level Rowena and Chris permitted.

When Chris abruptly stroked the bristle brush across the tightly stretched skin of her abdomen, Harriet gave a startled cry and pressed herself down into the bed as she tried to evade him. Chris simply pressed the brush harder against the tender skin and smiled at Rowena as the younger woman shuddered.

The initial shockwaves startled Harriet, but then as blood coursed through the veins beneath her skin the sensation started to arouse a peculiar pleasure, different from any she'd known before. Thrills of dark excitement ran through her and when Rowena began to use the baby brush on Harriet's arm again while still continuing to tease her nipples with the finer brush Harriet's entire body started to scream for a climax, a release from the relentless build-up of tension.

Chris and Rowena were too experienced to let this happen. Time and time again Harriet felt her body gather itself together for the blissful explosion, and every time at the very last second one of the brushes would cease to move and the moment would be ruined until eventually Harriet was reduced to tears of frustration.

'Let me come, oh please let me come!' she begged them.

Chris bent his mouth to her ear. 'It's a punishment, remember?'

'I can't stand it any longer,' she moaned, but they both knew that she could. They changed rhythms and places, they brushed over her hip bones with the baby brush and up her calves with the bristle brush. They even allowed the finest brush to tease inside her inner lips. brushing briefly against her swollen clitoris so that her breath snagged in her throat and she wrenched her fastened body upwards trying to trigger the elusive orgasm. Again they were too clever for her – the brush had already been removed and her vulva moved restlessly against nothing.

Lewis continued to study them all. He had never seen a woman as swollen with desire as Harriet. Between her outspread legs he could see tiny beads of moisture, a clear indication of her arousal, and the whole of her upper body was flushed with sexual excitement while her breasts were larger and the veins in them more prominent than ever before.

He tried to imagine what such tension must be like, but it was impossible. All he could do was watch, and wait for the moment when he could take advantage of the cruel game Rowena and her half-brother were playing.

Harriet lost all track of time. It was as though the two of them had been toying with her for hours, and her body never seemed to understand the game. Despite constantly being let down, despite the continuing frustration and the terrible aching emptiness this caused, it responded to their every touch. She tried to stop it, to tell herself that there was no point and they weren't doing it to pleasure her, but still her skilfully trained body was misled by them as it searched frantically for the shattering moment of satisfaction their attentions promised.

Finally Lewis couldn't stand it any longer either. 'My turn I think,' he said quietly and the other two watched as he removed the final item from the table.

Chapter Nine

LEWIS CAREFULLY PULLED the soft latex ring over his penis until it was resting comfortably at the base. All around the ring were soft goose feathers designed to titillate the woman's clitoris as the man thrust. He knew from experience how well they worked, and the thought of the finely tuned Harriet at last receiving their soft caress on the most sensitive part of her body made him tremble. Slowly he approached the bed. 'Untie her,' he ordered Chris.

Chris frowned. 'She's meant to be kept like that.'

'Only for your pleasure. I prefer her loose.'

Rowena gave a small sigh. It was always the same; Lewis would never play games the way she liked them, not even now when so much was at stake. She nodded at her half-brother and he reluctantly released Harriet. 'What about the blindfold?'

'Leave that on for now,' replied Lewis, picturing the blissful shock that awaited Harriet when he finally penetrated her.

Harriet rubbed at her wrists, trying to restore the blood flow. Her flesh was screaming for attention, and the pressure in her body made it seems as though her skin had shrunk in the wash and was now too tight for the swollen flesh constrained within.

Lewis knelt over her, his legs outside hers, and looked down at her, savouring the moment. Her face was slightly flushed and damp with continual arousal, her hair tousled and her lips swollen and pink, but it was the desperate straining movements of her body that most clearly demonstrated her terrible need for sexual release.

More excited than ever before, Lewis bent his mouth to her ear. 'Bend your knees up towards your chin and rest your ankles on my shoulders, as close to my head as you can manage,' he told her.

At the sound of his voice, low and sensuous, she shivered and her legs moved up until she could feel the sides of his face with the insides of her feet.

Carefully Lewis balanced his weight on one arm. He then wrapped the other around her legs, just below her knees, so that he could control their movements and change the sensations for her once he'd entered.

Harriet's breathing quickened as she felt the soft velvet head of his erection nudging against her outer sex-lips and then he was gliding smoothly into her and at last the aching void was filled.

No sooner had she started to relish the feel of him deep within then she noticed another sensation as well. A light tickling feeling over her clitoris, like butterflies' wings brushing gently against it. When he withdrew a little the sensation stopped, but with every movement it started again, and sometimes he would rotate his hips so that the clitoris was stimulated even more and each time he did this Harriet heard herself gasping with pleasure.

At last the build-up towards release began again, but this time she knew that it wouldn't be stopped, that she would finally gain the satisfaction Chris and Rowena had refused her, and her body tried to rush towards its goal.

Lewis slowed the pace. His arm gripped her legs tightly so that she could feel him within her more, but her clitoris received less direct stimulation from the feathers. Then, as the darts of arousal from that tiny mass of nerve endings slowed he would release his grip a little and allow the feathers to touch her once more.

Without thinking Harriet reached up blindly for him and her hands went beneath his upper arms and gripped the back of his shoulders. He felt her fingers digging into him every time the feathers did their work and her body strained towards a climax, then when he withdrew the pressure of her fingers eased but she tried to pull him down towards her, seeking more physical intimacy from the position.

Toying with her like this, giving her such pleasure while at the same time increasing his own, was as wonderful for Lewis as it was for Harriet. Harriet though had been played with for too long, and soon she grew frantic and started to twist her lower body in order to increase the tempo of the pulse beating behind her aching nub.

Lewis decided to change position and delay her gratification just a little longer. Ignoring Harriet's pleas he disentangled their limbs and then knelt back on the bed with Harriet's hips positioned between his outspread thighs, before lifting her feet on to the front of his shoulders.

Her hands clutched at his knees and she moaned, pleading with him to end her torment. 'In a minute,' he whispered as his hands slid over her outer thighs and belly. Her muscles contracted violently at the touch and she pressed herself against him.

Lewis knelt up and the movement meant that he penetrated her very deeply while at the same time the feathers worked their usual magic against the sensitive tissue around her swollen clitoris. Before she could catch her breath he leant back and his erection pressed against the top wall of her vagina.

Harriet felt a deep ache start inside her, a blissful sweet ache that she didn't want to lose and she tried to move herself again. 'Keep quite still,' he said softly. 'Just wait.'

Harriet forced her writhing body to remain motionless, and Lewis kept still as well, concentrating simply on maintaining the pressure against her G-spot. He knew that if he kept the pressure constant for long enough she would almost certainly climax. Slowly her breathing quickened and her mouth opened slightly as the ache turned into something far greater.

Now it was ecstasy and it spread slowly upwards throughout her lower belly. When he saw her nipples tighten Lewis knew that her long-awaited orgasm was only moments away.

For Harriet the waiting, the stillness and the darkness caused by the blindfold were all part of the glorious sensation that was sweeping over her and then without warning the pulse behind her clitoris started beating frantically and her whole body drew in on itself as it prepared for the moment of release.

As she hesitated, balanced on the very edge of satisfaction, Lewis gently slid a hand beneath her buttocks and then pressed one fingertip against the rim of her anus. Again the pressure was firm and constant and combined with the pressure on her G-spot the result was incredible.

At last, after all the waiting, Harriet's body succumbed totally to the build-up of myriad sensations and the burning heat of her orgasm tore through her. Her arms and legs thrashed around wildly, her limbs totally unco-ordinated in the final moment of sexual gratification.

Gradually the tremors of the orgasm slowed, and Harriet started to breathe more evenly, but then Lewis let his finger slip inside the rim of her anus and he ran it gently around the inside so that the dying embers of the climax were re-kindled and yet another violent wave of pulsating contractions tore through her. This time she let herself scream aloud, unable to control herself in any way, so totally was she in the grip of her body's sensuality.

As the second huge orgasm ripped through her, Harriet's vaginal walls contracted furiously and Lewis was no longer able to keep control. He held back for as long as possible, relishing the sensation of the pulsations that were gripping him, but finally his hips thrust furiously and then he was spilling himself into her, his climax going on and on until it seemed as though she would drain him of every drop of fluid.

When his last involuntary twitch had died away Lewis lowered himself on to Harriet, and she felt her breasts squash against his chest as he moved himself around, pressing against her as though trying for a closeness that was physically impossible. She clutched at him, trying to let him know that she wanted the closeness as much as he did.

Rowena and Chris watched the two of them and while Rowena felt jealous of Harriet, her half-brother was jealous of Lewis. He would have liked to see her writhe and scream for him in the way she had for his brother-in-law. His own erection was painfully hard now, and he was impatient for the night's games to continue.

'Isn't it time we all took part?' he asked casually, trying to conceal his eagerness from Rowena.

Lewis rolled off Harriet, lying by her side with one arm beneath her shoulders. He removed her blindfold and when their eyes met his softened in response to the look in hers. Harriet smiled. Lewis didn't; he would have liked to, but now was the wrong moment and he knew it.

Watching Harriet smile Rowena vowed to make sure the night ended as she'd planned. 'Come along, Lewis,' she said sweetly. 'You mustn't be greedy. Harriet's having such a lovely time you must let us all share her now.'

'We all share each other,' replied Lewis. 'Harriet's one of the group, not the focal point.'

'You could have fooled me,' murmured

Rowena, averting her head as she spoke so that only Chris heard.

Harriet gazed at them all. 'I've never . . .' Her voice tailed off. It seemed ridiculous to start saying she'd never taken part in an orgy when she'd spent the past few hours being aroused and satisfied by three virtual strangers, but then she'd been passive. She wasn't sure she could take an active part when they were all involved.

Lewis looked thoughtfully at her. 'What's the matter, Harriet? Don't you find us attractive?'

'Yes, of course.'

'And haven't we given you a lot of pleasure?' asked Chris.

Harriet nodded.

'Then you must reciprocate,' said Rowena. 'Don't tell me you've still got some inhibitions left? Not after the past half hour!'

Harriet wanted to tell them that it wasn't a question of inhibitions, she knew she'd lost them long ago. It was a matter of feelings. She loved Lewis, she didn't love Rowena or Chris, and that meant that it was more difficult to lose herself in sensations. She responded more easily when her emotions were involved. Even when Chris and Rowena had been arousing her, she'd known that Lewis was watching, and hopefully being aroused by her. To make love to the others simply for their pleasure wouldn't be as easy.

'Don't disappoint me, Harriet,' murmured Lewis.

She smiled, knowing deep down that it wouldn't be too hard. Her sensuality was such that once her body was aroused again it shouldn't be difficult, it was only the prospect that was alarming. 'I'll try not to,' she promised.

'We don't have to stay in this one room, do we?' asked Chris. Lewis shook his head. 'Good, then let's go!' He grabbed Harriet by the hand and pulled her out through the door, along the landing and down the flight of stairs, stopping halfway down.

Rowena and Lewis were just behind them. All four of them were naked but the house was warm and Harriet realised that she was beginning to feel comfortable without her clothes, less self-conscious than ever before.

Chris stood with his back to the wall. 'Lie on your back on the stairs for me, Harriet,' he said. Rowena laughed. Puzzled, Harriet did as he asked. Chris then stood over her with his legs between her thighs and she drew one leg up so that her inner thigh was pressed against his outer leg. He raised his inner leg upwards, resting the knee on the same stair as Harriet's head.

Harriet saw at once what was intended as his erection bobbed just above her face. Reaching up a hand she slid it along his shaft, while at the same time Chris bent his outside leg. This had the effect of bringing his penis within reach of Harriet's mouth and also enabling him to stimulate her vulva with his shin bone.

Suddenly Harriet found herself tremendously excited by the whole experience. She could tell that Chris was desperate for her, that he wanted to come in her mouth and the sense of power this gave her was like an aphrodisiac.

She flicked her tongue along the underside of his shaft and sucked in her cheeks to create a vacuum within her mouth. The pressure on

185

Chris's penis was intense and his legs trembled with the effort of keeping control for a few precious seconds as her velvet mouth and slightly tentative hands worked on him.

Lewis stood a few stairs above them leaning against the wall while Rowena rubbed herself against him, her arms round his neck and her perfect breasts brushing softly over his chest.

Although it was only a very short time since he'd climaxed with Harriet, Lewis found that the feel of Rowena against him together with the sight of Chris moving in and out of Harriet's mouth was making him hard again and he gripped Rowena by the hips so that she could feel his burgeoning erection.

All at once Chris gasped and far too soon for his liking he was spilling himself into Harriet's mouth. She sucked greedily at the liquid, enjoying the musky taste of him, and when he thought he'd finished she stroked a spot at the very base of his spine that forced a few last drops out of him. He groaned at the wrenching final contractions.

Rowena was determined to have some satisfaction herself now. Aware of this, Lewis continued down the stairs past Chris, who was leaning slumped against the wall, and the prone Harriet, and went into the large drawing-room. Rowena, who had followed him, went up on tiptoe to kiss him but he put her away from him and started throwing the large cushions from the chairs on to the floor.

By the time the other two joined them the floor was covered and with a laugh Chris threw himself down on to the soft surface. Lewis guided

Rowena across and then the pair of them lay down facing her half-brother. Rowena leant back against her husband's chest and he supported himself on one elbow before sliding the other arm down the length of her side, lingering over her most sensitive areas until his hand closed about her upper thigh. He then pulled her leg back over his, tipping her on to her opposite side so that her sex was totally exposed to the watching Chris.

Harriet stood in the doorway watching. She saw Chris's hand move towards Rowena and then his fingers were carefully parting her outer sex-lips so that he could bend his head and use his tongue to part the inner lips.

Lewis glanced at Harriet. 'Come and join us,' he said with a smile. 'Sit by Rowena's head. I'm sure her breasts would like some attention.'

For just a second Harriet hesitated, but then, drawn by the excitement of the other three she moved to obey. She touched the redhead's firm right breast lightly and Rowena sighed. 'Not like that! Do it harder. I don't like soft caresses there.'

Harriet increased the pressure and at once Rowena's large nipples rose to twin peaks and Chris's tongue ran up and down the channel between her inner sex-lips in a soft movement that made her whimper with delight.

'Use your mouth on her,' Lewis suggested to Harriet. Bending her head she took one of the tight nipples between her lips and sucked on it. 'Nip it with your teeth,' continued Lewis. 'There's no point in wasting finesse on my wife, she doesn't appreciate it.'

His words excited Rowena and she rubbed herself against Chris's face. His tongue darted inside her for a moment, and then traced a quick path down her perenium before returning to the moisture-slicked inner channel.

Harriet waited for a few seconds and then she suddenly nibbled on the nipple imprisoned between her lips. Rowena gasped at the scarlet streak of ecstasy that shot through her and when she thrust her breasts further upwards Harriet bit her again.

At the same time Chris allowed his teeth to graze lightly against the stem of his half-sister's clitoris and at once she climaxed, shuddering violently for several seconds. Harriet released the other woman's nipples and watched her body shaking. She found it unbearably exciting, and suddenly wanted someone to pay her attention again.

Chris, lifting his head from between Rowena's thighs, knew from Harriet's expression how she was feeling and pulling her to her feet he drew her across the room to stand by one of the chairs. He bent her face down over the broad arm, her head hanging down in the space where the deep cushion had been, and before she had time to protest his hands were on her buttocks and he was separating the cheeks of her bottom.

Once she was fully open Rowena rubbed lubricating jelly all around the entrance to her rectum, occasionlly letting one small finger slip inside the rim, then she stood back and watched as Lewis, now fully erect again, positioned himself behind the girl.

Harriet held her breath. She knew what was going to happen, but not who was going to do it to her. When Rowena crouched at the front of the chair and began to massage Harriet's breasts she tried to turn her head to see which of the men it would be but Rowena caught her hair and kept her face down.

'It's a surprise,' she whispered. 'I expect you're hoping it's Chris. Lewis is so large, isn't he? Even I find it painful sometimes when it's Lewis. Not that I mind. I like the pain, but somehow I don't think you will.'

Lewis couldn't hear what his wife was saying, but he felt Harriet stiffen beneath his hands and knew that she was now tensed against him. Cursing beneath his breath he let one hand slide under her so that he could tease her clitoris, drumming lightly and insistently against the surrounding area until she grew slippery with excitement and her muscles relaxed.

Now he could let his swollen purple glans rest against that inviting puckered little opening and he circled his hips to encourage her to open more. Still the most secret of entrances remained closed against him. He stopped, uncertain whether or not to proceed, but then Rowena and Chris changed places and as Chris caressed the dangling breasts Rowena slid a well oiled finger into her husband's rectum, pushing until she could massage the prostate gland.

Immediately he was flooded with sharply intense sensations that nearly precipitated his climax and without thinking Lewis thrust blindly forward, his body intent on gaining its own satisfaction.

Despite the lubrication of the jelly and the stimulation that had preceded it, this violent intrusion made Harriet cry out with a mixture of

189

pain and shock. He was so large he seemed to be stretching her more than her body could stand and she tried to twist away from him.

Lewis grabbed her hips to keep her still and slowed his pace a fraction and then Chris pressed his hand upwards against her belly. He pressed and released, pressed and released, then lowered his hand until it was just above her pubic bone. There he repeated the process and now sparks of delicious pressure filled her belly and when his fingers went lower and parted her pubic hair he kept the heel of his hand firmly in place so that her bladder was still under pressure.

Harriet felt she would burst. There was a hot sensation in her belly, her clitoris was throbbing and the almost painful movements within her rectum were now starting to engender delicious thrills that lanced right through her.

At that moment Lewis climaxed and his spasmodic jerking as he spilled his seed into Harriet for the second time in the evening triggered her climax and she felt her internal muscles contract gratefully while the delicious heavy fullness swelled and swelled until at last she came.

Eventually she stumbled from the arm of the chair and lay down on the cushioned floor with Lewis next to her while Chris and Rowena stared at each other, their eyes bright with a strange yearning excitement.

'What would you like us to do for you?' asked Chris.

Lewis looked at his wife with interest. All of them present, except for Harriet, knew that tonight was the film's final scene. It had been decided long ago that out of a night's prolonged sexual interplay would come the plot's resolution.

Nights like this changed people's feelings and perceptions. Sometimes they discarded old loves and ways for new ones; at other times they decided that they no longer wished to live as dangerously as before, choosing instead to be secure in a single relationship. Exactly what Rowena and Chris were thinking Lewis had no idea; all he knew was how he felt. As for Harriet, as the nameless girl in the film her feelings had never been considered important. Now he knew better. Harriet had changed the entire plot but he had to accept it. If he didn't then he could no longer tell himself that his films reflected life. However much he might have wished for something different, things were the way they were. Rowena had this one last chance to shape the finale.

'I think I'd like us all to use the sauna,' said Rowena. 'It's my favourite place.'

'I've never been in a sauna,' said Harriet innocently.

'All the more exciting for you then,' said Chris smoothly, already picturing how she would look as she emerged from the steam room and was shown what awaited her.

Lewis nodded. He was pleased now that he'd had the foresight to instal cameras in most of the main rooms. All that he'd missed of the night so far was the sex that had taken place on the stairs, and that vision was printed so clearly on his brain that it didn't need cameras.

Chris put an arm round Harriet's waist and squeezed her affectionately. 'You'll enjoy this,' he assured her.

Harriet didn't believe him. There was too much suppressed excitement in his voice, but she couldn't understand why because Ella used saunas regularly and was always trying to get Harriet to join her, claiming they put new life into her.

The four of them walked past the swimming pool and through some doors to the far end. In front of them was a large cubicle with darkened windows and Harriet hesitated.

'It's just steam,' Lewis told her. 'You might find it rather hot at first but you'll soon adjust. There are slatted shelves for us all to lie on.'

Rowena went in first and Harriet followed. The almost suffocating heat rose up and she coughed, but the men were on her heels and she was hustled into the cubicle before she could voice any misgivings.

The steam swirled about them and it was difficult to see where the shelves Lewis had mentioned were. Then she felt his arms on her hips and he guided her towards one of the lower ones, pressing her shoulders down so that she didn't hit her head on the one above.

Harriet lay back. Sweat trickled down the valley between her breasts then along her ribs. The entire surface of her body was covered in a film of perspiration and it was difficult to breathe.

'Don't you think it's bliss?' enquired Rowena from above her.

'Not really,' confessed Harriet. 'It's too hot.'

'You'll cool off quickly in the next room!' laughed Chris, and she felt his hand grip her ankle and caress her calf. Above her Rowena gave a small sigh of pleasure and Harriet realised that

Lewis must be lying with his wife because she could hear the sound of flesh against flesh and the soft murmur of his voice.

When Chris's hands started to fondle her breasts she was sure that she was too drained by the heat to respond, but amazingly her nipples still sprung to life and encouraged by this he pressed his damp face between them, nuzzling at the inner surfaces.

'Time for the next room,' called Lewis.

Harriet was highly relieved, and let Chris lead her through the steam and out through a different door into the cubicle beyond. The cold hit her in an icy blast. Stunned by the change in temperature she backed away as goosebumps covered her skin and she began to shiver.

At the far side of the cubicle was a bath, but it wasn't full of water, it was piled high with snow. Harriet stared at it in astonishment, and then Rowena was climbing in covering herself with the icy flakes and laughing with pure joy.

'Aren't you going to join her, Harriet?' asked Lewis, his dark eyes unfathomable.

Harriet could feel her teeth chattering at the prospect. 'I don't think I can,' she protested.

'It's what they do in Finland,' he assured her. 'Believe it or not it's very invigorating once you take the plunge.'

Chris stood by the bath tub and waited. Rowena looked over at the shivering Harriet and smiled. If she hadn't done that, if she'd kept her feelings to herself, then Harriet might well have refused and left the three of them alone together but the sight of Rowena's pleasure at her discomfort spurred her on.

'All right,' she said briskly and then she was climbing into the freezing snow. For a moment she quite literally couldn't breathe as the biting cold snow covered her sweat-drained flesh.

Now the two men began to move the women around in the bath. Lewis worked on his wife, massaging the snow into her breast and belly, moving his hand between her thighs to press the freezing flakes against her sex mound and as he worked Rowena sighed voluptuously, relishing the shocking contrast after the jungle heat of the steam room.

Chris worked just as assiduously on Harriet. At first her body shrank from him, but then a wonderful glow started to suffuse her body and when he turned her on her face in the snow and rolled tiny snowballs up and down her spine every part of her began to tingle so that she felt more alive than ever before in her life.

'Our turn,' said Chris at last and the two women stepped out to let the men in. Now it was their turn to massage the snow into the men and when Harriet filled her hands with snow and then ran them up and down Chris's penis he gasped with excitement and reached up for her breasts, tweaking the rigid nipples and instigating blissful darts of excitement.

'How do you stop the snow from melting?' asked Harriet.

'The bath's really a kind of fridge,' explained Rowena. 'I paid a fortune for it, but it was well worth the money.' She looked at Harriet's body. 'You seem to appreciate it as well. I hope you like the final part as much!'

'I thought this was it,' said Harriet. 'Ella's never

said there was anything more.'

'Well, whoever Ella is she doesn't know everything,' laughed Rowena.

Lewis and Chris climbed out of the tub and then shepherded the two women out of the cubicle and back round the side until they were at the side of the swimming pool.

'Lie face down on the loungers,' said Chris, producing two blindfolds. 'It's always ladies first on these occasions.'

The blindfolds were fastened and Harriet and Rowena stretched out on the slatted loungers, whose soft cushions had been removed. The slats pressed into Harriet's breasts, already tender from the sauna, but she didn't like to protest because Rowena seemed quite happy with her position.

The air around the swimming pool was pleasantly warm, and Harriet slowly started to relax after the contrasting heat and cold of the sauna. Her limbs felt heavy, and the darkness of the blindfold lulled her towards sleep.

She was drifting off, her thoughts full of Lewis and the night's events, when her body was stunned by a fierce stinging sensation across her buttocks. She jerked back into wakefulness and started to move from the chair. 'Keep still,' laughed Chris. 'This is the best part of all.'

Again she felt the piercing stinging sensation, but this time it was on her upper thighs and she closed her legs to protect herself. 'What are you doing?' she gasped, and even as she spoke she heard the sound of something falling against Rowena's skin too.

'It's only the birch twigs!' said Chris. 'They get your blood flowing again.'

He was clearly an expert at applying the bunch of sticks because each blow fell in a slightly different place until the whole of Harriet's back was smarting and pricking. She wriggled and at once the slats of the chair pressed into her lower belly.

'Now turn over,' said Chris, the excitement clear in his voice.

Part of Harriet didn't want to. She felt that she should refuse, tear off the blindfold and walk out of the room, but she could hear Rowena's tiny cries of rising excitement and knew that her own body was slowly responding in the same way.

At first the burning stripes had been uncomfortable, close to pain, but already that was changing and she was trembling with the beginnings of that dreadful need Lewis had kindled in her. She tried to imagine how the twigs would feel falling on her delicate breasts and belly and suddenly she wanted to know, to experience it for herself and so she turned and Chris looked down at her long, slim body and his legs went weak with desire.

Lewis paused for a moment, despite Rowena's pleas, and glanced at his brother-in-law. It was impossible for Chris to disguise the lust on his face and when he felt Lewis's eyes on him he turned to look at him defiantly.

'Enjoying yourself?' asked Lewis coolly.

'Very much,' retorted Chris, and Lewis watched the fair-haired young man raise his arm high in the air and bring the birch twigs down across Harriet's unprotected abdomen. She jerked with the impact, but her nipples were visibly hardening and as the tiny red marks appeared on her skin she thrust her belly up as though begging for more.

Chris was happy to oblige, and Lewis had to look away, angered both by Chris's excitement and Harriet's response. His blows on Rowena increased in force and she squealed with delight, lifting her buttocks high into the air to present an easier target for him.

Harriet was in an ecstasy of excitement. Her breasts were aching for what she now thought of as the caress of the birch twigs, but Chris continued to apply them to the lower part of her body until she grasped her breasts in her hand and pushed them up with a moan of need.

Seeing her like that, begging him to strike her in the way he liked best, Chris longed to take her there and then without consulting the others. He no longer cared about the rules of the plot, he simply wanted to take Harriet but first he allowed the twigs to strike her where she so clearly wanted them. The crispness of the blows across her breasts precipitated a sudden and unexpected orgasm in Harriet whose body shuddered and trembled before her arms and legs sprawled limply over the sides of the lounger.

At this Chris lost control. He hurled himself on top of her, moving roughly against the marked skin and nipping at the flesh of her throat and shoulders. Harriet, lost in the world of darkness and pleasure, was taken by surprise. She tried to push him off because this wasn't what she wanted, but Chris was beyond stopping. He reached under her and she felt his fingers moving urgently between her buttocks. Clenching herself against him she went to close her legs but found that he had a thigh between them and his erection was already nudging at the entrance to her vagina. He was heavy and rough, his hands careless of her needs as he struggled to achieve his own gratifaction.

'Stop it!' cried Harriet. 'I don't want you. Get off.'

Lewis, who hd been applying the birch twigs to Rowena's inner thighs, was suddenly alerted to what was happening. He dropped the switch and crossed over to where Harriet was struggling.

'What the hell do you think you're doing?' he asked Chris.

'She's enjoying it,' muttered Chris, still trying to force the cheeks of her bottom apart.

'Get off her,' Lewis's voice was filled with icy contempt. 'Can't you ever do what you're told?'

'She's not yours,' panted Chris, pressing down on Harriet's shoulders.

'She isn't yours either,' said Lewis coldly. 'Harriet belongs to herself. Now get off her.'

Rowena tore off her blindfold, sat up and looked over at her half-brother. 'What are you doing?' she cried in disbelief. 'That wasn't part of the script.'

Chris stared at his sister in a daze of sexual frustration. 'I want to do it my way. I want to hear her scream like you scream for me. I want . . .'

'You bloody fool,' said Lewis scornfully. 'She isn't like your half-sister. Any idiot could have worked that out for himself.'

'She is!' insisted Chris. 'She liked the twigs, she liked the pain, she . . .'

'Hurt *me*,' said Rowena softly. 'Come here, Chris. I want you to hurt me now. Please, I need you.'

Harriet lay quite still, more shocked by what she was hearing than by anything that had happened to her since she came to the house. They were talking as though this was some kind of play or film, not real life. And as for Chris, how he could have thought she wanted the kind of thing he and Rowena did she couldn't imagine.

Lewis watched his wife closely. She was holding out her arms to her half-brother and her need was there for them all to see. Very slowly Chris got up off Harriet and stumbled over to Rowena.

'You can do anything you like to me,' she whispered. 'Take me to your room. I want you to do everything you can think of. Take me further than we've ever gone before. I need you, Chris; she doesn't. She's no different from Lewis.'

'But if I had her, you could stay with Lewis!' protested Chris. 'We'd both be free then. Isn't that what you wanted?'

Rowena shook her head. 'What I thought I wanted and what I need are two different things.'

'But I want Harriet!' he protested.

Rowena stared at him. 'You can't do! Don't you understand, she isn't like us and she never will be.'

'I'd change. I'd be what she wanted. She excites me, Rowena. There's such sensuality in her response – she's so open to new experiences it makes everything more exciting. Like starting my sex life all over again.'

Rowena looked at her husband, her eyes bewildered. 'You can't both want Harriet!' she said in horror.

Lewis gave a twisted smile. 'Why not? I never promised you a happy ending.'

Chapter Ten

HARRIET STILL DIDN'T understand what was happening. She turned to Lewis. 'What do you mean, "happy ending"?'

Furious, Rowena decided to attack both men in the way that would hurt them most, by telling Harriet the truth. 'You don't really think my husband is in love with you, do you?' she sneered. 'He isn't in love with anyone. Lewis lives for his work, and you were just a part of it.'

'But I didn't do any work for him,' protested Harriet. 'Only a few letters and phone calls. It was you who employed me.'

'When I *employed* you it wasn't to write stupid letters for either of us. You were chosen because Lewis thought you were attractive, and exactly right for the role of innocent pawn.'

None of this made any sense at all to Harriet, who hadn't understood a word Rowena said. 'Lewis wasn't there when you interviewed me,' she protested.

'He was watching through one of his two-way mirrors. I'm sure you know all about them, after all you did use one to watch me with Chris, didn't you?'

'How do you know that?' gasped Harriet.

Rowena laughed. 'Because it was all part of the plot, darling!'

'What plot? You aren't making any sense.'

'Lewis's film, the one I'm meant to star in, is about a brother and sister who are in love with each other. In the film the sister marries but the husband can't stop her continuing her affair with her brother. Both he and his wife want the relationship to end, only the woman is too caught up in the dark sensuality of her incestuous affair. Are you with me so far?'

Harriet nodded. It was beginning to make a horrible kind of sense.

'Good. Well, Lewis had the brilliant idea of bringing the film to life, and only writing the script as events happened. We had the perfect cast here, except for one vital ingredient – the other woman. He thought it needed an outsider, a catalyst, and that this young woman's presence would force all the characters to re-appraise their lives.

'Of course, in order for it to work the men had to become sexually involved with her, which Lewis did rather too convincingly I'm afraid, and then the heroine would decide which of the men she wanted the most. I was meant to choose between Chris and Lewis after watching them both with you. Do you understand now?'

Harriet stared at Lewis. 'So you never really felt anything for me? You were just playing out this charade in order to make your film truthful, is that it?'

'It's called *cinéma vérité,*' said Chris helpfully.

'I call it a cheap, despicable trick,' said Harriet furiously. 'How dare you take someone into your home and then use them physically and emotionally for your work! Haven't you any conscience at all?'

'Not much,' admitted Lewis.

Harriet jumped to her feet. 'I hate you all. I think you're sick, and if this is what they call art I don't want anything to do with it. I hope the film's a flop and you never work again.'

Lewis reached out an arm and grabbed her by the wrist. 'Don't you see, Harriet, you changed everything. What Rowena says is true, but once you were here, once I got to know you, it didn't go the way I'd planned.'

'Really? How disappointing for you!'

'No, it wasn't. I didn't mind. Harriet, I do feel something for you. Sure the first time I took you to bed it was acting, but once we were together, once we'd made love, it changed. I tried to tell myself it hadn't, that I was just caught up in the role-playing, but deep down I knew even then. I don't want to lose you, Harriet. You mean more to me than any woman's ever meant.'

'According to your wife that isn't saying very much,' retorted Harriet. 'Tell me, does your work still come first?'

'No!' he protested, and Rowena drew in her breath in astonishment. 'Harriet, if you leave, I'll come after you. I can't let you go. When I saw Chris on top of you just now I could have killed him. As for watching you with him earlier, on the stairs, it was agony because I felt that you should be with me. I didn't want to go on with it all any more.'

'But you did, didn't you?' Harriet pointed out. 'You never stopped and told me the truth.'

'There was too much riding on it, I couldn't. But now it's finished, we can—'

'It's finished all right,' said Harriet, fighting back her tears. 'I'll never forgive you for what you've done to me. I want to leave now.'

'Wait!' interrupted Chris. 'Let me come with you. There's so much I could teach you. We'd be happy together once you admitted the truth about yourself. You know that you're fascinated by me, I can tell by your responses. Don't back away just when you're finding out who you really are.'

'None of you knows anything about truth,' retorted Harriet. 'You don't live in the real world, and you never will.' As she fled from the poolside the other three looked at each other in silence.

Up in her bedroom, Harriet started throwing clothes into suitcases, her heart pounding with shock and grief. She knew that nothing they'd told her had made any difference, that she was still as obsessed by Lewis as he claimed to be by her, but she didn't know how she could ever trust him again, even if he meant what he'd said about coming after her.

As for Chris, she shuddered at the thought of a lifetime with him, although she also knew that there was a part of her, a part only just beginning to emerge, that did take pleasure from some of the things he did. But she didn't love him, and the knowledge that she did love Lewis made his betrayal all the more terrible.

In Rowena's bedroom husband and wife sat on either side of the bed. Lewis was staring moodily out of the window while Rowena sat with her head in her hands.

'How could it have gone so wrong?' she complained bitterly.

'It didn't go wrong,' said Lewis shortly. 'This is what happened. There never was a right or wrong ending.'

'But what about me?' she demanded. 'I'm meant to be the heroine. If you think I'm going to star in a film where I end up losing both men to some naive English girl with long legs you're making a big mistake.'

'You wouldn't be the star,' he said flatly. 'Whoever plays Harriet would be the star.'

Enraged, Rowena threw a book at him. It hit him on the back of the head and he turned on her, his eyes dangerously dark. 'You were the one who started this,' he said softly. 'If you remember, you begged me to make this film. "I want to be free of Chris" you wept, and I believed you. But it wasn't true, was it? You didn't want to be free of him at all, you wanted to humiliate me. All the way along it was Chris you were going to stay with. That was the ending you had in mind, but Chris has spoilt it by falling for Harriet himself.'

'I did want to be free of him!' protested Rowena.

'You're a rotten actress and a rotten liar. When I go through the films your face will give you away, but the few times I did see your expression I could tell that it was Chris you were most involved with.'

'What film?'

'You don't think I committed everything to

204

memory tonight, do you? I filmed it all, and I intend to watch it carefully. Then I'll send for Mark and give him the ending.'

'What's going to happen to us all?' asked Rowena despairingly.

Lewis shrugged. 'Right at this moment I honestly don't care.'

'Do you really love Harriet?' asked Rowena incredulously.

Lewis sighed. 'I suppose I do. I certainly can't contemplate living without her.'

'But why? We had a good life together, didn't we? And we're in the same business, we talk the same language. Harriet won't understand what you do. She'll be jealous of your work.'

'I was jealous of Chris – it didn't mean our marriage wasn't good for a time.'

'If you were jealous then you must have loved me!' exclaimed Rowena.

'No, it was my pride that was hurt. No man likes to think a woman prefers another man's style of lovemaking, especially when it's her half-brother.'

'She isn't even beautiful!'

'She's less obviously beautiful than you,' admitted Lewis. 'You're incredibly sexy-looking, but deep down, Rowena, I don't think you enjoy sex as much as you say. Not the kind of sex I enjoy anyway.'

'I only married you because you were handsome and famous,' said Rowena viciously. 'And you're right, your style of lovemaking never did suit me, but as long as I had Chris too I was all right. Now your bloody film's ruined everything. You say you can't live without Harriet – well I can't live without Chris. I don't care about acting, I don't think I ever want to make a film again, but I must have him. I need the charge he gives me, the excitement that you've never understood.'

'I understand it,' said Lewis. 'It just isn't my style. For a change, yes, but not all the time.'

'Then we'd be well rid of each other. Unfortunately Chris has decided he'd rather have Harriet, and Harriet doesn't want you.'

'Harriet did want me, until you decided to tell her the truth,' said Lewis angrily.

Rowena smiled sweetly. 'Don't tell me you'd have started your relationship based on a lie. That would be highly immoral!'

'Whatever happens you and I are finished,' said Lewis, getting to his feet.

'And who will you get to star in your film?'

'Believe me, once the script is completed I won't have any trouble with casting. It isn't as if you were a big draw any more. I was doing you a favour.'

Rowena scowled. 'As it turns out it was a favour I could have done without.'

'That's what's exciting about a venture of this kind. I have to admit, this isn't a twist I'd ever have thought up for myself.'

'Make sure you thank Harriet before she leaves then. I'm sure she'll appreciate having been such a help to you.'

Lewis slammed out of the room.

Harriet was closing her last case when she heard a tap on her door. Her heart missed a beat as she imagined Lewis standing on the other side. Despite all that had happened she knew that she wanted to see him one final time.

'Come in,' she called.

Chris entered. 'Are you really leaving?' he asked.

'Yes,' said Harriet curtly, almost in tears now that she knew it wasn't Lewis.

'I'd like to come and see you, after you've gone.'

'There's no point. I don't want to see you.'

He moved closer and his hands gripped her tightly round the shoulders. 'You know I can excite you. Earlier, beside the pool, you loved it when I used the birch twigs on you. That's only the beginning, Harriet. There's so much more I can teach you.'

'I'm sure there is, but I don't want to learn it.'

'Your body does. I can feel your nipples hardening at the thought,' he murmured, and his hands roamed over her breasts which were covered by the thin cotton material of her tie-blouse.

'All right, since you seem to need me to spell it out I will,' said Harriet. 'Perhaps you're right, maybe there are things that you do that excite me, but I don't want *you* to do them.'

'You want Lewis, don't you?'

Harriet stayed silent.

'He won't ever let you explore your darker side. He wouldn't do it for Rowena, that's why she kept turning to me.'

'No it isn't!' shouted Harriet, furious with all of them, but most of all furious with her own body for letting her down at a moment like this. 'You and Rowena are tied together by far more than that. You're incapable of living apart. Even if I did love you, which I don't, you wouldn't stay faithful to me. You'd keep running back to your half-sister, because you aren't two people, you're two halves of one.

'I saw that for myself the first time I watched you together. Like it or not, Chris, you and Rowena are inseparable and no one but her will ever understand or appreciate you properly. Why won't you accept that?'

His light blue eyes stared at her. 'Perhaps because I'm afraid of what we'll do to each other,' he said at last.

'You both thrive on fear. You need that edge to everything you do. Think about it, Chris. Once you'd taught me all you know, where would we go from there? It's more than sex, you two are emotionally bonded for life. Your needs and desires are the same – no one will ever be able to satisfy either of you half as well.'

'You mean you aren't prepared to be as honest as she is about your sexuality,' he said contemptuously.

'No,' she said quietly, 'That isn't what I mean. I think I understand myself very well now, but if you want to think that's what I'm saying then fine, go ahead and think it. The bottom line is that you and Rowena are meant for each other, and there isn't any way out. You may not always be happy together, but you'd be far more miserable apart.'

Chris released her. He paused by the door. 'I thought you were special, but you're not. You're pathetically conventional, and you'd have bored me in a few weeks. I only hope Rowena will forgive me.'

'Don't worry,' said Harriet, turning her back on him. 'Rowena knows very well that she can't live without you. Now please get out of my room.'

'Just remember this, Harriet,' said Chris softly. 'You still haven't achieved your full sexual potential. If you do stay with Lewis, you'll have to encourage him to be more adventurous or you'll end up bored by him.' With that he closed the door softly behind him.

After he'd gone Harriet sank down on her dressing-table stool and stared at herself in the mirror. She didn't look very different from the day she'd come to the house for her interview, but inside she was a completely different person. If anyone had told her what she'd learn about herself during her time here she'd never have believed them.

Lewis hadn't only stolen her heart, he'd taken away her innocence as well but she was shocked to realise that she didn't care. She liked the person she'd become, liked the way her body responded to all stimulation and the new ecstatic pleasures she'd discovered. The trouble was, if she lost Lewis then where would she find another man who understood her body and its needs so well?

Unlike Chris, Lewis didn't knock on Harriet's door. Instead he walked straight into her bedroom, and found her gazing at herself in the mirror. She turned to look at him, her eyes expressionless. 'What do you want?'

'I've come to apologize.'

She raised her eyebrows. 'Isn't it rather late for that?'

'I never meant to fall in love with you, Harriet. It just happened. Then, when I admitted to myself how I felt it was too late. I couldn't tell you the truth or the film would have been ruined. I had to let events run their course. I was going to explain it all to you afterwards.'

'I don't suppose you'd have put it quite as bluntly as Rowena.'

'No. Because Rowena was angry she tried to hurt you. I never meant that to happen. You must have been able to tell that you were important to me.'

'I thought I was,' she said sadly.

Lewis walked up behind her and laid his hand on her shoulder, staring into the mirror at her. 'You still are,' he murmured, bending down so that his chin rested in her hair. She felt his hands sliding down over her breasts, and the difference in the sensation compared with when Chris had touched her was vast. This was a caress, an expression of feeling, and she pressed herself against him.

'Let me love you again,' he begged, unfastening the tie of the blouse.

'I don't think . . .'

'I don't want you to think,' he said sharply, and then he was lifting her up and carrying her towards the bed. He unfastened her blouse but left it on so that her breasts thrust out through the opening. Looking into his eyes she knew without doubt that she'd been right. He did love her, and he desperately wanted her to love him in return.

Slowly and sensuously he unfastened her Indian cotton skirt and eased it over her hips. She was naked beneath it and he pressed his mouth to her pubic mound while his hands moved upwards along the sides of her body.

Harriet's breathing quickened and she knew that she was going to respond, to accept his

210

lovemaking with gratitude because this was what she wanted. However it had started out, she knew that by the time it ended she had emerged the winner.

Lewis stripped off his own clothes and then sat at the top of the bed, his back supported by the headrest. His erection stood up proudly and without taking his eyes from Harriet, he let himself slide down the bed until he was flat on his back with his knees raised.

Once he was still, Harriet climbed on top of him. She positioned her knees on either side of him and lowered herself on to his erection, allowing him to enter her very slowly, a fraction of an inch at a time. Whenever he tried to move she would raise herself so that he slid out of her again.

Lewis quickly realised what he had to do and forced himself to lie still until at last he was fully inside her. 'Lean back against my legs,' he whispered. Harriet did, and when Lewis shifted slightly this meant that he was penetrating her as deeply as possible.

'I'm going to bring myself to a climax,' she murmured, staring directly into his eyes. 'You mustn't come before me.'

'And what will happen if I do?' he asked with a smile.

'I shall leave, like I said before,' she replied.

The smile faded from his face. 'Harriet, don't joke about it.'

'I'm not joking. You've played enough sexual games with me. I thought you might like to experience one for yourself. I'm sure your legendary self-control will come to your assistance.'

Lewis wasn't so certain. His testicles were

already drawn up tightly against his body and there was a dangerous tingling sensation in his glans which meant that his orgasm was very near.

'You have to watch me,' insisted Harriet when he closed his eyes.

Lewis obeyed, and watched as she parted her outer sex-lips, revealing herself fully to him. His mouth went dry when her fingers carefully spread the inner lips apart and then she was running one finger along the shiny delicate pink flesh of her inner channel.

Harriet forgot the man beneath her, forgot how hard he was struggling for control, all she could think about was the rising tide of sexual heat.

Suddenly she held out her hand to Lewis. 'Lick my finger,' she said breathlessly. He flicked out his tongue and tasted the delicious tang of her arousal. With a smile she returned the saliva-moistened fingertip between her thighs and let it move in slow circles around her clitoris.

Lewis felt that he would explode at the sight. Her eyelids were heavy, her cheeks flushed, her whole body taut and ready for the climax she was instigating. The tingling in his glans increased and his hips twitched slightly.

'Not yet,' whispered Harriet, remembering the times he'd made her wait for satisfaction.

Lewis groaned. He was certain he couldn't control himself much longer, but now Harriet was moving her free hand behind her and as one hand continued to tease her clitoris and surrounding flesh the other lightly tickled his swollen testicles.

'Harriet, no!' he begged.

She smiled to herself at the expression of anguish on his face, and then her clitoris began to throb and suddenly her own climax took over and her body tightened so that she knew release was only seconds away.

Lewis knew it too and prayed she'd hurry because he'd never been balanced on the edge of gratification for so long before. To his relief her body abruptly bent forward as the first muscular contractions took hold of her and then she was twisting and turning on his erection as she cried out with pleasure and release.

Now Lewis too could come and he thrust forcefully upwards, knowing that he was filling every inch of her and as her orgasm began to wane he moved her roughly up and down on him. Her sensitive nerve endings were reactivated and as his hot seed exploded into her she climaxed again, shuddering and moaning until at last they were both still.

Lewis helped her off him and drew her down to lie on top of him. 'Does that mean you won't leave me?' he asked at last.

'Not yet,' she said with a smile.

'We'll go back to the States. Rowena and I will get divorced, the marriage was really over long ago. There's so much I want to show you.'

'I've enjoyed your film,' she said softly. 'If it's a success, will you repeat the experiment?'

'Using other characters, you mean?

'Some of them could be new, but sequels are popular. Maybe the fictional Harriet and her lover could figure in the next one too.'

Lewis nodded in appreciation. 'I think that sounds a very good idea. You'll have to give me time to think about it though. Besides, the first film might not be a success.'

Harriet ran her hands over his chest, tweaking his sensitive nipples. 'I'm sure it will be. How could it fail with so many twists in the plot?'

'A good question,' agreed Lewis, wrapping his arms around her. He loved her, yes, but already his thoughts were on the film, the script and now the incredibly exciting possibility of using Harriet in another piece of *cinéma verité*.

'What will happen to Rowena and Chris?' asked Harriet as she drifted off to sleep.

'I don't think we have to worry about them,' replied Lewis. 'When I passed Chris's door it sounded as though they were both very active. I imagine they'll stay here in England and live their life behind closed doors, the way they've always wanted to.'

The one thing Harriet knew for sure was that she must never let Lewis become complacent about her. He was a man who liked a challenge, and although she sensed that her need for him was just as great as his was for her she didn't intend to let him know that.

'I hope I like America,' she said, trying to suppress a yawn. 'I should do. As long as I don't get bored.'

'I won't let you get bored,' promised Lewis, snuggling up behind her so that they fitted together like two spoons. 'I have some very exciting things in mind for us both.'

Harriet smiled to herself. She hoped he had because she knew that in some ways Chris had been right. There was still a lot that her body wanted to learn, and if Lewis wouldn't teach her then hopefully he'd make sure they got involved with people who would.

Epilogue

'*I CAN'T BELIEVE* it!' exclaimed Mark, watching Lewis adjust his bow tie in front of the mirror.

Lewis frowned. 'What can't you believe? The fact that I'm getting married again?'

Mark laughed. 'That's the one thing that does make sense. If Harriet had ever given me so much as a second glance I'd have snapped her up, I can tell you.'

'Lucky for me she didn't then!' exclaimed Lewis wryly.

'I meant the film's success,' Mark continued. 'You're the first director ever to make an art film and turn it into a massive mainstream box office hit.'

'If you'd known what was going to happen perhaps you wouldn't have made such a fuss about the ending when you were writing it,' said Lewis. 'I nearly had to type the last scene myself if I remember correctly.'

'It just wasn't what I'd expected,' protested Mark. 'But you were right, as usual.'

'We'd better go down,' said Lewis. 'I can hardly

be late for Harriet because I'm talking business on our wedding day!'

They went down the massive staircase of his Beverly Hills mansion and out on to the lawn where over two hundred guests were assembled.

'Have you thought any more about a sequel?' asked Mark.

'Today you're meant to be my best man, not my scriptwriter.'

'But have you?'

Lewis glanced at his watch. 'Harriet's late. How many hours does it take to put on a wedding dress?'

'A bride's always late. Have you?' persisted Mark.

'Of course I have.'

'And?'

Lewis glanced anxiously towards the house. 'Where is she?'

Mark put a hand on his arm. 'She isn't going to run away, you know! Relax. Tell me about the sequel.'

Running his hands through his dark hair Lewis gave in. It was better than fretting in case Harriet had changed her mind. It had been difficult enough to persuade her to marry him. Now that the wheels were all in motion it would be disastrous if she changed her mind.

'At the start of the film, Helena – our heroine from *Dark Secret* – is getting married,' he said slowly. Mark stared at him, his eyes suddenly alert. 'Her husband's still a workaholic, and they go away on their honeymoon with a business colleague and his wife of ten years. The colleague, who's also a friend, lusts after Helena and has

216

done ever since he first set eyes on her.'

'Does the husband know this?' asked Mark.

Lewis smiled. 'Of course. But he knows, you see, that his new wife needs excitement and new experiences if she's to be really happy so he encourages her to get to know his friend very well indeed.'

'What's the friend like?' asked Mark.

'On the surface an extremely courteous and charming Englishman. Underneath it's a rather different story.'

'And what happens?' asked Mark.

Lewis shrugged. 'Who knows? I'll probably mail you the first few scenes while we're away.'

'You're not working on your honeymoon!'

'Here she is!' exclaimed Lewis. 'Doesn't she look incredible?'

Mark looked towards the house and saw Harriet gliding across the lawn towards them. She was wearing an elegant straight white dress in taffeta with a lace bodice and peplum, enhanced by a taffeta sash. In her hands she held a spray of salmon and white rosebuds and matching flowers were entwined in her gossamer-fine headdress.

'She looks fantastic!' agreed Mark.

Throughout the ceremony Lewis never took his eyes off her. Later as they mingled with the guests, most of whom were strangers to Harriet, he kept her hand imprisoned tightly in his as though he was terrified she'd disappear if he released her.

Harriet was relieved when they finally found themselves alone for a brief moment. Lewis had drawn her into his study, ostensibly so that she could freshen up her makeup, but the moment

217

they were alone he began kissing her passionately, pressing his body urgently against hers and murmuring incoherently in her ear.

She was overwhelmed by love for him and let her head fall back so that he could kiss and nibble at the soft white skin of her throat.

'Say you love me!' he said fiercely.

'You know I do,' responded Harriet, her knees trembling at the thought of the passion they'd be sharing on their honeymoon.

'Say it!' he repeated. 'You never actually say the words.'

'I love you, Lewis,' she whispered.

He gave a sigh of satisfaction. 'I know I've neglected you over the past few weeks, but I've been so busy. Once we get away it will be different.'

'I understand,' she assured him.

Lewis straightened her headdress and teased a strand of hair down over her forehead. 'There, that looks better, much sexier!' Laughing she took his hand again and they went out into the hallway.

A man was standing there, examining one of Lewis's paintings. When he heard the study door open he turned and smiled at the couple.

'Edmund!' exclaimed Lewis, holding out a hand. 'Now nice to see you. Harriet, I don't believe you've met Edmund, have you? He's one of my closest friends, and more importantly a fervent supporter of my work. He's putting the money up for the next film.'

'The sequel to *Dark Secret*?' she asked.

'Yes.'

'Hardly a high-risk project then,' laughed Harriet.

The man smiled at her. 'No, but I did back *Dark Secret* as well, and that certainly was a risk so I think I'm entitled to a less worrying investment this time round!'

His voice surprised Harriet. She'd grown used to Americans now, but he was clearly an Englishman with the beautifully modulated tones of an expensively educated one.

'You're English too!' she laughed.

He nodded. 'We'll have to form an alliance, Harriet.'

Something in the way he spoke caught her attention, and Harriet looked at him more carefully. He was tall, although not as tall as Lewis, and very slim with brown curly hair, dark eyes and an extremely sensuous mouth.

'I'd like that,' she said slowly.

At that moment a very tall blonde woman came in from the garden and slipped her arm through Edmund's. 'There you are, sweetie! I've been looking all over for you.'

'Harriet, this is my wife Noella. Noella, I'm sure you recognise Lewis's lovely bride.'

'Sure I do. Welcome to Beverly Hills, honey.'

'Do you miss England?' asked Edmund, his eyes warm.

'Yes, desperately,' confessed Harriet. 'That's why Lewis is taking me back there for our honeymoon.'

'Is that right? Whereabouts are you staying?' asked Noella.

'Cornwall,' said Lewis. 'I've always wanted to see it, and Harriet spent a lot of time there as a child.'

'What a coincidence,' cried Noella, glancing at

her husband. 'We're off to Cornwall next week too.'

'It's hardly a coincidence,' said her husband quietly. 'Lewis and I have a lot to discuss over the next few weeks. It seemed sensible for us to be close so I decided to combine our long-awaited trip with his honeymoon.'

Harriet stared at Edmund and then back at her husband. 'You mean you're going to work on our honeymoon?'

He squeezed her hand. 'I wouldn't really call it work, sweetheart. Edmund and I need to finalise a few details concerning the sequel. I know how interested you are in that, so I didn't think you'd mind.'

A thrill of excitement ran through Harriet. Now she understood what Lewis had meant when he'd told her that their honeymoon would be something she'd never forget. She looked at Edmund again. He was definitely attractive, and she sensed that beneath the urbane surface there was much more to him than met the eye.

'You don't mind, do you, Harriet?' he asked with a half-smile.

Harriet shook her head and looked up at her new husband. 'I can hardly wait,' she assured him. Lewis bent his head and kissed her full on the lips.

Edmund stood watching silently for a moment and then turned and left with Noella. He was content. His turn would come.

Sisters Under the Skin

Vanessa Davies

Chapter One

LOUISE ANDREWS WAS lying alone in the wide bed, her eyes closed but her ears fearfully alert. She was waiting for the tell-tale sound of a key turning in a lock, the sound she had come to dread over the past few months.

'How often have you lain here like this?' a voice in her head enquired.

'Far too often,' came the sardonic reply.

Louise sighed and switched on the bedside lamp. The clock said almost midnight, so the pubs would be closed. That meant Martin would be home soon. She shuddered at the thought of him lumbering into the bedroom, reeking sourly of whisky. If he tried to kiss or paw her she would slap his face.

As if she didn't have enough to worry about already. The letter from the building society had come that morning, threatening repossession of their house. Anger rose in her as she remembered how hard she had worked to pay the mortgage. But she couldn't do it alone. And now her husband was both unwilling and unable to spend his remaining money on anything but drink.

Suddenly Louise heard the sound that chilled her heart. Putting out the light she huddled down under the duvet, hoping to convince Martin that she was asleep. She heard the familiar bang of the front door and the soft swish of his jacket as he let it drop to the floor, followed by the dull thud of his footsteps as they came straight towards the bedroom. He coughed and cursed, then flung open the door and flicked on the light-switch.

'Don't pretend you're asleep!' he snarled, pulling the cover right off her so that she lay naked and exposed to the glare.

Louise shielded her eyes with her hand and pulled the duvet back to her waist. 'Leave me alone. I'm tired!' she murmured, trying not to antagonise him.

His dark, drink-bloated face loomed over her, eyes red and cloudy, mouth contorted and emitting a draught of whisky breath. 'I'm tired too. Tired of being given the brush-off. You're my wife, Louise, and I've a right to my conj . . . to my connub. . . to screw you whenever I feel like it!'

'You're drunk,' she accused him. 'And I'm exhausted. I'm going to sleep in the spare room.'

She swung her legs over the side of the bed and rose unsteadily, but he grabbed her wrist and forced her back down onto the mattress. 'Sleep in there if you like, but first we're going to make love, my sweet.'

He was slurring his speech, and somehow that got on her nerves more than his clumsy movements or foul breath. Louise just wanted to get away from him, but she knew he could turn even nastier when he was in that state. As far as her befuddled mind could make out she had three choices: to make an escape bid and barricade herself in the spare room, to face up to him and risk a violent confrontation, or to give in for the sake of peace and quiet.

Wearily she settled for the last option. At least it would be over soon and then, perhaps, she could slip off to the other bed and get some sleep away from his loud snores.

'That's better!' he grinned, seeing her lie back and look up at him in submission. He took off his shoes, undid his belt and pulled off his jeans. She could see his prick rearing aggressively in his pants. Wherever did the idea that alcohol made men impotent come from? With Martin it had the reverse effect, making him more randy than ever.

The bedsprings groaned, protesting on her behalf, as he knelt over her and thrust his forefinger between her thighs. 'Just testing the water,' she imagined him saying in his usual vulgar way, although he hadn't uttered a word.

Despite her silent anger Louise felt herself opening up to him, yielding to his intruding finger out of sheer habit. His mouth was slobbering over her breasts now, making her nipples stiff and tingly. She looked down and saw his stubby penis rearing with impatience, then felt it knocking against the hard nub of her clitoris as he made several attempts to guide it into her. To think that I once enjoyed this, she thought.

While he thrust back and forth she tried to relax, even to feign pleasure, but all the time she was wishing it was over. A part of her was deeply sad that she was no longer in love with her husband, that she had lost all hope of ever recovering those rapturous feelings she'd once had for him. Her body still remembered, though. The reflexes that signalled her arousal were all there: her breasts taut and hard-nippled, her clitoris engorged and throbbing. It was a weird feeling, being betrayed by her own flesh.

At last he spurted inside her with a loud groan, then rolled off her and straight into oblivion. Louise lay there inert for several minutes, afraid of rousing him. She felt the juices dribble out of her and slowly her body returned to normal, the swollen tissues ceasing to throb. Beneath her fatigue remained a dull anger, twinned with hopeless despair. What on earth was she going to do? Clearly she couldn't stay with him. Not when their marriage was such a travesty. But where could she go?

Into the spare room, right now. Already Martin was working up to one of his snoring marathons and there would be no peace for her that night if she stayed beside him. Slowly Louise slipped off the bed and padded out of the room, closing the door behind her.

But once she was in the tiny boxroom that served as a guest bedroom sleep evaded her. It wouldn't be long before they lost the house, and then what? Although Martin still had his job, Louise was unsure what her own future held since the company she worked for had recently been taken over and there were rumours of redundancies. Just how much more could she take?

If only some escape route could be found, some way of chucking everything in and starting all over again. Louise knew that was wishful thinking. Even if they gave up the house she would still have her share of the debt to pay off. Eventually her financial worries would be over, but that left the far more important matter of her marriage. It was over in all but name, she knew that. But did she have the guts to face a divorce, on top of everything else?

Then she thought of Gina, and the germ of a plan began to grow in her mind. Gina was her half-sister, the daughter of their mother's first husband, and they had shared a stormy ten years of childhood, culminating in the older girl running away from home at sixteen. After that Louise had only heard from her sister sporadically, but six months ago she had seen a photograph of her in the evening paper.

Straining to recall the details, Louise summoned up a mental picture of Gina on the arm of some wealthy-looking Arab, which hadn't surprised her in the least. Now she remembered that the pair of them had opened some kind of club in the West End that had sounded a bit sleazy. While many of the details remained vague, making Louise wish that she had kept the article, she thought she remembered the name of the club: *Seventh Veil*, that was it.

Out of curiosity Louise crept down to the living-room and found the Yellow Pages. There was a box advertisement under the heading 'Night-clubs' which announced that the *Seventh Veil* was a fully licensed venue providing 'intimate entertainment' for a 'select clientèle'. Louise was intrigued. What if she picked up the phone, dialled that number and asked for Gina? Before she knew it she was doing that very thing.

A suave but suspicious-sounding male voice answered. When she asked for Gina he wanted to know who was calling.

'Her sister.'

'Her *what*?' the man said in disbelief. Louise felt affronted. Okay, so they hadn't had much to do with each other over the last few years, but it was painful to realise that Gina never mentioned her. 'Excuse me, I didn't know she had one,' he added semi-apologetically. Even so there was an unpleasant undertone to the man's voice that disturbed her. He was as good as accusing her of lying.

'Please tell her that Louise is on the line,' she said coldly. 'If she's not busy, that is.'

'Gina's always busy. But if you really are her sister I'm sure she can spare you a few minutes. Hold the line, please.'

It was a long wait, but eventually Gina's throaty voice could be heard saying, 'Louise, is it really you? Fancy hearing from my kid sister after all this time. And after midnight, too!'

'I'm sorry if I'm ringing late. . .'

Peals of laughter came. 'Late? My goodness, darling, we never close before three a.m.! But I suppose this is well past your bedtime, isn't it? Still working for that dreary company and married to that dreadful man?'

Louise felt her hackles rise, but she controlled herself and took a deep breath. 'Yes, by the skin of my teeth. Look, I know this is an awful cheek, Gina, but I've simply no one else to turn to. I need somewhere to stay. Just for a week or two, while I sort myself out.' She hesitated before adding, 'You're right about Martin, he's a real loser. And our house is about to be repossessed.'

'You poor thing!' Much to Louise's surprise her sister sounded genuinely sympathetic. 'Of course you can stay at the flat. We've a spare room. Look, why don't you go there now? I'll be back in a couple of hours.'

The idea of a moonlight flit was suddenly extremely attractive. Louise was fully alert, her senses awakening at the prospect of an adventure. 'Could I really? But how would I get in?'

'No problem. You'll find the spare key in the garden, hidden in a statue of Venus by the pool. You know my address, don't you?'

'Are you still in Holland Park, where I sent the Christmas card?'

'That's right. You pop along there right now, and I'll see you as soon as I get back. Help yourself to coffee, booze or whatever you fancy. Oh, there's Ahmed looking daggers at me. Sorry, I have to go. I'm supposed to be with a client. See you soon, though.'

Louise crept into the bedroom where Martin was still snoring loudly, dead to the world. She grabbed a bundle of underwear from a drawer, swept an armful of her clothes and some shoes out of the wardrobe, then went into the bathroom where she hastily freshened up. She dressed herself in a shirt and jeans then retrieved her travel bag from on top of the hall cupboard and packed her things.

Her conscience pricked her as she was about to leave and she wrote a brief note for Martin, telling him she would be in touch. Then, after checking that she had enough cash, she phoned for a taxi and sat hugging her bag just inside the front door, waiting for it to arrive.

The journey across London was swiftly accomplished at that time of night. Gina lived near the park in a large old house that had been converted into flats. Louise entered through wrought iron gates and found herself in a gravelled area containing a central pond, tubs filled with plants and a few rather pretentious-looking statues. She peered at them in the faint light from a towering street-lamp. There was a laughing faun, a rearing unicorn and . . . yes, a small statue that must be Venus, standing in mock-modesty on a shell.

Louise approached and looked beneath it, but there was no sign of a door-key. She reached out and touched the cold stone, convinced that Gina must have meant some other statue. But there were no others remotely resembling the Goddess of Love. Letting her fingers rove over the fluted interior of the shell, Louise grew impatient. Was this some trick?

Then she recalled her sister's exact words: Gina had said 'hidden *in* a statue'. Smiling to herself, Louise let her fingers trail down between the tiny buttocks and then felt between the hard, smooth thighs. A tickling thread brushed her knuckles. She took it between her thumb and forefinger and gave a tug. Out came the key, tinkling against the stone. It had been hidden right inside the anatomically correct figurine.

Giggling softly, Louise crossed the forecourt and used the key in the slot marked Flat 4 to let herself in. She found herself in an elegant hallway, with a marble-topped gilt table and lush pink carpeting that stretched on up the wide stairs. Gina lived on the second floor.

When she entered the apartment and switched on the light Louise was impressed. The main sitting-room was vast and high-ceilinged, and looked as if it had been furnished by an interior designer, with everything just so. Louise wandered round examining the tastefully selected antiques that blended with the more modern furniture, admiring the quality of the furnishings and the subtle understatement of the colour scheme.

Beneath her admiration, however, she was disturbed to detect an unmistakable streak of envy. Defiantly she poured a large gin and tonic from the art deco-style drinks cabinet in the corner and sank into the comforting embrace of the deep sofa, pulling off her shoes. Old feelings were reawakened as she contemplated the fruits of her half-sister's success. 'Ill-gotten gains, more like,' she muttered to herself, taking a long sip of her drink.

All the information Louise had about Gina's career since leaving home had been in the form of rumours, gossip and very occasional meetings. Her sister wasn't one for keeping in touch by letter or phone, and the only time she'd had direct contact with her relatives was at her father's funeral which she had attended briefly, avoiding the aftermath of tea and sympathy. There was no doubt that she was the black sheep of the family, but exactly why this was Louise had never been able to discover.

What she did know was that her sister was far more daring and extrovert than Louise could ever be. She got that from her half-Latin father, of course. When Gina was sixteen and Louise was ten she remembered dark hints being dropped about 'boys'. The elder girl often stayed out late, resulting in angry scenes between Gina and her stepfather Peter, who was their mother's second husband, and Louise's own father. Soon afterwards the precocious fledgling had left the nest, and life at home became very dull. Whatever else Gina had done she'd certainly provided welcome entertainment for a bored ten-year-old girl.

Later, when Louise had reached puberty herself, she missed having her sister around all the more. Sensing that she would have been able to answer her own questions about 'boys', she resented more than ever the fact that Gina had walked out on them. She was also curious about the woman that her sister had become. Still, maybe she could make up for some of that lost time now.

Rising from the depths of the sofa, Louise refilled her glass then wandered off on a tour of the flat. There was a well-equipped kitchen, large enough to take breakfast in, and a luxurious bathroom with a whirlpool bath. There were two doors to the bathroom, the one she'd come in by and another one on the other side that she presumed must lead to a bedroom. Filled with curiosity, she went over and opened it.

It was obvious at once that this was the master bedroom. Decorated entirely in softest pink, with subtle lighting, its air was full of the heady scent of jasmine. Louise was startled to see that the ceiling was covered in mirrored tiles. A king-sized bed dominated the room, and she was somewhat surprised when she noticed a pair of handcuffs hanging from the headrail. She walked over and stroked the exquisite silk cover, relishing the way her bare feet sank into the thick-pile carpet that felt like swansdown between her toes.

Louise was starting to feel deliciously naughty. Like when she had crept into her mother's bedroom as a child and tried on her clothes and make-up. She crossed to the velvet curtains hanging from a brass rail and drew them across, exposing Gina's clothes. And what clothes! There were very few examples of what you might call everyday wear, and only a handful of conventional evening dresses.

The bulk of the collection was made up of exotic and erotic garments in satin, velvet, leather, vinyl and latex. Fascinated, Louise drew out a red latex number with a lace-up back and a see-through panel of black net set into the bosom. She tossed it onto the bed then found an equally outrageous mini-dress in shiny turquoise satin with diagonal slashes of black lace across the breast and crotch.

Her fingers lingered amongst the sensual materials, caressing and scrunching them to feel their sleekness, so eerily like her own skin. Some Louise held up to her cheek, others she draped over herself, trying to imagine how she would look in them. There were accessories too. At the bottom of the wardrobe she could see shiny patent shoes with impossibly high heels, and coiled on hooks were studded leather belts and strange-looking harnesses made of leather, rubber and chains.

'What a weird sex life my sister must have,' she thought, feeling a voyeuristic glee at the thought of her and her partner making love in that very bedroom. She wondered which one of them wore the handcuffs. All she knew about Gina's current partner was that he was called Ahmed. The photo in the paper had been too blurred to make out his features properly. Louise's curiosity grew as she remembered the words on their club ad: 'intimate entertainment'. Gina certainly seemed to be an expert at that if the evidence in her bedroom could be believed.

'I wonder where she keeps her underwear,' Louise thought, and a thrill went through her.

It didn't take her long to find it. There was a row of drawers inside another wardrobe and as she drew them out Louise found sets of bras, panties and suspender belts neatly arranged inside. She pulled out a couple of bras in black lace then realised with a shock that the scanty cups were designed to go *under* the nipples, not over them. The thought proved irresistible. Quickly Louise took off all her clothes and tried on the black bra. Her shapely breasts were thrust upwards, the nipples hardening as they jutted over the supportive padding. She postured in the huge mirror that almost filled one wall, feeling like a calendar girl.

Soon she found some matching undergarments: a skimpy pair of open-crotch panties and a rubber suspender belt. A little more rummaging produced some shiny black plastic stockings which she proceeded to roll up her calves and thighs. The sensation was amazing, like having her legs wrapped in cling film.

Louise finished her second gin then went back to the wardrobe where she selected a pair of black shoes that were about her size. She squeezed her feet into them and sashayed back to the mirror, where she posed seductively, giggling all the while. She hadn't enjoyed herself so much in ages! If only Martin could see me now, she thought. But he was so strait-laced he wouldn't begin to understand what a kick she got out of making herself look so sexy. Impatiently she banished all thoughts of her husband from her mind.

Her eye was drawn back to the two dresses on the bed and she decided to try on the red latex one. The combination of alcohol and fatigue was putting her into a reckless mood, added to which she was feeling decidedly randy. There was something wickedly exhilarating about going through her sister's things without her permission. Especially things like these!

It was quite a struggle getting into the figure-hugging dress and almost impossible to lace up the back. Somehow Louise managed by pulling the ends over her shoulder and tugging, then she knotted them loosely. She looked at herself in the mirror and was shocked to see how low-cut the back was, revealing several inches of buttock cleavage. When she stood back and surveyed herself from the front she gasped with amazement at the vision in the mirror.

Every curve of her body was visible beneath the clingy vinyl, but the biggest surprise was to see her breasts beneath the black netting, pushed up into great peachy mounds by the platform bra. Louise had never imagined she could look so blatantly voluptuous – not without the aid of plastic surgery, anyway. She lifted up one side of her shoulder-length brown hair so that her bosom was tilted provocatively, crossed one thigh half over the other and pointed her toe in a classic pin-up pose. Then she turned round and bent foward, surveying herself over her shoulder as she wiggled her bottom.

Sensing that her voyage of discovery was not yet over, Louise noticed that there were several large drawers under the bed. They were obviously intended for bed linen, but she had a feeling that Gina would have found some other purpose for them. . .

The first drawer she pulled open contained a collection of small whips and riding crops. Louise took one and tried it out. She took up a stern attitude in front of the mirror, looking haughtily down her nose at herself. Had this implement actually been used on someone's backside? If so, whose? She tapped it experimentally against her own behind and felt the faint sting even through the taut plasticised material.

Another drawer yielded a clutter of chains and manacles. Presumably they went with the hand-cuffs. A third produced an assortment of masks and hoods. She took out a kind of black highway-man's mask edged with frilly lace and fixed it round her head. Gazing upward she saw herself in the mirrored ceiling and the effect was startling, as if she were taking part in some weird ritual.

The last drawer Louise opened made her gasp too, but it also brought an excited flush to her cheeks and a very urgent tingle between her legs. She had uncovered a hoard of dildoes and other sex toys whose striking resemblance to male organs and ingenious design left her in no doubt as to their function.

Tentatively she drew out a huge, flesh-coloured vibrator and ran the artificially ribbed contours across her palm. There was a discreetly-placed switch at the end and when she turned it on the thing leapt into buzzing, throbbing life. It squirmed about in her hands like a live thing. Hastily she turned it off and placed it on the bed. Her fingers moved amongst all kinds of other devices: rings with fleshy rubber prongs attached, pairs of ivory-coloured balls joined by a thread, double dildoes. Most of their uses were blatantly obvious but some she could only guess at. What was also obvious was that she was looking at the assorted paraphernalia of a life devoted entirely to sexual pleasure.

Picking up the large dildo again, Louise felt a languid weariness overcome her and she closed the drawer then lay down on the bed. The duvet cushioned her body deliciously, making her stretch and yawn. She took off the too-tight shoes and the clammy stockings, then began absently stroking her naked thighs with the smooth tip of the artificial glans. Almost without realising it she flicked the switch with her thumb and the noise of an angry mosquito filled the room. Now she could feel it vibrating against her inner thigh, sending electric shock-waves throughout her nervous system. She'd never experienced such a strange sensation before.

Louise felt very woozy as she lay there, drunk and tired but also in a state of high arousal. Her earlier session with Martin had failed to satisfy her, leaving her hungry for what she hadn't had in a long time – a fully satisfying orgasm. The cunning little toy in her right hand was all too tempting. It wasn't long before she was allowing it to nose under the hem of the red dress and over the suspenders towards her already fully awakened vulva.

With a great sigh Louise felt the shuddering tip of the dildo reach her yearning clitoris and she gave a moan of satisfaction at the first stirring contact. Below the nub of hard flesh her pussy felt completely liquid. She moved the fake penis around until she reached the spot that gave her most pleasure, then allowing it to have its head. Soon she was desperate to feel the thing inside her, filling her up. The thick shaft slid easily between her labia and deep into her warm, expanded sex.

By pressing the vibrator upwards, Louise found that she could still apply the necessary friction to her clitoris while she moved the dildo around inside her. She kept it there with one hand while she used the other to caress her breasts through the window of black netting, moving across the bulging slope of flesh to her exposed nipples. The slightly abrasive feel of the material was very stimulating.

Louise arched her back and whimpered as her clitoris throbbed in sympathy with her nipples, and she began to move the thick plastic shaft in and out more rapidly. Her efforts became even more frantic as her lust intensified and soon she was totally oblivious of her surroundings, helplessly caught up in her inexorable rise towards orgasm. All the frustrations of the last few months were driving her on, clamouring for the sweet release into oblivion.

The first spasms of her climax made her cry out,

not in triumphant fulfilment but out of a still more desperate longing. It was a paradox that even in the midst of her satisfaction, even with that thick penis substitute plugging her, she still felt achingly hollow inside. Faintly dissatisfied with herself she pulled the vibrator out of her, silenced it with her thumb and threw it to the end of the bed. For several minutes she lay there sprawled and open, letting the air cool her raw and tingling pussy. Then she turned over on her side and, filled with an exhausted relaxation, finally fell into a deep sleep.

Chapter Two

GINA PUT DOWN the phone and went up to Ahmed, smiling wryly. His dark brown eyes narrowed in suspicion. 'Who was that?'

'You'll never guess. My kid sister!'

'You never told me you had a sister.'

'She's my half-sister, to be precise. Same mother, different dad. I think she's in a bit of a state, so I said she could stay with us for a while.'

Ahmed shrugged. 'As long as she doesn't get in the way.'

'I don't think she will. From what I remember of her, Louise wouldn't say boo to a goose.'

He grinned. 'The submissive kind, eh? Well okay, but if she pokes her nose in where she's not wanted, she'll be out on the street, understood?'

Gina nodded, adjusting her bra. It was a shell-pink satin bra with peepholes through which her tawny nipples protruded. Her only other garments were a minuscule pair of matching panties and suspender belt, black fishnet stockings and shiny black high-heeled shoes. Ahmed's dark eyes smouldered briefly at her before he turned and went into the office behind him.

Proceeding down the corridor, Gina went through a door that took her back into the hushed atmosphere of the Seventh Veil. Subdued lighting afforded a degree of anonymity to the clients who sat at round tables, mostly alone but sometimes with a male friend or two and, very occasionally, with a woman. Even in the semi-darkness it was obvious that most of the audience were Arabs, although there were a few Englishmen too.

Near the door where Gina entered was a raised platform that served as a stage. Six girls were already dancing there to a slow, insinuating beat and soon Gina joined them. She exchanged a smile with Janice, who had only been with them a week but was learning the ropes fast. This was the part of the evening where each girl showed off her talents so that the watching men could choose their favourite. For Gina, though, it was a mere formality. Her man had already been chosen for her by Ahmed. He was a wealthy Egyptian on a brief visit to London who had agreed a fee that was far above anything the other girls could command.

Languidly Gina swayed her hips to the music, enjoying the sensual movement of her muscles, feeling herself relax and become the erotic creature of the night who was now her second self. She was aware of the taut swelling of her breasts filling out the satin bra, and of the hard nipples protruding through their wanton apertures, and she knew that every man in the place desired her. When they discovered that she was already booked they would envy that lucky man, and he would be happy to pay over the odds for her. It was a procedure she had been through many times before. If you wanted the girlfriend of the owner to perform exclusively for you then you paid top dollar, and no arguing.

The pace of the music quickened and Gina rolled her pelvis more suggestively, enjoying the discreet massage that the muscular contractions gave to her sex. She had been to belly-dancing classes and could rival the best of the Arabian dancers, but in the club she performed only a modified version. The clients didn't want to see just an imitation of what they could get at home. What they came to Seventh Veil for was blatant eroticism coupled with a personal service, and the club was already getting a reputation for delivering the goods.

Through the dim lighting Gina surveyed the men's faces as she danced, trying to home in on her target. She could see a man in a long striped *djellabah* sitting at a side table, apart from the rest, and she sensed from his aloof bearing and keen attention to her dancing that he was her client. A burst of excitement flared through her loins. Here was a man who was probably a millionaire, feasting his eyes upon her as if she were his prospective bride. He could look all he liked, and for a handsome sum he would get a very close look indeed, but how far it went was up to her, not him.

Already Gina was wondering what she would grant him, but on the whole she decided she was feeling rather tired and, besides, she was curious to know whether Louise had really followed her directions and ended up back at her flat.

No, let that proud bastard salivate over her as much as he liked, tonight she would keep him in suspense – and later Ahmed would turn him down when he made his discreet enquiries. He would just have to learn that not every woman who acted the whore could be bought. Sometimes that gave her the most pleasure of all.

Gina slowly danced her way towards the man's table, her body glistening with a film of sweat and exuding a mixed aroma of perfume, perspiration and musk. She saw his pupils dilate with interest, and his legs shifted beneath the long white robe. When she was about a metre from his table she paused and stared directly at him, hips still gyrating, her brown eyes giving him just the kind of bold come-on he would find most intriguing.

A waiter cleared the low table next to his chair, leaving only the white cloth on top, and with an agile bound she was soon on top of it. Gina had no worries about falling off, as the table was bolted to the floor and she was well practised in the art of dancing in a restricted space. She watched with a smile as her client's eyes travelled from her shapely ankles up to her long, lean thighs. Out of the corner of her eye she could see that Janice had come to dance for the man at the next table. While she was happy to perform for the man who had paid for her, she didn't like her clients being distracted by neighbouring dancers. But soon the Arab was far too interested in what was, literally, under his nose to bother about what was going on around him.

Concentrating hard to keep her balance, Gina wiggled her body right down until she was squatting before her client and he was looking straight at her bosom. He gave a barely perceptible sigh, which turned into an embarrassed cough. This was his first time at Seventh Veil. She doubted it would be his last. Her hands went to the front fastening of her bra and she snicked it open, letting her breasts hang free beneath the loose pink satin cups with the full extent of her cleavage exposed. She had been blessed with an almost perfect pair, medium-sized and with very long nipples. They were firm and smooth, incredibly inviting to a man's touch, but this man would not get to handle them.

Gina teased him, raising her shoulders to lift the dangling garment and let him peek at the taut slopes of flesh beneath, then letting the bra flop down again. He gave an audible groan and she chuckled, enjoying his discomfiture. Her well-defined pink lips pouted as if she were taking pity on him. She lifted up the satin and let him gaze his fill on the naked delights beneath, then she half-covered herself again and slowly, with great control, swivelled her way back up to a standing position. Her hands smoothed down her hips, drawing attention to the pink triangle that concealed her mons, framed by the long black suspenders. She saw him run the very tip of his tongue between his lips and a tremor of lust took her by surprise.

Balancing carefully on one leg she held up her foot for him, smiling and nodding to indicate that he might remove her shoe. First the Egyptian pressed his lips to the shiny black toe, then he eased it off her heel and placed the shoe in his lap. He repeated the procedure with the other one then placed the pair carefully on the carpet beside his chair. His hands returned to his lap, where Gina was sure she could detect slight movement beneath the flowing robe. Was the man wearing any underwear at all? Somehow she doubted it.

Standing on tiptoe, Gina twirled around to the music and showed him her buttocks, leaning forward and thrusting them almost in his face. She began to caress them, letting her fingers slip right under the leg of her panties and stroke the deep chasm between her cheeks. This seemed to get him extremely aroused. She could hear his breath coming in sharp, ragged bursts as he ravished her with his eyes. So he was a bum man, was he? Well, she had a treat in store for him!

Turning again, Gina decided to free herself from the bra. She removed it and let it hang from her fingers, dangling against the tip of the man's nose. He sniffed it appreciatively and she let it fall into his lap. Eagerly he caught it up and pressed it to his face, eyes closed, breathing in the lingering vapours. Then he looked up and saw her hands lifting her bare breasts for his inspection, the pinkish-brown nipples already jutting and stiff. He moaned, and his hands dropped to his lap again, still clutching the skimpy garment like a totem.

Slowly she unhooked the suspenders from her stockings and began to roll them down, with his dark eyes watching every inch of her flesh as it was uncovered. Peeling the last few inches off her toes she dangled the stocking before him then let it fall into his lap. Again he gathered it up in both hands and pressed it to his face, inhaling deeply. She repeated the process with the other stocking and then undid her suspender belt and let it fall to the table. Now only a scant few inches of pink satin covered the last vestige of her modesty.

It was time to slow the pace. Gina always liked this part, where she had them really lusting after her but she denied them that last glimpse. It made her feel both sexy and powerful. She smiled to see him gazing up at her like a supplicant, his eyes roving all over her body, the hands in his lap moving restlessly over what she was now sure was a giant erection beneath. She turned slowly, bending forward a little so that her pert buttocks were displayed to advantage, and heard him groan again. Definitely a bum man.

Well, she would give him what he wanted – but slowly. First her hands slipped beneath the top of her satin pants to cup her bum cheeks, clutching and stroking them as she gradually allowed the pink covering to slip down. Gina glanced down over her shoulder at him and saw that he was holding his erection firmly beneath the thin cotton of his robe. His dark eyes were staring at her with glazed intensity. Leaning forward a bit more she parted the two halves of her behind and gave him a peek at the rosy crevice between them, which elicited a sharp gasp of surprised gratification.

Moving her hips in a slinky rhythm, Gina rotated her bum at him and let her panties finally slip down her thighs. She daintily stepped out of them and threw them back over her shoulder into his lap, then she turned round with a winsome smile and presented him with her totally naked body. She watched his face contort for a few seconds, his hands moving furtively, and then he made a series of groaning noises and she knew that, for the time being at least, her client was satisfied.

Leaping nimbly down to the floor Gina gathered up her scattered undies and whipped the white cloth off the table around her naked body like a toga. She gave the Egyptian a brief kiss on his fevered brow as the waiter moved in to settle the account. Then she flitted off through the other tables, like a ghost in the white sheet, until she could slip through the exit and into the dressing-room at the back of the stage.

Ahmed was waiting for her there. 'How did it go?' he asked. 'Was he satisfied?'

Gina unwound the tablecloth and sprayed her face and bosom with delicately scented toilet water as a quick freshener. Soon the room was full of the aroma of lilac. 'I should say so!' she grinned.

He came up and kissed her cheek. 'Good, then he'll be back.' His hand crept up to the lower slope of her breast which he stroked delicately.

Gina removed his hand with gentle firmness and went to put on a pair of white cotton pants. She didn't bother with a bra but slipped into the loose comfort of grey cotton track-pants and hooded top. 'I want to go home now,' she announced. 'Will you come too, or do you have to stay on a while?'

'No, I'll be back after I've had a word with chummy-boy. See you in five minutes.'

He kissed her briefly on the mouth but it was enough to rouse her libido. She usually felt randy after she'd been performing all night, and Ahmed reaped the benefit. Tonight, though, there was another dimension to her excitement. She was

247

keen to get back and see if her kid sister was there.

Gina's curiosity about how she looked these days was growing by the minute. The last time she'd seen her was at her wedding, when Louise had been the traditional blushing bride. What a farce! She'd almost turned down the invitation but then had taken pity on her sister at the last minute. Well, it seemed her prediction that Martin would turn out to be as big an idiot as he looked had come true.

They got back to their Kensington flat at two in the morning. Gina knew at once that Louise had arrived because she'd left the light on in the living-room. A quick inspection also revealed that she'd helped herself to a gin and tonic, leaving both bottles out on the cabinet.

'Maybe she's in the spare room,' Gina said, giving Ahmed a wink.

He followed her as she went to find out, but before she reached the spare room Gina noticed that a faint glow was coming from her own bedroom. She pushed the door open. The room looked a mess, with her wardrobe curtains flung open and the drawers pulled out from under the bed. But it was what was on top of the bed that made her gasp aloud.

Louise was lying there wearing her own red latex dress, which was hitched up around her waist to reveal black suspenders and open-crotched panties through which the pale pink lips of her pussy could be clearly seen. She glanced at Ahmed, whose eyes were nearly popping out of his head. 'The little minx!' she whispered. Then she noticed that lying beside her sister on the bed was her favourite vibrator. The glistening film over its plastic glans left her in no doubt that it had provided good service.

'What a cheek!' she giggled, tiptoeing over to the bed.

Ahmed murmured, 'If you ask me she's just asking for a severe spanking.'

Gina turned, her finger against her mouth. 'Well, well, well! Who'd have thought it? My naughty little sister!'

After pulling the duvet up over her sister's sleeping form, Gina led Ahmed back towards the door. 'Let's leave her to sleep it off,' she said once they were out of the room. 'We can use the sofa bed just for tonight.'

'I don't care, as long as I get to have you,' he grinned. 'It's a good thing I didn't come back from the club alone, or I wouldn't have been able to resist her. What a sister!'

'Now don't get the wrong idea,' Gina cautioned him. 'I know she looks pretty raunchy right now, but that's not the Louise I remember. It could be she's just drunk and in a state over the break-up of her marriage. I don't think she's normally so . . . uninhibited.'

When they returned to the living-room Ahmed was so eager to make love that he practically tore the clothes off Gina. They ended up on the floor, with each of them mouthing the other's private parts. Gina groaned her approval of the solid dimension of her lover's penis as it worked its way towards the back of her throat. She relaxed and let the huge glans move in rhythm while Ahmed's tongue played delicately around her engorged clitoris.

It was such a relief, after all the tensions of the evening, to feel herself being coaxed towards orgasm by the man who knew exactly how to make her come. Gina let her tongue move lazily up and down his shaft while Ahmed began the regular pattern of licking and sucking that never failed to induce an orgasm. His hand reached for the nearest breast and tweaked her already rock-hard nipple, notching up her arousal to fever-pitch.

With unconscious grace Gina began rotating her pelvis to bring herself to the brink, at the same time tasting the first bitter juices that seeped from her lover's glans. Maybe they would climax together, she thought dreamily. It was good to do that straight away, before they fucked. Her fingers caressed his balls, feeling them tighten in readiness to expel his seed, and she knew her own orgasm was imminent. When she felt his finger thrust inside her she squeezed hard and the throbbing excitement rose to exquisite, unbearable heights until there was a sudden change and she was swept into the cataclysm, her whole body shuddering as the rippling first orgasm intensified and then, very gradually, diminished.

The first few drops of his ejaculation tickled her throat before he withdrew and spurted over her naked breasts, rubbing the viscous mess all over her nipples the way she liked it and prolonging the last few seconds of her ecstasy. She looked up at him, eyes shining, and murmured, 'It looks like we're both turned on more than usual tonight. I wonder why?'

He laughed and turned her over, starting to massage her plump buttocks and making the whole of her rear end glow with delicious warmth. 'She doesn't look like you,' he said. 'Not from what I saw of her, anyway. Her tits are smaller, and her pussy lips are all pale and virginal-looking.'

'I wouldn't be surprised if her wimp of a husband never satisfied her. Maybe that's why their marriage is on the rocks.' Gina got onto her knees with her rump thrust provocatively in the air and let Ahmed caress her thighs, itching for his fingers to move into the slick chasm between them. He was in no hurry, teasing her labia with the lightest of fingertip brushes before he finally moved in.

'Ah!' she groaned her approval, feeling a hot wave of renewed sensuality pass through her at the first firm caress of his fingers. She looked back over her shoulder and saw that his erection was growing again. He deftly unrolled a thickly ribbed condom down its length. She shuddered in antici-pation and she began to rotate her buttocks in automatic response.

There was one last fondle of her buttocks and then Gina felt the hard nose of his prick easing between her labia. She gave a long sigh as he penetrated her deeply, filling her up and making her arch her back and throw back her head in cat-like delight. Ahmed's hands moved to her belly, clutching at her smooth flesh while his mouth nibbled at the nape of her neck, sending her into new paroxysms of bliss.

Gina felt herself rising towards a second climax. Ahmed's right hand moved up to her breast while his left moved down to her mons, where he proceeded to give her clitoris exactly the kind of delicate friction that would speed up her progress. Gina ground her buttocks against his stomach in a fast rhythm, encouraging him to increase the pace of his thrusts so that the rubber profiles on the condom would give a good massage to her vaginal walls. He took the hint and soon they were both thrusting hard in pursuit of the ultimate pleasure.

This time, however, Ahmed was so excited that he jumped the gun, coming with spectacular force and triggering Gina as the violent spurts made him gasp out loud. She rode the tidal wave of her orgasm with spectacular abandon, screaming out her rapture as her whole body convulsed in fiery spasms and finally collapsing onto her knees when all the wild energy was spent. They lay together on the carpet for a while, quietly nuzzling each other, until Gina decided to pull out the sofa and get the bedding from its innards so they could get some well-earned rest.

'Tomorrow we'll find out just what Louise has been up to,' she murmured, as she snuggled against Ahmed's warm, hairy chest and waited for sleep to envelop her.

It was Louise who found them in the morning as she stumbled into the living-room with several mischievous demons using her head as a pin cushion.

'Oh sorry!' she gasped, waking Gina at once although Ahmed remained sound asleep.

Gina noticed that Louise was wearing her dressing-gown. She grinned and slipped out of the covers, pulling on her leggings and sweatshirt. Once they were both in the kitchen she closed the door behind them then gave her sister a hug.

'Hi! Good to see you.'

Louise pulled a face. 'I can't look too good this morning. Not after last night. I'm afraid I drank rather too much of your gin.'

'No problem. You sounded pretty fed up on the phone. Want to talk about it?'

'Later, perhaps. Right now I could murder for a cup of coffee.'

While they waited for the coffee to perc Gina gave her sister a quick inspection. Despite her rumpled, hung-over look, Louise had retained her pretty face and good figure. The light brown hair that now hung dishevelled to her shoulders was obviously well cared for, and could easily be restored to glossy stylishness. Her complexion was clear and even, her eyes still that intriguing mix of green and brown, and the generous curve of her upper lip was balanced by a sensual full-ness in the lower one.

Gina's gaze dropped to the high, protruding breasts and the slim waist accentuated by the tightly-tied belt. Whatever tribulations her kid sister had undergone she hadn't turned to bingeing, at least. She found herself assessing Louise as a potential dancer for the club and gave a wry smile, turning her attention to the coffee.

With a hot drink inside her Louise visibly relaxed. 'It's really good of you to put me up. I don't know what I'd have done without you. I was at the end of my tether last night.'

'Was Martin being violent towards you?'

'Not exactly. I just can't stand being around him any more. We're horrendously in debt and stand to lose the house, but he's still drinking and gambling. I felt I had to get away.'

Gina knew Ahmed wouldn't tolerate having her around for too long. They needed the flat to themselves, especially when they brought special clients home.

'You're welcome to stay here for a week or so, but it might be best if you started looking for a place of your own.' Then she remembered what Louise had been wearing when she found her last night, sprawled on her bed. She grinned. 'I know you've already been exploring my wardrobe. That was really rather naughty of you.'

Louise clapped her hand to her mouth. 'Oh, my God! I'm awfully sorry. I was half out of my head. I'd never have behaved like that normally.'

'Well, at least you have no illusions about what line of business I'm in. The club that Ahmed and I run entertains businessmen. Mostly foreigners on business trips to London. We hold some specialist nights, so I have an extensive collection of costumes.'

'Not just clothes,' Louise pointed out, the hint of a twinkle in her eye.

'No, we do offer a full range of services. Fortunately I'm in a position to pick and choose my clients. We run an upmarket operation, Lou. Our clients are very wealthy and we're as careful about admitting them as any gentleman's club.'

'You charge a lot, then?'

Gina nodded. 'Oh yes, our girls are very well paid.' She paused, eyeing her sister soberly for a moment. 'Tempted?'

Louise gave a laugh of derision. 'You can't be serious!'

'Oh yes I am. We have several dancers paying off their debts by working for us. And it won't take them that long. Once they're back on their financial feet they can stop doing it, if they want to. Only I've a feeling that most of them will carry on. They get to enjoy it after a while.'

Louise pulled a disbelieving face. '*Like* it? Surely a whore is a whore, whatever level she's operating at.'

Gina poured them both more coffee and lit herself a cigarette. She saw her sister make a slight grimace and remembered that her smoking had caused quite a few rows before she'd left home.

'I don't think you quite understand. Okay, sometimes our girls do sleep with the clients, but not as a matter of course. They're first and foremost erotic dancers. They strip off and perform at the tables. If they want to take it further with a particular gentleman that's entirely up to them, but they don't have to.'

'So they're more like strip-tease artistes?'

'Yes, except that they are all excellent dancers and they strut their stuff right in front of the clients. The men get a close-up view of what's on offer. But they can't touch, not unless the girl gives them explicit permission. We're very strict about that.'

'I see.'

'Maybe you'd like to come along one night and see for yourself?'

She saw Louise shrink back into her seat. 'Oh no, I don't think so.'

Gina shrugged. 'It's up to you. Do you have a job at the moment?'

'Yes, but maybe not for much longer. They're

planning to lay off some staff.'

'Well then.'

The women were interrupted by the sudden appearance of Ahmed, who came in wearing a towelling robe and yawning. He gave Louise a nod and made for the coffee pot.

'Say hello nicely, Ahmed!' Gina said sternly.

'It's okay, I expect he's tired.' Louise broke in. 'I'm sorry I stole your bed, Ahmed. It won't happen again.'

'You bet!' Ahmed grunted. 'What shall we do with her, Gina? Smack her bottom, that's my suggestion.'

Gina pretended to be affronted. 'I want none of that talk in front of my little sister. She's not one of the showgirls, Ahmed. She's led a sheltered life, haven't you, Lou?'

'I suppose so. By your standards, at least.'

Ahmed swallowed most of his coffee in one gulp then said, 'Well she'll get her eyes opened while she's here, won't she?'

Gina said nothing, but privately resolved to keep the pair of them apart as far as possible. Not that she was jealous, it was more that she wished to protect her sister. Despite the gulf between them she was family, after all, and as she grew older that was starting to mean something.

'Well, if you don't mind I'm going back to bed,' Ahmed announced. 'I like a lie-in on a Sunday morning. Coming, Gina?'

Louise said, 'Go ahead, I'll be okay. I think I'll take a walk, maybe buy a newspaper. Shall I take a spare key?'

Once Louise had left, Ahmed fell on Gina and dragged her back to the bedroom. He pulled down her leggings and was soon inside her, pumping away deliciously. Gina groaned and wriggled her way towards a climax, but as the familiar feelings accelerated inside her she couldn't help wondering whether the presence of another woman in the flat had turned her lover on. He wasn't usually this randy after a late night.

Still, who was she to complain?

Chapter Three

IT WAS STRANGE going to work from Gina's flat for the first time. Inconvenient, too. Louise had to take the Underground halfway across London and then walk, which meant getting up an hour earlier than usual. Obviously she couldn't carry on like that for long.

When she looked for flats in the evening paper, however, she was horrified by what she would have to pay out in rent. There was no way she could afford that on her salary, especially as she hoped to shoulder her share of the mortgage debt as well. She phoned Martin from work and left a brief message on the answerphone telling him that she was okay and would be coming back to the house to fetch her things at some point.

Meanwhile, Louise tried to keep out of her sister's way as much as possible. She didn't get back to the flat until around seven, by which time Gina and Ahmed were preparing to go to the *Seventh Veil*. On Monday night she was invited along, but she declined, saying she wanted an early night. Even so, she couldn't help feeling curious about what went on at their club.

After a ready-made supper, courtesy of Marks and Spencer, Louise thought she would watch some television and looked around for the remote control. She eventually found it in a cupboard (evidently they weren't great TV watchers) but on the same shelf were some photograph albums. Curious to see if they held any family photos, she took the pile out and sat down on the carpet to look through them.

The first one she opened had some pictures of Gina's father in the front. She had inherited his dark, Latin looks and probably his fiery temperament too if their mother could be believed. Flicking on through the pages Louise came across some photos she recognised. There were some shots taken of the pair of them in the back garden of the Pimlico house, Louise smiling brightly and Gina scowling. It had evidently been taken in the summer because they were both in bikinis, Louise still flat-chested and little-girlish at nine, while Gina had already blossomed into a buxom teenager with a slim waist and long, lean legs. No wonder all the boys had been after her, Louise thought.

There were photos from a seaside holiday in Devon too, the last time she remembered them all being together, her mother and father and the two girls. It made her sad to think how the whole family had broken up soon after, with first Gina and then her own father leaving home until only she and her mother were left. Two years later, their mother had died of cancer. Louise thought that was why she'd sought out Gina once her marriage failed – she had no one closer to turn to.

Putting aside the family album Louise picked up a second one. A tingle of excitement went through her when she realised that these pictures had been taken at the club. The first few showed girls dancing on a stage in various states of undress, and Gina was amongst them. From their positions it was clear that they were making some very sexy moves, and in the dimness beyond several pairs of eyes could be seen gleaming with intense concentration.

Louise turned the page and saw photos of individual girls dancing on the table tops for appreciative males. She was amazed to see how close they got to their clients, thrusting their naked breasts right into the men's faces. Although she was embarrassed by the blatant exhibitionism she was also fascinated. How did it feel to have that much power over a man, to prance before him on a 'look but don't touch' basis and make him salivate at the sight of your naked body? She couldn't possibly bring herself to do it, of course, but she was still intrigued by the idea. Maybe Gina would tell her about it in detail sometime.

But there were some still more intriguing photographs to come. In another album she could see Gina in what looked like fancy dress at some kind of party where everyone wore outlandishly sexy clothes. Her sister wore a kind of black rubber corset with holes cut in it for her breasts, a tiny pair of spangly silver panties and thigh-high shiny boots with spiky heels. Her hair was fluffed up to form an enormous halo around her head and she had great panda eyes and red lips.

When she turned the pages of the same album

Louise found many more peculiar photos: Gina dressed as a nurse, Gina dressed as a school-marm, caning an overgrown schoolboy's behind; Gina dressed in an elegant ball gown and wielding a serious-looking dildo. The variations filled several pages and left Louise totally flabbergasted. This was another world, and one she wasn't sure she wanted to explore in real life. Yet to see it recorded by the camera was a fascinating experience.

Louise replaced the albums in the cupboard and turned on the television but her mind was still on those extraordinary photographs. Then she noticed a pile of videos on a shelf and her heartbeat quickened. Chances were she knew exactly what kind of videos they would be. She got to her feet and went over to read the labels on their spines.

They were labelled after the days of the week and Louise guessed they had been taken at the club. Gina had said they held special theme parties so they must be films of the proceedings. With trembling fingers Louise took down one subtitled 'SV – Fetish Night'.

The video opened with a crowd of people laughing and joking, playing to the camera. Louise spotted Gina at once. She had on an extraordinary pair of shoes, so high-heeled they must have been extremely uncomfortable to walk in, and what looked like a couple of plastic bags fashioned into a bikini. The camera followed her on to the stage, where there were other girls dressed in high-heeled shoes, all very shiny and bright. Gina sat down on the kind of low stool you get in shoe shops and a red-haired woman came up and knelt before her, almost as if she were worshipping her feet. She removed one of the shoes reverently and began to kiss Gina's toes.

The video grew even more bizarre. The red-haired woman took Gina's shoe and began to masturbate with its pointed toe. Louise found that bit so weird that she fast-forwarded until she came to a new scene. Men were being invited up on stage to have their penises fondled by women wearing rubber gloves. Again, this was more than Louise could take. She removed the video from the slot in the machine and gingerly picked out another one.

This one, subtitled 'Bed Time', was totally different. It was an intimate film of Gina and Ahmed making love in the same bed in which Louise had slept when she arrived. At first she felt guilty watching it, like a voyeuse, but then she told herself that they were used to doing it in front of other people, so why worry?

As she watched her sister performing fellatio on her lover, and then lowering herself with great enthusiasm onto the hard spike of his erection, Louise felt something akin to envy. Gina was so uninhibited, so obviously enjoying herself in a sensual and voluptuous fashion. Had it ever been like that between her and Martin? Not that she could remember, and certainly not in the last couple of years.

Now, watching Gina use her pelvis with supple grace, groaning with delight as Ahmed's fingers crept up to caress her huge nipples, Louise admitted to herself that she'd been missing out. Their love-making was going on and on, a far cry from the five or so minutes of frenzied activity that she had known with Martin. Often she had been left unsatisfied afterwards but he had ignored her needs and selfishly gone straight to sleep. Even bringing herself off with the vibrator had been a more thrilling experience than most of her times with her husband.

Self-pity threatened to overwhelm her so she stopped the video and put it back in the cupboard. Then she decided to have a bath. She made full use of the expensive toiletries she found, luxuriating in the scented water and satin-smooth body cream. The erotic sights she had seen that evening had made her yearn with unsatiated desire, but she had no idea how long she would have to wait to find a new partner. Then she remembered her sister's impressive collection of sex aids. Did she dare make use of them again?

Louise glanced at the clock: half past eleven. She knew it would be hours before the pair of them came home from the club, so she went into their room and pulled out the drawer from under the bed. This time she examined the contents more closely. Amongst the various sizes and shapes of dildo she found a pot of cream called 'Afrodisiana'. Squinting at the small print she saw that it was supposed to contain extracts of rare African plants that worked as aphrodisiacs. It was recommended for use in conjunction with a dildo. She unscrewed the lid and put it to her nose. It smelled kind of mossy and herbal and half of it had already been used.

She chose a thick wand of ivory plastic as her penis substitute, lay down on the thick-pile carpet (somehow Gina's bed seemed taboo after seeing that video) and opened up her robe. After the relaxing bath her skin felt warm and smooth, inviting to the touch of her own fingers. She'd borrowed a pillow for her head and felt perfectly comfortable, a deep-down feeling of anticipation making her glow all over. Tonight she would discover what it meant to be a truly sensual woman.

Louise put her finger into the pot and spread the cool cream over her labia. It felt icy cold at first but then it began to burn a little, like cool fire. She felt the delicate tissues start to tingle and throb until her clitoris became ultra-sensitive, bulging out from between her labia. She stroked it gently and the most wonderful sensations flooded through her, making her squirm and moan in delight.

Forgetting all about the dildo that lay at her side, she continued to stroke herself with light, fluttering movements of her fingertips. The deep need for fulfilment soon made her rub more firmly as the slippery nub swelled up, demanding more of her. It was just like scratching an irritating itch, only a hundred times more satisfying. She could feel herself becoming more and more wet, flooding her inner labia with sticky juices and making it easier for her fingers to slide back and forth over her clitoris that was becoming ever more hungry for stimulation. Like a ravenous animal it reared and stiffened at her touch, frightening her with the violence of her own need.

Yet however long she persevered her climax seemed just as far away. She was stuck on a high plane of arousal, but no amount of friction seemed to take her higher to that final, blissful release. Her wrist ached and she wondered how much longer she could keep going. Then she remembered that the cream was supposed to be used in conjunction with a dildo, and she reached for the hard implement at her side. Over and over again she plunged it into her heated vagina, clenching her muscles to draw it in and then pushing out to expel it again. Her body was beyond her control, acting out of some fevered instinct that was pushing her towards a conclusion she both craved and dreaded.

At long last the sensations suddenly intensified, propelling her into a self-obliterating orgasm that set the lower half of her body convulsing with almost painful contractions. Louise gasped and moaned her way through the experience and then lay limp and exhausted, her heart pounding rapidly in her chest and her limbs trembling. She had no idea how long she had been lying there by the time Gina returned.

'Oh, you wicked girl! When the cat's away the mouse will play, is that it?' she said with mock reproof when she walked in through the bedroom door.

Louise opened her eyes and tried to sit up, but she flopped back down onto the floor again, utterly spent. Gina frowned as she picked up the pot of cream. 'You haven't been using this on yourself, have you?' Louise nodded. 'You silly thing! You should have asked me about it.'

'Why?' Louise asked, faintly.

'It's for internal use only. You put it on the end of the dildo and it gives you a stronger climax. But if you use it too soon, or put it on your clitoris, the effect can be quite painful.'

'You can say that again!'

'You poor thing! Still, that'll teach you to play with fire, won't it?'

'I'm sorry, Gina. I've got no excuse this time. I wasn't drunk or anything, I just. . .' To her dismay Louise felt the tears start to roll. Comforting arms supported her and thrust a tissue under her nose. She was aware of Gina's musky perfume and felt a faint aftershock of arousal.

'I know what you need,' her sister said. 'A hot chocolate laced with brandy. Then we can talk, if you want.'

While Gina went into the kitchen to prepare the drinks, Louise cried into the tissue. She felt such a fool, apart from anything else.

Wrapped in the warm robe, Louise went through to the living-room and sank into the huge sofa where Gina soon joined her. As she sipped the rich, sweet drink she began to relax again.

'It's all right, you know. I don't mind,' her sister said, grinning over the top of her mug.

Louise smiled back. 'You weren't supposed to find out. I thought I'd be safely tucked up in bed by the time you returned from the club.'

'I knocked off early. Thought you might want to chat. You're in a bit of a state really, aren't you, Lou?'

She nodded. 'I'm starting to realise what a total shit Martin is. And I've been putting up with it for so long. I should have left him years ago.'

'I did warn you. At your wedding, if I

266

remember rightly. Still, I'm not going to say "I told you so" because there's no point. The question is, where do you go from here?'

'I've no idea. When I think of all the money I owe it's frightening. I can't go on managing alone on my salary, and what if I lose my job?'

'You know, I think you really should consider joining us at the club. It's not as bad as you might think. Of course, you have to dance with some conviction, act really sexy. But half the time it's just that, an act. You may be going through the motions but your mind can be somewhere else.'

Louise drained her mug, savouring the pool of liquid chocolate at the bottom. Should she tell Gina about seeing the photos, the videos? She decided against it. Her copybook was already blotted enough for one night. 'I'm not like you, Gina. I've had no experience of that sort of thing. You've always been more adventurous than me.'

Gina gave a naughty smile, her brown eyes gleaming. 'But it seems to me that you have a healthy curiosity about sex, Louise. Why else would you go snooping around my bedroom?'

'I'm curious, yes. But I'm also a bit afraid.'

'What of? Maybe you fear that you'll become insatiable, throwing yourself at every man who comes your way.'

Louise made a wry face. 'I don't think there's much chance of that. I'll be lucky if Martin hasn't put me off the male sex for life.'

'Is that why you're going in for so much DIY these days?'

Following a spontaneous urge, Louise threw a cushion at her sister. Gina caught it with a laugh and threw it back. Her fingers played with a strand of dark hair as she tucked her bare feet under her in the big armchair. 'You know, you really should come along one night,' she continued. 'Just to see things for yourself.'

'I might.'

Gina picked up a cigarette pack from the dresser and took one out. 'How about tomorrow? It's a normal night – normal for us, anyway. Nothing too outlandish going on. And Ahmed will take care of you, see that you're not harassed or anything.'

Louise glanced at the clock. 'Well, if I'm going to take up your offer I'd better make sure I get to bed now. Otherwise I won't be able to keep my eyes open.'

She rose and went over to give Gina a kiss on the cheek. 'Thanks for everything. I don't know what I would have done without you.'

Lying in the spare bed, Louise reflected on the differences between them. Just how much experience had her sister packed in during the past twelve years? She really did feel like the naive younger sibling, even though they were both adults now. And yes, she was curious about Seventh Veil and what went on there. Maybe she should overcome her scruples and take up Gina's invitation to attend.

After all, she was starting a new life now, one without Martin. A wave of misery threatened to swamp her as she thought of their failed marriage, but there was something exciting about it too. They had married too young, everyone had said so, but the bonus was that she was still young enough to enjoy life and find someone new.

At work the next day a cloud of gloom hung over the offices of Newbolt & Co. Rumours abounded of imminent redundancies and Louise knew she could be in the firing line – literally! Everyone was watching the personnel manager like a hawk, trying to read his inscrutable expression, but nothing happened. Even so, when the end of the day came there were no sighs of relief, only groans at the thought that the suspense would continue.

Travelling back to Holland Park in a crowded tube train Louise reflected that she could really do with something to take her mind off work that evening. Provided she had time for a rest she would go with Gina to the club and check it out for herself. The flat was empty when she arrived, so she took a quick shower and left a note on the kitchen table saying she was taking a nap but would like to accompany them to Seventh Veil later.

When Louise awoke from her slumbers she could hear Gina singing to herself in the kitchen. She got up and went in to find her cooking pasta.

'Thought you might like something before we go,' her sister smiled. 'It'll be a long night. But I'm really glad you've decided to come. You'll enjoy it, I can guarantee!'

Ahmed was already there, it seemed, and Gina had to perform that evening but she promised that Louise would be well looked after. When she expressed doubts about her limited wardrobe Gina offered to let her wear any of her clothes.

'Nothing too conspicuous though, I suggest. Not unless you want to stand out in the crowd, that is.'

After much deliberation, Louise decided on a slinky velvet dress in hyacinth blue. It was smart and sexy enough for evening wear without being too obvious. She let Gina do her hair in a new, swept-back style that accentuated the heart shape of her face. It was a nice feeling to have her big sister brush her hair again, reminding her of the days when they still lived together.

'Come on, we're going to be late and Ahmed will be mad at me,' Gina announced at last. 'He hates it when I keep a client waiting.'

They took a taxi all the way to Park Lane where the club was situated in a basement. 'Near to all the posh hotels,' as Gina explained. The doorman smiled and inclined his head as they walked in. Louise's eyes took a while to adjust to the dim light and somewhere in the heart of the complex she could hear the thumping beat of some raunchy music. Gina moved through the corridors and offices greeting everyone until Ahmed appeared.

'Where the hell have you been?' he said.

'Ssh, don't be a spoilsport. We're here now. What's on my agenda tonight?'

'Ravi wants a personal, Hamid wants a feelie and Chuck wants a special.'

'Well he can't have one. Tell him next time. He can have a feelie tonight.'

'Okay. Oh, there's a new guy called Shamooz. Top brass at Technoleum. Be nice to him.'

'Right. Where's he sitting?'

'Table seven. Lucky for some! Now you go and get ready. The girls are well into their routine. Take the solo spot. Don't worry about your sister, I'll take care of her.'

Louise listened to their exchange in wide-eyed amazement, wondering what it all meant. When Gina disappeared into the dressing-room Ahmed took her by the elbow and steered her through a door on the left and into a large dark room in which only red lamps burned except at the bar and on stage. The ruby glow cast over everything took some getting used to, but when Louise sat down with Ahmed at an empty table and looked towards the more brightly lit stage her eyes soon became accustomed to the weird half-light.

Ahmed clicked his fingers at a waiter who came up at once. 'Champagne!' came the order. Louise didn't want to argue. Instead she looked with increasing wonder at the girls who were gyrating semi-nude on the small platform. Their erotic dances and minimal costumes were obviously designed to show off their very attractive bodies. Then she noticed some business going on between a client and one of the waiters. It wasn't long before a girl was wending her way from the stage to his table, and Louise realised that the clientèle could order more than just drinks.

'We like to have our waiters acting as go-betweens,' Ahmed explained. His tone was oddly formal, like that of a tourist guide. 'That way no one is offended and the business is conducted with propriety. A system of discreet hand signals is used.'

'I see. And what range of services is on offer, exactly?'

'The basic consists of a table dance only, with no touching. A lap dance allows the girl to slide into the man's lap and wriggle about. No touching is permitted. Both these dances take

271

place in public. There is a private area where a client may have a "feelie", which allows touching above the girl's waist only. Naturally, that is the most expensive of all.'

'And afterwards?'

Ahmed's black eyes met hers sternly. 'That is entirely between the girl and the client.'

The cold way he talked about the 'girls' was rather chilling, but Louise supposed he had to keep a rational business head. However it suggested that if she should decide to join his staff she could expect no special privileges for being Gina's relative.

'Watch Janice!' Ahmed commanded, nodding in the girl's direction. 'You will see what a basic dance entails. Generally it lasts about five minutes.'

'Is that all?'

'It is quite long enough to satisfy most of our clients. The preliminary dancing on stage acts as a kind of appetiser, you see. By the time an individual girl arrives at their table the men are already well aroused.'

The table dance began with the girl asking the man to help her up. She put one high-heeled shoe into his palm for a few seconds then stepped nimbly onto the table where she proceeded to undulate her body. She quickly removed the top half of her bikini so that her small breasts were on view. For a while she danced topless, caressing her nipples and rousing them to hard pink points. Then she let her hands slip down to her stomach and made faces at the man while she slipped her fingers into her panties and appeared to play with herself.

Louise looked around her, peering into the shadows where most of the audience sat with their eyes intently focused on the stage. Only a few were distracted by the sight of the table dancer who was now inching down her pants to display her sand-coloured pussy. The man she was dancing for leaned forward in his chair to inspect her more closely. She wiggled a few more times, dangling her discarded garments in front of the man's nose, then skipped down from the table and wrapped her naked body in the table-cloth, teasing her client with her eyes as she did so. There was a glimpse of her bare rump as she dashed off towards the stage door, weaving between the tables.

Turning her attention back to the stage Louise noticed that Gina had appeared, resplendent in a kind of jewelled bikini and shiny silver stockings, held up by white furry suspenders. Looking back at Ahmed she noticed his eyes widen, and his lips curved into a kind of proprietary smile.

'She looks great, doesn't she?' Louise said.

He nodded, but at once rose from his chair. 'Excuse me for a moment.'

She saw him go over to a man sitting in the corner and hold a brief conversation. Her gaze returned to the stage where it was already evident that Gina was a star amongst the dancers. Where they merely wiggled, she gyrated; where they acted slinky, she was voluptuous; where they were vulgarly sexy she was exquisitely erotic. Gina was a class act, and no mistake.

'I wonder how much *she* makes a night,' Louise thought, and was instantly ashamed of herself. It was none of her business.

Slowly, seductively, Gina came to the front of the little stage and began to descend the steps. All the men's eyes were on her as she made her slow, sinuous progress across the room, moving her body with proud grace. It was obvious that everyone was envying the man who would have her special favour that night. The man in question sat smugly awaiting her with Ahmed at his side, and soon she was standing in front of him. A waiter came with a light bamboo screen and placed it around the table, but he left an opening through which Louise could see what was going on.

Ahmed picked up the champagne bottle, poured the man another glass and handed it to him, then helped Gina onto the low table. Louise had the feeling that some pre-arranged programme was being acted out as the dance began. She could just see her sister's dark eyes flashing in the glare from the stage but her body had turned a rosy pink all over from the dim reddish lighting.

Some of the other girls were moving from the stage to various tables around the room, but Louise found it impossible to look anywhere else. She was fascinated by the sight of her sister's lithe body as it twisted and turned on the high heels, her hips swaying extravagantly while her stomach moved in rippling circles. Her hands were under her breasts, lifting them up for the man's inspection, and then she began slowly working the thin straps down her arms, accentuating the deep ravine that divided her bosom.

Ahmed resumed his seat at Louise's side. 'That

man's bought himself a feelie,' he announced matter-of-factly, shifting his chair to get a better view. 'But I doubt he'll be using his hands very much. Watch.'

Gina wriggled out of her bra straps so that the cups were held up by sheer will power. She knelt down and the man moved closer so that his nose was almost in her cleavage. With agonising slowness she turned down the top of one bra cup. Lower and lower it went until the brownish areola of her nipple was exposed. Then she did the same with the other one. The bra hung there provocatively, almost revealing all but not quite, while the man stared at the tops of her nipples with avid concentration, still clutching the half full champagne glass.

Louise saw her reach behind her back and unclasp the spangled bra, letting the cups sag a little. Like shy children her breasts remained hiding behind the sparkling satin until, with a triumphant smile, Gina lifted the garment right away and exposed her fine bosom completely. The man's groan of delight could be heard even above the music. He reached out with his free hand and pulled gently at her long, distended nipples. Then he stroked her right breast and squeezed it a few times.

Louise was practically on the edge of her chair, imagining how it would feel to be in her sister's shoes right now. With another smile, this time one of complicity, Gina took the champagne glass from his tremulous hand and dipped her finger in the bubbles. She pinched her left nipple, making it gleam with the wine, then repeated the process with the other one. At once the man leaned forward and took the nipple into his mouth, sucking the champagne from it vigorously. She poured a little between her breasts and it began to run in a narrow rivulet which he eagerly lapped up.

Laughing with abandon, Gina emptied the rest of the glass over her breasts and the man went crazy, licking and sucking at her abundant flesh like a man thirsting in the desert. Louise couldn't help giggling. She looked at Ahmed, who gave her a tight-lipped grin then said, 'You'd never believe what he's prepared to pay for the privilege.'

'Is that all he gets?'

'Yes. Gina won't do any more tonight. Although what she's got planned for the big cheese is a bit more exciting. That counts as a feelie too, but the word covers a multitude of sins.'

Ahmed gave a strange dry laugh, almost like a cough, and lifted up the champagne bottle from the table. 'Some more of this, or has that spectacle put you off?'

Louise held out her glass and he filled it almost to the brim. She was feeling reckless tonight – and very horny. The spectacle of so much uninhibited behaviour was catching. A part of her wanted to kick off her shoes and dance on the tables too, with or without her clothes. How wonderful it would be to perform for the whole room, to have all those men cheering and whistling just for her!

Surprised by her sudden streak of exhibitionism, Louise turned back to her sister. The man had evidently had his share because Gina was coming down from the table and taking his face between her breasts for one last, voluptuous squeeze as the waiter hovered, ready to take the screen away. She was laughing and smiling all the way back to the stage door, but as she passed Louise's table she gave her a wink.

'Do you want to go and talk to her?' Ahmed said. 'She has about ten minutes before her next performance.'

'Okay.'

Ahmed led her through the door and into the dressing-room where Gina was leaning over a basin washing her breasts with scented soap. 'Oh hi!' she grinned, turning round as they entered. 'Won't be a tick.'

Louise found it strange that she had reverted to her everyday self so quickly. She seemed no more fazed by what she had just done than if she were taking a break from a supermarket checkout. She sat waiting on a chair until her sister was ready to talk.

'Well what did you think of that little exhibition, Lou? Not so bad really, was it?'

'No, it seemed very quick really. Once you'd got your top off, I mean.'

'Oh, he was well on the way by then. In fact, I think he probably came when I poured the champagne over my tits. Kind of sympathetic magic, wouldn't you say?' She giggled.

'You talk about it so . . . ordinarily. But I thought you were very good. I admire your . . . artistry, I suppose you'd have to call it.'

'Artistry, I like that.' She threw the back of her hand across her forehead, striking a dramatic pose. 'My dear, how I suffer for my artistry!'

'Don't make fun of me. I'm trying to pay you a

compliment without sounding too daft.'

'There's nothing to it, honestly, Lou. A few wiggles and a bit of teasing and they're happy as Larry. You could learn to do it. Any woman could, given the right coaching.'

'Maybe.' Louise sounded doubtful. 'But you have to have the nerve, don't you? To carry it through in front of all those men, I mean.'

'I can just about remember my first time. I was terrified, I admit that. But you know what saved me? I imagined them all as little puppy dogs that needed training! You're their mistress, I told myself. If they step out of line you must tap them on the nose, but if they're good little chaps you can reward them with a titbit. And, do you know, it worked a treat!'

Ahmed put his face round the door. 'It's Shamooz next,' he reminded Gina. 'So you mind you pull out all the stops. We want to turn him into a regular customer.'

'Have you put him in the hot seat?'

'Jerry's moving him there right now.'

Gina turned to Louise. 'The hot seat is the only private one in the club,' she explained. 'That's where we do the really intimate stuff for our top clients. I'm afraid you won't be able to see what's going on from where you're sitting, but Ahmed will take you into the office and you can watch from there.'

'From the *office*?'

Ahmed gave a cunning little grin. 'Closed circuit camera. We have to keep a watch on our clients somehow, especially when they're in the hot seat. If anything untoward happens and a girl loses control of the situation I can send someone in straight away.'

Gina was doing a quick costume change. She put on a pair of black stockings and suspenders, but without knickers. Then she slid a red mini-dress over her head but wore no bra. She thrust her feet into high-heeled shoes and sprayed perfume down her cleavage and around her thighs until the dressing-room reeked of the not-so-subtle aroma. Seeing Louse's wrinkled nose she explained, 'It's Egyptian perfume, "Lily of the Nile". Clients adore it, but it's a bit overpowering for my taste.'

She blew Louise a kiss and flitted from the room. Ahmed held out his hand. 'Come on, Louise. You and I are going to watch a little peepshow!'

Louise felt her heartbeat quicken as she followed him into the nearby office. It had been one thing to sit with him in the other room, with all those other people there. But would he behave as impeccably behind the office door, with no one else around? What if he became uncontrollably aroused by the sight of his wife pleasuring that rich client? Would he make a play for her?

She began to wish that she'd stayed safely back at the flat, after all.

Chapter Four

THERE WERE TWO armchairs in the small office and a screen was placed high up in one corner. While Louise took her seat Ahmed pressed some buttons and a shot of Gina walking across the main room came up. Although the lighting was quite dim the lascivious looks of the men as she sashayed past their tables was plain to see. Some turned to see where she was heading and watched her disappear behind a partition at the far end of the room.

Ahmed pressed another button which evidently activated a hidden camera. A man was sitting there in the enclosure, looking around. His eyes lit up when Gina entered with a broad smile and a pert wiggle of her hips. They exchanged a few words but couldn't be heard over the closed circuit system.

Louise glanced at Ahmed who was sitting with his hands steepled beneath his chin, surveying the screen thoughtfully. 'This is a man we really need as a regular client,' he murmured, half to himself. 'He's just been posted to London for six months and if he likes the club there's every chance he could bring in some more clients.'

Louise said nothing, disliking the man's mercenary tone. Did he have to be so cold about everything? She didn't know how he could bear to sit there watching his girlfriend making out to all those men without being disturbed by the sight. On the contrary, he appeared to relish it. He's just a pimp, she thought. Yet Gina seemed perfectly happy with the arrangement too. It was all very strange.

The scene progressed, with Gina waving her body back and forth before the avid gaze of the man called Shamooz. He was dark and thick set, with squarish glasses behind which his staring eyes were magnified. Louise could see that he was wearing an immaculately cut suit and expensive-looking shoes. When he moved his arm she caught a glimpse of a stylish watch on his wrist and a flashy diamond ring. Again she found herself wondering just how much this little entertainment was costing him.

'Come on Gina, get on with it. We haven't got all night!' Ahmed muttered, as Gina turned her back on Shamooz. She thrust out her behind and slowly raised the hem of her skirt to reveal her naked buttocks. She waggled her behind at him, then let the hem fall again.

'Better give him a fondle soon, or he'll lose interest,' Ahmed muttered.

Louise felt more relaxed now she realised that all his attention was on the performance Gina was giving. He seemed to have completely forgotten about her. She sat back in her chair and watched her sister turn until she was facing Shamooz again. This time she began to unzip the back of her dress, letting the front fall to reveal the plump tops of her breasts. The man said something and she nodded, leaning forward until her deep cleavage was revealed. He reached out and felt her breasts for a few seconds before she whisked them away and turned her back on him once more.

Gina lifted her skirt and stood close enough for him to caress her smooth derrière. She raised her arms and the front of her dress fell down about her waist but the man was too absorbed in fondling her buttocks to notice. He half rose from his seat and kissed her back, but she frowned at him over her shoulder and he stopped. For a while Gina danced out of his reach, still with her back to him, then she began to turn to each side, giving him a glimpse of her bare breasts. The long nipples stuck out provocatively and Shamooz uttered a sigh. Although she couldn't hear it, Louise could plainly see his mouth opening and his chest heaving with frustrated desire.

At last Gina gave him the full frontal view he craved and for a while she lifted her breasts and played with her own nipples, getting him more and more aroused. Then she slowly came up to him and let him grab hold of them himself. At once he thrust her right nipple hungrily into his mouth while he grasped the other one, pulling her pelvis close to his face with his other hand as if he were afraid that she might dance out of his reach again. Louise could feel the sexual heat seeping through her body, making her tingle in all her secret places.

'That's right let him suck you!' Ahmed

muttered, glancing at his watch. 'But don't forget he's going to want more for his money than that.'

'Will she go to bed with him then?' Louise asked faintly.

Ahmed gave his short, sharp laugh. 'No way!'

'But what if he offered enough money, would she then?'

'We've already told him that Gina is unavailable for any out of hours activities. That will only make him want her more, of course.'

Again Louise was shocked by the calculating nature of the man, but it was hardly her place to criticise. The vision on screen was getting hotter as Gina shrugged the remains of the dress down over her hips and eventually let it fall to the floor in a puddle of red silk, exposing her naked mons. She had shaved her pubic hair quite extensively, stopping short of becoming totally smooth. Only a small dark tuft now guarded the entrance to her pussy. Still wearing her suspender belt and stockings she slowly moved towards Shamooz once more. By now the poor client could hardly contain himself and was literally on the edge of his seat, his hands suspiciously restless in his lap.

Gina stood with her legs apart, looking down at the man who had paid for the privilege of touching her intimately. Now he would get his prize. She took his hand and guided it towards her open crotch. Louise smothered a gasp of surprise as she saw Shamooz lean forward, an incredulous look on his face, and slip his finger between her labia.

Wiggling a bit to let him inside her, Gina began to squeeze her muscles and gyrate her pelvis. It was extraordinary to watch because whereas, normally, it would have looked as if he were in a position of power, invading her private parts, now it was quite the reverse. Gina was taking the man's finger and playing with it mercilessly, satisfying herself in the process.

'That's right,' crooned Ahmed. 'Give him what he wants, sweetie. Just enough to whet his appetite for next time, no more.'

As Louise watched the man's face contort with what looked like agony, Gina seized his head and held it against her stomach as he gasped and moaned, smiling down at him. Eventually he withdrew his finger and sucked on it with relish while she backed away, saying something with a smile. He grinned back at her, and she pulled the mini-dress down over her head. Then she took his balding head in both hands and kissed it, before leaving the booth. Shamooz sat there looking dazed for a while then adjusted his fly and stood up.

'One more satisfied customer – I hope!' Ahmed smiled. 'Do you mind if I leave you for a few moments? I have to talk to Mr Shamooz, make sure that everything was satisfactory.'

Louise sat back in her chair, feeling strange. She'd been indulging in various forms of voyeurism lately, but she was fed up with feeling sexy all on her own. With a weary sigh she reminded herself that being alone, and entirely responsible for her own life, was something she would just have to get used to now.

However, she wasn't alone for long. The door soon opened and Gina entered, gleaming with sweat, her body covered by a robe. She flopped down onto the chair that her lover had just vacated. 'Phew! There must be an easier way of earning a living!' she grinned.

'You said anyone could do it!'

'Absolutely right. But not everyone can do it *well*. And there was a lot riding on that particular encounter. The prestige of this place is built on clients like that.'

She lit a cigarette, giving a long sigh as the smoke issued from her lips. Louise said, 'But don't some of the men go too far? I mean, try it on.'

Gina pursed her lips and blew out a stream of smoke. 'You'd be surprised how little trouble we get. Must of our clients do seem to respect the rules. And of course there are plenty of men around to protect us if anyone does overstep the mark.'

'What you did, just then – do all the girls go that far?'

'Not unless they want to. It's entirely up to them. Some draw the line at any physical contact. Others are prepared to go all the way, and all shades in between. That's the beauty of the job – you're in control.'

'So I could just dance then, nothing more?'

'Well, you'd have to remove your clothes, obviously. But that's all.'

'I see.'

She made it sound tempting, but Louise was still doubtful. Gina had been doing it for ages, that much was obvious, yet despite her token protests she must enjoy the work to carry on doing it. While Louise didn't like to bring up the question of money, she couldn't help wondering what else the girls got out of it.

Gina's break ended abruptly when Ahmed reappeared. 'Ravi's getting restless so get your bum in gear. He only wants a table dance, but he's got two mates with him. Table nine, okay? But do a turn on stage first, get the old anticipation going.'

'Right.' Gina stubbed out her cigarette and gave Louise a quick smile before leaving the office.

'Okay?' Ahmed said. Louise nodded. He gave her a mock bow. 'You may go back to your table now, madame!'

She followed him back into the main room where they sat at the table with a 'reserved' sign on it. All over the room girls were performing for their clients, showing off their assets at close range, some on top of the tables and others on the floor or on a little podium. Every exotic dancer seemed to have her own unique style but they all obeyed one rule: maintain eye contact with your client. They were flirting and teasing them to the limit, making the men who had paid for their services feel special.

When Louise asked herself the question 'Are these women being exploited?' she had to admit that there was no evidence of that. They went as far as they wanted to go, they were protected both by the rules of the establishment and by the waiters and doormen, whose eyes were everywhere, ready to spot the first hint of anything untoward. The girls were made up to look beautiful, their scanty costumes enhancing their undeniably lovely bodies. The more Louise saw of what went on the less she felt she could condemn it as sleazy or degrading.

Still, there was a considerable difference

between being tolerant of others and practising the same behaviour oneself.

By the end of the evening Louise had modified her views about the Seventh Veil and she said as much to Gina and Ahmed as they rode home in a taxi. They seemed pleased, but were preoccupied with discussion of what had gone on that evening. It was clear that the club was central to both their lives, and they had little life apart from it. When they got back to the flat Gina made them all a drink and they sat around in the lounge. Although she was tired, Louise didn't feel ready for bed. Her 'normal' routine, the one she had been following for the past three years of her marriage, had been disrupted and it felt a bit like jet-lag.

'So, Louise, what are your first impressions of our little business?' Ahmed asked, his eyes glinting keenly at her as he sipped a Brandy Alexander.

'I suppose you provide a good service. High-class, I mean. The girls looked very pretty and they were good dancers. And the men seemed very well behaved.'

'That's because they regard it as a privilege to be allowed entrance. We offer high-class entertainment and they pay a high price for it. To be a member of the Seventh Veil club confers some prestige.'

'For the girls, too,' Gina said. 'They can earn up to five hundred pounds a night, or more.'

Louise raised her eyebrows in surprise.

'Of course it depends on what service they offer. Those girls who are only prepared to dance probably earn nearer a hundred and fifty. But for the ones who are proper lap-dancers the sky's the limit. They're not only paid in cash, either. Sometimes they get gifts of jewellery.' She held out her right hand for Louise's inspection. A large emerald flashed on a gold ring. 'I got this from a client who became quite a friend. He left it to me in his will, bless his heart!'

Louise was stunned, and a little envious. Ahmed was watching her closely. He said, 'Aren't you interested now, Louise? You could pay off your debts in no time. Get a down payment on a decent new place.'

'I'd train you,' Gina said eagerly. 'From the look of you it wouldn't take long. You have a good figure and you move gracefully. Do you like dancing?'

'I used to.' Louise's reply was tinged with sadness.

'Well then, you'd probably enjoy it. And I think you could do with some fun in your life, as well as some cash. Tell me I'm wrong!'

'She might like to come to one of our party nights,' Ahmed said. He rose from his chair and Louise felt a slight tremor in her stomach when she saw where he was heading. 'We have a video you might like to see. . .'

He took down the box marked 'SV – Fetish Night' and slipped the video out. Then he frowned. He took down another box and examined its contents too. 'Gina, have you been looking at these?'

She shook her head. 'No. When would I find the time? You know how busy I've been.'

'In that case, how come they've been put back in the wrong boxes? You know how particular I am about that.'

He gave Louise a penetrating look. She felt her cheeks grow hot and knew that her guilt must be evident, which only made her blush all the more.

'I see!' Ahmed walked towards her, a weird smile on his face. 'You've been watching them, haven't you? While you were here alone and we were at the club. First you raid your sister's wardrobe and private drawers, then you make free with our video collection. What a mischievous little creature you are!'

Louise felt a flutter once again in the pit of her stomach that was half excitement, half fear.

She looked to Gina for support, but her sister had that same mysterious smile on her face. 'Yes, I think you've gone just a bit too far this time. You only had to ask, my dear. But helping yourself behind my back . . . well, we don't tolerate that kind of behaviour do we, Ahmed?'

'We certainly don't. But how are we going to make sure it won't happen again? I think we're going to have to punish her, don't you?'

Louise wriggled in her seat as Ahmed came far too close for comfort, perching on the broad arm of the sofa. 'What do you mean?' she asked faintly.

'Don't worry, it won't take long. Gina and I favour the "short, sharp shock" approach, don't we, darling?'

'We certainly do!'

Gina got up and went to open a drawer. She took out a small, supple cane and Louise gave a gasp of dismay. 'Oh no! You don't intend to use that on me, do you?'

'That's exactly what we intend.' Ahmed's smile

broadened. 'Stand up, like a good girl.'

'But this is ridiculous. I'm not in school now!'

'Unfortunately, as you know, caning is no longer allowed in schools,' he said. 'Personally I think that's a bad thing. Fortunately it's still permitted between consenting adults in private.'

'But I haven't consented.'

Gina flexed the cane with a smile. 'You will when you know the alternatives. I cannot tolerate the taking of liberties and you have taken several in the short time you've been here. Either submit to punishment, as a symbol of your determination to keep out of trouble in future, or you'll have to leave, first thing tomorrow. The choice is yours.'

Louise looked from one to the other in horror. They were talking in a tone and language that she could hardly decode. If this was a game it was a game of bluff, and she didn't know whether to risk calling theirs or not. Nervously she rose from the chair and watched as Gina handed Ahmed the cane then came up to her.

'Let me help you, Louise. I promise it will all be over before you know it, and it won't hurt – much. Now lift up your dress, which I must remind you is actually *my* dress, you ungrateful hussy.'

'No, Gina, this is quite ridiculous. I. . .'

'You know the terms, Louise.' Ahmed said sternly. 'And the more you prevaricate, the more strokes of the cane you will receive. Now hurry up and do as you're told.'

She could tell he meant it. As she hesitated, Gina lifted up her dress for her and summarily pulled down her panties. Louise didn't resist, not even when she was made to bend over and brace herself against the arm of the chair. She tensed her buttocks as Ahmed went to stand behind her while Gina looked on with amused approval. A deep embarrassment seized her and she closed her eyes.

Yet behind her apprehension Louise felt her pulse fluttering wildly and knew that, at some basic level, she was perversely enjoying it. Humiliating as it was to bare her behind to a man she hardly knew, it seemed trivial compared to what she had witnessed at the *Seventh Veil*. And surely he would not hurt her, would he? A few light taps were the most she expected.

So it came as a shock to hear the loud swish of the cane as it descended and to feel the sharp sting as it made contact with her vulnerable flesh. She winced and contracted her buttocks. Ahmed gave her another stroke, and then another until Louise felt her behind begin to smart horribly. 'That's enough, surely!' she pleaded, hearing the cane being raised again.

'That is for us to decide, not you,' Gina told her. 'Another three, I think, Ahmed.'

'I agree. Three more should be sufficient for a first offence.'

Louise tensed her behind as the next torment came and the next, keeping her cheeks as taut as possible until he had finished. She remained there trembling, tears springing in her eyes at the pain, but just as she was about to pull down her skirt her sister said, 'No, wait Louise. I'll get something to make you feel better.'

Out of the corner of her eye she saw Ahmed return the cane to its drawer then go and sit down again. He took up his glass as if nothing had happened, and resumed sipping his brandy cocktail. For a few dizzying seconds Louise hated him intensely, but then Gina returned.

'Stay still, I'll rub this ointment in,' she told her. 'It will soothe you.'

Although she wanted nothing more than to get to bed and bury her head beneath the pillow in shame, Louise submitted to the last indignity. The cream was deliciously cool after the heat generated by the beating, and soon she began to feel much better. Her sister's fingers were gentle, and the pain was already subsiding to little more than a tingle. A surprisingly pleasant tingle, she was soon to discover. When she drew up her panties and sat down gingerly on the chair again a feeling of warm satisfaction flooded through her lower regions.

'How do you feel?' Gina asked.

'Peculiar.'

'Don't worry about it, Louise. That was just Ahmed's way of finding out if you were into being caned. We have CP and fetish nights at the club, you see, on Thursdays.'

'CP?'

'Corporal punishment. Some of the English businessmen can't get enough of it. We get other types in too, MPs, judges. You'd be amazed.'

'Some like to beat, others like to be beaten,' Ahmed explained. 'And they'll pay good money for the privilege, too.'

'So whether or not you decide to take part in our other activities you might like to consider that,' Gina said.

Suddenly Louise felt terribly tired and confused. She gave a yawn then said, 'I . . . I don't know. I need time to think about it.'

'Take all the time you want,' Ahmed smiled, rising to his feet. 'I'm going to bed now. Good night.'

He threw Gina a meaningful glance and Louise realised that she was keeping the lovers apart. She rose too, and went to use the bathroom. Looking in the mirror as she scrubbed off her make-up, she couldn't help wondering whether she would be able to face herself in the mornings if she took up Ahmed and Gina's offer of work. Her hazel eyes looked back at her candidly and her full lips gave a little sexy pout, just to see if she could do it. She grinned then began brushing her teeth.

The following day she was struck once again by the atmosphere of gloom and doom in her office, but now she experienced it in contrast to the 'workplace' she had visited the night before. Her impression of *Seventh Veil* had definitely been of job satisfaction for the workers, not to mention all those satisfied customers! At Newbolt & Co, however, it was quite the opposite. The work was boring, the pay was bad and the prospects even worse.

In her lunch hour Louise made a quick tour of the employment agencies, just to see if there was anything better available. But there wasn't, and by the time she returned to the office she felt more depressed than ever. The rumours were still flying around but now they had escalated beyond selected redundancies to include the whole firm going bankrupt!

How marvellous it would be to just give in her

notice now, to walk out on the whole damn lot of them. If she decided to take up Gina and Ahmed's offer she could do just that. So why was she hesitating? Was she scared about what Martin would think of her?

It came as a shock to realise that she was. But why should she care, now that he had ruined their marriage? She no longer loved him, and what she did with her life from here on was entirely up to her. The debate raged off and on in Louise's head all afternoon and she was no nearer to solving it by the time she left the office.

But as she travelled back to Holland Park she started to feel differently. Far from being worried about what Martin might think she actually started relishing the idea of shocking him. Seeing what went on at the club, both live and on the video, had opened her eyes to how other men and women behaved, what they enjoyed doing, and it left her own past love-life looking pretty feeble. Why shouldn't she be more adventurous, for a change?

So when she arrived back and her sister enquired about her day, Louise surprised herself by replying, 'It was lousy. So lousy I've decided to take up your offer and work at the club. But I won't give up the day job. Not just yet, anyway.'

Gina gave her a warm hug. 'I'm so glad. You won't regret it, I promise you.'

'Shall I come along tonight, then?' Louise asked.

She was disconcerted when her sister said, 'No, not tonight. Why don't you phone in sick tomorrow and we'll go shopping and buy you some clothes, get your hair done and put you through a few dance routines. But tonight you need to rest. You look washed out.'

'Do I?' Louise sighed. It was hardly surprising. She'd had more excitement in the past few nights than in the past few years. This was life in the fast lane, but it would take some getting used to.

'But mind you behave yourself when we leave you alone tonight!' Gina grinned. 'Tell you what, I've got a dance video somewhere. Why don't you use that to limber up a bit, if you have the energy?'

Louise did as she was told and thoroughly enjoyed herself, prancing about like a go-go dancer in one of the clubs she used to frequent before she met Martin. In the good old days, she thought wryly. She went to bed exhausted at eleven and slept through soundly until eight the next morning.

Feeling only slightly guilty Louise phoned the office and told them she had a migraine. She wished she had the confidence to give in her notice, but it was too soon. What if she got cold feet and couldn't go through with being a table dancer? Then she would have burnt her boats. It only emphasised how different she felt from Gina, who had walked out of their house at sixteen with no money, no job and nowhere to go. Now look where she'd got to!

They set out around ten and went straight to Soho, where Gina generously provided her sister with several appropriate outfits for her new career. After a pub lunch she took Louise to see Dino, her own hairdresser.

'You hair could take lightening,' he announced when she was in his salon with a towel around her shoulders, a sitting target. 'Your skin will tone nicely, and I think you'd look great as a blonde.'

'A blonde!'

Dino and Gina grinned.

Louise opened her mouth to protest, but then shut it again. What was the point of telling herself she should live more adventurously if she balked at every new thing? She would go with the flow, see where it took her.

Even so, she was very startled when she first saw her new self in the mirror. The golden halo made her eyes look very green – and her eye-brows very dark.

'It suits you,' Dino assured her. But then he would say that, wouldn't he, Louise thought.

'You'll need new make-up,' Gina told her. 'I can help you with that. And we'll get your brows lightened a bit too. Soon no one will know you weren't born blonde.'

'Except when I take my clothes off!'

Gina smiled. 'Well, there are ways round that too.'

She'll be wanting me to have breast implants next, Louise thought grumpily as they travelled home on the Tube. But beneath it all she felt enormously excited at the prospect of her new life. In some magical way having a make-over was giving her more confidence so that by the time the crunch came it would no longer be the old Louise that was taking to the floor, dancing sexily and then removing her clothes. Maybe she should change her name as well!

Chapter Five

'*I THINK "LULU"* suits her new image perfectly, don't you Ahmed?' Gina was looking at her sister as she spoke, giving her a conspiratorial smile. Only the two of them knew that had been Louise's baby-name. Now it was about to resurrected as her working alias.

After a weekend of intensive training, Louise had shaped up really well and Gina was trying to persuade her lover that she was ready to appear at the club. Monday nights were always quieter, less intimidating, and she knew that would make her sister's first public performance less of an ordeal. She could do her five-minute dance routine and then be invited to perform before one of the regular clients, who were more likely to be tolerant of a nervous newcomer.

'It will do,' Ahmed replied, his black eyes narrowing as he took another professional look at Louise. She was going through her dance to the tune of 'Light my Fire', shaking her tight little butt and thrusting out her pert breasts with more abandon than previously. It wouldn't take her long to get the hang of it, Gina decided. Maybe they did share some wild strand of their mother's genes after all!

Louise flopped onto the sofa, looking exhausted, and Gina told her to make sure she got to bed early. 'You can come along tomorrow night and make your début,' she told her.

'Already? But surely I'm nowhere near ready yet!'

'This isn't the London Palladium!' Ahmed grinned. 'You won't be judged on your dancing ability – not much, anyway.'

'But I don't feel confident enough. Maybe I'd be all right on stage, but dancing at the tables where they can see me close up . . . surely that's far more nerve-wracking?'

Gina took hold of a spindly-legged chair and placed it next to a coffee table in the middle of the room. 'Okay, when you've got your breath back, dance for Ahmed. Pretend he's a client. Pull out all the stops and give it everything you've got.'

She went over and put the dance track on again while Ahmed went to sit down. Louise got to her feet, smoothing down the fringe of her bikini pants and straightening the straps of her bra. Gina made her go to the other side of the room and walk across to him.

'Fine, look him right in the eye as you cross the room. Be bold. This man has paid for the privilege of seeing your beautiful body. Show it off!'

Gina continued to watch critically as her sister sidled up to Ahmed and thrust out her spangled rump, proceeding to rotate her hips and thrust her mons upwards in a smooth rhythm. She felt oddly proud of her. The mousy little creature that had blushed and stammered when she'd been caught red-handed in her bedroom had been transformed into a sexually confident woman. On the outside, at least. What kind of sex-life she would have now that she was finally separated from that dork of a husband was anybody's guess. She would certainly have plenty of offers if she worked regularly at the club.

Slowly Louise removed the tiny bra and revealed her plump, pretty breasts. Gina saw the enlargement of Ahmed's pupils, a sure sign that he was titillated, and wondered if he was growing attracted to her sister. He hadn't shown much interest in her when she'd first arrived, but there was a certain vulnerable openness about her now that she imagined most men would find appealing.

The pace of the music increased and so did Louise's dance, her breasts jiggling up and down before Ahmed's intense gaze. She had her hands down the front of her panties now, teasing him before she took them down, and there was a definite erotic charge in the air. Looking at her face, Gina realised that Louise was actually enjoying it. Her eyes were a bright and seductive green, and her pink lips were soft and open as if ready to be kissed.

'She's doing it much better now, isn't she?' Gina said to Ahmed, going to stand by his chair and absently stroking his dark hair. 'Is she turning you on?'

'Definitely. If I were a client I'd want to touch her now.'

Gina put out her hand and felt his erection. She smiled up at Louise, who was inching the panties over her hips. 'You see? You're getting him really hard.'

At once Louise averted her gaze, her cheeks reddening. 'Maintain eye contact all the time!' Ahmed barked, making her freeze.

Gina tried to reassure her. 'He's right, Lou. You must keep looking at him, and carrying on with your act, no matter what. Don't let anything put you off. Try talking dirty to her, Ahmed. She must get used to that sort of thing.'

'I want to suck your tits,' Ahmed began, in a feigned gruff voice. 'And then I want to stick my fingers up you, back and front, and give you a good seeing to. Get 'em off, girl. Let me see what your bare bum and naked pussy look like, so I can imagine screwing both of them.'

Although Louise carried on with what she was doing, the smile and the air of confidence had vanished. 'Smile!' Gina said. 'Look as if you're still enjoying it. If you don't, how can you expect him to?'

Louise made an effort and the glow slowly returned to her skin and eyes. She was now completely naked and was stroking her own breasts, hips and thighs with sensual abandon, successfully ignoring the stream of words that was issuing from Ahmed's mouth.

'Good, that's very good!' Gina said. 'Keep looking at him and smiling, no matter what he says. He can't touch you, remember. Not this time, and never without your consent.'

At the end of the performance Gina gave her a hug. 'You did very well. And you're unlikely to have to deal with that sort of talk. Usually our clients are very polite, paying you compliments and making you feel good. I just want to be sure that you won't be fazed by anything.'

'I can't promise that,' Louise said ruefully.

Ahmed said, 'We'll make it as easy as we can for you tomorrow. We'll find some really nice guys for you, don't worry.'

Later, in the taxi on their way to the club, Gina asked Ahmed what he'd really thought of Louise's performance. He gave a slow smile. 'Well, she has a certain shy but brash quality, like a teenage virgin trying to be sexy. It's very appealing, actually. I'm sure that some of our clients will go for her in a big way.'

'Mm, interesting. But do you think she could ever be persuaded to go further?'

Ahmed looked thoughtful. 'I'm not sure. It depends how she's handled, and on her early experiences at the club. That's why we must be very careful. I've been thinking about who usually comes on a Monday, or who might be persuaded to come. There's Jojo, of course.'

'Yes, I thought of him. And Sirhan. He's good-looking, and very sweet.'

As the pair of them discussed various options Gina became quite excited. She was remembering her own early excursions into the world of exotic dancing, how timid she had been at the start and how very bold she had become since. It amused her to think of her little sister following the same path.

The following evening Gina found herself in a taxi again, this time with Louise beside her. Ahmed had gone to the club earlier to make the arrangements, and while they were alone Louise confessed to being horribly nervous.

'I'm so afraid that something will go wrong,' she admitted. 'Or that they won't like me or something.'

Gina gave her a sisterly hug. 'Don't worry, you'll be fine. I'll introduce you to some of the other girls and then you'll feel part of the team. Treat it like any other new job and just do your best. You'll soon feel at home.'

When they got to the club Gina took her straight to the dressing-room where Janice and May, a Chinese girl, were getting changed. It seemed a good idea for Louise to meet them, since Janice was one of the newest dancers at the *Seventh Veil* and May was one of the longest-serving.

'What number are you?' May asked her. She was referring to the number by which the girls were identified, and to which they would respond when any of the waiters held up that number of fingers.

'Number seven.'

'Ah, the luckiest number of all!'

Soon all three girls were chatting away and Gina felt free to go off and find Ahmed. She didn't usually work on Monday nights but often turned up at the club anyway, to socialise. Besides, she liked being near her lover. Seeing him from across a darkened room still gave her a thrill. She smiled as he gave her a thumbs-up sign from the bar and walked over to join him.

'Is everything okay?' she asked.

'Sure. Jojo's out of the country right now, but Ali and Sirhan will be here. So will Jules.'

'Jules!' Gina smiled. 'Ever the gallant Frenchman. He'll probably kiss her hand at the end and make her feel like a princess.'

'They all know she's a novice. We'll see how she copes with those and if anyone else asks for her I'll vet them. I've told all the staff.' He took Gina's face between his hands and kissed her on the lips. 'She's getting a really easy ride. I hope she appreciates it.'

'Oh, I'm sure she does.' Gina threw him one of her intimate smiles. 'And I do, too.'

'Well I'll think of some way for you to show your gratitude later!' he grinned, before drifting off again.

Gina offered her sister a brandy before she went on stage and Louise gulped it down. Then Janice took her hand with a smile. 'Come on, it won't seem nearly so bad once you're up and running,' she smiled, her blue eyes warm and encouraging.

Louise made a face, tweaked her costume, then took a deep breath. 'Okay, I'm ready.'

Gina watched them go then lit herself a cigarette and put her feet up for a few minutes. There wasn't much she could do to help her sister now – she was on her own. She remembered what her first night had been like: she'd almost wet her knickers with worrying. But the darkness had been her friend, together with the bright lights on stage. Looking out into the room all she'd been able to see was the dull glow of the table lamps, while the dazzling brightness that surrounded her had lifted her spirits, made her feel special. A bright bubble in a black void. Was that how Louise was feeling now?

After a while she sauntered through the swing

doors and joined Ahmed at the bar. From the back of the room they watched Louise going through her paces with the other seven girls, each of them dancing in their own individual style. She didn't look at all out of place. Turning to Ahmed Gina said, 'She's doing okay, isn't she?'

He shrugged. 'This is the easy part. We'll see what Jules thinks of her later.'

Gina looked over to where Jules was sitting, his eyes on the stage. She had danced for him herself. He was a sophisticated Frenchman but his tastes were surprisingly simple: he required beauty and innocence, or at least the appearance of it. And her sister had both in spades. Now he was beckoning the waiter over, a mere formality since he and Ahmed had already agreed terms.

The waiter held up both his hands, displaying seven fingers. It took a while for Louise to realise that she was being called and when she did she faltered momentarily in her routine but soon recovered. With slow deliberation she descended from the stage and began to slink her way across the floor to where the handsome Frenchman was sitting with his cigarette in one hand and his wine glass in the other, awaiting her arrival.

Gina joined Ahmed at a nearby table from where she could see the proceedings. Trying not to stare too obviously she nevertheless managed to glimpse her sister's swaying butt as she reached her goal and paused, giving Jules a long smouldering look. Good girl, Gina thought. She saw Jules smile faintly, taking in every inch of Louise from top to bottom and back again. Was he hoping that some day he would get more than just a strip-dance from her? Such a fantasy would certainly enhance his enjoyment of her performance.

The question was, would Louise be secretly reciprocating that fantasy?

Not tonight, Gina decided, she would be far too nervous. But that was what made all the difference between a dancer who was just a stripper and one who was really special. With a fond smile Gina remembered the first time she'd really wanted the man she'd danced for. He had been a young German student, brought along by his wealthy uncle to sample the decadent delights of his favourite London club. The young man's hair had shone a bright, beautiful blonde beneath the subdued lights, much as Louise's hair was shining at the moment. He had been tanned too, with sapphire eyes and a perfectly sculpted mouth. Even now warmth filled Gina's loins as she thought of him.

She had been working for Ahmed but had not yet become his mistress, Gina recalled. There had been no particular man in her life, yet she had yearned for that innocent youth with an indecent passion. Her dance for him had been sultry in the extreme, full of wild passion and libidinous implication. His uncle had seemed taken aback, as if he had got far more than he'd bargained for. She had offered the blond beast everything: her ripe breasts, her pulsating pussy, but through it all he had sat there remote and expressionless, making her want him even more.

Afterwards the uncle had lusted after her himself but she had graciously declined. Her purpose had been to inflame the nephew, that infuriatingly cold and distant young man with the pale cicatrice on his cheek that was his badge of courage. For weeks afterwards Gina had hoped that he might return, preferably alone, to sate himself visually on her charms and then to sample them in the flesh, but he had never come again.

Instead the uncle had returned, months later, on his next business trip. Gina had overheard him talking to Ahmed. 'That absurd boy!' he had expostulated in his thick German accent. 'He was mixing in bad company, you know, so I bring him here to make a cure. I think so many lovely girls, he will lust for them and be saved from his bad friends. The girl she dance like a dream, like Salome before Herod, but is he made hard? Not one bit of it, whereas I! Now he lives with a transvestite in Hamburg. Ah well, I try my best! You have a saying, how goes it? You may lead a horse to water, but cannot force the beast to drink.'

Gina smiled to think of it. But by then she and Ahmed had become lovers and her dream of the beautiful blond German had faded into oblivion. . .

'Look!' Ahmed whispered suddenly. 'Your sister is getting into the swing of it, I think!'

Louise had removed her bra and was dangling it provocatively in front of Jules's nose. He was regarding her with amused tolerance, as one might humour a child. All the same his eyes were fixed on her luscious pink nipples, hard as sugared almonds on the vanilla cones of her breasts. She turned her back on him and pretended to pull down her panties but then stopped halfway and flung her arms in the air, revolving slowly until she was facing him again.

'She'll have to perform a few more tricks to please Jules!' Ahmed commented.

'Oh, she doesn't have to do much. Not this time, anyway. Her amateurishness is what appeals to him. I remember him telling me how much he loved to see the new girls trembling and blushing through their routines, and how disappointed he was when they became slick and professional after a few weeks.'

Gina watched as her sister's taut buttocks appeared and she stepped deftly out of what remained of her costume, holding it coyly in front of her pubis while she turned back to face her client. Jules nodded and smiled at her. Encouraged, she let the last vestige of her modesty fall to the floor and the Frenchman gave her a spontaneous round of applause.

Some of the others in the room looked round and one in particular appeared very interested in Louise. He just kept on staring at her, and alarm bells began to ring in Gina's head. 'Who's that guy over there, in the blue suit?' she asked Ahmed.

He peered through the gloom, screwing up his eyes. 'Where? Oh, Mikey!'

'What do you know about him?'

'He runs a chain of casinos. I think he's only been once before. Tanya took him home with her as far as I can recall.'

'He seems very interested in Louise.'

'Good.'

'No, Ahmed, you don't understand. . .'

But he was already on his feet, going off to greet a regular. Gina turned back towards the room and saw that Louise had ended her show and was making for the exit. As she passed Mikey's table he reached out and took her hand, stopping her in her tracks. Gina stiffened, anxiously. But Ahmed had also noticed what was happening and was making towards the man.

Gina watched the men greet each other and then Ahmed sent Louise off backstage, engaging the other man in conversation. She got up and followed her sister through the swing doors, soon finding her in the dressing-room gulping down lemonade.

'How did it go?' she asked. 'It looked fine from where I was sitting.'

'Oh God, I was terrified!' Louise finished the bottle and gave a little hiccup. 'Honestly, Gina, I don't know where I'll ever find the nerve to go through that again.'

'Nonsense! The first time is always the worst. Give yourself a rub down with cologne. I find that a marvellous tonic. Then you'll be ready to meet Ali. He's a nice chap, you'll like him.'

'Someone stopped me on my way out,' Louise said, her eyes wide with apprehension. 'He said he wanted me to do something for him. I've no idea what he meant. I don't think he speaks English very well.'

'Don't worry, Ahmed will sort it out. If he decides the man is too demanding he won't let you dance for him. You can trust him.'

She left Louise spraying herself with cologne and went back to the bar, where she found Ahmed talking to Jules. The Frenchman kissed her hand with his dry lips as she joined them, saying, 'Your sister is quite charming, Gina.

Where have you been hiding her all this time?'

'She's only my half-sister. We lost touch for a while, but I shan't let that happen again.'

'It is good to see her following in the family tradition! Will she progress, do you think?'

Gina knew at once what he was hinting at. 'For the moment she's content to dance, Jules. And I shan't push her. She must find her feet in her own way, and in her own time.'

'And very pretty feet they are too,' he murmured. 'Oh look, she has come back on stage. Now we are in for another treat, I think.'

For a while Gina watched her sister, then she saw Ali arrive. He waved her over.

'So, I am to have the pleasure of your sister's company tonight?'

'Yes, Ali. Be nice to her. It's her first night.'

'Ah, you make her sound like a virgin on her wedding night.'

Gina laughed. 'Dream on, Ali!'

They both watched as Louise gyrated on stage, her slender waist swaying and her stomach undulating as she moved her pelvis. Mikey, the casino tycoon, lit a fat cigar and leaned back in his chair, watching her through narrowed eyes. Although she tried to remain objective about the clients, Gina didn't like him much. There was something arrogant about him, something corrupt, as if he thought he was above the law. She reminded herself to get a profile on him from Tanya sometime.

When he snapped his fingers at the waiter Louise gave a startled look in his direction and Gina was instantly alert. The waiter held up seven fingers and Gina held her breath. When Louise began to descend from the stage she hurried to Ahmed's side.

'No, Ahmed! She mustn't dance for him,' Gina whispered urgently. 'Only for the clients we arranged. Go and stop her.'

'It's okay, she can give him what he wants. The man's hot for her, and if she dances for him tonight he'll come back tomorrow.'

'But I don't trust him. She's too inexperienced. Let her dance for Ali now instead.'

Ahmed turned away from her, his face hard. Gina knew better than to tackle him in that mood. She said nothing more, only watched the scene unfolding before her in helpless suspense. Her sister had reached Mikey's table now and was beginning her naive little dance, but already he was reaching out and trying to touch her, his strong fingers grasping eagerly at the flying fringe on her tiny briefs.

'My turn next?' Ali enquired pleasantly.

Gina shrugged. 'Who knows? Ask Ahmed.'

She was angry with her lover, very angry. It was important to give her sister an easy ride on her first night, but that Mikey character could prove to be a loose cannon. Gina saw Ahmed chatting to another client with his back to the stage, ignoring what was happening with Louise. Mikey made a grab for her and one of the waiters hovered uncertainly, but then Louise twirled round and almost bumped into the man's chair.

A stream of obscenities could be heard throughout the room. Louise paused, her face pale and strained, wondering what to do. Gina took a few steps towards them but then her sister pulled herself together and forced a smile. She resumed her dance, but Mikey was sitting there with a face like thunder, his arms petulantly folded across his chest. Gina looked at Ahmed: he was still absorbed in conversation, ignoring what was happening in the rest of the room. Her anger grew and she turned to Ali for sympathy.

'Ahmed should never have let her dance for that man!' she said in an undertone. 'I don't know how he got talked into it.'

'Money talks, my dear, you should know that by now.' Ali took her hand and squeezed it briefly. 'Never mind, when it's my turn to enjoy your lovely sister I shall make her feel like a queen!'

Gina threw him a grateful smile. 'I'm sure you will, Ali dear.'

Louise had removed her top now and was holding up her breasts for Mikey's inspection but he was muttering under his breath at her. Even so his eyes were on her nakedness, feasting gluttonously. This is the first and last time she performs for him, Gina vowed to herself. She went to sit at a vacant table near to where the dance was taking place. If no one else was going to look after her sister she'd have to do it herself.

Now that Gina was within a few yards of Mikey, his vulgar comments were audible.

Louise continued bravely, starting to roll down her pants but taking her time. She had closed her eyes now, presumably to blot out the vision of his lecherous face, but he took umbrage, swearing at her to look at him. She stared back like a zombie and continued her dance, stepping out of her costume and waving it provocatively at him.

Gina knew that it was only the approaching

end of her ordeal that was keeping Louise going. Her lower lip was trembling ominously and her eyes were moist. She longed to intervene, yet it was not her place. At the first sign of physical trouble a waiter would come to Louise's rescue, but as long as the problem was one of language and attitude nothing could be done. She caught her sister's eye and smiled encouragingly at her, but it only seemed to make matters worse. Louise looked as if she were about to burst into tears.

At last the dance ended, but as she bent to pick up her scattered garments Mikey reached out and pinched her naked behind. 'Ow!' Louise exclaimed. She backed away, fear and indignation written on her features. Swiftly Gina rose from her chair and went over. She took her by the elbow and began to usher her firmly towards the door.

'Come on, Lulu!' she said. 'Time for your break, I think!'

As soon as they were outside the confines of the club Louise began sobbing. Gina put her arm around her and led her into the dressing-room then shut the door.

'That beast!' she exclaimed through the tears. 'He pinched me, Gina! I wasn't supposed to let him touch me, was I?'

'Of course not. Look, don't worry about it. I'll make sure it doesn't happen again.'

But Louise was in a state. She trembled constantly and kept breaking down into tears. 'I can't do any more tonight,' she kept saying. 'Please don't make me go on again!'

'Okay, I'll take you home,' Gina said at last.

It was a disappointment to Gina. She'd hoped

to see her sister dance for Ali and Sirhan. Still, that could wait until another occasion. She knew that both the men would be tolerant. They had been attending the club ever since its opening and were now considered friends as well as clients.

As they rode back in the taxi Gina did her best to reassure Louise that she had done nothing wrong. The fault had been with Mikey and, to a lesser extent, with Ahmed for allowing the unfortunate incident to take place. It felt a bit strange having to act as mother to her own sister. She was used to mothering the new girls, considering that part of her job as Ahmed's personal assistant and the most experienced dancer on the premises.

But now, as she put her arm around Louise, she was reminded of when they'd been girls together and a sadness overwhelmed her. At the time she left home she had been thinking only of her own future. It hadn't occurred to her that, in depriving Louise of an elder sister, she had been changing the course of her life too. Would she have rushed into that stupid marriage if Gina had remained to advise her? The guilt she felt about that was compounded now.

She thought that Louise would want to go straight to bed, but instead she wanted to talk. They chatted for ages, mostly about old times, and were still up when Ahmed returned from the club. He didn't look pleased. Almost as soon as he entered he took a twenty-pound note from his wallet and handed it to Louise with a scowl.

'That's your night's wages!'

Gina leapt to her feet. 'Ahmed, that's unfair!'

He turned on her impatiently. 'I don't think so.

She's lucky to get anything after the way she behaved.'

Louise seemed cowed. She thanked Ahmed for the money and started towards the door, but he hadn't finished with her yet. 'I hope you're proud of yourself!' he snapped. 'You let me down badly, both with Ali and with Sirhan.'

'It wasn't her fault,' Gina intervened.

But Louise stopped her. 'Yes, it was. You're quite right, Ahmed, I did let you down. And I'm very sorry. I let that man rile me, but it won't happen again.'

Gina snapped at Ahmed, 'See? You've put her off the whole idea now. You should never have allowed her to dance for Mikey.'

To her astonishment, her sister said, 'No, Gina, it's not put me off. What happened tonight has just made me all the more determined to succeed, that's all.'

Ahmed's face broke into a smile. He took Louise by the hand and led her to the sofa, where he sat down beside her. 'You see, Gina, your sister has spirit! I admire that greatly. The only way we learn is by making mistakes. The weak ones amongst us give up when that happens. The strong learn from them. And Louise has shown us tonight that she is one of the strong ones.'

Gina had to agree. Her sister's spirit was remarkable. But she fancied that she should have some of the credit in helping Louise get over her ordeal.

Louise began asking Ahmed questions. Mostly about how much she could expect to earn on a normal night. They hadn't discussed business in such detail before, since she had yet to sign a contract, but it was clear that Louise had now decided to take the job seriously. She wanted to know how hard she would have to work to earn the kind of money she needed to pay off her debts.

'You'd have to do at least ten clients a night to earn two hundred just from table dancing,' Ahmed told her.

'And for lap dancing?'

He shrugged. 'Maybe five, six.'

'And if I did the next thing, let them touch me?'

'You could earn up to a hundred per client.'

Gina saw a faint gleam in Louise's hazel eyes. Something had changed in her this evening. Far from being intimidated by her experience with Mikey she had become all the more determined to win through. Was it the spirit of revenge she saw mirrored there?

Chapter Six

LOUISE DECIDED THAT in order to do her job at the club properly she had to give in her notice at Newbolt's, so she did just that. She told no one there what she was now doing for a living. They were a part of her old life, the one she'd shared with Martin. In one fell swoop she had left it all behind, together with those dreary office clothes that were still languishing in her old wardrobe.

When she phoned her husband he'd asked, truculently, what he was supposed to do with her clothes now that the house was being repossessed.

'Get rid of them however you like, give them all away,' she'd told him.

'And the rest of your things?'

'I'll come over sometime and sort them out.'

She chose a time when she knew he'd be out of the house. For two hours Louise sifted through the debris of her past, finding surprisingly little that she wanted to retain. It proved a cathartic experience. Soon afterwards she rang her solicitor and instigated divorce proceedings. All of which was a great boost to her self-confidence.

Next time she went to the club she danced for Ali, Sirhan and four others besides, earning over a hundred pounds. It wasn't quite the riches she'd imagined but it was a very good start. The trouble was there were only three nights in the week when she could do it. The others were 'Theme Nights' and she didn't yet feel ready to join in the various weird goings-on. Still, if she wanted to earn big money she would have to move on, sooner or later.

But her libido was up and rising. Despite the fact that she wasn't getting any sex, Louise found herself becoming more and more randy as she relaxed into her new role of exotic dancer and became more expert at it. The dormant desires within her were being slowly awakened, and she was enjoying the process. After a particularly sexy session she would come home and make good use of the vibrator Gina had given her, needing to satisfy her urges before she could sleep.

She loved seeing the men getting all worked up as she teased them, especially if they were men who attracted her. And she began to dream of giving them a little more, one day. Then, one night, Mikey walked into the club again and Louise felt all her new-found confidence evaporating. The very sight of him made her shudder with loathing. Yet there was a weird attraction too, as if she and he had some unfinished business.

Louise did her best to ignore him but halfway through the evening Ahmed took her aside.

'Mikey was asking for you,' he began, and a

cold dread seized her. He grinned. 'Now don't worry. He wanted to apologise for upsetting you before. He says he was a very bad boy and wonders if you'd like to punish him.'

'What?'

Ahmed grinned. 'You know, like I punished you. Remember?'

Louise blushed. 'You mean. . .'

'That's right. Strictly speaking that should happen on one of our CP nights, but since he asked specially you could do it now if you liked. In privacy, of course.'

'I . . . I don't know what to say!'

'Either yes or no will do for now. If you agree, have a word with Gina and she'll help you organise it.'

Louise couldn't help smiling at the thought of getting her own back on Mikey. Her humiliating experience with him still haunted her, despite her success with other men. It would be good to get him out of her system. She nodded. 'Okay. I'll do it.'

'Good girl! Meet Gina in the office in ten minutes. She'll tell you exactly what to do.'

While she waited, Louise kept looking across to where Mikey was drinking and smoking his cigar. Now that she'd made her decision she began to look forward to thrashing his behind, making him whimper. If only she'd known that was his bag she would never have let him upset her before.

Gina was ready in the office with an array of whips. She made Louise practise on a cushion until she found the one that felt easiest to wield. It was a small, thick-handled one that made a satisfying crack when she whisked it through the air.

'You can get him to come in here if you like,' Gina suggested. 'Try a bit of role-play.'

'How do you mean?'

'Well, this could be the boss's office. You could be punishing him for sexual harassment of a young female employee, or something. Use your imagination.'

Louise smiled. 'Okay. I'll try.'

Gina looked her up and down. 'You're not dressed for the part, though. Pity we didn't know about this before we left home, then we could have come prepared. Hey, I have an idea!'

She disappeared and returned a few minutes later with a dark green overall. 'I found this in the cleaner's cupboard,' Gina giggled. 'Put it on. Let's see how you look.'

When Louise was dressed in the overall her sister scraped back her hair into an elastic band and then found a pair of cheap sunglasses in the desk drawer. She popped out the lenses and handed them to Louise. 'Go on, put them on. Hey, that's not bad. Not bad at all. I'll go and tell Ahmed you're ready.'

While she waited, Louise felt a glow of arousal that filled her whole being and was one stage further on than sexual. She couldn't recall ever feeling quite like this before. In her life men had always been the bosses, the ones who told her what to do and made the decisions that she had to fall in with. She'd had to stand by helplessly when her father left home, when her husband gambled and drank away the mortgage, and when her manager had said there would have to be some redundancies.

Now she could reverse all her feelings of

helplessness with a few swift strokes of the whip.
The prospect was intriguing. She began to plan
how she would do it, and her excitement grew.
Then she heard a sharp tap on the door and took
her place behind Ahmed's desk, the whip hidden
on her lap. 'Come in!' she called in a loud, stern
voice.

Mikey entered, looking sheepish. He stood
before her with his bald head bowed and his arms
clasped in front of him. In a small voice he said,
'You wanted to see me, madam?'

'Yes, I certainly did!'

Louise placed the whip on the desk where he
could see it and rose from her chair. She walked
slowly round the desk, enjoying keeping him in
suspense. Then she stopped about a foot away
from him. She stood tall, throwing her shoulders
back and her chest out, and at once felt a surge of
real power go through her like an invigorating
shock.

'You insulted me. What do you have to say for
yourself?' she asked at last.

He raised his eyes a little, keeping his head
down. 'I am sorry, madam.'

'Being sorry is not enough. You must be
punished. Six strokes of the whip, I think. Take
your trousers off and put your hands on the
desk.'

'But, madam. . .'

'No arguments! If you don't do as you're told at
once I shall double the punishment.'

Quickly Mikey took down his black trousers
and bent forward, bracing himself on his arms.
Louise decided she wanted to see more of his
rump. She made him bend right over and rest his

320

head on his forearms. Then she seized the elasticated waist of his Y-fronts and pulled it down, revealing his well-covered buttocks. She picked up the whip and raised her arm in the air, relishing the moment. Then she brought it down smartly.

Mikey yelled, and clenched his buttocks tightly. She lashed at him again and this time he groaned in resignation. Louise smiled to herself. How she would like to do this to Martin! The thought brought new satisfaction to her soul as she struck again, making his corpulent flesh quiver.

Mikey turned his face towards her. 'Please, madam, isn't that enough?'

'No!' she snapped. 'Not nearly enough. You insult me even to suggest it. Six strokes is the absolute minimum for abusing a lady, don't you agree?'

'Oh, yes! Certainly, madam!'

'All right. Now tell me how wicked and ungrateful you have been to take advantage of my innocence. Get onto your knees and tell me.'

Louise was amazed when he obeyed her without question. Another wave of exultation went through her as he began to grovel at her feet. 'I am a worm, madam, a worthless creature. I dared to touch your perfect body, and for that I should be punished most severely.'

'Quite right. So bend down with your face on the floor, as if you were worshipping.'

He looked so ridiculous with his great white moons stuck in the air that Louise had to stifle a giggle. Beneath his belly hung his insignificant genitals. She brought the whip down again. He moaned and prostrated himself further until he was almost lying flat.

'Two more!' she announced. 'But first tell me how unworthy you are to even be in the same room as me.'

Mikey played his part to perfection, telling her that she was as far above him as the sun was above the earth. He swore that he would never insult her again but only be her slave, if she would let him. Louise gave him his last two lashes and then kicked him with the point of her shoe for good measure. He stared up at her in abject adoration before hurrying to obey the order to pull up his trousers.

'Now leave me, you disgusting creature!' she said, throwing him a last look of contempt. He bowed out of the room backwards, hands clasped before him, as if from a royal presence.

While she was getting out of the overall Gina returned. 'That creep seems very pleased with what you did. I overheard him telling Ahmed that you were a priceless gem in our collection of jewels!'

Louise giggled. 'I enjoyed it. And I wasn't nervous at all. It just seemed to come naturally to me.'

Gina gave her a searching look. 'In that case you might. . .' She seemed to change her mind. 'But it's early days yet. I don't want you to take on too much at once.'

Louise enjoyed the rest of the evening more than usual. Her session with Mikey had evoked a new sense of her own power, which was extremely satisfying. She danced with greater confidence and was bolder with her clients. She found that she could imagine touching them, being intimate with them in ways that hitherto she hadn't dared dream of.

'You're coming along fine,' Ahmed told her as they went home together. 'Maybe you'd like to try lap dancing soon?'

'Don't push her,' Gina warned.

'Of course not, it's entirely up to Louise. Still, the offer is there whenever she wants to take it up.'

Louse wondered vaguely what the 'offer' was, but since she was rather befuddled by drink and very tired she let the subject drop.

On Friday night Gina told her that she would be going away for the weekend.

'One of our most wealthy clients wants to take me to Paris in his private jet,' she smiled.

'Lucky you!'

'Don't worry. I've worked for it. But I hope you don't mind being left in the flat by yourself. Ahmed will be there too, of course, when he's not at the club.'

'Oh no, I don't mind. I quite welcome it, actually. It will give me the chance to catch up with myself, to take stock. Everything seems to have happened so fast.'

It was true. In just over a month Louise had changed her life around completely and she still didn't quite know who she was. She had lost touch with her old friends, the house she used to live in had a 'For Sale' board outside and Martin had gone into a rehab unit. Sometimes, in the depths of the night, Louise felt very alone and scared by all the irrevocable steps she had taken.

On the plus side, she really appreciated being with her sister again. They were growing closer then they'd ever been. Not that they'd had much time to chat, but at the club Gina's friendly presence had made all the difference. And the few heart-to-hearts they'd had at home had definitely helped to heal old wounds.

So when Louise awoke on Saturday morning and realised that Gina was gone a wave of bleakness threatened to swamp her. She went into the kitchen and made herself a black coffee and some toast, then Ahmed sauntered in wearing his dressing-gown. Louise felt a tingle of anticipation strike her, making her feel self-conscious. It was the first time they'd been alone together in the flat. He sat down on the stool, legs apart, and Louise tried not to look at his lean, naked thighs.

'Well, Louise,' he grinned, 'what are you going to do today?'

'Oh, I don't know. I'll go shopping, maybe.'

'And tonight?'

She shrugged. 'Stay in and watch TV, I suppose. I could do with an early night.'

'I would invite you to join me at the club, but I'm not going.'

'You're not?' Louise stared at him, suddenly apprehensive.

'No, I'm leaving Karl in charge. I thought maybe you would like to come for a drink or maybe go to another club, in the West End.'

Louise felt nervous. It didn't seem right that Ahmed was asking her out while Gina was away. 'It's all right, thanks, Ahmed. I'd rather stay here.'

'Okay. Then let me cook you a meal. Something Middle Eastern.'

She squirmed on her stool, wondering how to get out of it. The thought of spending an evening in with Ahmed was unnerving, but she had no option. 'Please don't go to any trouble.'

'It's no trouble,' he smiled, his dark eyes subtly insinuating. 'I would enjoy it. It's not often I get the chance to cook.'

For the rest of the day Louise was out, looking for somewhere to live. She'd decided that she couldn't impose on her sister for much longer, but she knew that it was really Ahmed she was seeking to avoid. Somehow he made her feel decidedly uncomfortable. Was it because she secretly fancied him? Or was it just because she believed he was attracted to her? It was hard to tell.

After buying various papers and looking in some estate agents' windows she concluded that she couldn't afford to live anywhere in that part of town but must look in the cheaper areas: Shepherd's Bush, perhaps, or Earl's Court. The prospect of tramping the streets inspecting run-down flats and bedsits was depressing.

She just had to earn more money, and soon. Fortunately she was in the right job, she just had to pluck up the courage to take the next step. Lap dancing, the intimate contact between her crotch and the client's fly. She'd seen the other girls doing it and it didn't look too difficult, but it seemed to be on the other side of a hard-to-bridge gap in her confidence. Well, she would just have to overcome her scruples. At fifty pounds a time she couldn't afford not to.

Reluctantly, Louise made her way back to Holland Park. When she opened the door of the flat with her spare key a delicious aroma filled her nostrils and Ahmed appeared, waving a wooden spoon. 'Hi! I'm glad you returned now because it's nearly ready.'

She smiled, already feeling more relaxed. Ahmed offered her a drink and she chose Pernod. It made her think of Gina in Paris. She went through to her room and found some loose-fitting velvet trousers and a silky top to change into, then she went into the bathroom to freshen up before dinner. As she sprayed on some of her favourite perfume Louise asked herself just what she thought she was doing, preparing herself as if for a date.

She had no answer to that.

The meal was excellent, full of subtle spices and washed down with some superb wine. Louise enjoyed chatting to Ahmed about her childhood with Gina, what she remembered of it anyway. When the conversation went on to her unhappy marriage, however, she became quite tearful and put up no resistance when Ahmed put his arm around her on the sofa.

'Poor little Lulu,' he said soothingly. 'You've had a rough deal, haven't you? But eveything will be better now. You are enjoying your life with us, aren't you?'

'Oh yes!' She smiled at him through her wet eyelashes. 'It's marvellous being reunited with Gina again.'

'Well, we are happy to have you here,' he smiled. Louise thought how nice he looked when he was smiling. She liked the way his soft, black hair flopped over his forehead too. And there was something very attractive about his slight but undoubtedly masculine body. She could quite see why her sister had fallen for him.

326

'I started looking for a place of my own today,' she said.

'There's no hurry. At first, I admit, I wasn't keen on the idea of you staying here. But since you've joined our staff at the club it has been quite convenient, hasn't it? Are you happy about working there?'

'Oh yes, I am now. It took me a while to get used to it.'

'It is the same for everyone, even those girls who have worked as dancers before. We have a different way of working from other places. And a more exclusive clientèle.'

'Like Mikey?' Louise gave a cheeky grin, which he returned.

'Yes, even Mikey. He might be an old rogue but his ill-gotten gains entitle him to the same services as anyone else.'

'I've been wondering . . . about this lap dancing.'

'Yes?' Ahmed's mouth was very near hers now, making her feel dizzy.

She pulled away from him a little. 'I thought I might try it. Only I don't know exactly what to do. I've watched the other girls, but I'm still nervous of doing it myself.'

'Would you like to practise?'

Louise felt a dark thrill pass through her. 'What, now? On you?'

He laughed. 'Why not? I don't see who else you've got to practise on.'

'Well, I don't know. . .'

'There's nothing to it, honestly. You've already danced for me, anyway.' He got up and went over to the hi-fi system, selecting a CD. When he turned round his gaze was intensely compelling. 'Dance, little lady! Let go of your inhibitions and dance for me as if I were a client. Then you will come and sit on my lap and continue dancing!'

Slowly Louise rose from the couch and kicked off her shoes. It felt strange dancing in her clothes and soon she was stripping to her underwear. Her head felt muzzy and her nipples and clitoris were tingling inside her silky bra and drawers as she kept looking into Ahmed's black, knowing eyes. He crooned his approval now and then, keeping up her morale. Not that she really needed it. Dancing for him made her feel deliciously seductive and womanly.

At last, when she was wearing only her tiny silk pants, he beckoned her towards him. She noticed that he had taken off his shoes and socks. She slid onto his lap and he whispered, 'Now put your feet on the floor and slide up and down my thigh.' As soon as she did so he gave a groan. 'I think we'll make this a "feelie", shall we?' Without waiting for her reply his hands cupped her breasts, making her moan with arousal. The friction of his rough trousers on the delicate swelling bud of her clitoris was most titillating, and Louise found that she could alter the pace and angle of her movements at will, rising and falling as well as moving forwards and backwards.

Suddenly she ground her mons hard against his crotch and heard Ahmed groan again. His mouth fastened on one of her nipples, making her shudder. Locked into an ascending spiral of excitement Louise turned around and waggled her rear against the bulge of his fly, where his cock was evidently straining towards a climax too. His hands seized her breasts and his mouth gave a soft nip to her neck, making her squirm with ecstasy and throw her head back against his shoulder. 'That's the way!' she heard him whisper. 'Now we're cooking, no holds barred!'

It was only when his expert fingers found her clitoris that Louise realised the full potential of the new position. Her efforts became more frenzied as her own libido increased in leaps and bounds, taking her near the limit of her endurance. Between the twin cushions of her buttocks she could feel the hard prominence of his penis, now thrusting against her, and she had a definite urge to make him come. His nails were scratching delicately at her nipples while his thumb worked her clitoris in firm circles, increasing the erotic tension to fever pitch.

'I thought I was the one who was supposed to be doing all the work?' she said, gasping as she turned to grin at him.

'You're doing fine, just keep going,' he replied, his voice thick.

But she wanted closer contact with that secret weapon he held concealed in his trousers. Feeling it through his clothes was no longer enough, she wanted to see it, touch it, taste it. Abandoning all her remaining reserve she hopped off his knee and knelt before him, her erogenous areas still throbbing with desire, and went to undo his zip.

'You must charge more for this, you know,' he grinned down at her.

She returned his gaze saucily. 'Well, are you willing to pay?'

'Oh yes! Name your price, little lady!'

Louise slid the zipper down and proceeded to extricate the short, thick shaft from his underwear. She encircled its base with her thumb and forefinger, then bent her lips to the glossy pink glans. Ahmed's fingers continued to play with her breasts as she knelt there and soon she managed to manoeuvre herself onto his naked foot, where his big toe first played very dextrously with her clitoris and then managed to find its way right inside her.

As she proceeded towards a climax, with that wicked toe alternately invading her and rubbing her clitoris, Louise's enthusiasm for the act of fellatio grew. Soon she was sucking and swallowing at the shaft while she licked back and forth across the glans, her fingers cupping his balls within his pants. She felt them tighten and knew that he was on the brink of orgasm. A few last movements of her lips and tongue made him come, spurting wildly, and the sensation of his hot convulsions triggered her into similar excesses.

The sole of Ahmed's foot was stuck firmly between her thighs, his toes rapidly clenching and unclenching which was producing the most exquisite stimulation for Louise's pussy and rocketing her into one of the most prolonged and intense orgasms she'd ever experienced.

'Oh God!' she moaned gruffly, as the bliss went on and on. She was dimly aware of Ahmed collapsing onto the sofa and removing his foot from her crotch, but that didn't stop the amazing waves of sheer ecstasy. She wallowed in them, forgetting everything in her self-abandon, until the tide began to diminish and she became more aware of her surroundings in general, and of Ahmed in particular.

Scrambling up beside him on the sofa Louise curled up with her head against his chest, pulling open the bottom of his shirt so that she could feel the warm, hairy flesh beneath. His arm encircled her and she could feel his breathing slowing, becoming more regular. A deep and drowsy satisfaction filled her veins.

Some time later she came to and realised that she must have dozed off. She was alone on the sofa, with a blanket draped over her, and there was the sound of running water in the bathroom. Sleepily she got up and rescued her clothes, which were strewn all around. She took them through into her room and got into her dressing gown. By then the sound of the shower had stopped and Ahmed was emerging.

Louise blushed as she remembered what they had done together. She had now gone through all the delights on offer at the *Seventh Veil* with Ahmed. Whether she could go through those same acts with a complete stranger only time would tell.

'Louise!' he smiled, his face lighting up as he saw her. 'You fell asleep.'

'I know.' She gave a yawn. 'Suppose I'd better get to bed.'

He came up and took her into his arms. 'I'd ask you to sleep with me, but I don't think either of us would get much rest tonight.'

She gave him a startled look. 'What about Gina?' she asked quietly.

'Oh, she wouldn't mind.'

'How can you be so sure?'

'Because we have an agreement. We're not bound to each other. We love each other, but that doesn't mean we can't have sex with other people.'

'Doesn't it?' Louise frowned in disbelief. She'd like to hear Gina's side of the story sometime. What they had just shared was undoubtedly a sexual experience, even if it had gone under the guise of 'vocational training'!

Ahmed seemed to read her thoughts. 'You don't have to worry about upsetting Gina. And I have to tell you that your technique is sensational! You can dance in my lap any time.'

Louise gave him a wry look and passed on into the bathroom. While she brushed her teeth she felt some of her former excitement return. Working at the *Seventh Veil* she had the opportunity not just to earn money through satisfying the clients, she could discover new urges of her own, and satisfy them too. Free to experiment with sex, she could explore her secret, inner world without shame. It was an intriguing prospect indeed!

Yet there was still a nagging voice that told her this was all too good to be true. Surely Gina would feel some degree of jealousy if she knew how her lover and half-sister had been behaving behind her back. It would be easy to pass it off as 'just practising' but in her heart Louise knew it had been much more than a mere rehearsal. After a while she had forgotten all about technique and followed her instincts. She had lost her detachment and become completely swept away by the feelings that had overwhelmed her. What they had taken part in that evening had not been a simulation but the real thing!

The next morning Louise stayed in bed until she

heard Ahmed go out, around ten, to get the Sunday papers. Then she dressed quickly and went out herself, going in the opposite direction from the newsagents. Try as she might to dismiss the episode with Ahmed as lightly as he appeared to have done, she couldn't help feeling horribly guilty. She would have felt quite differently if she'd been able to discuss it with her sister beforehand, or even performed for Ahmed in front of Gina, as she had before.

It was a pleasant morning and Louise took the Underground to Camden, where she and Martin used to browse around the market on a Sunday morning. She even recognised some of the stall-holders, but the familiarity was only superficial. The changes that had been wrought in her personality and lifestyle meant that she viewed the remnants of the past as if she were in a foreign land.

For a while she wondered about the old Louise: what had motivated her to stay in a loveless marriage for so long? Why had she been content to settle for less? However guilty she might feel about it now, the plain fact was that the sex she'd had last night with Ahmed had been fantastic. She felt her sexual education had only just begun, and the years she'd spent with Martin had been wasted ones as far as discovering her sensual potential was concerned.

Poor Martin. Going past the stall where they'd bought several knick-knacks for the house she indulged herself in sentimental regret for a few minutes. Then she pulled herself together. It was time to go back to the flat and discuss her future with Ahmed. She'd been staying there too long without paying rent. Either she should start paying her way, or she should move out.

And she also had to work out a regular schedule at the club. Now that her repertoire was enlarging she must decide which nights she would attend, which services she would offer, and what prices she could command. Fired by the thought that soon she was going to get her life in order, in a practical and financial sense at least, Louise strode out confidently towards the nearest Tube station.

Chapter Seven

THE WEEKEND IN Paris had been wonderful fun. David had taken Gina on a tour of the most disreputable night-clubs he could find, for a non-stop orgy of titillation. And she had been happy to continue on a more personal and private basis when they dragged themselves back to their luxurious hotel in the small hours.

But now she was glad to be home. As the chauffered Rolls dropped her off outside her apartment block Gina wondered what had been going on in there while she was away. Had Ahmed managed to seduce Louise yet? Maybe her sister was already feeling deliciously guilty, dreading her return and not knowing how to face her. She giggled at the idea. Poor Louise! She was so naive.

Louise was there alone. She'd washed her hair and was sitting in her drab towelling dressing-gown watching television. She started guiltily when Gina entered, making her suspect that something had, indeed, been going on. Smiling, Gina walked forward and gave her a kiss on the cheek. 'No, don't get up. I'll make some tea. Would you like some?'

'Er . . . no thanks.'

Louise looked edgy, her cheeks flushed. She glanced only briefly at her sister and then looked back at the screen. Gina walked into the kitchen, still smiling, made herself a drink then returned to the living-room. 'So, what have you been doing while I was away?' she asked.

'Doing?' Louise jumped like a scalded cat. 'Nothing. Nothing much, I mean.'

'Well, aren't you going to ask me if I had a good time in Paris?'

Louise flicked the remote to silence the set, then turned around. 'Of course, how rude of me!' Her tone grew warmer. 'What did you do? Where did you go?'

'Oh, we mostly explored the night life. Transvestite clubs, strip joints, sex shows. All the usual tourist sights!'

Louise giggled, but the strain was still there around her eyes. 'Were any of them like *Seventh Veil*?'

'One or two perhaps. Let's just say I picked up a few good ideas and inspirations. Where's Ahmed, by the way?'

Louise averted her gaze. 'I don't know. He had to go out. Said he'd be back by eight. He's not going to the club until ten, and he thought you might like to join him.'

'Did he go last night?'

'No, he didn't, as a matter of fact.'

'I thought perhaps he wouldn't. The pair of you had a night in then, did you?'

She saw the flush creep into Louise's pale cheeks again, proof positive that something had been going on between them. Gina sipped her tea thoughtfully. She would wait for her sister to tell her in her own good time. Because she definitely would, eventually.

'Ahmed kindly cooked me a meal,' Louise said. 'And we talked about my future in the club.'

'You did? What conclusion did you come to?'

The hazel-green eyes were looking straight into hers now. Behind the slight uncertainty Gina detected a new pride and optimism. 'He thinks I might be ready to try some lap dancing.'

'And what gave him that idea?'

Gina held her sister's gaze, willing her to tell her the truth. She knew Ahmed too well to believe that he'd simply had a conversation with Louise. She'd noticed the empty wine bottles in the kitchen, the dirty glasses. Most telling of all, she could sense a new defiance in the girl. It was written on her face as plain as day: yes, we did it, but what do you care, coming back from your dirty weekend in Paris?

She saw Louise take a deep breath. 'Well, we discussed it and he suggested that I might like to try.'

'Ah!'

She continued, very fast. 'So I did, and it was okay. He said . . . well he said my technique was fine and he thought I could manage to satisfy the clients. . .'

'Did you satisfy him?'

Louise looked scared. 'What?'

'Did you make Ahmed come when you wriggled in his lap? Or did it take a bit more than that to get him off?'

The scared look intensified. 'Gina, I didn't go to bed with him. . .'

Gina smiled. She was enjoying this. 'No, you

did it right here on the sofa, didn't you? What was it, a hand-job, a blow-job or did you, as we used to say, "Go all the way"? Come on, you can tell your big sister.'

Louise had her knickers in a twist now, all right. The look on her face was priceless. Gina knew she was being cruel, but she was so much enjoying seeing all that unnecessary guilt and suffering. One day they might share the joke. But for the moment she would savour the sense of power it gave her, this rare confrontation between her own free-loving lifestyle and the vestiges of her sister's moral code.

'Look, Gina, I'm really sorry. I'd had too much to drink last night and one thing led to another. But I didn't let him go all the way, honestly I didn't. It was only a blow-job.'

'Oh, that's all right then.' She's infused a note of irony into her voice, just for a tease.

Louise gave a rueful smile. Her blonde hair was almost dry and, fluffed up around her face, gave her an angelic look. 'I'm looking for somewhere else to stay. I think it's probably best if I moved out.'

'Why, because you got a bit carried away with Ahmed? Don't be ridiculous!'

'It's not just that. . .'

'Look, I know you can't afford a decent place yet. Why don't you build up your savings for a couple of months and then start flat-hunting? Besides, I like having you here. I'm in no hurry to get rid of you.'

Louise looked sheepish. 'I thought you would be, when you knew what had happened between me and Ahmed.'

'What, when I was having such a great

338

weekend with David? Look, Ahmed and I aren't possessive about each other, okay? We can't afford to be in our business.'

Suddenly Gina had a great idea. She gave a huge grin and plonked herself down on the sofa beside Louise, putting her arm around her shoulders. 'Hey, guess what? I'm going to give a party! Right here in the flat. We haven't had one for ages, and it will be fun to introduce you to some new people.'

She didn't mention her hidden agenda, which was to get Louise used to mixing with uninhibited types who were as happy in a threesome as in a couple, had affairs with both sexes, and who didn't mind what anyone else did as long as everyone was happy. Her sister had a few lessons to learn about the swinging scene before Gina could feel comfortable about her attending a Fetish Night at the club.

It would be fun planning another party at home. The club events were essentially business, with the clients paying for their privileges. This would be a chance to catch up with old friends and to experiment with new delights. Gina couldn't wait to tell Ahmed, sure that he would be as pleased as she was with the idea.

She told him about it on the way to work that night. 'I want Louise to meet more people, so I've decided to hold a party.'

Ahmed smiled. 'Good idea.'

'I gather you two have been getting better acquainted.'

'Of course. Wasn't that what you expected?'

'Absolutely. But you will treat her carefully, won't you? She's the only sister I've got.'

Ahmed kissed her. 'Don't worry, it was her

idea. Anyway, she enjoyed it as much as I did.'

'And you really believe she's ready to move on?'

'Yes. More to the point, she thinks so too. I'll tell Jules she's ready to give him a lap job tomorrow night. He'll enjoy that. When are you thinking of holding the party?'

'How about a week on Saturday?'

'Perfect. Now tell me what you did in Paris.'

Gina sat back in her seat and re-crossed her long legs. 'Well, the most thrilling moment was when we were at the *Boîte de Chatte*. They made what they called a *Cascade de Baisers*. It was a human pyramid – you know, like the 'Halifax' ads – but every row was kissing the row above in the most intimate places!'

'How on earth did they manage that?'

'They sat with their legs over each other's shoulders, boys and girls in alternate rows and each facing a different way. It was very ingenious!'

'I think that's a bit beyond us at the *Seventh Veil*.'

'Maybe, but it's given me an idea. . .'

For the rest of the journey Gina let her imagination run free. She was always the one to come up with the innovative ideas, while Ahmed thought of ways to put them into practice. It was the perfect patnership. On Sunday nights they often put on special shows, and Gina was always looking for new angles. The current *Showgirls*-style sexy ballet was wearing a bit thin.

All through the evening Gina kept taking time out to compile her guest list. The invitations would be designed by her arty friend Sara, who loved to draw erotic subjects. Gina's last party had been a great success and her friends were always asking her to give another. Well, she would surprise them all this time by introducing them to her kid sister!

First, though, Louise had to make some progress at the club. When Gina took her along on Monday night she sensed a new excitement bubbling away below the surface of those greeny-brown eyes. She wanted some tips about lap dancing, but Gina told her that she should follow her instincts.

'Just remember that the man's penis is your guiding star, so to speak. You should try to keep in contact with it at all times. And if he starts to lose his erection make sure you do something to get him excited again, even if it's only whispering dirty words in his ear.'

'Isn't it a bit messy when they come?'

'They don't always. Sometimes a client will want a lap dance to get him in the mood for a blow-job later. Or they might just want a bit of a tingle. But if they expect to come they generally wear a condom.'

Louise twisted a strand of her blonde hair absently around her finger. Her eyes were bright with anticipation. 'I think I'm going to enjoy this! Ahmed said that both Jules and Ali want me to dance in their laps tonight. Since I know them already I shan't be so nervous.'

'Some men are happy just to sit there and let you get on with it. Others want to touch you, but you should agree a fee in advance. Let Ahmed handle the money side for now.'

To Gina's surprise Louise suddenly gave her a

hug and a kiss. 'You're both being so good to me! I'm sure you don't treat all your new girls with kid gloves like this.'

'Maybe not quite so much. But we do like to make sure everyone settles in well. No point in having disgruntled girls working for us.'

For a while that evening Gina was too busy to take much notice of Louise. David turned up unexpectedly, wanting to be entertained in private. She was flattered that he'd come back to her so soon after their Paris jaunt and they spent an hour closeted in the Ladies. It was one of his little fetishes to enjoy making love on a toilet seat while other women urinated in the cubicle next door.

Returning to the club, Gina saw that Jules was already getting his lap dance and, from the look of him, enjoying it immensely. Louise was astride his thighs, her pert buttock's sliding back and forth to the tune of 'Future Love Paradise'. Every time one of her nipples neared his lips he would make a play for it, sometimes slyly catching it for a few seconds when she would pause and slide back from his lap with a reproving grin, telling him to behave himself.

Gina looked around the room and saw that at least half a dozen other clients were paying close attention to what was going on at table ten. She had a feeling that Lulu was going to be very popular – and very busy – over the next few weeks. Of course the novelty factor had to be taken into consideration, since every new girl caused a bit of a stir. But after a while things would settle down. She would have her quota of regulars, some passing trade, some new clients.

She would be doing some table and some lap dancing, and maybe, eventually, get to sleep with some of the clients she most fancied. But it would be a long time before she got to the stage Gina herself was at, where a client became more like an old friend and would take her on trips abroad with him.

Sighing as she recalled the long, winding road she'd taken to get where she was today, Gina went to join Ahmed. He grinned at her approach and nodded towards table ten. 'She seems to be the main attraction this evening!'

'Well she is managing rather well, don't you think? But then she's had expert tuition!'

They continued to watch in silence as Louise increased the speed of her movements. She was sweating now, red-faced, and clearly near to climaxing herself. Jules had his eyes open wide and his hands clenched tightly, staring intently at her firmly fleshed breasts. She held them together and, bending her head, licked down her exaggerated cleavage. Even from a distance Gina could see his thighs shuddering and hear her sister's gasps as she joined him in the ultimate ecstasy.

A spontaneous round of applause broke out amongst those who had been watching their progress. Gina gave Ahmed a wry grin. 'A veritable star in our midst!'

'I knew she would be,' Ahmed said quietly. 'From the first moment I saw her. There is one hell of a sensual woman, but she's not been given the opportunity to express it.'

'That stupid husband of hers!'

'Precisely. We shall just have to make sure she reaches her full potential now, won't we?'

343

Over the next few days Louise's burgeoning sexuality started having a subtle effect on Gina. It was as if, being half-sisters, they were sharing the experience in some measure. While it had all started with Louise learning from Gina, now the reverse seemed to be happening. Gina felt herself becoming almost innocent again, her senses re-awakening, and the old habits that she'd acquired over years of dedication to sexual gratification, her own and others', were now being cast off in favour of experimentation and discovery.

The most marked improvement was in her love-life with Ahmed. While Louise lay in the spare bed – perhaps dreaming of new pleasures, or pleasuring herself with one of her sister's toys – Gina found everything she did with her lover exquisitely fresh and exciting. They'd done a few drugs together, but this was different, better. Fresh and innocent as young love, the pair of them spent hours in simple positions and movements that once they would have scorned. And when she came Gina felt herself opening up more and more, attaining multi-orgasmic heights where each new peak of pleasure seemed to merge with the next. So that when the time came for the party she was at a level of sexual awareness such as she hadn't felt in years.

On the morning of the party she enlisted Louise's help to get the flat ready. She had bowls of condoms strategically placed, and her armoury of sex aids on display. There were videos for viewing in the bathroom, along with the massage oils. In addition she would throw open her wardrobes to anyone who fancied a spot of dressing-up, including, of course, Louise.

'Can I wear this?' Louise asked, holding up a long silky black dress. It was slit to the waist on both sides and had panels of sheer black chiffon over the breasts. Gina knew it would look fabulous on her sister. Probably even better than it did on her. She nodded, smiling wistfully.

While Ahmed slept, preparing himself for the rigours of the night, the two girls enjoyed getting ready together. After they'd showered, Gina washed and styled Louise's hair. She piled it up on her head and let just a few tendrils fall down about her face.

'It's good to start a party with your hair up,' she told her. 'Then you can look so much more debauched when you let it down!'

'Brilliant! I'd never have thought of that,' Louise grinned.

'Now for the dress. I suggest wearing just some black silk panties underneath and a matching suspender belt, with sheer black stockings.'

'I wasn't going to wear anything.'

'Some principle. Put them on so that some lucky person can take them off later.'

'Is there anything else I should do?'

'Apart from make-up, which I'll help you with in a while, you must choose your perfume carefully. Which one makes you feel most sexy?' Louise produced the bottle from her toilet bag. 'Good. Put it behind your knees, around your navel, between your breasts, inside your elbows and behind your ears. Then you'll float in a veil of perfume all night.'

While Louise put on her make-up base Gina got into her own party gear, a catsuit in paper-thin red latex that accentuated every curve and cleft of her body like cling film. The exciting part about her costume was the presence of camouflaged flaps that gave access to her erogenous zones at the flick of a finger. She painted her lips bright red and slicked gloss over them, then applied the smoky eye shadow and thick black mascara that she knew made her look like a siren.

'You look fantastic!' Louise declared, seeing her in the mirror as she lifted the mascara wand to her lashes.

'Thanks. No, let me do your eyes! They're going to look amazing. Trust me!'

Before Gina had finished the doorbell rang. 'Oh God, someone's early!' she moaned, rushing in to wake Ahmed. He had already showered and only needed to fling on his white pants and matching loose shirt to be presentable. While he answered the door Gina rushed back into the bedroom to put the finishing touches to Louise's make-up, straining to hear the voices of the guests as they came into the hall.

'Sounds like the Girl-Lees.'

'Who are they?' Louise asked. Thanks to clever shading her eyes looked a vivid green now without a trace of brown. Her cheeks were pink with excitement and her lips dewy and moist. I could fancy her myself, Gina thought.

'A bunch of Chinese transvestites from Soho. Cabaret act. They're all called Lee.'

She laughed to see Louise's pretty eyes almost pop out of their sockets. 'Oh, you'll see a lot of strange sights tonight!' she promised her.

The guests started arriving *en masse* soon afterwards and began helping themselves to drinks. Gina introduced Louise to a few people but soon she got caught up in the action and had

346

to leave her sister to fend for herself. She was challenged to play 'hunt the sausage' by an old cross-dressing friend of hers, and soon found out that he'd had the 'op'. A spot of foreplay with a vibrator followed.

Then a couple of lesbians invited her to join in their bathroom frolics. They all stripped and began sloshing soap and water around until their bodies were slimy and wet. They were joined by several other men and women, some of whom liked to watch and others who took part in what was rapidly developing into a free-for-all. People crawled in and out of the slithering mass of bodies at random, enjoying the sensation of being caught up in a kind of human slush pile. While they were groping and stroking and poking each other two people stood at the door with camcorders, filming it all.

Feeling ready for something new, Gina squeezed herself back into her catsuit and went back into the sitting room. The place was jam-packed with familiar bodies being very familiar with each other. She was soon grabbed by Charles, who loved to lift up her 'cat-flap' as he called it and taste her pussy. They lay sandwiched on the sofa between two couples who were engaged in some heavy petting, while on the floor Ahmed was giving head to a sexy black girl that their mutual friend Yvonne had brought along. Gina reached down just as Charles began to flick his tongue rapidly across her hot clitoris and toyed with Ahmed's erection for a few seconds before her own orgasm took her by surprise.

Afterwards she lay back, recovering, and surveyed the scene of debauchery in front of her.

While almost everyone in view was engaging in some more or less erotic activity she was quite startled to see one couple standing in the corner, drinks in hand, merely chatting as if at a conventional party. She was even more surprised when she realised that the girl was Louise. But who was she talking to? Squinting through the semi-darkness Gina finally identified him as Rick Morley. He was a one-time porn star and they'd once been in a low-budget skin flick togther. She couldn't even remember inviting him.

There were some loud groans at her feet. She looked down to see that Ahmed was having his balls sucked by a woman with huge breasts. Another woman was rolling a ribbed green condom down his erection. Well, he was having a good time anyway! She rose and wandered into the kitchen where good use was being made of her dips, but no one was bothering to use the corn chips.

'Gina! Wonderful party!' someone gushed in a drunken tone. Hands were placed over her eyes from behind and two giggling women began to search for a way into her private parts, while the man – she thought she recognised the voice of 'Dirty' Harry – started whispering obscenely wonderful suggestions into her ear. It wasn't long before her nipples and vulva were exposed and her three eager assailants proceeded to have their wicked way with her while a fourth plied her with with wine.

Several more orgasms later, Gina staggered from the kitchen back to the living-room and was amazed to see Louise still in conversation with 'Rick the Dick'. She managed to fight her way through to them and slapped her sister on her silk-clad rump. 'What are you doing standing here yacking like a couple of party-poopers?' She grinned. 'Hi, Rick! Made any good movies lately?'

'I've given it all up, Gina,' he replied gravely. God, he has gorgeous eyes too, she thought. I wish I could remember what we did together in that daft film.

'What did we do together in that daft film?' she asked him.

'Oh, the usual, I expect.' He smiled indulgently at her.

'It might have been usual for you, but it wasn't for me. Not at that time, anyway. I was only in it for the money. I expect you were too. I mean, it wasn't any fun was it, standing there starkers in some draughty room with me having to fluff up your erection when all I wanted was a decent cup of tea. . .'

Gina paused, aware that something was wrong. There was a definite atmosphere, but she couldn't quite make it out. Both Louise and Rick were standing there patiently, as if they were humouring her. Had she said something out of order? She mentally reviewed the conversation. Seemed pretty normal to her. Then she worked it out. She was excess baggage, not wanted on voyage, *persona non grata*. In short, she was playing gooseberry.

'Er, I've got to see a man about a condom,' she muttered, backing away. 'Have fun. Byeee!'

'Extraordinary,' she murmured as she slid through the crowd. Someone caught her round the waist and began kissing her passionately. 'Oh Dave, I never knew you cared!' she grinned when he let her get her breath back.

Dave was wearing his karate kit. 'Ever done it

349

in the Teh-Khwang position?' he enquired. She shook her head. 'Want to try? It confers great strength. Heaven below, thunder above.'

'Try Alka-Seltzer!' she giggled, and moved on.

Returning to the sofa, Gina sat down and Ahmed fetched her a glass of wine. He sat beside her and began to caress her right breast through the open flap. She sipped her wine contentedly, drinking in not only the alcohol but also all the sights, smells and sounds around her. She felt like a bubble of calm in a whirlpool of sexual activity. The Girl-Lees were giving blow-jobs to all comers; three lesbians were making love with frantic energy while someone filmed them; Angus was taking Pauline from the rear while she pleasured another woman with a dildo; Claudia was giving Sal a lesson in fellatio on a banana. . .

'Great idea!' Ahmed smiled, bending to kiss her exposed nipple. 'Another one of your successful society balls I think, Lady Gina.'

But as her eyes skimmed about the room, growing jaded at the sight of so much flesh, so much dissipation, so much blatant exhibitionism, Gina was suddenly shocked by encountering the most erotic sight of all. There, still in the corner and still talking, were the two people who were oozing the most sexual electricity in the room, despite the fact that they weren't touching at all. For a moment Gina felt infinitely sad, and terribly envious. In a split second of intuition she realised they were sharing something that no other couple at the party was experiencing: the lightning flash of an overwhelming attraction for each other.

But the next time she looked towards that corner they had gone.

Chapter Eight

LOUISE HAD BEEN feeling a bit like a wallflower at the party before Rick came along. The people that Gina had introduced her to wanted her to join them in a blindfold session in the bedroom but she hadn't felt ready for that. She'd wandered into the kitchen to get herself a drink and found two women doing disgusting things with the avocado and cream cheese dip, so she grabbed a glass of wine and went back into the living-room. It didn't take long for her to feel out of place there, too.

She just wasn't used to having sex with strangers in such a random way. It was one thing to be doing it in the club, where there were rules and people to enforce them, but quite another to join in some freaky orgy with people she didn't particularly fancy. Maybe she wasn't drunk enough. Louise finished her wine and started to head back to the kitchen for a refill. Before she could get there, however, Rick appeared.

'Would you like some more wine?' he smiled at her, his handsome face appearing like a beacon of light in the darkness. 'I was just going to get some myself.'

'Thanks, I'd love some.'

Their fingertips touched as he took her glass, sending a spasm of pleasure up her arm to her neck, from where it ricocheted down her spine. That was when she realised he was someone special. She awaited his return in a warm glow of anticipation. When his face loomed once more out of the steaming mass of bodies all around Louise felt her heart leap in her chest.

'There you go. Hope it's drinkable. Cheers!'

He had dark brown curly hair and startling blue eyes with long, sweeping lashes. His nose was straight and quite narrow, but his mouth was very generous. Louise couldn't take her eyes off his lips. They were broad and looked dewy soft, and he had a simply gorgeous smile. She wanted him to grin like an idiot at her forever, showing off those strong white teeth and filling his eyes with dancing light.

'My name's Rick,' he told her, and she murmured hers in return. 'Hi, Louise. Are you a friend of Gina's?'

For some unknown reason she didn't want to admit kinship. 'Sort of,' she smiled.

'And I'm sort of an ex-colleague. We did some filming together, quite a while back now.'

Knowing Gina, Louise had a pretty shrewd idea of what kind of film that would have been. But again she had the urge not to go into it. There was no way she could explain her reticence, except that she was feeling strangely protective of this fragile new friendship.

'What are you doing now?' she asked, somehow

sensing that was a safe question.

'Mostly modelling assignments.'

'I can see why!' Rick actually blushed! It endeared her to him even more. 'What have you done recently?'

'Well, I'm in *Arena* magazine next month. Modelling men's clothes.'

Instinctively she took note of what he was wearing: a pale blue sweatshirt that emphasised the strong curvature of his chest, loose-fitting linen trousers and the latest in trendy trainers. He held himself with the casual grace of someone used to displaying his body, and she began to wonder what he looked like under his clothes. A buzz of excitement travelled along her veins at the thought.

When Gina came up and began her brief, brash conversation with him Louise felt the warmth of their earlier contact slip away and a jealous coldness took its place. She tried not to give in to it, but she was terribly afraid that the spell might be broken.

So when her sister moved off again and Rick turned back to her with another of his dazzling smiles she felt greatly relieved. 'So you used to work with Gina. . .' she began, for want of anything else to say.

'Let's not talk about work, past or present, yours or mine,' Rick said firmly. 'What do you think of this wine? It's Californian. I was there just last month, drinking this very same tipple in a bar overlooking Fisherman's Wharf.'

They chatted on about places they'd visited, places they'd like to visit, and soon Louise felt as if she was talking to an old friend. Sometimes she became aware of what was going on around them and it seemed unreal, like a movie set. But mostly Rick held her attention one hundred per cent, his blue eyes searching hers with an acute sensitivity to her mood. He smiled often, irresistibly, and made her laugh too. Although she didn't give it much thought, Louise knew that the attraction between them went far more than skin deep.

At last he noticed her empty glass again. 'Would you like some more wine?' he asked, his voice so low that she had to lean towards him to hear it through the hubbub of voices, laughter and background music. She hesitated. Something in his tone suggested he might have an alternative in mind. 'Well. . .'

'I'm enjoying talking to you so much, Louise. But obviously this isn't the best place. Why don't we find somewhere quieter?'

'I don't think Gina thought about having a quiet room.'

'No, but I've got one. And it's only ten minutes' drive away. How about it?'

She understood that he was inviting her to his place, and knew what that might mean when they gave in to the physical imperative. But it was years since she'd felt such an overwhelming attraction to a man. Rick was drop-dead gorgeous, but he was sweet too, and funny, and warm. Best of all, he wanted to get to know her. It seemed too good to be true, but if it was only a beautiful dream she didn't want to let it go before she'd explored all the possibilities.

Louise followed him through the overheated crowd to the hall, where more couples were draped around in various conditions and positions. She took her jacket off the hook near the door and slipped it over her shoulders, then left the flat without a qualm. There had been no point in trying to tell Gina or Ahmed where she'd gone. They were both in the throes of some more or less mind-blowing experience and wouldn't take in what she said anyway.

Outside it was chilly and Rick put a protective arm around her as he led her to his car, a shiny silver BMW. 'I got this with the proceeds from my movie star days,' he said ironically, seeing her admiring the vehicle. 'This and the flat are all I have to show for it, but I'm far happier with what I'm doing now.'

Inside the car Louise felt her tensions drain away and a delicious, drowsy relaxation fill her limbs. Rick's vibrant presence, accentuated by a hint of some sultry cologne, was making her feel something more than mere arousal. She felt sexy too, of course, more than she cared to focus on. But there was also a feeling of cosy familiarity, similar to how she'd felt with Martin in the heyday of their marriage. How was that possible, after knowing someone barely half an hour?

As the car sped through the dark, deserted streets Louise stopped puzzling and just enjoyed it. She knew she didn't have to put on an act with Rick, didn't have to make smart comments or try to impress him. They talked about ordinary, mundane things, like their favourite biscuits or kids' TV programmes. In no time at all they were drawing up outside a large house in Chelsea made of dark red brick, its white front door covered with brass furnishings. 'I have the garden flat, otherwise known as the basement!' he grinned, leading the way down a flight of stone steps.

The flat was not as spacious as Gina's but Louise felt very at home there. Rick opened some wine and put on some music. After they had chatted for a while he suddenly said, 'You look wonderful in that dress, Louise. D'you know what I wanted to do with you at the party?'

She shook her head, fiery cheeks compounding her embarrassment. He smiled, taking her hand. 'I just meant it would have been nice to dance with you, that's all. Can we do it now?'

Rick raised her to her feet and pulled her into his arms, where she floated dizzily around the room. The music was a slow ballad and Louise rested her head on his shoulder while her legs entwined with his and their hips swayed in unison, taking her into a realm of quiet contentment. She was aware of the powerful masculinity of his body, of the sex energy that was dammed up in him waiting to explode, but for the moment she was happy to rock gently in his arms and await developments.

When the music ended they stopped dancing and tender fingers tilted up her chin. Louise held her breath as his mouth descended, touching hers so gently at first that the hairs stood up on the back of her neck. His palms were smoothing over her shoulders, and her nipples were brushing lightly against his chest through the thin material. She looked up into the naked flame in his sapphire eyes and a great shudder of desire went through her.

He must have felt it too. Suddenly his mouth

was pressing more firmly, his tongue between her lips, and his embrace tightened, squashing her breasts against him. He reached down and felt through the open sides of her skirt to her stockinged thighs. Nimble fingers released her suspenders and the stocking-tops slipped down, giving him access to her naked flesh. He groaned faintly as his fingers smoothed a path up her inner thigh and found the silken pouch that covered her sex, already moist with her secretions. Louise longed for him to go further, but instead his hand came up to her breast and held it, his thumb rotating on her stiff nipple beneath the veil of chiffon.

'Louise!' he murmured, his lips still on hers. 'I'm so hungry for you, but I think I'll get indigestion if I eat you all at once!'

She giggled, slipped her hand beneath his loose shirt to feel the warm skin of his back. 'And I think I'm going to collapse if we carry on like this standing up!'

To her surprise he lifted her right off her feet and carried her into the bedroom where he laid her down on his bed. It was dark in there, but he lit a lamp then sat on the bed looking down at her. 'You're very special to me,' he whispered. 'Don't ask me why. I just know.'

'I feel the same way,' she smiled, gazing into his eyes where the golden lamplight was mirrored within the deep blue of his gaze.

Louise stretched out her legs languidly, enjoying the chance to rest them. Carefully he removed her shoes and then began to massage her toes through her stockings. She sighed and leaned back against the pillow, transported into bliss. His capable hands moved up her shins to where her stocking tops lay rumpled, and slowly pulled them down over her knees and finally over her feet until her legs were bare.

'Silky dress, silkier skin,' he murmured, his lips kissing her thighs with titillating softness. Louise felt all kinds of desires coming to birth in her. She longed to explore his body, to feel his firm buttocks beneath her palms and caress the sinewed strength of his thighs. She wanted to know what his secret dimensions were, the size and shape that men set such store by. But she held all those urges at bay, not wanting to spoil things by grabbing too much too soon. Instead she took her cue from him, letting him set the pace. He had started a slow-burning fire in her that would continue till dawn if he let it.

Lazily his hands lifted the black silk panels of her skirt to reveal the dangling suspenders. His hands went beneath her bottom and found the hooks that secured the garment. She lifted her pelvis and allowed him to undo it, discard it, opening up her pubic area to view.

The tiny triangle that held her pussy now held his gaze. For several seconds Rick looked down at the scrap of black silk before covering it with her skirt again. Louise felt a pang of disappointment. She moved her thighs and the silk rustled insistently, but his hands were no longer there. Instead they had travelled up to her neck, stroking it softly as his lips returned to hers.

This kiss was different, more sensual. For a few seconds she tasted the buttery tang of the Chardonnay on his lips then his tongue slid into her mouth in a delicious foretaste of what she hoped was to come. Lovingly Rick began to explore the inner recesses of her mouth with the tip of his tongue, and at the same time he was stroking her body with the silk of her dress, moving it around her stomach, breasts and thighs. Louise gave a voluptuous sigh. Her mouth was full of sweet saliva, mingling with his. She ran her hands down his long, muscled back and found the tight mounds of his buttocks which she stroked appreciatively.

His kiss deepened, growing more passionate as Louise clenched his behind and moved her pelvis up in a yearning bid to make contact with his body. His thighs moved over hers, pinning her down, and she felt the weight of him pressing hard against her. His tongue probed more deeply along the length of hers. She moved her lips against his, sensing the new urgency that had risen within him and which she could easily match.

Soon his mouth was travelling away from hers to the soft column of her neck, making her squirm with ticklish delight. Rick had his hands on both breasts now, kneading them, making the already hard nipples crave the touch of his fingers, his lips. Louise grew impatient with her dress, wanting him to tear it off her, but still the barrier remained between them. Then one hand found its way into the opening at her waist and lightly caressed her stomach beneath the silk and travelled up her midriff to brush against the lower slope of her right breast. Louise's whole body felt taut and strained, her breathing suspended as she willed him to carry on up and touch her rigid, aching nipple.

But his fingers travelled back down to her belly again and there they stayed while he bent his head and grazed the rosy tip of her breast with his teeth through the chiffon. She sighed and he mouthed it eagerly, although the feel of the wet stuff against his lips must have been strange. It clung to her breast where his saliva dampened it, stuck to the contour of her nipple.

'You're lovely in this dress,' he repeated. 'I can hardly bear to take it off you.'

'And I can hardly bear to keep it on!'

They laughed at each other, full-throated and free, their faces throwing radiance back and forth. Louise felt utterly happy, completely centred on her own pleasure. She turned over onto her stomach and let him unzip her, but then he spent ages just stroking her back through the opening and sweeping his hand over the smoothness of her rump. One finger slipped down between her buttocks, taking her pants with it. They stayed at the top of her thighs while he moved back up to pull down the straps of her dress.

Louise lifted her torso and felt the top half of her dress being pulled down over her breasts to her waist. It finally bunched around her hips while he pressed her down again and began to stroke her back once more. This time his fingers crept around to the side of her breasts, flattened beneath her. She moaned as the delicate skin responded to his feather-like strokes. The slow heat between her thighs was intensifying, sending out warm flurries of desire that confused her brain and befuddled her senses. I want him, she thought, like I've never wanted anyone before.

And the great thing was, he seemed to desire her just as strongly. As soon as she turned over onto her back Rick was at her feet and kissing his way up her legs until he reached her pubic mound. His kisses there, over the silk, were slow and reverent and she thrust her mons at him eagerly. But he went on to lick around the hollow of her navel, excruciatingly ticklish, then moved on upwards. Louise gave a long, grateful sigh as he at last reached her naked breasts and took first one, then the other nipple between his lips, rolling them gently and darting his tongue in and out. She felt his teeth graze them softly and she arched her back as the keenest of thrills passed through her. Her hands went to the top of his head where she ruffled his dark curls, and then she began tracing the delicate curves of his ears with her nails.

'This is heaven!' she breathed.

'Almost!' Rick replied, looking up at her from the comfortable cushion of her breast with a cheeky grin.

He continued his sensual mouthing of her breasts until Louise could bear it no longer. She wanted him naked, wanted to see the whole of his body at once, but she was too shy to mention it. The roughness of his sweatshirt was brushing against her stomach and his trousers felt coarse against her smooth legs. He had taken off his shoes, but his socks were still on his feet. Beneath his clothes she could sense that his body was muscle-packed but lean, the body of a man who knew how to look after himself.

'Please, Rick. . .' she begged, hoping he would know what she meant. He drew back, sat up and gazed at her. His brows were very straight and dark, a frame for the piercing blueness of his eyes beneath.

Now they were lifted quizzically. 'Louise?'

She sensed how much he liked saying her name. 'Can't we take our clothes off now?'

'You want me to?' With a swift, easy gesture he stripped off the shirt and revealed his top half. Louise feasted her eyes on the broad expanse of chest with just a smattering of dark hair in the deep ravine between his pectorals. She took in the solidly developed arms, and the lean abdomen that led down to a slim waist. His skin was lightly tanned, and it gleamed with health and vitality.

'Oh Rick!' Louise put out a tentative hand and laid her palm against his chest. She had never seen a man so beautiful in the flesh. He held out his arms to her and she pressed her face to the warm, flat pillow of his torso. It was like sheltering against a friendly rock.

He stroked her cheek protectively as Louise nestled in his arms, feeling archetypically female and submissive. Not that he was trying to dominate her. But set against all that impressive brawn she couldn't help feeling small and vulnerable. The emotions that were welling up inside her were unfamiliar, coming from some primal level of consciousness that she'd never plumbed before. They brought with them an overwhelming desire to be taken by this man, to be penetrated to the very core of her being.

'All right, you win,' he smiled, pulling the dress right off her until she only had her panties left half on. His hands roved freely and rapidly about her body, making every nerve-ending beneath her skin tingle fiercely. Louise lifted her mouth to him and he kissed her, drinking deep of her saliva, their tongues performing a loving dance. Then she felt his hands go to the rolled-down scrap of silk about her loins and finally uncover her sex, the soft-centred heart of her desire for him – and the focus of his desire for her.

Louise closed her eyes as he bent his head towards the junction of her outspread thighs. Gentle fingers parted her labia and she felt his warm breath on her opened vulva, a delicious prelude to the touch of his mouth. The tip of his tongue probed between her outer lips and found the deep chasm which was already filling with her juices. She moaned as he dipped into it, his hands slowly caressing her inner thighs, and a flood of pure joy went through her.

The lapping tongue moved upwards, found her distended clitoris and began to lick it hard, making Louise cry out in rapt approval. She could feel his hands stroking her behind, and then a finger found its way right round into her open sex and pushed straight in, as far as it could go. Her hips bucked in a reflex urge towards him as he delved deeper inside, his tongue still flicking rapidly across her throbbing nub. She squeezed on his finger and her arousal heightened.

Louise was very near to a climax now, and it wouldn't take much to push her over the edge. What it took, in fact, was for Rick to move one hand up to her straining breast and tweak her nipple. There was a flash of electricity that went both up to her ears and down to her toes simultaneously, then she felt the first shuddering spasms ripple through her lower regions, gathering force and breaking over her like a tidal wave. She spiralled through a series of wild convulsions that left her breathless, her pussy hot and pulsating, her chest heaving. Again and again she felt the powerful torrent of pleasure course through her. Then the ecstatic cycle began to subside and she sank into a state of profound relief.

When she returned to consciousness she was lying in Rick's arms. He was still wearing his trousers and socks, she noted with some amusement. Seeing that her eyes had opened he kissed her forehead then drew gently away. 'You're wonderful, Louise,' he whispered. 'But I have to be up early tomorrow, for a photo shoot – more's the pity. So I'll sleep in the spare room, not to disturb you.'

'It's all right. . .' she began, but he had already got up from the bed.

'Sleep well!' he smiled, switching off the light.

Louise was far too tired to argue. Alone in the darkness she tried to make sense of what had happened to her that night, but soon succumbed to sleep.

When she awoke in an unfamiliar bed, she quickly scanned through her memory of the night before and was overwhelmed by happiness. Rick, where was he? Then she remembered. He'd had to leave early. A blanket of disappointment threatened to engulf her so she got straight out of bed and opened the blinds. The décor of the room was classy but understated, a tasteful setting for the bed which she now realised was antique, with a marquetry design on the headboard. Probably a family heirloom or something. There was a door leading from the bedroom into an en suite bathroom.

After showering, Louise felt better. She got into her dress, feeling quite incongruously clad for daytime, then went out into the hall. A door opposite led into a small but well appointed kitchen and there was a note for her on the pine table: *Louise – that name will be just a kiss away from my lips all day! Please find your taxi fare on the dresser. Will phone tonight. Ricky xxx*

She put on the kettle and made herself some tea, feeling like an interloper. There was evidence of Rick everywhere: in the letter addressed to him on the mantelpiece, in the half-eaten pot of yoghurt in the fridge, in the green rubber boots by the back door. Somehow she hadn't thought of him as a gardener and yet, when she looked through the kitchen window, the garden was ablaze with flowers and tubs of herbs on a small patio.

Then she went into the sitting room and saw the current copy of *Arena* on the coffee table. She couldn't resist flicking through it but it took her two goes to discover the advert with Rick in. He looked so different with his hair swept back in dark waves, his eyes half closed against the bright sunlight, wearing an oatmeal linen suit and navy shirt. She smiled down at his face and vowed to buy her own copy forthwith.

Much as she would have liked to linger there, discovering more of Rick's personality through his surroundings, Louise knew she must get back or Gina would be worrying about her. She phoned for a taxi and reluctantly took the money on the dresser shelf since she'd left her cash at home. Then she pulled her jacket on, doing up the buttons to conceal her breasts. Conflicting feelings were making her want to get away, to reflect on what had happened without the subtle influence of being in Rick's flat to sway her mind.

The cab driver gave Louise only a cursory glance before whisking her off to Holland Park. When she opened the door to the flat mayhem met her eyes. As well as the usual post-party debris there were people sprawled all over the hall. She tiptoed through to her room and found a couple fast asleep in her bed. Feeling increasingly annoyed, and wishing she'd stayed longer at Rick's, she peeped in at the sitting room. The Chinese transvestites were piled in a promiscuous heap of satins, black wigs and naked limbs.

Frowning, Louise returned to her room and rescued a pair of jeans and a T-shirt, together with some underwear and shoes, then went into the bathroom which was mercifully empty. The only room in the flat that was, she supposed sourly. She dressed herself in more suitable clothes, picked up her shoulder bag from behind the door in her bedroom and hurried out as discreetly as she had entered.

For several hours she walked around the Sunday morning streets, buying a newspaper and trying to read it in the park. But her thoughts kept drifting back to Rick like homing pigeons. She knew that what they had shared last night could end up being a one-night stand, the aftermath of a party where everyone was prepared to let their hair down and lose their inhibitions. Don't kid yourself that he feels the same as you do this morning, she warned herself. But his note had promised that she would remain uppermost in his mind all day. Was he just a Don Juan, getting a perverse kick out of pretending to have 'romantic' feelings when he had no intention of seeing her again?

Although they'd talked almost non-stop – until the kissing had begun, of course! – Louise realised that she knew very little about him. She knew where he lived, but she could never bring herself to turn up there uninvited. Maybe Gina could tell her more about him.

But a strange reluctance overtook her when she thought about telling her sister. Louise had an urge to keep her experiences with Rick to herself, at least for the time being. She didn't know why, exactly, but she feared that Gina might ridicule her if she confessed to being in love with him. For that was definitely how it felt. Could she trust such extravagant emotions, when she was still married to another man. The thought was sobering.

Yet why should her heart care if she were divorced or not? Her love for Martin had died years ago and this new love had come upon her unawares. She hadn't been looking for a new relationship, not consciously anyway. And after all, Rick had made all the running, inviting her to his flat and then kissing her so sweetly and making love to her with such controlled passion. Whatever he had been seeking last night it was not a cheap thrill for himself. If she had tender feelings for him, she could be certain they were reciprocated. So went her reasoning process, on and on, round and round, until she tired of her own confused logic. Time would be the arbiter of both their feelings, she decided. She would just have to be patient.

Returning to the flat around noon she found most of the guests gone and Ahmed making toast for the four hangers-on who remained in the kitchen.

'Ah, Louise! There you are,' he smiled. 'Where did you get to?'

'I just popped out for a paper,' she said. It was only a white lie, but she felt her cheeks colour a little as she said it.

'How about some coffee? Toast?'

'No thanks, I had some earlier. Is Gina still asleep?'

'In bed, not asleep. Here, take this tray into her, will you? I reckon she deserves a rest this morning.'

Amidst a chorus of 'hear-hears' Louise went through to the main bedroom. Gina smiled when she entered and sat up, plumping up the pillows behind her shoulders. 'There you are! Ooh, breakfast in bed. Come and sit down and tell me how you enjoyed the party.'

'Very much,' Louise smiled, taking her seat beside the bed.

Gina's eyes had a red-rimmed look. Her dark hair hung in tousled strands to her bare shoulders where a couple of love-bites were visible, and there was a general air of lassitude about her. She drank from her coffee cup thirstily. 'The last time I saw you Rick was with you, then you both vanished. What did you get up to, you naughty girl?'

Louise thought quickly. 'Nothing much. We

went outside for some air and walked for a while. He's very nice, isn't he? When I came back I was really tired so I found a quiet corner and went to sleep.'

'Really?' Gina was frowning at her. 'That doesn't sound like much fun. Didn't you get off with anyone?'

'I had a few flirtations!'

'Is that all?' Gina sounded more than disappointed. As if Louise had let her down.

'I found it a bit much, to tell you the truth. I've never been to anything like that before. You could hardly expect me to join in with gay abandon – or straight abandon, come to that!'

Gina stared at her thoughtfully for a few seconds, then nodded. 'Mm, I suppose you're right. It was a bit of an experiment as far as you were concerned. Ahmed was afraid you mightn't be up to it just yet. But that means our party nights at the club are probably not a good idea for you either.'

Louise had hardly thought about her work at the club since meeting Rick. Right now she felt less than enthusiastic about it, but presumably she would change her mind come Monday night. 'I'm sorry. . .'

'Don't be, it's okay.' Gina reached out and clasped her hand. 'You've done really well so far, Lou. But now you know what company I keep maybe it would be best if you looked for somewhere else to live before too long.'

Louise nodded, feeling unaccountably miserable. Suddenly her whole life had come under scrutiny once more and she didn't much like what she saw. Last night had changed things, perhaps irrevocably, and she felt as if she were in limbo, unable to go forwards or backwards. She couldn't wait for Rick to phone that evening. Just to hear his voice would be a tremendous relief. Until she did she couldn't be sure of anything any more.

But then a dreadful thought struck her. What if he didn't phone that evening? Or didn't get in touch with her at all? What if she never saw him again in her life?

Chapter Nine

GINA WASN'T ALTOGETHER surprised when Louise decided to do no more than table dancing at the club for the time being. She knew that inviting her sister to that party had been a tactical mistake. Even so, she was a bit worried about her. Louise was acting strangely, spending a lot of time alone in her room when she was in the flat, going out at all hours and sometimes staying away all night. When Gina had tried to ask her about it she'd been rebuffed.

'If you're seeing a client behind Ahmed's back, watch out!' she told her grimly.

Louise had insisted, 'Oh no, it's nothing like that. I've just been spending nights in my old house, sorting things out.'

Gina didn't believe her for one minute, but she didn't press it. Relations between them were cool these days, and she didn't want to make the situation any worse. But when Louise told her she was moving out and gave a fashionable Chelsea address her curiosity was aroused once more. 'Surely you can't afford to live there on your own.

Are you sharing, or what?'

'Yes, but my flatmate won't be there very often. It's perfect for me right now.'

Her tone was still distant and Gina decided not to pry. But she might just call round there on the off-chance sometime.

Right now, however, she had other matters to occupy her. Ahmed had hired a new girl at the club and he was showing more than just a professional interest in her. Gina had to admit the girl was exceptionally good-looking. Her name was Yasmin and she was half Indian and half English, with pale coffee-coloured skin, long black lustrous hair and grey eyes. All the men were mad about her, and when she danced the snaky undulation of her slim hips, the suggestive thrustings of her pelvis and tight little bottom, and the controlled flexing of her pert rounded breasts awakened unexpectedly strong lesbian longings in Gina herself.

For a while she acted as house mother to the girl, who had never done anything but dance in discos before. She didn't need much tuition, having a natural talent and sex appeal, but she did need help in handling the men. Gina had never seen anyone get so much unwanted attention, so she kept an eye on the proceedings to make sure the girl wasn't pestered.

One night she saw Ahmed shepherding Yasmin out of the club just after midnight. Her shift wasn't supposed to end till two, so Gina went up to see what was wrong. 'Are you feeling ill, darling?'

Yasmin turned her beautiful, sooty-fringed eyes towards her and giggled. Gina recognised that look of schoolgirlish wickedness and turned a strange mixture of hot and cold inside. 'Ahmed, where are you taking her?' she asked softly.

'Home. We need to work on a few routines.' He patted the girl's rump affectionately. 'This young lady has ambitions, and I mean to see that she achieves them!'

Gina felt her heart racing as she struggled to maintain her cool. 'Good. Well, I'll be home in an hour or so. See you both then.'

It was a well-worn code, that she and Ahmed had used a dozen or more times. Sometimes, when they met a particularly sexy woman at the club or at a party, they would take her home with the idea of making love in a threesome. Usually the girl in question knew exactly what she was letting herself in for, and was fully acquiescent from the word go.

This time, though, her lover frowned back at her. 'I'd be grateful if you'd stay to lock up tonight, Gina. And when you return, please don't disturb me. I expect I'll be quite exhausted.'

Yasmin gave a knowing smile, stoking the fire of Gina's fury even more. Ahmed simply wasn't playing the game. He wanted this lovely creature all to himself, and was deliberately excluding her. Well, she wouldn't give in that easily!

Although she remained at the club for another hour, Gina could barely control her anger. It wasn't just that she felt cheated of a few hours of sensual pleasure, satisfying as that would undoubtedly have been, but she couldn't stand the thought of Ahmed having Yasmin all to himself, instead of sharing her. The idea that she could be simply jealous took some time to develop, but when she faced it Gina was quite shocked. She had lived for so long with the idea that she and Ahmed had an open relationship, free from the possessive pettiness that other couples displayed. But there was no mistaking the gnawing pain inside, compounded of her frustrated longing and a poisonous envy.

Unable to stand it any longer Gina finally handed the keys over to Karl, promising him a bonus for staying the extra hour, and took a taxi home. She entered the flat as silently as possible, removed her shoes and tiptoed through the hall, listening for any sound that might give her a clue as to their whereabouts. It didn't take long to work out that they had already graduated to the bedroom.

Softly Gina turned the handle of the door which Ahmed, in his arrogance, hadn't bothered to lock. She peeped through the crack and saw the couple on the bed, gilded with subdued light from the bedside lamp. It made a pretty scene. Ahmed had music playing too, soft and low, and a scented candle filled the air with jasmine as a tribute to the girl. All to put Yasmin in the mood, Gina thought sourly. Not that she looked like she needed it.

Hatred threatened to engulf her as she stood at the door, spying on the couple that she'd previously hoped to join. She knew there was no point trying to barge in on their love-making. There had been a steely look in Ahmed's eye that told her, unequivocally, 'I'm having this one all to myself.' Instead she drew some small satisfaction from the fact that, unknown to them, they were being watched.

Yasmin had stripped to her panties and Ahmed was completely nude. They were lying side by side, the girl fondling his erection while he played with her breasts, tweaking the dark brown nipples to hard points. Gina sensed that they hadn't got to the main action yet. They must have been taking their time. Maybe she'd been practising her lap dancing on him, or giving him a blow-job. As she gazed intently at the couple she felt a hot surge of lust hit her groin, taking her by surprise. She pressed her fingers to her delta over the thin skirt she was wearing and felt her clitoris throb when she located it.

Rubbing herself gently, Gina watched Ahmed remove the girl's white pants and reveal her luxuriant black pussy. His fingers dabbled for a moment or two in the crevice beneath, smearing the juices first over her pubic hair and then her gently rounded stomach before he moved back to stimulate her nipples. Yasmin gave a loud sigh and bent her mouth to his glans, moving round to push her pussy into his face. Gina couldn't see him actually licking but she could tell from the look on the girl's face that she was enjoying it very much indeed.

Ahmed was enjoying it too, if the size of his prick was anything to go by. It reared up and thrust itself into the round red 'O' of Yasmin's mouth. Her plump breasts were pointing downwards and soon his hands had grasped them, kneading them and drawing out the hard nipples while he sucked her off, making her lovely beige butt wiggle with twofold satisfaction.

Suddenly Gina realised that she was missing a trick here. Reluctant though she was to interrupt, however temporarily, her voyeuristic thrill, she left the doorway and hurried back on stockinged feet into the living-room. There she opened a drawer as quietly as she could and found what she was looking for. With a cunning smile on her face she returned to her vantage point at the bedroom door.

She lifted the black box to her eye and pressed a button. The shutter slid open, its slight click masked by the gentle notes of music issuing from the other black box beside the bed. Gina pressed again and there was a brief flash, but Ahmed and Yasmin were too preoccupied with each other to notice. He was thrusting his distended organ in and out of her open mouth at great speed, and she was bucking her hips in a frantic effort to match his accelerating libido. Suddenly she sat right back on his face with a loud cry as the white spray fountained from his glans over her breasts and stomach. It hung there in glutinous pearls as she orgasmed over and over, her stomach muscles rippling and her breasts shaking.

Gina felt her own insides quiver in sympathetic response to the other woman's pleasure but beneath her erotic excitement there was still that jealous anger. She took another couple of photos then retreated from the door. Going back into the living-room she paced around for a while, trying to control her mounting frustration. What she felt like doing was filling a bucket of icy water and thowing it over the pair of them, like a couple of randy dogs. Yet she knew that would only provoke Ahmed to the point of throwing her out of both the flat and the club. Sometimes it irked her that she was still so dependent on him. She had plenty in the bank, but nowhere else to go. What on earth would she do if her job at *Seventh Veil* came to an end?

When she'd calmed down a little Gina reflected that she had, after all, gained some vicarious satisfaction from spying on them. Her clitoris was still hot and throbbing, her nipples stiff and tingling, and she could feel how wet and ready her vagina was. Maybe if Ahmed bundled Yasmin off in a taxi soon she could reap the benefit of all that stimulation and have a monster session with her lover. If he had any strength left, of course.

It was time to find out. Gina returned to the bedroom door, still armed with the camera. She smiled to see that they were still at it, this time with Yasmin on top. The girl was rising and falling to the slow, voluptuous beat of the music, grinding her mons against his as she hit the root of his shaft, then remaining poised for a few seconds as she hovered above his cock, her pussy-lips caressing the sensitive glans. Ahmed was groaning as his roving hands alternated between her rotund buttocks and equally globular breasts.

Once more Gina struggled to quash the fervent desire to join them. She fantasised about sitting behind Yasmin as if they were riding the same horse, her labia spread against those warm, smooth buttocks and her clitoris rubbing between them. Her hands would be cupping those firm breasts from behind, playing with the adorable nipples, and her lips would graze on the delicate skin of her neck. Ahmed would find it extremely arousing of course, and would soon come. Silly man, why couldn't he see how good it would be for him if they were a threesome?

But perhaps he was breaking her in gradually, Gina thought, deciding to wait a while before suggesting such a bold venture. The idea that such delights might be hers in future made her feel much better, and the wild urgency of her desire returned in force. Now she envisaged herself with his prick inside her, sucking the sweet fruit of Yasmin's pussy as she rode Ahmed to her own delicious destination. She took some more photos then put the camera on the floor so she could ease the sudden upsurge of her sexual appetite.

Gina pulled up her skirt and put her hand down the front of her panties. Her pubic hair felt damp, and her clitoris bulged out so that her fingertips found it easily. She let out an involuntary gasp as the sharp sweetness of her arousal flooded through her, but neither of the others seemed to hear a thing. Through heavy lids she glimpsed them. Her lover had now decided to assert himself and had swivelled round to plunge into Yasmin from above, his penis and swinging balls clearly visible between his outspread thighs as he performed. Beneath him Yasmin thrashed and moaned her way towards a second shattering climax, her head turning this way and that on the pillow in her desperate quest for fulfilment.

The sight was too much for Gina's overloaded sensory system and she began to come in a flurry of hot spasms that had her moaning and swaying, one arm supporting herself against the door jamb. When the feverish orgasm subsided it was all she could do to pick up the camera and crawl on her hands and knees into the sitting room. She put the camera back in the drawer then flopped, exhausted, onto the sofa and was soon lost to the world.

Some time later Gina awoke to silence. She got up and switched off the lamp in the sitting room then looked at the clock: almost three a.m. Feeling she had a perfect right to make her presence known now she walked into the hall and found the main bedroom door wide open. The bed was empty, and Yasmin's clothes had been removed. A surge of cold anger swept through her. Had the pair gone off into the night together, to continue their dalliance undisturbed?

Gina stripped off her clothes and fell into bed, too tired to bother about what Ahmed was doing right then. The next morning, however, she was surprised to be awakened by voices. It didn't take her long to discover that Yasmin was still in the flat. Annoyed, she pulled on her robe and went into the kitchen only to find the pair of them laughing and joking over coffee.

'Good morning,' Gina said frostily.

Ahmed gave her a smile and a peck on the cheek, but his eyes still had that coldness in them that she'd detected last night. 'Morning, Gina. Hope you don't mind Yasmin staying.'

Gina poured herself some coffee from the pot then retreated to the corner. 'Not at all.'

But she did mind. And, increasingly, she had the idea that there was some hidden agenda. She finished her breakfast without saying much, then went to shower. When she came out of the bathroom, Yasmin was gone. Ahmed was still in the kitchen drinking coffee, a thoughtful look on his face. 'I'd like to talk to you, Gina,' he said.

She felt her heart plummet. Something in the tone of his voice told her that he had a plan in mind, one that he expected her to object to. He came straight to the point. 'I've offered Yasmin the spare room. She's gone to get her things then she'll be coming back this afternoon.'

'What?'

Gina could hardly believe he'd done that without consulting her. Okay, so it was technically Ahmed's flat, but didn't she have some rights as a sitting tenant, at least?

The look on her face made him continue, swiftly. 'She's been given notice to quit and she has nowhere else to go. It will probably only be for a few weeks. But while she's here I want you to be nice to her, okay?'

Gina's first reaction was outrage. But there was still an over-optimistic part of her that refused to be silenced. 'I see. You want a *ménage à trois* for a while, is that it?'

But if she'd had any hopes of sharing Yasmin with him they were quickly dashed by the stubborn look on his face. 'Technically, I suppose so. But I meant what I said last night, Gina. I'm keeping Yasmin all to myself. Do you have a problem with that?'

She struggled to control her feelings, pausing to light her first cigarette of the day. 'I'm not sure, I mean, where will you sleep? If you and Yasmin intend to take over our bed. . .'

'No, don't worry. We'll use the spare bedroom. I've no intention of humiliating you or anything, Gina. It's just that . . . well, Yasmin is rather special to me, that's all. It's a long time since I've wanted a woman so much.'

'I see.'

Gina drew nervously on her cigarette, her mind racing. 'In other words, I'm no longer the number-one wife. Is that it?'

'Gina. . .'

He put out his hand to her but she could see in his eyes that it was so. That awful, empty rage took her over inside and she felt sickened. 'What if I don't cooperate? I get kicked out, I suppose.'

'There's no need to react like that. After all, I was willing to let your sister stay here. . .'

'That was different!'

'Have it your own way. I've told you what will happen, and that's that.' He rose from his stool, wiping the toast crumbs away from his mouth with a serviette. For some reason the gesture provoked her uncontrollably. She picked up a mug containing coffee dregs and flung the brown mess over him, then walked out. Hot waves of adrenalin were flooding through her veins as she grabbed her coat from the peg in the hall and left, slamming the door behind her.

Gina walked round and round the park with long, rapid strides for about ten minutes before she began to calm down. Rational thought was still lacking, however. Three bloody years, she kept telling herself. That's what I've given him, and how does he repay me? Trading me in for a younger model. What a sad fucking cliché!

Slowly the desire for vengeance grew in her, and a plot began to hatch. It even made her smile. If she was going to lose her lover, her home and her job in one fell swoop then she might as well go out with a bang. It was her own stupid fault for tying up every aspect of her life with Ahmed. But

381

there were other men out there, men who still found her attractive and desirable. She thought of David, with whom she'd had such a good time in Paris, and her mood lightened a little. But first she had some unfinished business to deal with. Walking with slow deliberation she turned back towards the Gothic-style house which now, looming through the dank mist of an autumn afternoon, looked to her more like a prison.

Louise stretched out in the luxurious bed and gave a long sigh of contentment. Rick had gone off early on a fashion shoot and she'd had a late night at the club, so it was good to be able to relax while the mellow autumn sun fell across the duvet in one big, golden swathe. She switched on the clock radio by the bed and some light, upbeat music filled the room. Today she would go to that Italian deli and buy the ingredients for a delicious pasta dish. She simply loved cooking for Rick. She loved doing anything for him. In fact, she simply loved Rick.

Although Louise still had her debt and divorce hanging over her she was at last on the road to recovery. Once her share of the mortgage arrears was paid she would stop working at *Seventh Veil* and find a more respectable job again. Rick had no idea what she did there. Or, if he did, he kept it to himself. She'd told him that she worked in an exclusive club, and he'd questioned her no further. Perhaps he'd rather not know.

She had also managed to conceal the fact that Gina was her sister. At some level Louise felt guilty about it, though she hadn't lied. When Rick had asked her to move in with him, after knowing her for less than a month, Louise knew that her life was about to take a totally new direction and she didn't want anything to spoil it. She'd already made one major break with the past and soon she would make another. Her destiny was linked with Rick's from now on.

Everything seemed perfect between Louise and her new lover. Their first dates had been wonderfully romantic – clubbing followed by midnight walks by the Thames, cinema visits followed by sexy suppers *à deux* – and always ended up with the most superb love-making. Now lying in bed, Louise was getting all hot and bothered just reminiscing. Her fingers trailed between her smooth thighs as she recalled their second session.

They had drunk quite a lot of wine that evening, and returned to Rick's flat eager to get their hands on each other. Louise started to tear the clothes off his back, but Rick gently stopped her and they'd taken things more slowly. When she was completely nude he ran her a frothy bath and washed her all over like a baby, arousing her gradually as he soaped her in all her intimate places. Then he had taken her through to the bedroom wrapped in a warm, soft towel and, very tenderly, unwrapped her like a birthday present.

Rick proceeded to consume her like a luscious fruit, his lips travelling all over her super-clean body and finally coming to rest between her thighs. His lips and tongue were expert in their caresses, knowing exactly how much pressure to apply and where, when to speed up and when to slow down, when to give all their attention to her pulsating clitoris and when to drink from the pool of her juices or dive deep into their source. After he had licked her to an exquisite climax she'd begged him to allow her to undress him, but he'd seemed strangely reluctant.

'What's the matter, Rick?' she asked him, ready to reassure him about his penis size if that was what was bothering him. It couldn't have mattered less to her.

As it turned out that was exactly what was bothering him, but not in the way Louise had expected. First he'd let her strip off his shirt to display his handsomely muscled torso once again. Then he'd undone his belt and fly and stepped out of his trousers. Her eyes had fallen automatically to the red Calvin Klein briefs and what she saw made her gasp. Beneath the cotton she could plainly detect the outline of a huge erection, far bigger than she'd anticipated.

He'd noted her surprise with a wry grin. 'Yes, I am rather . . . well endowed. It's a mixed blessing, though. Sometimes I think all women want me for is my big dick.'

'Is that why you didn't want me to see it straight away?'

He nodded, his blue eyes clouding a little. 'I was afraid the same might be true of you.'

Louise stared back at him incredulously. 'How on earth can you say that, after the way we've been together?' Her eyes had started to brim with tears. The thought that Rick might not trust their budding relationship as much as she did was too hurtful.

But he took her into his arms and kissed her forehead, smiling radiantly again. 'I was hoping you'd say something like that.'

'Silly!'

Louise tapped him playfully on the end of his nose and soon they were kissing again. This time she could feel his erection thrusting upward between their bodies, and her desire to become better acquainted with his penis grew to irresistible proportions. Slowly she slid down his body, her lips grazing his flat stomach, until she was squatting at his feet. Then she carefully lowered the pants over his mighty organ and took it between her palms.

It looked and felt like some exotic plant: a long, thick stem culminating in a pinkish-mauve bulb. Even the faint, delicious smell issuing from its glazed eye seemed vegetable rather than animal. Instinctively Louise leant forward and cradled it between her breasts. Rick closed his eyes and threw back his head with a moan as she bent her mouth and gave his glans an experimental lick. It was like sampling a hot ice-cream cone. She opened her lips wide until they encircled his helmet just above the ridge.

Although she managed to get about an inch of his shaft inside her mouth Louise found that stretched her to the limit. All her senses were on full alert as her tongue was flattened against the invading flesh. She could taste his bitter-sweet juices, smell his increasingly musky odours and feel the firm rigidity of his erection as it moved in and out off her lips at a cautious pace. Wondering how it would feel making similar progress into her pussy was an awe-inspiring thought, and a bit frightening. She was grateful to Rick for his gentle restraint and her desire for him intensified.

'Oh Louise, let me do something nice to you

too,' Rick pleaded, from far above her, his hands caressing her dark blonde hair.

They moved onto the bed and were soon embracing side by side, legs entwined and the thick staff of his penis pressing urgently against her belly. An overwhelming curiosity now seized her. Just what was it like to have such a huge member inside you? Already she imagined she could feel her vagina loosening and stretching to accommodate the giant penis, lubricating oils flowing free and making her vulva feel slick and welcoming. Rick's hands on her breasts were only increasing her hunger for him, filling her with cravings that only full penetration would satisfy.

Rick must have sensed her urgent longing because soon he produced a condom from beneath the pillow and began to roll it down his cock. Must be an extra large size, Louise thought as the latex stretched to its fullest extent, forming a second skin over the long shaft. He smiled up at her, his blue eyes sending her sweet signals of love and lust. 'It's probably best if you go on top,' he murmured. 'Then you can control the depth of thrust.'

Louise needed no encouragement to straddle him and place that shiny pink dome between her eager pussy-lips. She gasped as she felt the tip of it engage in her entrance but Rick made no move to push in further. He was letting her take the lead. She wriggled about for a bit, getting the feel of its warm strength against her soft and dewy vulva, taking the measure of it. She bore down on him experimentally and felt herself widen, opening up to him. Slowly she let herself rise and fall against his glans and each time it was a little easier to let him in. The best thing was the feel of his great shaft pressing against her clitoris as she moved.

'You have wonderful self-control,' she smiled down at him, her gaze lingering on the tanned and handsome contours of his face and chest.

'I've had to develop it. But with you it's harder than ever. You can't imagine how much I want to be inside you.'

'Oh yes I can!' she insisted with a smile.

The sensation of slowly easing him further in was exhilarating. Louise felt the soft tissues around her entrance stretch and give, allowing the huge shaft to slide in between her inner walls. She didn't have to contract her muscles to feel him. The massage that her G-spot was getting was fantastic, and already she could feel the blunt end of him nudging against her cervix. Louise kept the rest of his shaft at bay with her fingers while she slid gently up and down with sighs of bliss. It was heavenly.

Rick was getting off on it too, his breath coming in ragged bursts and his eyes glazed. She guessed it wouldn't take him long to come now and slowed down to make it last longer. He reached up and took her breasts into his hands, warming them. His thumbs began working her nipples up into hard, tingling studs and Louise knew that it would soon be her turn to reach that point of no return.

'Your pussy feels wonderful to my prick!' he grinned up at her.

The words almost triggered her right away, but she stopped moving and just waited a few seconds, relishing the feeling of being filled to maximum capacity. Every square inch of her internal skin was in glorious contact with firm, hot flesh and as she began to bear down on him once again the first shuddering hints of the pleasure to come rippled through her lower regions, making her gasp with renewed satisfaction.

'I think I'm about to come!' she murmured, squeezing his erect penis as hard as she could.

Instantly her orgasm strengthened, and the wild ripples that ran up and down the end of his shaft were enough to bring on his climax too. Making fierce animal noises, the pair of them wallowed in pure ecstasy together, firmly docked, and Louise began to feel as if something more than just a physical bonding was taking place. She seemed to be giving herself up to him, allowing their two consciousnesses to flow and merge until each knew what it was like to be inside the other.

When the spell faded, Louise lay snuggling up to his broad chest and knew that something wonderful had happened. A part of her was still fearful that it wouldn't last. After all, she'd known Rick such a short time. But she told herself that even if things didn't work out between them she wouldn't have missed the experience she'd just had for the world.

But things had gone from strength to strength since then. Louise sang gaily as she went about getting dressed and tidying up, looking forward to the meal she planned to cook before she left for the club that evening. She was so looking forward to the day when she would no longer have to work at *Seventh Veil*. Tired of saying no to the constant requests for lap dances and blow-jobs, she found it hard even whipping up the enthusiasm to perform a table dance these days. Fortunately she was no longer the 'new girl' since Yasmin had arrived. That took some of the heat off. The men were buzzing like flies around that honey pot, including, she'd been amused to notice, Ahmed. It was a good job Gina was not the jealous type.

Hard as it had been to tear herself away from Rick that evening, Louise arrived at the club on time. She was thinking about the brief session of love-making they'd managed to fit in when her lover returned from his photo shoot at seven, and her body was still hot and tingling with the after-effects. Maybe that would help her to dance better that evening. It was the sort of stimulus she needed these days.

After paying the taxi driver, Louise walked through the car park and into the back door of the building. She was about to enter the dressing-room when she noticed it was completely empty. That was odd: it should have been full of girls getting ready for the night's show. She went towards the swing doors that gave access to the main club room, and hesitated. There was a strange buzz of voices on the other side. None of this was normal, something was up. But what?

Warily she pushed the door and slipped through. A huddle of girls stood in the centre of the floor, some half dressed, staring at the walls with blank incomprehension or wide grins on their faces. Louise squinted at what they were looking at and gave a sudden gasp. All around the room were pinned poster-sized photographs of two people making love in various positions. At first she thought it was just some new idea for the décor – until she recognised the couple featured there: Ahmed and Yasmin!

Mystified, she rushed up to ask Janice, 'What's all this about?'

She shrugged. 'No one knows for sure. It was like this when we arrived. We don't know who put them there, or if it's meant as a joke or what.'

'If you ask me, it's no joke,' Sarah put in. 'I reckon someone wants to embarrass the pair of them. And I've a good idea who that might be!'

'What do you mean?' Louise asked, nagging doubts forming at the back of her mind.

'Look, if they've been put up maliciously we'd better start taking them down,' Janice said. 'Ahmed won't be pleased when he arrives. And neither, I should imagine, will Yasmin.'

'Too late!' Sarah muttered.

All eyes turned towards the swing doors, through which the man in question had just entered, closely followed by Gina.

Chapter Ten

GINA'S HEART WAS thudding loudly in her ears as she followed Ahmed in through the swing doors. She saw the other girls surveying her handiwork and her pulse rate speeded up even more, this time with annoyance. She hadn't counted on there being an audience for her little photo show. If only Ahmed had arrived at the club earlier!

But now everyone knew about his affair with Yasmin, evidence of which was blazoned over the walls in all its blatant glory. Not that anyone would care – except for the parties concerned, of course. She saw her lover turn ashen, his eyes contracted into steely points as he swung round and faced her. 'Is this your doing?' he snapped.

'What if it is? Don't you think it livens the place up a bit?'

Ahmed's hand flipped out at speed and caught Gina across the cheek. Her eyes smarted as the spot began to burn and she put her hand up to cover it. But worse than the physical pain was the disgrace. She had a brief glimpse of Louise's stricken face as she turned away. Ahmed had never struck her before.

'Bastard!' she muttered, making for the swing doors.

Behind her she heard him call out, 'Tear them all down, girls! I don't want to see a single scrap left on those walls when I come back into this room.'

Gina broke into a trot, desperate to get away from him, but as she reached the dressing-room door rough hands pushed her through and slammed the door behind them. Ahmed caught her wrist and twisted it painfully, making her cry out.

'What's the meaning of this?' he snapped. 'How dare you make a laughing-stock of me and poor Yasmin in front of the other girls!'

Fear had Gina gripped by the throat so she could hardly speak. She stared wildly at him, realising how far down the path of jealousy she had gone. But why? For three years she had accepted that he was free to screw whoever he chose, as indeed she was herself. Why had everything changed with Yasmin?

The same question seemed to be surfacing in Ahmed's mind as he stared into her face, searching for clues to her uncharacteristic behaviour.

'What the hell do you think you're doing, Gina?' he asked her, quietly now but in a more menacing tone. 'You're acting like a jealous cat. What's going on?'

She shook her head, near to tears. 'I don't know, really I don't. It's not like me, I know. But when you brought that girl back to the flat something seemed to snap in me.'

Ahmed's expression was still cold, but he had

loosened his grip on her. 'You spied on us and took photos. That I suppose I can understand. But to put them into the public domain, that is completely out of order. I'm only glad that Yasmin hasn't seen them, poor girl.'

'Where is she?'

'She wasn't feeling too good this evening so I told her to stay at home.'

Gina felt relieved. It was Ahmed she'd wanted to get at, not Yasmin. Even so she would probably get to hear of it. Suddenly she felt horribly ashamed of what she'd done. A sense of unreality took hold, as if she'd been in some altered state and suddenly returned to normal.

Then she remembered that Yasmin was going to be staying with them, indefinitely. Her old anger returned in a flash. 'I can't put up with her living with us for much longer,' she said.

Ahmed's eyes darkened again. 'In that case, you'll just have to move out.'

'*Me* move out?'

'Yes, you. I've promised Yasmin she can stay, and there's nowhere else for her to go. She's young and vulnerable, Gina. You can look after yourself.'

'I don't believe I'm hearing this! Three years I've been living with you, and now you're throwing me out without a qualm.'

'No, you can stay. As long as you are nice to Yasmin. Those are my conditions.'

'While you fuck her under my nose, is that it?'

'It's never bothered you before.'

Their argument was becoming circular. Again the weird sense of unreality had returned, together with the scary prospect that Gina could ruin her entire life in one fell swoop if she wasn't careful. She endeavoured to pull herself together. 'If I were to move out, you'd still let me work here at the club, wouldn't you?'

He gave her a strained smile. 'As long as you behaved yourself. The question in my mind now is how do we undo what's been done this evening. I think we need some kind of damage limitation exercise, don't you?'

Gina felt a sense of foreboding. She knew that look on Ahmed's face meant something. But what? She began to get out of her clothes and into her working togs. But Ahmed was still turning things over in his mind. When she had changed Gina lit a cigarette and sat opposite him, trying to appear unconcerned, but her pulse was racing.

'I know,' he said suddenly, his eyes brightening. 'Since your crime was public, your punishment shall be also. I shall see that you are thoroughly disciplined on Thursday night.'

Gina shuddered. Thursday night was Fetish and CP night. Up to now Gina had always been the one to administer chastisement, not receive it. She was well known as a dominatrix, and the clients queued up to be thrashed by her own fair hand. Ahmed could not possibly have devised a more humiliating punishment. Or, she grudgingly admitted, a more fitting one.

It was hard getting through the rest of the evening. The other girls were wary of being seen talking to her and she felt shunned by everyone, including Louise. Not that her sister had been over-friendly of late. Gina had found out, through the club grapevine, that her sister was living with Rick Morley and was angry that Louise hadn't told her directly. After all, she knew both of them. But when she'd tackled her about it all she'd got were pursed lips and shrugged shoulders.

Despite the frosty atmosphere in the club that night, Gina went through the motions with her regular clients but when the time came to go home she felt relieved. As she and Ahmed rode in silence through the streets of the capital, she couldn't help wondering how much longer she would be calling the Kensington flat 'home'.

During the next few days Ahmed did his best to keep her and Yasmin apart. Not that Gina had any desire to talk to the girl, but it was painfully obvious that he would not let the pair of them be alone for a minute. What was also plain, although less obvious, was that Gina had been subtly demoted from her position as his chief consort. Now it was Yasmin who joined him in the master bedroom while Gina had to make do with the spare bed. Yasmin also shared candlelit suppers with him, while she had to make do with a tray in what was now her room. Gina's charge card at her favourite department store was terminated, while Yasmin went on extravagant shopping sprees. Without having to say a word, Ahmed was making it clear that the process of degradation had already begun.

By Thursday night Gina was secretly in a state of trepidation. She tried her best to hide it, not wanting Ahmed to think that she feared him. But inside she was shaking. As she was getting ready to go to the club Ahmed entered the spare room where half her costumes were now stored in the small wardrobe. He went through them quickly, selecting what he wanted her to wear.

'I think this white silk and lace bra with the matching G-string,' he said, casually tossing them at her. Inwardly, Gina shuddered. The outfit offered no protection whatsoever to her buttocks, being little more than a thong around her waist and between her buttocks. Over it he wanted her to wear a black silk mini-dress with white apron and cap.

'The French maid's outfit?' she said, frowning. 'Isn't that just a bit too traditional for your taste, Ahmed?'

He merely smiled pleasantly at her, adding a frilly white suspender belt, sheer black stockings and black high-heeled shoes to the pile on the bed. Dutifully Gina put them on. No doubt he was planning some kind of playlet to entertain their clients. They wouldn't need a script. The ritual used a form of words that they had perfected over the years and each would take their cue from the other.

The Seventh Veil was packed that night and Gina had the uneasy suspicion that Ahmed had been spreading the word about her public penance. She knew the evening would be a test of her nerve and she was steeling herself to remain cool and in control. She couldn't see Yasmin but all the regular fetish girls were there, each distinguished by her costume. The submissives wore dog collars and chains, some with rings through their nipples; the rubber addicts sweated in latex catsuits; the bondage girls, some hooded, were confined in leather outfits with buckles and straps. It was a bizarre scene but, to Gina, a familiar one.

Less familiar was the skimpy costume she was

wearing herself. Normally she wore full dominatrix gear such as her tight-laced black rubber corset, Madonna-style bra with holes for her lipsticked nipples to point through, studded leather G-string and leggings or zippered lederhosen and, of course, her most vicious-heeled shoes. Her make-up would accentuate the image with black or scarlet lips and she would always ensure that her hair was elaborately styled, supplementing it with hairpieces where necessary.

Tonight, though, the tiny skirt and minuscule G-string left her feeling uncomfortably open and vulnerable. Her hair was drawn back in a simple French plait under the white cap and she was showing only a little cleavage in the square-necked dress. Ahmed nodded his approval as she mingled with the crowd, a tray of party canapés around her neck. The clients murmured compliments too, often in a knowing tone, and Gina was aware that the tension was mounting all around. The cabaret was due to start at eleven, and around that time everyone made sure they had a drink and a seat at one of the tables, preferably with a companion who shared their particular passion by their side.

As usual Ahmed took the stage to introduce the proceedings. He looked immaculate in his dinner jacket and Gina felt a faint stirring of the old attraction he'd had for her as she waited in a state of mixed trepidation and excitement for her cue. The first entertainment featured the 'pony girls' who trotted obediently around the small stage, tossing their long blonde manes before a riding mistress who flicked their rumps with her whip and made them go through their paces. They were followed by a masturbatory episode of foot fetishism, and then a performance by 'Nudini', self-styled 'Bondage Queen', whose act managed to combine escapology and strip-tease as she struggled out of a coiled mass of ropes and chains.

Gina knew her moment was coming when Ahmed took the stage again and help up his hand for silence. He put on his best MC manner and breathed into the microphone. 'Good evening, ladies and gentlemen. Tonight we have, as the climax of our show, something very special. As most of you know, for quite some time our premier pussy-cat here at the club has been the lovely Mistress Georgina. Take a bow, Mistress!'

He waved in her direction. Embarrassed, Gina rose from her seat and gave a mocking curtsey, which everyone applauded. Then Ahmed resumed his spiel. 'Well, from time to time Georgina has committed a few little peccadilloes. After all, she's not perfect. Who is? But I have to say that just recently our little pussy-cat used up her ninth life. Yes, she did. Which means that tonight she is going to have a little taste of her own medicine.'

The men started to whoop and cheer, causing Gina's heart to flip anxiously. It was all she could do to appear unconcerned. She picked up one of the titbits from the tray she had placed on the table and popped it into her mouth. It was like chewing on chalk.

'Georgina, would you come up here on stage please?'

She rose slowly, deliberately, smiling back at

the grinning faces all around as if the act had been well rehearsed and she knew exactly what was in store for her. Her progress towards the platform was laden with sexual emphasis as she swayed her hips and wiggled her bum. Ahmed held out his hand and pulled her up the two steps until she stood beside him, hands on hips, surveying the crowd with a knowing grin.

'Tonight, gentlemen, you will have a rare treat!' Ahmed promised, smiling suavely. 'You will see the Mistress of Correction well and truly corrected. Note that she is not wearing her usual costume, but one far more suited to her new submissive role.'

The men whooped again, and some of the girls had the temerity to cheer. Gina scowled at them, and Ahmed wagged his finger. 'Naughty, naughty! Now I want you to kneel before me, Gerorgie, and show how willing you are to subject yourself to discipline.'

Gritting her teeth, Gina did as she was told. The carpet had been removed and the wooden platform was hard under her knees. She was afraid of snagging her tights but she stayed there, head bowed, until he bade her rise again. Behind her she could hear someone moving furniture about. When she got to her feet she saw that the whipping frame had been brought on by two of the girls, and she began to tremble. Always, in the past, she had been the one to administer the whip or the cane but never before had she been subjected to the same treatment.

Strong hands seized her and led her over to the frame where she would be secured. The two girls wore only leather harnesses and tiny G-strings.

They stripped off her maid's uniform until she was in her underwear, then strapped her wrists and ankles to the frame. The bra was a half-cup and her breasts spilled out of it, allowing her rosy erect nipples to peep through the steel bars. Then they pushed the button which made the frame slowly revolve, turning round so that she was facing the audience and then presenting them with her almost naked *derrière*. The men cheered loudly, keyed up for the spectacle.

A fleeting thought went through Gina's mind as she rotated in suspense: thank God Louise isn't here! It was a relief that Yasmin was nowhere to be seen either. As long as her humiliation took place only in front of clients and fetish girls it wouldn't seem so bad. She waited patiently for Ahmed to finish addressing the audience and produce his whip or cane.

'If you're going to be pussy-whipped,' he was saying, 'then there is only one appropriate instrument: the cat o'nine tails!'

One of the girls brought the instrument to him on a red velvet cushion. He took it and brandished it, the nine thongs rearing from the stout leather handle like vicious snakes. When Gina glimpsed it she shuddered at the prospect of those cruel lashes biting into her defenceless flesh. The frame made one more revolution and there, stepping onto the stage, she caught sight of a figure that made her gasp. The girl wore a shiny black leather collar, gauntlets, a tight-laced corset, and leggings all studded and linked with silver chains. Her shoes were black patent, also laced and with very high heels. Although the girl's identity was concealed beneath a frilly black rubber mask, Gina knew in an instant who she was.

So this was to be Ahmed's final humiliation of her! The significance of choosing Yasmin to administer the whipping was not lost on Gina. He was spelling out, in no uncertain terms, what she had feared: that her heyday as his lover and partner was over, and a new star was about to take centre stage.

Yasmin walked towards him slowly, her hips swaying seductively. The wave of applause reached its height then died away, to be replaced by hushed expectancy. Gina caught a glimpse of her tormentress as she swung round on her heel, whip in hand, and began to walk towards the frame with her bright red lips curved into a smile. Gina felt herself breaking out into a sweat. Her pulse was racing and her mouth was dry, but there was nothing she could do about it. All she could hope for was that, when the time came, she would not lose her nerve.

The strains of 'Hard-Hearted Woman' could be heard as Yasmin took up her position on the small podium, from where she could easily lash out at the naked buttocks spread out on the metal bars. For a couple of revolutions Gina was in suspense, her wrists and ankles already beginning to chafe. But then she heard a cheer as the new dominatrix raised the black leather handle and prepared to strike. No sooner was her behind within reach than Yasmin struck. There was a staggered crack as all nine lashes hit the air and then the stinging points landed on her naked behind like pepper shot. Gina flinched involuntarily, clenching her buttocks against the pain.

As the crowd came into view again Gina could see the men staring at her lasciviously, taking in every second of her agony. She stopped focusing on them and gazed sightlessly into the crowd, willing her eyes not to let her down by watering. As the torture-scaffold continued to rotate, Gina braced herself for the second bout of lashes, tightening her buttocks and holding her breath so that when the blows rained down on her poor cheeks again she would not cry out.

To her relief the impact of the second strike was less severe since several of the thongs missed their target, the smarting only lasting for a few seconds before a dull hot ache took its place. Gina's glazed eyes skimmed the crowd and then it was time to steady herself for the third assault. This time the thongs caught her equally on both buttocks and she could feel every individual impact. Despite her self-control she winced, and the crowd caught sight of it as she came into view. Catcalls and whistles followed, only making her all the more determined to maintain her steely demeanour throughout the session.

'Three down, three to go!' she heard Ahmed say. 'I must say our pussy-cat is standing up well to her sentence. And Madame Yasmin is wielding her power superbly! Let us have a round of applause for the beautiful new star amongst our galaxy of glamorous *grandes dames*!'

When she heard those words Gina felt despair seize her. He was as good as announcing to all and sundry that Yasmin was taking over from her, that she was being demoted. She struggled to keep a check on her anger, telling herself that now was not the time to show how upset she was. The whipping frame turned again, the bright spotlight exposing her body in every detail to the scrutiny of the audience. She could not afford to give anything away. Her face was set in a controlled mask, her muscles tense and her breathing shallow. Three more strokes: how could she stand it?

By a supreme effort of will she managed to endure unflinching to the end, even though Ahmed urged Yasmin to thrash harder and, at the final turn, she obeyed, the rawhide searing into Gina's behind like branding irons. But with it came immense relief, the knowledge that she had survived and, in some small measure, that she had achieved a victory over Ahmed. If he had expected her to break down in tears, or cry out in pain, he had been disappointed.

The two girls came on to undo her bonds and a spontaneous round of applause broke out, which Gina acknowledged with a bow and a wry smile. She then turned to Yasmin, whose glittering eyes were just visible behind the mask, and gave her a sneering grin before hurrying from the stage and straight through the swing doors into the dressing-room. There, finding herself alone at last, she burst into tears.

After a few minutes she pulled herself together and lit a cigarette. She found some cold cream and smoothed it into her throbbing buttocks, wincing as her fingertips touched the inflamed flesh. Her whole being was in turmoil, but one thing she was sure of: she couldn't go back to the flat tonight. It would be too degrading. What Ahmed and Yasmin had done to her that evening had robbed her of every vestige of self-respect.

She picked up her bag and began to look for her purse to see if she had enough cash for a hotel room.

Then she saw her small leather address book and had a better idea. She flicked through until she found Louise's phone number. That girl owed her one. At least one. Staggering off to the pay phone, Gina felt her heart lighten a little. She put in her coin and dialled the number. There was a long wait but eventually someone came to the phone.

'Hi, Rick. This is Gina!' she said, trying to sound as normal as possible even though it was past midnight.

'Gina? What do you want? We were just going to bed.'

He sounded suspicious. She tried to placate him. 'I'm sorry. I wouldn't normally have rung you so late but I'm at the club and I need a place to stay tonight. Just for tonight.'

'Well I don't know what Louise will say. . .'

'Just ask her then, would you? Please?'

There was some conversation that Gina couldn't make out, then Louise came to the phone. 'Gina, what's the matter? Is anything wrong?'

She sounded so sweet and concerned that Gina felt the tears well up again, but she stifled them and said, 'I've had a bit of a rough time and I need somewhere to go tonight. Can I stay with you, please?'

'Of course. But can't you tell me what's wrong?'

'Later, maybe. I'll get a taxi, be with you in under an hour. See you!'

By the time she got to the flat Gina was feeling a lot better. Her behind was merely sore, instead of agonisingly tender, but more importantly her spirit had been soothed too. Rick had already gone to bed when Gina arrived. He had an early morning shoot, but Louise also hinted that he'd left the pair of them alone to have a chat. For that, at least, she was grateful.

'It's good of you to put me up like this,' she began, sinking gingerly into the soft leather sofa. 'I just couldn't face going back to the flat tonight.'

'Well, you put me up when I had nowhere to go, so I'm only returning the favour,' Louise said coolly. 'What happened tonight? Were you at the club?'

'Yes. Ahmed decided to punish me for what I did the other night.'

'What, putting up those photos, you mean? I thought you were really stupid to do that.'

'I know. I suppose I wasn't thinking straight. Anyway, he's had his revenge good and proper now.'

'What do you mean?'

'I think he's trying to get rid of me and put Yasmin in my place. I suppose I should have seen it coming. After all, I've had three years. That's a pretty good innings, don't you think?'

Louise frowned, her hazel eyes looking genuinely concerned. 'You mean he's kicked you out of the flat?'

'And the rest! I was wondering if I could stay here for a couple of nights.'

'I see.'

Louise was still frowning, sunk in thought, and Gina reckoned she could guess exactly what was

405

going through her mind. 'It's okay, I'm not planning to move in with you and Rick. I just need breathing space, that's all.'

'It's not that. It's just . . . well, he doesn't know you're my sister.'

'Ashamed of me, huh?'

'Not of you, no. But I want to stop working at the club. I've had enough of all that. I want to start over again.'

'And I don't fit with the new image, is that it?' Gina found a cigarette in her bag and lit it, inhaling deeply. 'Well, don't you worry your pretty head about me. Soon as I can find somewhere else to live I'll go. It's not as if I haven't got money in the bank.'

'I'm sorry, Gina. You look like you've had a hard night. Do you want a drink?'

Gina gratefully accepted a brandy. She didn't want to talk about her ordeal at the club that evening. It didn't seem necessary. Especially if Louise wasn't going to be there any more.

'Have you told Ahmed you're leaving?' she asked her.

'Not yet. Rick is going to try and get me some modelling work.'

'Hah!' Gina smirked at her sister through the haze of smoke she'd just blown out. 'Only modelling you're likely to get through that man is topless, or worse. Wise up, Louise. Don't let men rule your life. Get back in control.'

Louise stiffened. 'You don't know what you're talking about. Rick and I really care about each other.'

'Don't kid yourself, girl. The only thing you care about is his big dick.'

406

'What would you know about it?' Louise flared, her eyes green points of anger. 'I knew you'd be like this. That's why I didn't want to tell you at first. You're so damned cynical, Gina. But this time you're wrong. It's more than just physical between us. We love each other.'

'Oh, that little four-letter word again! I suppose Martin was just a flash in the pan and this is the real thing. Isn't that how it goes?'

Louise made a visible effort at self-control. 'Look, you're obviously in no mood for a proper chat and I'm tired. Bed's made up in the spare room. I'll see you in the morning. Night.'

Gina waved her glass at her and put her stockinged feet up on the sofa. She leaned her head back against a cushion and closed her eyes. The sounds of water running in the bathroom lasted for around a minute then she heard Louise entering the bedroom. To fuck Rick the Dick. Gina giggled, the brandy taking effect. She wondered if there were any of the old videos about, the ones she and Rick had made together. That would definitely give Louise something to think about!

Chapter Eleven

'I'M GIVING IN my notice at the club tonight,' Louise announced. Gina looked at her sister's determined face and sighed. When would the silly bitch ever learn? Even if she couldn't learn from her own mistakes, she now had her sister's example to go by.

They were washing up the breakfast things. The flat was quiet and the kitchen was filled with a mellow light that filtered down from the street. It seemed idyllic, but as she dried a china plate with a tea-cloth Gina felt some elder-sister responsibility to introduce a note of caution. 'Are you sure you're doing the right thing? I mean, you still owe money on the house, don't you? And you've only just moved in with this guy. Talk about on the rebound!'

Louise gave a starry-eyed smile. 'Rick says he'll take care of everything. I only owe about three thousand on the mortgage now. He says I can consider it a loan. Once the modelling assignments start coming in I'll be earning that much a month. Imagine, Gina!'

'Yeah! Imagining is about as near as you'll get. Look, sweetheart, you're forgetting one thing. Rick the Dick made his money out of hard porn films. He's got the equipment, as you're no doubt well aware by now. Do you really want to end up making sleazy movies?'

'Rick's put all that behind him now. The modelling he does is all very respectable. I've seen his photos. They're in *Arena*, *Vogue*, *Harpers & Queen*. I'm not saying I'll get such prestigious work. Not at the beginning, anyway. But he's going to introduce me to his agent on Monday morning, and. . .'

Gina held up a weary hand. 'Spare me the details, darling! Let's just say I'll believe it when I see it. But in my opinion you're a fool to trust a man with a track record like that after only knowing him a couple of weeks.'

Louise turned away, tight-lipped, and began stacking the plates in a wall cupboard. After a while she turned and said, 'Well what are you going to do, anyway? If Ahmed asks after you tonight, what shall I tell him?'

'Tell him I'll be back at work on Monday. I just needed a breather. He'll understand.'

'And what about somewhere to live?'

'I'm going flat-hunting straight away. Any shopping you need?'

Louise frowned. 'No thanks, I'll get my own. Look, I don't mind you being here, Gina. But I wish you wouldn't poke your nose into my business, okay?'

'Okay. I'll get my bag and be on my way then.'

The flat-hunting went better than Gina had expected. She found a couple of rooms quite near the club. The district wasn't too savoury but the flat itself was very pleasant, so she put down a deposit and arranged to move in on Monday. Already she'd decided that she would continue working for Ahmed, even though they would no longer be lovers. It might even work better if theirs was a purely business relationship. After all, it was the clients who mattered most at *Seventh Veil*, not the internal politics of the staff.

She wasn't worried that he would turn her down, either. For all his faults, Ahmed was a fair-minded man and he would consider that Thursday night's little spectacle had more than compensated for her earlier misdemeanour. Gina smiled as she thought of how she could turn her new place into a love-nest for her regulars. The landlord probably wouldn't find out, and if he did then she could afford to give him a sweetener on top of the rent. Ten years in the business had taught her how to handle these things.

Rather than get in the way back at Rick's place, Gina decided to eat out that night. She returned to Chelsea around eleven, entered the flat with the spare key Louise had given her, and found Rick there alone in front of the television, a bottle of wine at his elbow.

'Hi, Louise gone to work?' she smiled breezily, hoping to pre-empt any trouble.

He threw her a suspicious glance. 'Yes. She was wondering where you'd got to, as a matter of fact.'

'I thought it best to leave you two love-birds alone, so I ate out.' She flopped down into an armchair and kicked off her shoes. 'Mind if I have a glass of your wine?'

He rose and fetched another glass from the cabinet, pouring her a generous measure. She took it and smiled sweetly up at him. 'Quite like old times this, isn't it, Rick? Remember when we used to drink that Spanish plonk to keep our spirits up? Or, in your case, your pecker. I thought alcohol was supposed to have the opposite effect, but with you it always worked a treat. Cheers!'

His blue eyes cooled as they looked at her. 'All water under the bridge now, Gina.'

'So I gather. Little sister has been telling me you've gone legit, as they say.'

'*Sister?*' He started out of his chair, a deep furrow between his brows.

Gina laughed. 'You mean she's not told you yet? Ashamed of me, probably. She has no idea how far back you and I go. Or how far we went, come to that!'

'Sisters?' he repeated, bewildered. 'You mean to say you two are related?'

She sipped her wine. 'Half-sisters, actually. Same mother, different fathers. We lost touch when I left home at sixteen, but she came looking for me when she was in trouble. Now it's my turn. Well, that's what families are for, isn't it?'

'I can't believe this. You're so utterly different.'

'In appearance, maybe. But we're the same under the skin. We both have our mother's flighty temperament.'

'That's incredible. But now you mention it, I can see some resemblance. Something about the eyes. And your figures are not dissimilar.'

'Well, you'd know all about that, wouldn't you? Tell me, Rick, is she a good lay, my sister?'

'God, Gina, you're disgusting!'

411

'It's a reasonable enough question. When she first came to live with us Louise was practically a virgin. She'd been married for three years, but she was still naive and inexperienced. Ahmed had to break her in so she could perform at the club. You do know that's what she does, don't you?'

Rick gave her a disgusted look. 'You haven't changed, have you, Gina? If there's a chance to spread some poison, you'll take it. And in answer to your question, yes I do know what work she does. She hasn't told me in so many words, but I know the scene and I put two and two together. Anyway, it doesn't matter now because she won't be doing it any more after tonight. If I can put all that behind me, so can she.'

Gina drained her glass. The wine seemed to go straight to her head, making her woozy. Being with Rick was reminding her of old times. Times she had once wanted to forget, but which now had a certain rosy glow about them. After all, it had been fun for a while, hadn't it? *Wild About Willy* – wasn't that the name of the one they'd won the porn Oscar for? She held out her glass for more wine and Rick divided the remains of the bottle between them.

'Don't you ever think of the old days, Ricky?' she asked him with a smile.

He gave a reluctant grin. 'Sometimes.'

'Me too. All those dreadful films we churned out. At the time I never bothered to keep the free copies. Now I wish I had. After all, they showed me at my most youthful and sexy.'

'You're not looking so bad now.'

She smiled at the unexpected compliment, and a flicker of the old Rick showed in his blue eyes. Encouraged, she asked, 'I don't suppose you've got our masterpiece, have you? It would be great to see it again.'

'As a matter of fact I have.'

He stood up and walked over to a cupboard. Gina's eyes followed his neat behind across the room. In the loose tracksuit he was wearing she could see the outline of his buttocks, tight and firm as ever. Something fired inside her, setting her libido on slow burn. She watched him take two videos out and hold them up, showing her the covers.

'Oh, *Wild About Willy* – you have got it!'

He grinned. 'That was the crowning glory of both our careers, wasn't it? No plot, hardly any dialogue, but plenty of action.'

'Remember that tacky awards ceremony, where the MC got completely pissed and dropped the Oscar? Whatever became of the golden dildo, by the way? Don't tell me you've got that too!'

'No, Old Shorty got that. Used it as a doorstop, or so he said.'

'Shorty Klein! Now there's a name I haven't heard for years. Whatever became of him?'

'Last I heard he was publishing a fetish mag. Shall I put this thing on, or what?'

'Oh, yes please!' Gina giggled, settling on the rug in front of the television with her back to the sofa. Rick put the video in the slot and pressed the remote, then came back to sit on the sofa just behind her. She leaned back, wanting some physical contact, and her shoulder brushed his thigh. Tacky music filled the room and then the credits came up, making her giggle as she recalled the rest of the cast.

413

While the video progressed, showing her arrival at the 'Mr Muscle' contest where Rick was supposed to be the main contender, Gina felt her old warm feeling towards him reviving. He had been the favourite of her male leads, always professional in his approach and never failing to deliver the goods. They'd had lots of laughs, too. Now, as they watched the fruits of their efforts, the giggles returned in force.

'Oh God, do you remember the problems we had with my nipples in that scene?'

'You mean when Shorty wanted them flaccid?'

'Yes! I was supposed to play the innocent, and he wanted to show my nipples slowly getting aroused as I watched you going through your poses. Trouble was, it was so damn cold!'

'I seem to remember someone's hair dryer being called into service!'

'The lengths we went to!' Gina giggled at the unconscious innuendo. 'Well, the lengths *you* went to, anyway! You never had any trouble performing on cue, did you? Fast forward to the locker-room scene, Rick. I want to see you in action!'

They watched in silence as Rick emerged from the shower with just a towel around his waist and found Gina there, wanting his autograph. The camera zoomed in on the enormous bulge below the white towel, then cut to show Gina's eyes opening wide with sexual curiosity and her tongue flicking across her red lips. It was strange seeing it all again, after so long. As the towel was slowly drawn aside and the full extent of his erection was revealed, Gina felt an unmistakable twinge of desire and her pussy began to feel wet and open. She shifted position so that she could clench her thighs and ease the sudden throbbing of her clitoris.

The atmosphere in the room had subtly changed from one of jokey reminiscence to erotic tension. Gina didn't need to wonder whether Rick was feeling as aroused as she was. Over the time they'd worked together they had developed a kind of sixth sense that allowed them to tune into each other's feelings. She was amazed to find it still there. Even without looking at him she could sense the electric charge around him, knew that his massive hardness on screen was matched in real life, and an even more urgent pang of lust struck her, deep within.

Watching herself now on screen as she took his stiff member between her hands and knelt to kiss the rearing glans, Gina knew that what had made their acting special had been the spark of genuine attraction between them. She kept her eyes fixed on the television, fearing the consequences if she turned to look at Rick. The scene progressed to full-blown fellatio. Gina smiled to recall how she had trained to be able to take as much of that thick shaft into her mouth as possible. Practising first on a rolling pin, she had then asked Rick is she could rehearse with the real thing, which had led to a very satisfying session at her flat one Sunday afternoon. Was he remembering it too?

'You were always the best at sucking cock, Gina.'

His voice, thick with desire, startled her and she turned round to see Rick looking down at her, his eyes smouldering with the kind of lust you couldn't fake. She was seized by an overwhelming longing to see that prodigious prick once more, and it seemed to coincide with his equally compelling urge to show it to her. His hand was at his fly, unzipping it as his other hand reached out for her. At the touch of his fingers on the nape of her neck Gina shuddered, her whole body responding eagerly to this first green light.

At the back of her mind was a warning red light, but it was faint and easily ignored. Now fantasy and reality were merging indistinguishably as the action in the room mimicked that on screen. Almost without thinking, Gina found herself kneeling between Rick's open thighs, her lips and tongue exploring the well-remembered contours and musky taste of that wonderful organ. So familiar was the situation that Gina could almost hear the whirring of the camera, was half expecting to hear Shorty's voice call out, 'Cut! That's perfect, folks! Another red-hot blow-job in the can!'

Rick's hands reached down and pulled her shirt out of her waistband, making her shiver with anticipation. Still working her tongue around his glans, she feverishly undid the buttons and shrugged out of the sleeves. Then she unhooked her bra, levering the straps down over her arms until her breasts were completely bare. He gave a groan and seized them with both hands, squeezing the ample flesh and making Gina moan in response. The video proceeded unobserved as they gravitated onto the floor, where they soon managed to strip each other of the rest of their clothing.

Lying on the rug, Gina spread her thighs wide for Rick to perform cunnilingus on her. 'You were always the best at this, too,' she told him throatily, as his tongue unerringly found her clitoris and began to give her the kind of stimulation she most appreciated. She could feel the wild surges her libido was making as the years melted away and once again they were Rick the Dick and Queen Gina, undisputed superstars of the porn movie world. When his tongue began to probe her sex and she felt herself on the verge of coming, Gina also felt a renewed pride in her own achievement. It was no wonder that she'd been the best in her day. She'd never had to fake an orgasm in her life.

It had been a quiet night at the club for once, and Louise was thankful for it. Knowing that she had to face Ahmed after hours and tell him she was quitting had put a dampener on her performances. So when only three requests for a table dance came, and she spent more time than usual dancing on stage, the loss of income was more than compensated for by her relief that she didn't have to go through the motions.

She also had more time to observe what was going on around her. With Gina absent it was obvious that Ahmed was grooming Yasmin to be a star performer. He was introducing her to some of the wealthier clients and she was putting on a sexy act for all of them, wiggling her tight butt and thrusting out her small but well-shaped boobs. Soon she would be progressing beyond lap dancing and into the private stuff, no doubt ending up entertaining selected clients at Ahmed's flat. In every way she was taking over from Gina, so how long would her sister stand for being out-ranked?

Not long, she suspected. But with her looks and experience Gina was well able to look after herself. Maybe she would set up on her own as a dominatrix, or find work in another exclusive West End club. Well, she was welcome to it. Although Louise had found the world of exotic dancing an exciting alternative to office work, the glamour had begun to pall and now she couldn't wait to give it up. Especially now she had Rick. Whatever else she felt about her sister, Louise would always be grateful to her for throwing that party!

By the time she came off stage at the end of the night, Louise was dreaming of a new future with the man of her dreams. She must have had a special glow about her because Ahmed stopped her in the corridor with a grin. 'You're looking pleased with yourself,' he commented.

'Oh Ahmed, I wanted a private word with you, please.'

'Okay, step into the office. I'll be with you shortly.'

While she waited Louise felt nervous. She couldn't help thinking of Gina's reaction when she'd told her she was stopping work. Was she in for another lecture, this time from Ahmed? Well, it was none of their business, she told herself defiantly. They knew nothing of the love between her and Rick. She trusted her lover implicitly, and she wouldn't let her optimism be dampened by anyone, least of all anyone who had an axe to grind.

But when Ahmed appeared and she blurted out that she wanted to give in her notice, he said, 'Well I'm not surprised. You're not really cut out for this work, are you, Louise? I could tell from the start. Once you'd got over the novelty value it became hard work. And then when you stopped doing lap dances I knew it wouldn't be long before you gave it up altogether.'

'You don't mind, then?'

He shrugged. 'No one's indispensable.'

Including Gina, she thought wryly. With a bright smile she said, 'That's all right then. How much notice do I have to give?'

'As a matter of fact I interviewed a new girl only yesterday. She's very keen but I told her I had no vacancies at present. If she's still available, she can have your job and you needn't come back. I'll phone you tomorrow.'

A wave of pure relief swept over her. She hadn't realised how much she was dreading having to carry on at the club. Ahmed was right, she'd never been cut out for it, not really.

As she rose to leave, he said with a smile, 'You and Gina are like chalk and cheese, aren't you? But you'll both do okay, in your different ways. The one thing you've got in common is guts. Good luck!'

Louise felt quite fond of him as she shook his hand. But something told her their paths were unlikely to cross in future.

As her taxi sped back across London, Louise was looking forward to being with Rick again. Hopefully Gina would have gone to bed, but she knew Rick would wait up for her. He always did, even when he had an early call. They'd probably sip some wine together, then start kissing and cuddling on the sofa until the urge to make love became too strong. Then they would hurry to get ready for bed, to share the passion she'd been looking forward to all day.

On weekends it was different. They often stayed in bed for hours on end, surfacing only to grab some fast food and keep up their energy for love-making. Louise hoped her sister had found a flat of her own by now. With any luck she'd be moving out tomorrow, leaving the place to her and Rick again. Not that she begrudged Gina a bed for the night. It was just that her cynical attitude to love was beginning to get her down.

Louise could hear the TV playing as she entered. It sounded like a steamy late-night movie. Good, that would have got Rick into the mood. Not that he needed any incentive! She took off her jacket and put down her bag then opened the sitting room door. Rick was nowhere to be seen, but over the back of the sofa she could just see the television screen. Forget mere 'steamy' – this movie was positively pornographic!

She stared at the image on the screen. A dark-haired naked woman was kneeling with her back to the viewer, her tongue snaking up the shaft of an enormous penis. It's as big as Rick's, Louise thought. The actress moved in between his thighs and took the organ between her breasts. The camera moved in too, giving a shot of the man's cock cradled in her cleavage, then it panned up his tanned, muscular torso and came to rest on his face for a few seconds. Although his eyes were closed in an expression of rapt concentration, Louise recognised him at once. But what was Rick doing, running his old porn videos?

Both fascinated and repelled, Louise stared at

the screen where the woman now had her head bent right over Rick's penis and was licking it enthusiastically while she rubbed her breasts up and down the shaft. Suddenly she looked up and winked at the camera. A shock ricocheted through Louise's body as she recognised her sister's face.

So this was what they used to do together! No wonder Gina had taken a sceptical attitude when it came to Rick settling down in a steady relationship. She'd known him in the days when he'd been prepared to have sex with anyone, and probably not just in front of the camera. But he had finished with the past and was starting a new life. Louise was confident that she would be a major part of that life too, wouldn't she?

Suddenly she realised that the moaning sounds she could hear were not coming from the screen. Louise stepped forward and rounded the end of the sofa, then stopped in her tracks with a horrified gasp. There, sprawled on the rug, were the naked bodies of Rick and Gina in the sixty-nine position, their enthusiasm for the task rivalling that of their screen performances as they licked and sucked each other towards a climax.

'No!' Louise yelled, seizing the first thing that she could find and throwing it at the pair. The cushion bounced harmlessly off Rick's rump but served its purpose of alerting them to her presence. Rick scrambled hastily to his feet, his handsome face a study in tortured consternation, while Gina continued to lie there on the rug with a sneering smile on her face. Right then, Louise didn't know which one of them she hated more.

'You bitch! You bastard!' she yelled, turning to

run from the room. All she knew was that she wanted to get away from that hateful scene of double betrayal.

But she didn't make it to the door. Rick's strong arms caught her in their embrace and, although she kicked and struggled wildly, held her firmly until she had calmed down.

'Louise, please forgive me!' he pleaded. 'We got carried away watching our old video. It doesn't mean a thing, honestly!'

'It means I can't trust you, either of you!' she snapped.

'Look, if we'd intended to deceive you would we have done it right here on the floor when you were due to return any minute?'

Louise was stunned for a few seconds, but she soon recovered. 'The fact is you *were* doing it. And if I hadn't come in right then. . .'

'Then the chances are that we'd have come to our senses and stopped. Honestly, Lou, it's the truth. We've both been drinking, and. . .'

'Ha, good old alcohol! The time-honoured excuse for behaving like a bastard. So you were both drunk. Well that's all right then, we'll forget all about it. Hope you don't have too bad a head in the morning!'

Seizing her chance, Louise stalked from the room and hurried into the bedroom. She shut and locked the door, wanting no more to do with either of them that night. Sobbing bitterly into the pillow, she ignored the urgent rapping at the door and, when everything at last went quiet, took off her clothes and crept beneath the duvet, feeling wretched. Confusion reigned inside her head as she replayed the images of her sister and her lover, images that merged with those of the video to make a vivid, true-life scenario that tormented her. Gina had warned her that love with Rick wouldn't last, but then she had been the very one to ruin it. Just what was going on? Had her sister acted out of jealousy?

It was hard to come to any other conclusion, but whatever Gina's motives Louise couldn't excuse Rick. He was the one who had hurt her most. She knew what her sister was like, knew how jealous of Yasmin she'd become and how she'd tried to take revenge on Ahmed. It was even possible to understand how she'd become the woman she was, given the kind of life she'd led since she left home. But Rick had seemed different. She'd taken his declarations and promises deeply to heart, believing him to be a reformed character. What an idiot she'd been!

Although her tears had subsided they had left an ache in her heart, and an emptiness in her soul. It was all over betwen her and Rick. She would have to move out, and she would still have her debt but no means of paying it off. Her divorce was coming up soon – how ironic! Her prospects, that had seemed so bright just a short while ago, had suddenly been reduced to nil. Wearily Louise turned on the pillow, *his* pillow, she reminded herself bitterly. She'd sold almost all her possessions in a futile attempt to make a small dent in her debt. Now she had nothing left to lose but her pride, and some good that would do her!

Eventually Louise drifted into a fitful sleep. In the morning she woke with a dull sense of foreboding and then remembered everything, triggering more tears. After an hour or so of self-pity she made it to the bathroom and splashed her red, puffy eyes with cold water then went into the kitchen, desperate for a black coffee. Today she would have to sort her life out, find somewhere to stay, see if Ahmed would take her back just for a few weeks until she found another job. The way she felt now she'd be prepared to do anything for the clients just to get enough money for a deposit on a flat.

When Gina came into the kitchen wearing her black silk robe Louise picked up her coffee mug and sprang to her feet, intending to leave. But her sister gave her a rueful smile.

'Wait, Lou. I think you and I should have a little chat, don't you?'

'Like hell I do! What makes you so sure I want to talk to you?'

'Because you're in an almighty mess and you've no one else to turn to, that's why. Now just listen for a few minutes, will you? I'm not used to apologising or explaining, so don't give me a hard time, okay?'

Louise sat down again and slumped over her coffee. She wouldn't look at Gina while she was talking but stared sulkily at the pine table top. One night Rick had made love to her on that table, while she was preparing a meal for him. She angrily quashed the memory and began to listen, despite herself, to what her sister had to say.

'What Rick told you last night wasn't quite true,' Gina began hesitantly. 'We didn't just get carried away, and we weren't all that drunk. At least, I wasn't. I made a deliberate play for Rick, led him on. It was me who asked him to put the video on in the first place, and once I saw that he was getting turned on I took advantage of him.'

'Why? To get at me?'

Louise met Gina's eyes. They looked sad and world-weary. Was it possible she could be genuinely sorry for what she'd done? Well, it was too late now.

'Actually I thought I'd be teaching you a lesson. I see now that was stupid of me. I wanted to show you that any man could give in to temptation, be unfaithful. Especially one who had lived the kind of lifestyle that Rick had. But I've been thinking about it since. . .'

'When, last night, while you were in bed with him, you mean?' Louise regretted her bitter outburst when she saw the look on her sister's face.

'I spent the night on the couch. Anyway, I realised that what you and Rick had was something I've never had, and I suppose I was jealous. It's not just physical between you and him, is it? When you threw that cushion at him and he looked up, I saw how stricken he was, how terrified that he'd ruined the one thing that really mattered to him. And I felt terrible too. I felt about the same as when I broke Mum's vase.'

'What?'

'Oh, you don't remember, I suppose. But it was why I finally left home. She had this precious vase, some kind of antique. We were having a screaming match and I broke it. The look on her face horrified me. I felt she wished I'd never been born, she hated me for coming into the world and spoiling her life. And I couldn't stand that feeling, so I just got up and left. The one thing in my life I regret is that I never went back to tell her I was sorry.'

There was silence. Louise stared at her sister, tears starting in her eyes. She rose slowly and went to give her a hug. The hurt inside her was still there, but for the moment it seemed less acute.

'Anyway,' Gina smiled up at her through tear-washed eyes. 'At least I can say I'm sorry to you. And I really mean it.'

Chapter Twelve

TRY AS SHE might, Louise couldn't forgive Rick for what he'd done. What Gina had said about men was proving horribly true. She'd been through the drink and debt scene with Martin, now she was going through the infidelity scene with Rick. Presumably next time came the violence. It was enough to put you off sex altogether. Maybe she should try women.

The trouble was she ached for him still, like an addict suffering withdrawal. Gina had gone to her new flat leaving the pair of them alone, but there was an atmosphere you could cut with a knife. Louise mostly kept out of his way and when their paths did cross she met every overture of his with a stony stare or, if absolutely necessary, a curt reply.

Ahmed rang to tell her that the other girl had taken her job and would be starting on Monday. Louise hadn't had the nerve to plead with him to take her back. Instead she went off on Monday morning to the Job Centre, pretending that she'd come straight from her old job at Newbolt's. The little matter of her P45 could be sorted out later.

When a temporary job at an estate agent's came in she jumped at it. Maybe they'd help her find a flat, too. She couldn't bear living with Rick any longer than was necessary.

Then he had to go away on a three-day shoot. Although part of her was relieved, once he'd gone Louise missed him terribly. Despite the fact that they'd hardly been speaking lately she had still grown used to seeing Rick about the place, and she still derived a sneaky pleasure from looking at his great body. Unbeknown to him she'd been through all his portfolios, drooling over the sexy images. If only the inner man had matched up to the outer one, she'd told herself with a sigh. Still, you couldn't have everything. Obviously Rick was a good bet for a one-night stand, but she'd made the fatal mistake of falling in love with him. End of story.

The job in the estate agent's was boring as hell, but at least it was only for two weeks. Louise found it hard adjusting at first. She kept wondering what her colleagues would say if they knew about her not-so-distant past. Then it occurred to her that the same was probably true of Rick. When he posed for those suave *Vogue* and *Arena* shots, did the ghost of Rick the Dick ever rear its ugly head? The thought seemed to bring her closer to him. Not that it made any difference. He was still out of bounds to her, both physically and emotionally.

That evening there was nothing to interest her on the TV so she began browsing through his video collection. Inevitably, after all the *Die Hards* and the *Rockys* she came across his own porn videos. They had names like *Good and Hard* and *Rocks Off!* and if they weren't in plain wrappers the covers bore pictures of impossibly pneumatic women and muscle-bound men. She flipped through them idly.

Then she found one with such an alluring picture of Rick on the front that she was instantly seduced. He was wearing nothing but jeans with the zipper half down, and his thumbs were in his belt. He had a gorgeous tan and his chest and hair were wet, as if he'd just been in the sea. Behind him was a beach scene, with Baywatch-style babes gazing adoringly at him. Louise slotted it into the player and pressed the remote. The same picture came up on the screen along with the title: *Adonis on Paradise Beach.*

Louise settled back on the rug and let the video run. She was soon mesmerised by the images of Rick bathing nude in a rock pool, being chased by nubile mermaids all over the beach and then dragged protesting into a cave where they each had their wicked way with him. As she watched the girls performing acts of fellatio on him, rubbing themselves with his penis and allowing him to tongue their pussies, Louise could feel herself becoming unbearably hot and randy. It was days since she and Rick had made love, and in the intervening period she'd felt too miserable to think of pleasuring herself. But now her libido had returned with a vengeance and she could hardly wait to satisfy it.

While the video presented her with yet more tantalising pictures of Rick *in flagrante delicto*, Louise started to pull off her tights. She could feel the dampness at her crotch and knew that she was already horny as hell. Just because she was through with men didn't mean she'd stopped being a sexual being, she reminded herself ruefully. Time for a spot of totally safe sex, without risk of disease, complications or heartbreak!

Her nipples were practically bursting through the cups of her bra by the time she pulled the lacy trimming down and got to them. She groaned with relief as she felt the hot little buds between her fingertips, but soon the throbbing in her crotch became equally unbearable and she put one hand down the front of her pants to feel the hard nub at the top of her pussy.

Through bleary eyes she gazed at the TV screen, where Rick was sucking the full breasts of some buxom redhead while he stroked her furry bush. Louise thought she knew exactly how the woman felt. The memories of all her nights with him returned to torment her, making her arousal seem more painful than pleasurable. Helplessly she called his name out loud, over and over, trying to ease the aching void within her soul as well as the fevered needs of her body. If only he were there with her now, in the flesh, not just a flickering image on the screen!

Then, somewhere in the back of her mind, she registered the familiar click of the front door as a key turned in the lock. Her hand froze, and her heart seemed to suspend its pulsing beat as she listened hard, intent on ascertaining whether her ears had played her false or not. Was it just wishful thinking that had conjured up the sound of someone entering the flat? A shiver ran down her spine as she heard the door open and close. There was a heavy tread and then the door of the room was opened.

'Louise? Are you still up?'

It *was* Rick! What was he doing back so soon? One thing was obvious: he couldn't see her from the door because she was on the floor in front of the sofa. The irony of it almost made her burst out laughing. Hastily she pulled up her jeans and pulled down her top, clicked the remote to obliterate the video and put her head up above the sofa. 'My God, you scared me! I thought you were an intruder.'

'I'm sorry. I tried to phone but it was either engaged or off the hook.'

Louise went to check. It hadn't been put back on its cradle properly. That was her fault. She'd called Gina earlier in the evening when she was feeling lonely, but there had been no reply. When she turned back to Rick she was blushing guiltily, not because of the trouble with the phone but for what she'd been doing when he came in. Her crotch still felt overheated and tingly. She made an effort to appear normal. 'What happened to the photo session?'

'The camea crew were in a road accident. Nothing too serious, but two of the lads had to stay in hospital for observation so Joe cancelled the shoot.'

'I see.'

Louise felt ridiculously awkward. The semi-silence of the past few days had been broken, but she still didn't know what to say to him. Her embarrassment deepened as he noticed the empty video case on the floor by the TV. A slow grin brightened up his face, making him look irresistibly boyish. 'So! No need to ask what you've been up to while I was away!'

He picked up the box, looking quizzically at the picture on the front. 'Adonis, huh? What happened to that guy? Wasn't he torn to pieces by jealous women or something?'

Louise trawled her memory. 'Killed by a wild boar, I think.'

'Oh. Well if I had the choice of being massacred by a gang of women who hated me, or killed by one single woman who loved me, I know which I'd prefer.'

His impossibly blue eyes were searching hers now, holding them with their dazzling radiance. Louise felt herself melt in the smouldering heat of his gaze, that was searing its way into her soul, purging her of all her fear and despair until only a deep, desperate longing for their previous closeness remained.

Rick came to sit on the floor beside her, his long legs in front of him. He sighed and stretched. It had been a stressful day for him. Louise fought the urge to offer him something to eat or drink, as she'd once have done. Instead she took the video out of the machine and replaced it first in its box, then in the cupboard. 'Well, I think I'll go to bed now then.'

She turned to the door but he leapt to his feet. 'Louise! Please don't go yet. I want to talk.'

Although she had stopped in her tracks her body was tense all over. She said nothing but just stood there in turmoil, like a potential suicide on the ledge. 'Talk' sounded so innocuous, but in her present state it could lead to other things, things she wasn't sure she wanted. Then she felt the firm touch of his hands on her shoulders and her heart sank. If he made any more moves towards her she was lost.

Gently he turned her round to face him. Louise tried to avoid his eyes but it was impossible. They drew hers irresistibly, with the blinding light of their candour.

'What happened between me and Gina was a stupid mistake. It was wrong of me. But it meant absolutely nothing. I want you to know that.'

'It might have meant nothing to you. To me it meant that I could never trust you.'

'I know, and I'm terribly sorry. If I could turn the clock back I would. But it was just. . .' He sighed, struggling to express himself. 'It was like a kind of reflex, you know? She wanted me to put that video on, and then it was so easy to slip back into the old ways.'

'But that's just the point. How could I be sure you wouldn't slip back into those "old ways" again?'

Rick led her to the sofa and they sat down side by side, but Louise couldn't relax. She sat there primly, as if she was being interviewed. Yet all the time her body was crying out for him in silent agony, wanting so desperately to be in his arms instead of an arm's length away.

'I don't know,' he admitted miserably. 'All I know is I've lost the most precious thing in my life through being stupid and careless. I had dreams for us, Lou. And now they're all shattered. And I'm shattered too.'

She knew how he felt, but a stubborn voice kept insisting that it was all his fault. He was the one who had spoilt it all, not her. Yet Gina was to blame too. Not just for seducing him, but also for putting doubts in her sister's mind. Louise asked herself if she would have reacted quite as strongly if those doubts and fears hadn't already been there.

'I don't know what to say,' she sighed. He reached out and took her hand. A flood of warmth went through her, breaking down her reserve. 'I feel sh . . . shattered too.'

Helplessly she let the tears flow and let herself be taken into his embrace where she gave full vent to her feelings. She soon realised that she was crying for complex reasons. Not just for herself, but for Rick and Gina too. They'd all, in their different ways, sold out on love. Gina had come to believe she would never have it; Rick believed that he'd had it and lost it; Louise knew that what once was sweet could so easily turn sour.

With the heat of his body enveloping her, Louise slowly felt her heart begin to melt. She hugged him close, wanting him so much, and the fears began to recede. His lips found the soft skin of her neck and deposited tiny kisses there that made her spine tingle. Deep inside she felt herself opening up to him again. It was a fragile truce, but it was a start.

Rick's mouth moved up and onto hers, parting her lips with his tongue until they were in full contact, their mouths engaged in lush and sensual kissing. The last dregs of Louise's bitter defensiveness leached away, leaving her willingly vulnerable to his advances. She clung to him in passionate abandon, letting his hands stroke her wherever they wanted, and soon she wanted to caress him too. She undid a button and slipped her hand through his shirt to find the smooth, honed flesh beneath.

'Oh Lou, I love you. Really I do!' His lips breathed into her ear, then returned to hers, letting her bask in the glow of his love. Their kiss

434

deepened, and then she felt his lips slide from hers to graze on pastures new.

Nudging its way beneath her top, his mouth travelled up to the warm divide between her breasts and made her groan with delight as his tongue probed down the sensitive cleft. She could feel her breasts straining against the bra cups, and put her hands behind her back to unhook the garment. Rick's lips moved to her nipples and a fountain of pure pleasure seemed to spurt up inside her, making her pussy feel liquid. The need inside her was compelling, and to her amazement she suddenly heard herself say, 'Please, Rick, kiss my pussy for me!'

Obediently he stripped off her jeans and panties, his eyes gleaming with anticipation as he stared briefly at her naked mons. She opened her legs for him and saw his gaze take on a new dimension of joy and wonder. But then, as he bent his head to do her bidding, Louise realised that something wonderful had indeed happened. She had asked a man to pleasure her, told him exactly what she wanted doing, and he had obeyed without question.

It was the first time this had happened to her. With Martin she had never dreamed of asking, only passively accepted what he did to her. Even while she was working at the club and revelling in the new sense of power it gave her, she had not known this unique satisfaction. Rick wanted to please her, wanted her to be happy, simply because he loved her. The knowledge came as a revelation.

'Rick, would you stroke me with your fingers there too?' she asked, experimenting with her new-found licence.

His tongue continued to flick across her clitoris while his finger played around her entrance, teasing her by entering a little way and then retreating, making her more and more hot for him. He put two fingers into her, then three. She thought about his penis entering her and shuddered hungrily. But perhaps it would be good to wait a while. Her pussy was wet and fully open, but she wanted to explore his body before she went any further.

Eagerly she swivelled round into the sixty-nine position, felt for the hard, thick erection and took it between her palms. It increased even more as she began to caress it with soft, sensitive fingers, revelling in its solid dimensions and the velvety texture of the skin.

'It's all yours to play with,' she heard Rick say huskily. Louise bent her head to lick across the domed tip. It leapt in her hands like a wild creature and she felt an answering flutter in her core that made her want him all the more. This time she didn't want to be on top. She wanted Rick to possess her utterly, to fill her with a surfeit of flesh so that she was utterly satiated, complete. Oh, how she ached for him!

Tenderly Louise held the rampant organ between her breasts, relishing the way it thrust into her cleavage, her lips and tongue tasting the salty sweetness that was beginning to issue from his glans. Rick was still paying homage to her pussy, preparing her with his lips, tongue and fingertips, gently stretching and softening the delicate tissues of her vagina to accommodate the length and girth of his organ. Soon she felt wide open, her slick entrance able to take his bunched fingers easily. She moaned out her desire and he groped for the condom in the pocket of his discarded jeans, then positioned himself to enter her.

With a deep sigh, Louise felt his glans slip between her labia and enter her. She pushed against him, hungry to feel him inside her, but he held back so that she wouldn't have too much of him too soon. Slowly he eased himself into her, triggering the most exquisite sensations as her desire for the most intimate embrace of all was gradually realised. Her vaginal walls caressed the thick shaft as it progressed further and further in and she could feel herself yielding to him, letting him penetrate her more deeply until his glans was lodged right up against her cervix and every inch of her was satisfyingly filled.

Rick began to move back and forth, sliding his shaft against her inner surfaces with infinite gentleness and giving her clitoris a good rubbing in the process. She sighed and leant back, her breasts thrusting upward, and soon felt his soft lips against her yearning nipples. His tongue savoured them, sucking and licking, until they swelled and firmed up even harder than before. The pulsating currents whirled from her breasts down to her stomach and on to link up with her clitoris, turning her body into one escalating circuit of desire that felt like it would overload if she didn't climax soon.

'Oh, Louise!' Rick moaned as his own relentless drive gathered pace.

Louise could feel the heat of him enveloping her like a tropical noon, and his raw, sexy aroma reached her nostrils, fuelling her arousal. She tightened her thighs to feel the thick root of his shaft moving back and forth, his balls slapping rhythmically, and she cried out in ecstasy at the sudden onset of her orgasm. Again and again her vagina seized his penis in a fierce embrace until she was aware of Rick shuddering and gasping, joining her in an ecstatic consummation that was utterly fulfilling.

For a while afterwards he lay in her, like a great ship docked in harbour, and Louise derived a bittersweet pleasure from their closeness. She'd got what she wanted: one last act of love with Rick. Whatever happened she would never regret it. But as the minutes ticked silently away and the afterglow faded, all the old insecurities started to return.

It was on this very rug, Louise reminded herself, that he and Gina had been making love just a couple of nights before. Well, he was a great lay, she had to give him that. But that was all he was, all he could ever be to her. She'd been foolish to imagine that their relationship was based on anything more than sexual attraction. Rick would always attract other women, and what man could help but respond when the most desirable women in the world – beautiful models, sexy film stars – would be throwing themselves at him on a daily basis. Louise had already seen that he hadn't the will to resist.

Then, quite suddenly, his voice came in her ear, interrupting her reverie.

'You know Louise, sex with you is wonderful. But it's not enough.'

'Oh!'

She was stunned. Did he have to rub it in quite

so cruelly? Anger drove her to her feet. She picked up her clothes and turned from him, cheeks burning, then dashed from the room. All she wanted now was to be alone, to recover from the latest humiliation as best she could.

Once inside the spare room Louise slammed the door behind her, threw her clothes on the chair and flung herself face down on the bed where she proceeded to sob her heart out. So loudly was she weeping that it came as a complete surprise, a few seconds later, to feel Rick's arms around her, pulling her close in an embrace so strong that she found it impossible to escape. To make matters worse, his blue eyes were sparkling with glee and his mouth formed a wide grin. 'You silly, silly girl!' he murmured, kissing each of her dewy eyelids in turn.

'Stop being so patronising!'

'I'm sorry, but you just don't understand!'

He loosened his grip on her and put his arm around her shoulders instead, drawing her close. Miserably Louise sat hunched against the broad expanse of his chest. The trouble was, she understood too well!

'When I said sex wasn't enough I meant that you're more important to me than just a good lay. Look at me, Louise please!'

Reluctantly she turned her head. His eyes were pleading with her to hear him out. And behind their mute appeal was an expression that she found quite irresistible: the sweet and sensual look of total adoration.

'When I say I love you, those aren't just empty words,' he continued. 'I want all of you, heart and soul. I want us to be together forever. I want to marry you. What more can I say?'

Louise let her breath out very slowly, seduced by his adoring face and wishing, with all her heart, that she could believe his beguiling words. But somehow she couldn't, quite.

'How can I trust you?' she breathed at last.

His gaze clouded. 'Oh God, I wish I knew! All I can say is that I never want to hurt you again, and I'll go to any lengths to avoid it.' His eyes drifted away from hers and he added, in a tone of quiet anguish, 'But that's presuming you'll give me a second chance. And you're not going to, are you?'

'I want to, but. . .'

'You do?'

It broke her heart to see him hovering so transparently between hope and despair. 'Oh Rick! If only I could!'

She clung to him then, wanting so badly to believe in the dream they'd once shared. But always the spectre of Gina came between them. Was it possible for them to make a new start?

Rick got up from the bed and began pacing up and down the room. 'Look, I have to say this, so please let me finish. What happened the other night with Gina was a relic of the past and I truly believe it won't happen again. But to make sure it doesn't, I have a proposition to make. I've been thinking this through, trying desperately to find some way to win you back, and I've come up with a kind of plan. I've started doing really well here in London, getting known on the modelling circuit and all that. But people have started noticing me abroad, too.'

'Really? Well that's great!'

Louise couldn't keep the sarcasm out of her

voice. She was thinking of her own future, which she'd successfully sabotaged, thanks to Rick. What chance did she have of becoming a model now, without his backing?

He held up his hand, a pained look on his face. 'I asked you to let me finish, Lou. Please! This is my last hope!'

'Okay.'

'As I was saying, I'm getting a reputation abroad too. Specifically in Paris. In fact just yesterday I had an offer from one of the men's fashion houses to model their next collection. The trouble was, I was so fucked up over you that I said I'd have to think about it. They've probably booked someone else now.'

'I'm sorry. . .'

'That's not the point. What I'm trying to say is that I'm willing to move abroad – Paris, Milan, New York, you name it – if only you'll come with me. We could start afresh, forget the past. I know you've got a lot you want to forget too. Then I believe our love could stand a chance. What do you say?'

Louise stared at him, her heart filling up with some new combination of emotions she couldn't quite identify. Foremost amongst them, however, was the first swoop of real optimism she'd felt in ages. 'Rick! Do you really mean this?'

'I may be shooting myself in the foot here, but yes.'

Fired by a new burst of energy, Louise got up and flung herself into his arms. 'Yes, yes, why not! What have I got to lose? There's nothing for me in London any more.'

'Are you sure?'

He looked so vulnerable, so unsure. Louise

441

stood on tiptoe and kissed his meltingly soft lips. 'Quite certain. It's what I need, a complete change of scene. Ring those Paris people first thing in the morning. See if their offer's still open. If it is, I'll come with you.'

She hadn't felt so excited in years. A new life with Rick was just what she needed. She'd be getting away from the emotional and financial mess of her marriage, away from Gina's cynical attitudes and the temptation to slip back into her sister's lifestyle. She would learn to trust again, to love without inhibitions, to find the happiness every woman dreams of.

'Oh Louise!' he sighed, his mouth pressing more firmly onto hers. She felt the warm energy of his desire flowing through her, and soon they gravitated back onto the bed where their kisses and caresses became more ardent. Rick's legs entwined with hers, the warm bundle of his sex falling between her thighs, and his right hand began caressing her breast, evoking faint echoes of their earlier passion. She looked down at his face and saw in his clear blue eyes no dark shadows. Only a sincere wish to make it work between them.

Even so he whispered, with a rueful smile, 'You know, my love, there are no guarantees.'

'Who needs guarantees? They're not worth the paper they're written on,' she said, thinking of her impending divorce. Then she grinned wickedly. 'Anyway, relationships can be judged by more than one yardstick.'

At which the yardstick in question began to stir into action.

Educating Eleanor

Nina Sheridan

Chapter One

'MICHAEL, YOU CAN'T honestly expect me to take this lying down? I put as much into that house as you did – more, in fact. If you want to keep it on, that's fine, but you'll have to buy me out. I want my half.'

Eleanor Dawes listened as her soon-to-be-ex husband proceeded to weave a predictable path from pleading to threats. Once upon a time, her stomach would have been churning by now and she would have acceded to his every demand, throwing in some extra concessions of her own for good measure. Now, though, she knew better and she let him burn himself out. When at last he fell silent again, she said calmly, 'My solicitor will be in touch with yours. Goodbye, Michael.' She placed the receiver quietly back onto its cradle.

The coffee she had made for herself just before the telephone rang had grown cold, so she went to make another. Michael had gone too far this time. The separation had already depleted her savings out of existence; if she didn't have a roof over her head in the form of this cottage she'd be virtually destitute.

Eleanor turned and smiled at the framed photograph of her grandmother which took pride of place on the shelf over the small dining table.

'You saved my life, leaving me the cottage, *Mam du*,' she said aloud.

A cat rubbed up against her lower legs and mewled plaintively.

'And you, Thomas,' she said, sweeping the black ball of fur up with one hand. 'Whatever would I do without you and Dylan to talk to?'

Dylan, the fat tabby who rarely budged from the best armchair, raised a lazy eyelid as she paused to stroke him en route to the sofa in front of the TV. *Pebble Mill* was starting and Eleanor settled back with her coffee and Thomas on her lap to watch.

Watching lunchtime television was Eleanor's way of breaking up her day when she was at work on a book. Today, she had the added satisfaction of having typed '*end*' on the last page of her manuscript. She refused to think about what she would do next, determinedly basking in the glow of a project completed. Normally, her agent would have already negotiated her a new deal so that she could start on the next book almost as soon as she finished the last, but what with the public scandal which erupted around Michael after he lost the by-election, and the upheaval of moving from London to South-West Wales, Eleanor hadn't managed to work out a new proposal.

It was a miracle she had been able to complete this book, she reflected grimly; her concentration had been sorely affected by the problems in her personal life. Unfortunately, she needed the income from her writing now more than ever, and if she didn't obtain a new commission soon she was going to have to find some other way of keeping body and soul together.

She sighed, only half watching the television as her mind went over the unpaid bills in the drawer of the bureau in the corner of the room. Living rent-free was a huge help, but there were other day-to-day expenses to be covered.

The television presenter introduced his first guest and Eleanor turned her attention to the screen. Her lip curled as she saw the man walking down the steps to join the presenter on the sofa.

He was tall with dark, wavy hair which had a habit of flopping over one eye in such a contrived fashion that Eleanor could imagine him blow-drying it to fall just that way. He was lean and fit-looking, his black jeans moulding the contours of his long thighs, his boots polished so that they shone dully under the studio lights. His mid-blue silk shirt was open at the neck, just enough to give the viewer a glimpse of curly black chest hair.

at his throat, but not enough for it to look as though a medallion belonged there. As he sat down, he tucked his black jacket back so that it didn't obscure the sight of his trim waist and neat black suede belt.

Marcus Grant had been attracting a great deal of publicity just lately. An American sexologist, he was famous for his ground-breaking research into sexual response and erotic potential. His subject matter, coupled with his smouldering, film-star looks, made him a media dream. Eleanor hated him, instinctively.

'Surely,' the interviewer was saying to him now, 'sexual desire is an emotion which some people experience more often than others?'

Marcus Grant leaned forward in his seat, his dark eyes like two liquid pools, inviting his audience to drown in them.

'On the contrary, Alan,' he replied, his voice like smooth Guinness, trickling over the senses. 'Although the initial experience of arousal can be said to be instinctive, the frequency, and the intensity with which it is felt, is a learned response.'

'So, are you saying that we can all learn to become more sexual animals?' the presenter asked, raising his eyebrows knowingly at the camera.

Marcus Grant looked straight into the camera lens so that Eleanor, and, no doubt, half the female viewers in the country, felt he was talking directly to her.

'Absolutely. I meet so many people – women in particular – who write themselves off as frigid when, in fact, with a little training and practice they could discover a whole new world of pleasure.'

Eleanor pointed the remote control at the television and erased Marcus Grant's face from the screen.

'Smug git!' she said aloud.

Feeling intensely uncomfortable, Eleanor decided she would take herself off for a brisk walk down to the post office where she could post her manuscript.

Upstairs in the small bedroom, she stripped off the baggy old tracksuit she wore at the word processor and pulled out clean jeans and a cotton jumper to wear over a T-shirt. Catching a glimpse of herself in the dressing-table mirror, she paused, her eyes assessing.

Her body hadn't changed much in the last ten years. At thirty she was still slender, still firm-breasted, and her bottom hadn't yet succumbed to gravity. Pulling her clothes on over her serviceable M&S undies, Eleanor thought with impatience of what the American had said. Michael had always said she was frigid. The truth was, she simply didn't have a very high sex-drive.

It had bothered her, when she was younger and her contemporaries had spent half their time at college getting laid. Now though, she was comfortable with herself and she doubted if, at this stage in her life, she was likely to change. Learned response indeed! Marcus Grant made women sound like performing monkeys, talking about *training* and *practice*. Eleanor guessed that it probably didn't occur to him that many women, like herself, were perfectly happy with the sexual drive they had been given, thank you very much!

The telephone was ringing as she ran down the stairs.

'Gloria!' she said as she recognised her agent's voice. 'How are you?'

'Fine. More to the point, how are *you*, stuck in that godforsaken place?'

Eleanor laughed, for she could almost hear the shudder in Gloria's voice.

'It is *not* a godforsaken place, Gloria,' she said patiently, knowing that she was wasting her breath. Anything outside the capital was the back of beyond to Gloria. 'It's more like God's promised land. You'll have to come and spend a weekend in the summer, and I guarantee you'll fall in love with it yourself.'

'That's very kind of you,' Gloria replied with heavy irony. 'Actually, I was ringing you about a job, not to discuss the merits of sheep versus cars. Have you finished the book?'

'I'm just about to post it.'

'Good. Have you ever heard of Marcus Grant?'

Eleanor sucked in her breath.

'Funnily enough, I've just been watching him on *Pebble Mill*.'

'*Pebble Mill*?' Gloria repeated, mystified.

Realising that her agent probably didn't even know there *was* such a thing as daytime television, let alone watch it, Eleanor changed the subject.

'What about him?'

'He's gorgeous, isn't he?'

'Hmm,' Eleanor said non-committally. 'So what about him?'

'He needs a co-author for his next book, *Becoming Sexual*. Naff title, but a sure-fire bestseller. Knowing you're free, I put your name forward and he wants to meet you.'

'What! You've already talked to him about me?'

'He knows and admires your work, and he's offering a good deal.'

Gloria mentioned an advance that made Eleanor's eyes water. If she took this assignment, she would be financially secure for the next twelve months. Could she bring herself to work closely with a man whom she loathed on sight?

'I'm not interested, Gloria.'

'What? Why not?'

'The subject doesn't appeal.'

'Oh, come on, Eleanor! At least meet the guy and see what he's got in mind. I know you're feeling a bit raw, after what happened with Michael, but this might be just the thing to take your mind off it. And I know you need the money . . .' she wheedled.

'Sorry, Gloria, but I won't do it. I have a feeling that Mr Grant and I just would not get on.'

451

'What makes you think that?' Gloria asked, clearly surprised.

'Only that he's the epitome of everything I hate in a man.'

'Explain.'

'Okay. For starters, he comes across as arrogant, overbearing and self-regarding. He obviously considers himself God's gift to womankind, and I object to any man who sets himself up as an expert on female sexuality. Is that enough for you?'

'I see. And you've surmised all this from watching him on the television?'

Eleanor felt herself flush.

'I've read interviews too,' she defended herself, somewhat lamely. 'Come on, Gloria – the way he talks about women, he can't be anything but an arrogant bastard, at best.'

'Point taken,' Gloria conceded. 'You've got to admit, he's got a cute bum, though.'

'Gloria!' Eleanor laughed in spite of herself. 'No. N-O. All right?'

'I'll leave you to think it over and ring you in the morning. Ciao for now!'

She rang off, leaving Eleanor feeling exasperated. She might be broke, but there was no way she was going to put her name to a book which encouraged women to 'train' their sexual responses!

Once she had delivered her manuscript to the post office and gossiped a while with the post mistress, Eleanor decided to take a walk along the beach. Spring was in the air and, although this part of Wales never became overcrowded even in the high season, now the beach was virtually deserted.

Though moving to Wales had been a necessity rather than a choice, Eleanor was glad she had come. The local people, whether out of affection for her grandma, or out of a natural antipathy to the Tories, had welcomed her into their homes and made her feel as though she really belonged. As English as she was, Eleanor was very aware of the honour that had been granted her and she was determined not to taint her new neighbours with the scandal she hoped to leave behind her in London.

As she walked along the firm-sanded beach, Eleanor's mind began to clear and she turned her thoughts to the proposition Gloria had put to her. It was true that she had made a name for herself as the author of several popular, accessible books about modern medical matters. She had discovered a knack for presenting often quite complicated medical research in an easily read style which meant she was often asked to contribute to magazines and television documentaries. Women in particular seemed to appreciate her straight-talking, unpatronising approach and, if it wasn't for Michael's avarice, she would be living quite comfortably on what she earned.

Her face clouded as she thought about Michael. He had been so passionately idealistic when she had first met him. Sweeping her along on the tide of his ambition, she'd stood by his side as he worked his way up in the party, finally being elected to the Commons. From whence he proceeded to destroy himself, dragging Eleanor down with him.

'You're looking very pensive, *cariad*.'

Eleanor almost jumped out of her skin as the deep, lilting voice sounded close to her ear.

'Rhys!' she laughed. 'I didn't hear your footsteps on the sand.'

'You were so deep in thought I doubt if you'd have heard me if I'd been walking on gravel!' he said. 'Come and have a cup of tea with me at Mrs Williams's place.'

Smiling, Eleanor tucked her hand comfortably in the crook of Rhys's arm and walked with him towards the steps leading up to the roadway. His arm felt strong and steady and dependable and Eleanor was surprised to realise how pleased she was to see him.

'No work today?' she asked him, eyeing his ragged jeans and the baggy, shapeless sweatshirt he wore.

'I'm playing hookey,' he told her. 'Actually, I wanted to see you.'

'Me?'

'Yes. I was thinking that you'd be needing the services of a good lawyer if the story in today's

Mirror is true.'

Eleanor frowned.

'I haven't seen any newspapers today,' she admitted.

Sensing Rhys's discomfort, Eleanor steeled herself for the worst.

'Here,' he said, pulling the folded tabloid out of his back pocket. 'You'd better read it yourself.'

Eleanor sat on the edge of the sea wall and opened the paper at the page Rhys indicated. Michael smiled back at her from a wedding photograph, a younger, more trusting version of herself on his arm.

'Oh no!' she whispered.

Tory Wife Drove MP to Suicide Attempt ran the headline. *The Truth surrounding Michael Dawes' Sham Marriage.*

Eleanor felt sick. Folding the newspaper, she handed it back to Rhys and covered her face with her hands. After a moment, she felt his touch, tentative on her shoulder.

'You could sue for libel, El. You've suffered enough without them blackening your name like this.'

Eleanor looked up into his handsome face, so full of concern for her, and struggled to smile. She had known Rhys Jones since they were both in nappies – his family had lived across the street from her grandmother and the two of them had been inseparable during every summer of their childhood. She could still catch an occasional glimpse of the tow-headed, freckled-faced boy in the man sitting beside her now. Only now his hair was blond, his face interesting rather than cute, handsome but with the same unusual light-blue eyes which seemed to see everything.

Rhys had been the object of her first crush, they had shared their first kiss, their first date and their friendship had endured over the years so that Eleanor knew that Rhys was the one person in all the world on whom she could rely. He was always there with a word of encouragement, a smile, a hug, and now he was offering himself in a professional capacity.

'I don't want to sue, Rhys,' she told him now. 'It would only prolong the unpleasantness. You know, Michael actually had the nerve to ring me this morning to harangue me about the house. He must have been disappointed by my lack of reaction!' She laughed bitterly.

'I am going to need a good divorce lawyer though – do you think your colleague Amy would represent me?'

Rhys nodded.

'Of course. But I would strongly advise you to issue a restraining order on this kind of thing – scum like this shouldn't be allowed to get away with it!'

Eleanor appreciated the outrage expressed on her behalf, but still she shook her head.

'It will be Duncan who's behind all this. If I sue I'll be playing straight into his hands.'

Rhys regarded her thoughtfully for a few moments.

'Why are they doing this to you, Eleanor? I can't understand it.'

Eleanor shrugged wearily.

'I get the impression that Michael blames me for having to resign. And I suppose he has a point – I was responsible, at least indirectly, for his affair becoming public knowledge. So far I've had all the public sympathy. He and Duncan think I should sign the house over to Michael as some kind of compensation for his career going down the tubes.'

'What kind of warped reasoning is that?'

Eleanor smiled at him, both amused and warmed by his vehemence.

'As you say, it's warped. But there doesn't seem to be a lot I can do about it. It's not as if I have a public position, so they can't really harm my career. Spreading nasty rumours about me isn't going to get them anywhere – sticks and stones and all that. I prefer to ignore it.'

'And hope they'll go away?'

'Perhaps.'

Rhys sighed, his large, warm hand reaching for hers and enclosing it.

'All right,' he said. 'Come on – I'll walk you home.'

'What happened to that cup of tea you promised me?' she protested half-heartedly.

Rhys's eyes scanned her face and she sensed

that she had grown pale.

'You can make us one at home,' he told her and they walked back to the cottage in companionable silence.

Waiting for the kettle to boil in her tiny kitchen, Eleanor could see Rhys through the open door, sprawled in an armchair with Thomas on his lap. Dylan eyed him disdainfully, but then even he leapt up onto his knee after a few minutes. Rhys had that effect on women as well as cats, she mused to herself – no one could resist him for long. And yet Rhys had remained steadfastedly single, content, it seemed, with his lot.

He smiled at her now as she handed him a mug of tea. He had the kind of smile that lit up his light-blue eyes from within, making them twinkle sexily.

'Why have you never married, Rhys?' she asked him as she sat opposite with her own steaming mug.

'You know I'm waiting for you, El,' he replied. He smiled as he said it, but Eleanor was aware that the smile didn't quite reach his eyes.

'You deserve better than me, Rhys,' she said quietly. 'What happened to that girl Sara you were serious about?'

'She couldn't measure up. Why are you always doing yourself down, *cariad*?'

Eleanor shifted uncomfortably in her chair. Normally she avoided intimate chats with the attractive man who was now regarding her so seriously, but, despite her protestations that she ignored such things, the malicious newspaper article had caught her with her defences down.

'It never was very good between Michael and me, you know,' she said softly.

Rhys made an impatient sound at the back of his throat.

'Hardly surprising when you consider his secret.'

Eleanor shook his head.

'Michael wasn't homosexual before he met me.'

Rhys regarded her with amazement.

'Is that what he told you? Eleanor – think about what you're saying. It's not your fault. None of it is your fault.'

'I know that in here,' she agreed, tapping the side of her head. 'But I can't help but wonder, if I'd been better at . . . at the intimate side of our marriage, maybe he'd not have looked elsewhere.'

Rhys put down his mug and came to kneel on the floor in front of her. Eleanor knew that, for his sake, she ought to move away, but something kept her still. His touch, as he reached out to smooth her long hair away from her face, was gentle, full of tenderness. Eleanor felt a tightening in her throat, an unwelcome stirring in response to his nearness. She could feel the warmth of his body even from this distance, could smell the clean, salty tang of his skin. It made her feel dizzy and weak and she pulled herself together with an effort.

'You're a good friend to me, Rhys,' she said, a

slight quiver in her voice betraying the effect he was having on her.

Rhys grimaced and allowed his hand to drop to his side.

'But nothing more,' he added, his voice flat and expressionless.

'Does there have to be more?' Eleanor asked him, her eyes pleading. What on earth had possessed her to allow this conversation to develop? 'I value your friendship.'

'As I do yours. But I have to ask you, Eleanor – is there really no chance for me with you? Would you never consider marrying me?'

Eleanor felt her heart constrict. She had sensed this question brewing ever since she'd come home to Wales and she had been dreading it. She was fond of Rhys, loved him even, as a sister loves a brother, but she couldn't give him what she knew he wanted. She had a feeling that he would settle for less, but she thought too much of him to offer anything less than he deserved. Picking her words carefully, she sought to turn him down without jeopardising the friendship she valued so highly.

'Rhys, if there was any chance of my marrying again, believe me, it could only be you. But there isn't any chance. I'm happy on my own.'

'You weren't destined to be alone, Eleanor. You're far too sensual a woman to be content to lead a celibate life.'

Eleanor shook her head.

'Life is a lot less complicated without sex,' she told him.

'You're wrong, Eleanor. Just because it wasn't good between you and Michael doesn't mean it could never be good at all.'

Eleanor shook her head.

'Rhys—'

She gasped as suddenly, without warning, he pulled her into his arms and kissed her. At first she was too surprised to respond, then she felt the warmth of his lips moving over hers, coaxing them apart, and she knew that she didn't love him as a sister does a brother at all. There was nothing in the least bit filial in the way her head swam and her body responded to the sweet, curiously familiar taste of him. It was good, so good, and she wanted it to go on.

She gazed at him, wide-eyed, as he broke away.

'Something for you to think about, Ellie,' he said, a note of bitterness in his voice that wounded her.

'It was just a kiss, Rhys,' she protested.

He seemed to be about to say something, then his shoulders sagged and he dropped his eyes from hers. With a sigh, Rhys stood up. He looked down on her for several minutes. 'I'd best be off,' he said, regret colouring his tone. 'I'll tell Amy you'll be coming into Carmarthen to see her. Try not to worry too much, Eleanor – these things have a way of working themselves out.'

Eleanor had the feeling that he was talking

about himself as much as her battle with Michael and she smiled sadly. If only he could meet someone else, some loving girl who would make him happy – nothing would give her more pleasure. She frowned as her heart gave a little somersault at the thought. The sensation was far from pleasurable.

'Goodbye, Rhys,' she said softly, closing the door behind him.

It hurt her to think that she had disappointed him again. The image of his crestfallen face stayed with her. She refused to think about the kiss, and how it had shaken her. Perhaps it would be easier for him if she went away for a few days. The divorce was going to be expensive and Gloria had offered her a way to solve both problems. It struck her as ironic that she was even considering working with Marcus Grant, but the idea was looking more appealing by the minute.

Gloria was ecstatic to hear from her again so soon.

'I thought that maybe a confirmed celibate might be able to give a new slant to a book called *Becoming Sexual*,' Eleanor told her wryly.

Gloria snorted.

'I doubt you'll want to stay that way for long once you meet the delicious Mr Grant,' she told her. 'He called by the office less than an hour ago – he's very keen to meet you.'

'Really?' Eleanor was unimpressed. 'Well, it can't do any harm for us to meet. We might hate each other on sight anyway.'

'I doubt it,' Gloria said pointedly. She proceeded to give Eleanor details of Marcus Grant's hotel and promised to ring her when she had set up a meeting.

Later that night, Eleanor lay in bed, unable to sleep. Rhys had telephoned to see that she was all right and the memory of his dear, familiar voice still warmed her. Gloria had confirmed that she was to meet Marcus Grant at three the following day and she had set the alarm so that she could be up to catch the early train.

Her whole body felt prickly and no matter what position she took up, she could not make herself comfortable. She began to stroke her arms, comforting herself, enjoying the warm slip of her palms over her skin. They were inconvenient, these occasional bouts of sexual tension, but they were easily assuaged by a little gentle masturbation. Sex with oneself was so much less stressful without the fear of disappointing a partner.

Closing her eyes, Eleanor imagined that they were Rhys's hands smoothing and stroking her skin, edging their way down over her stomach to the silky-soft skin of her inner thighs. The tender, sensitive flesh between them was moist and warm and she sighed as her fingers fluttered across the delicate folds.

From the limited experience she had had with

Rhys before, she knew that he would be a gentle, unselfish lover. She imagined him now burying his face between her breasts, kissing the skin and sucking the burgeoning nubs into the hot, wet cavity of his mouth.

Her breasts hardened and crested as she thought of it, her legs sliding apart on the cool cotton sheets, her labia opening. With the middle finger of her right hand she traced the slippery channels of flesh, teasing herself until she could bear the suspense no longer.

Her clitoris was a hard, smooth promontory which hardened still more under her fingers. Eleanor found her breath catching in her chest as she rubbed it, manipulating all the little nerve endings until they quivered with life.

She imagined Rhys closing his lips over the little nub, worrying at it with his tongue and his teeth, and she felt the tension build, moving inexorably towards climax. Once she had passed the point of no return, once her body was slick with sweat and her breathing was rapid and harsh, she pushed herself on, reaching for that moment of altered consciousness, the release which her body craved.

Eleanor lost control of her mind just before she lost control of her body. Instead of seeing Rhys pleasuring her with his fingers and his tongue, a sudden, harsher image forced its way into her head, of Michael as she had seen him that fateful afternoon, ploughing into the body of Duncan, his private secretary. Even as her mind recoiled, her body made the jump into orgasm and she came with a sob, closing her legs on her own hand and curling up into a ball.

Tears of shame sprang to her eyes as she acknowledged that, once again, the image of her husband and his lover had acted as a trigger to her own orgasm. How could she find something which so appalled her so unbearably arousing?

If Rhys could see into her mind, *then* he would understand why she couldn't make him happy. He'd recoil from the truth, his image of her forever tarnished by the knowledge of her darkest fantasies.

She jumped as the telephone rang, fumbling for the receiver in the semi-darkness.

'Hello?' she said, aware that her voice was smoky with spent passion.

There was a deep chuckle at the other end of the line.

'You sound as though you've been having a good time,' a voice which was strangely familiar said.

'Who is this?' Eleanor said, embarrassment and guilt making her sharp. She sat up in the bed, pulling the covers around her protectively.

'You don't know me, Mrs Dawes, but I believe we are to meet tomorrow afternoon. My name is Grant. Marcus Grant.'

Of course it is, Eleanor thought angrily. Who else would be arrogant enough to call a stranger at this time of night?

'Do you know what time it is?' she said icily.

'It's just after eleven. I'm sorry – did I wake you?'

He sounded genuinely surprised and Eleanor softened a little.

'I always go to bed early,' she said.

'Oh. Well, I hope you won't be too averse to a few late nights when we begin work,' he said.

'Mr Grant, we haven't even agreed on a contract yet,' Eleanor reminded him coolly. 'Was there a reason for your call?'

'Of course. I was hoping to put back our appointment to four rather than three. Would that be convenient?'

'Yes, that would be fine.'

'Good. I'll leave you to get back to what you were doing . . . Eleanor,' he said with a casual insolence that took Eleanor's breath away. She was about to tell him to mind his own business, but she realised that he had already replaced the telephone.

Lying back on the pillows, Eleanor stared up at the darkened ceiling. Why did he have to phone her at that moment, of all times? She groaned inwardly. He can't have *known*, she told herself rationally. Yet he had known, she could tell by the timbre of his voice as much as by his words.

Perhaps she should call the meeting off altogether – it was obvious they weren't going to get along. Then she thought of Rhys and her

466

empty bank account, and she knew that turning down this assignment would be tantamount to both emotional and financial suicide.

She'd meet with Marcus Grant tomorrow, she decided, and she'd interview him as carefully as he would no doubt interview her. And she would make it perfectly clear to him that she considered the assignment to be purely professional, that innuendos such as those he had uttered on the telephone were strictly off-limits.

That decided, she settled down into the bed and closed her eyes. But it was a long, long time before she fell asleep.

Chapter Two

THE GRIMY, RAIN-WASHED streets of London came as a shock to Eleanor as she stepped off the train at Paddington. After the lush, green peace of Pembrokeshire the city seemed to exist on one discordant screech of sound which hurt her ears and made her feel disorientated.

Strange, how quickly she had adapted to her new home, she thought as she allowed herself to be swept along by a tide of commuters towards the taxi rank. The hotel was easily reached by Tube, but Eleanor felt she simply couldn't face the idea of battling her way to the right platform before squashing herself into an airless carriage with countless strangers.

Sitting back in the relative comfort of a black cab, she gazed out of the window at the people rushing by and recalled how she had once been one of them, among them, always in a rush. Now her life was so much gentler, the pace much more conducive to writing. Sometimes, at home, she wondered if she missed the metropolitan life. Now she knew that she did not, and she relaxed into her seat with the smile of someone glad to be a mere visitor.

It wasn't strictly necessary to go straight to the hotel since she wasn't due to meet Marcus Grant until four, but Gloria had booked her a room so that she could stay overnight and Eleanor had requested that a copy of Grant's latest book be left at reception for her. After the long journey, she intended to have lunch courtesy of room service while she read it.

The hotel was a surprise. From what she had seen and heard of Marcus Grant, she expected him to have chosen somewhere modern and efficient, but essentially soulless. Instead she found herself deposited outside the dignified façade of a tall Edwardian terrace, guarded by an elderly doorman in full dress uniform.

'Allow me to carry your bag, madam,' he said at once, walking unhurriedly down the steps to greet her.

His smile was cool and professional and Eleanor agreed with a gracious nod. Inside, the foyer was lit by a single enormous glass chandelier embellished with countless crystal droplets which tinkled discreetly as the door opened and closed.

The man who checked her in was as stiff as the

469

doorman and Eleanor found herself responding to the porter's cheery grin far more warmly than she might otherwise have thought was wise.

After the formality of her greeting, Eleanor's room came as another surprise. Tastefully decorated in shades of pink and soft dove grey, it was furnished in sumptuous style with well cared-for antique furniture. The room was dominated by a huge brass bed, the head and foot boards of which were wrought of the most elaborate ironwork. The bedspread was of faded pink satin and was piled with cushions of various shapes, sizes and fabrics. It looked so inviting that, ignoring the small desk by the window, Eleanor kicked off her shoes and made herself comfortable.

Grant's book was called *Women's Secret Lives*. There was a brief biography of the author on the back flap of the jacket, listing his academic credentials and repeating praise for his work by obscure journals, the pedigree of which Eleanor didn't trust. There was a small, black and white photograph of him staring moodily into the camera. Eleanor could feel the smoulder emanating from the page.

Given her own ambivalence about sex, Eleanor found the subject-matter intensely uncomfortable. The book began with a treatise on the potential in women to develop a rich fantasy-life, sometimes at the expense, so the author suggested, of their own long-term relationships.

The following chapters described, in quite toe-curling detail, the fantasies that various women had allegedly described to Marcus Grant for the sake of his research. The thought of divulging her most intimate thoughts to a man like Grant, as these women apparently had done, made Eleanor feel quite ill.

Her eyes widened as she read of women who fantasised about things Eleanor had never dreamed could be conducive to sexual pleasure. Doggedly reading every word in the interest of being fully informed about Grant's work when she met him, Eleanor soon became aware that, whilst her conscious mind was often repelled by the acts described, her body was actually responding.

One scenario in particular caught her imagination. The woman telling the story was introduced as 'Jennifer', a suburban American housewife in her thirties, happily married with what she described as a 'normal' sex life and two school-age children. The story was told verbatim.

'My favourite fantasy starts with my husband coming home after work one night with new clothes for me in a carrier bag. Now, my man *never* buys me clothes, I doubt he even knows what size I take, y'know? So this is like, real fantasy territory, right from the start!

Anyways, he tells me he's arranged for an overnight babysitter and that he's taking me somewhere real special – somewhere I've never been before. Now, I don't say too much, don't ask too many questions cos I don't want him to go changing his mind. So I run me a bath and afterwards I rub perfumed cream into my skin so that it's all soft and sweet-smelling, then I go over to the bed where I've the left the carrier bag.

Inside is this dress – red it is, and long, down to the floor – and I can't believe my eyes. I ain't *never* worn a dress like this before! It turns me on, y'know? Just thinkin' that my old man can picture me in a beautiful dress like this, it makes me wet knowing how he sees me. Because buying me this dress, well, it shows he don't think of me as no dowdy wife in my housecoat and slippers like I usually wear. He sees me as the kind of woman who'd wear a dress like this one.

There's more stuff inside the carrier bag. Satin panties that come up round the waist and a matching bra all trimmed in lace. They're red too, but real pretty, not tarty. Well, I put the bra and the panties on, then I slip my feet into a pair of mules, trimmed with red feathers. Those mules have the highest, spindliest heels you ever did see and I feel like I'm gonna fall right off when I stand up.

Then I put the dress over my head and it falls like a silk curtain over my body. Phew-ee – you should see me in that dress! My husband, he wants to pull into a motel, but I say, no way! You promised me a night out, and a night out is what I'm gonna have.'

Eleanor made herself more comfortable on the cushions, intrigued by where this story might lead. She found herself growing to like the interviewee and she could imagine Jennifer stepping out in all her finery, her husband as proud as punch, stealing a few hours away from the children and the cares of their everyday lives.

There was no intrusive commentary breaking into the account and Eleanor found herself approving of Marcus Grant's methods of allowing his subject to speak for herself. This way he allowed Jennifer's personality to leap from the page, and drew the reader in to her story.

Pleasantly surprised by this revelation, Eleanor read on.

'When we draw up in front of this swish restaurant downtown, I can hardly believe it! Loyd and me, we swank into that place, and everyone turns to look at us. I can feel their eyes on me as the head waiting guy shows us to our table. All the men in that room want to be in my man's shoes, and all the women, I can feel their envy. Tonight I am *hot*, you know what I'm saying? [Laughs.]

We eat – oysters that slip down our throats, juicy medallions of beef, still pink in the centre, tiny potatoes all covered in melted butter – and all the time we eat each other with our eyes. I take off one of my shoes and walk my bare toes up the inside of Loyd's leg to his crotch. He's got an erection so hard I swear the material of his trousers is strainin' fit to bust!

"Jennifer," he says, "Jennifer, what you tryin' to do to me, girl?"

But his eyes, they're all dark and smoky and I can tell he's loving every minute. I lean forward to tell him *exactly* what I'm trying to do, but I don't get the chance, because just then, the lights are turned down real low and a spotlight falls in the centre of the room. There's a blast of music, then this gal dressed in feathers and sequins appears in the light and starts to dance.

Well, it's so unexpected, y'know, in a place like that, so fancy an' all. For a minute I just sit there, stunned. I can feel a change in the room, like everyone's getting excited, watching this girl in the middle of the room. And I'm thinking, I can bump and grind as good as that any day!

After a few minutes, I notice that Loyd isn't watchin' the dancer at all – he's watchin' me. And I say to him, I say "What?" and he says, "You can dance better'n that, girl," just like he's read my mind.

Well, I'm feeling so horny by now, I stand up from the table and walk over to the girl. I hear the buzz of excitement that goes around the room, but I don't pay no mind, I'm too busy looking at the girl. She's got her top off already, and her titties are like two little poached eggs, no bigger than that, but sweet.

She smiles at me and waves me over. I start to copy her moves, giving a little shimmy that drives the audience wild.

"Hey, baby – show us what you've got!" they shout.

I laugh and dance harder. I've never felt so alive, so free. It's like nothing matters, like I can't hear nothing, can't feel nothing except the music. The beat is driving through me so that I feel like I'm vibrating. And out there my man is watchin' me and wantin' me . . .'

Eleanor felt uncomfortable. What Jennifer was describing was anathema to her: the mere thought of displaying herself in public in such a way filled her with fear and horror. And yet, vicariously, it seemed that she could feel the other woman's excitement, could identify with her arousal.

But it was too close to the ambivalence she felt about the scene she had witnessed between Michael and Duncan. Disgusted on the one hand, yet unbearably aroused on the other. Such feelings filled her with shame.

Shame, however, did not seem to be in Jennifer's often colourful vocabulary and Eleanor turned her attention back to the text.

'I'm hot; I can feel the sweat running down my sides and between my breasts. It feels like the most natural thing in the world to reach behind me to unzip the dress to my waist. The audience go wild as I ease the straps down over my arms and let the dress drop down to my waist. The rush of cool air against my skin brings me out in goose bumps. My breasts are quivering in the satin cups of my bra and I lean forward to give everyone a better look.

I can't see no faces, but I can feel those eyes on me, lusting after me. God, I feel good! I pull the zip down all the way now and the dress falls in a silky pile round my ankles. The other girl, she reaches out and holds my hand so that I can step out of it. Then she dances round me and unhooks the clips of my bra. My tits are bigger than hers, firm with nipples that stand out proud.

So there I am in my red satin panties and my come-an'-fuck-me shoes, bumpin' and grindin' and struttin' my stuff. And I feel like I'm on fire, like I could take on any man in the room. Hell, I could take on *every* man in the room! [Laughs.]

This girl, though, I soon find out that she's got other ideas. She comes round and stands right in front of me and I find myself staring into her eyes. They're big and blue, like a doll's and there's something in them that makes me feel kinda weak at the knees. Then she puts her

476

arms around me and starts kissin' me.

Well, I ain't *never* been kissed by another gal before. I don't know what to do, so I just stand there and let it happen. It's good – her lips are soft and big and she knows just how to tease my mouth open so that her tongue can get inside. I can feel the tips of her nipples brushing oh-so gently against mine and I feel the shiver runnin' right through to my insides.

Then I feel a tap on my shoulders, and there's my man, come to take over. The girl smiles and steps back, though I know that the way she's looking at me, so disappointed, is the way I'm looking at her too. Except that I'm glad Loyd has come to claim me back.

He picks me up, like I was light as quicksilver, and he carries me off to a room in the back of the restaurant where there's this big, squashy sofa. And then we have the *best* sex we ever had.'

Eleanor put the book aside and lay back on the pillows, staring up at the uneven ceiling. Though she emphatically did not want to do any of the things that Jennifer described, she felt warm and heavy-limbed, aroused in a way that she didn't quite understand.

Jennifer's *joie de vivre* leapt off the page, her enjoyment, her sheer exuberance reaching out and pulling Eleanor in. It was an uncomfortable feeling. If she had had any doubts that the subject matter with which she would be expected to work would not suit her, then reading Jennifer's story had dispelled them.

And yet she was intrigued, fascinated even, by the focus of Marcus Grant's work. What had drawn him into it in the first place? What conclusions had he drawn from his research so far? *Could he help her?*

The rogue thought popped into her head, taking her breath away. Is that really what she wanted – to 'retrain' her own sexual responses? Eleanor lay back on the pillows and closed her eyes. She could feel the slow burn of sexual arousal churning gently through her veins. Surely that was evidence enough that the raw material was there?

It was as if a small light was being shone into the innermost recesses of her mind. Bruised as she was by the ignominious way in which her marriage had ended, she had found it easier to opt for celibacy than to contemplate starting all over again with someone else. Even when Rhys had opened his heart to her yesterday she had refused to even admit the possibility that it might be different with him.

Opening her eyes, Eleanor glanced at the small carriage clock placed discreetly on the dressing table. It was three o'clock already. If she was to be as alert and poised as she wanted to be when she met Marcus Grant, she had better get her skates on; there would be time enough to explore this alien train of thought later.

In the small ensuite bathroom, she showered and towelled herself dry, conscious of the image of her naked body reflected back at herself in the mirror tiles which lined one wall. As the steam cleared she eyed her neat, naturally slender body, looking at herself as Jennifer had, assessing. Did she have the kind of figure that could carry off a long, red dress like Jennifer's?

Slowly, Eleanor ran her hands down her sides, tracing the shape of her body. Her skin was warm and soft, still slightly damp, and her palms slid easily over the surface. In proportion with the rest of her, her breasts were neither small nor large, but firm, the areolae wide and pink, smooth in the steamy heat of the bathroom.

The indentation of her waist was gradual rather than dramatic, her stomach softly rounded in a natural, feminine way that pleased her. Her hips flared gently from her waist, her bottom high and reasonably pert, the hair at the apex of her thighs dark and plentiful. She would have like longer legs, but had no complaints about the shape of the ones she had.

Altogether, it was a pleasant enough package, if unremarkable. Allowing her long, dark hair to fall over her face, Eleanor pouted at her reflection and undulated slowly, as if to music. What would it feel like to have all those eyes watching you dance? Attempting a sultry expression, she moved her shoulders the way Jennifer had described. Her breasts shook, her nipples hardening in response to the sudden movement, and Eleanor put her hands squarely over them, feeling them quiver against her palms.

In the mirror, she saw that she looked like a startled doe and she began to laugh.

'Ooh, you sexy creature, you!' she said aloud, blowing herself a kiss and laughing as she turned away. But although outwardly she laughed at herself, she was aware of a tiny corner of her mind that was excited by the possibility of change.

In the bedroom Eleanor began to dress. With the interview in mind, she had brought with her a smart, light-weight grey suit. The skirt buttoned neatly at the side of her waist, the hem reaching just below the knees. Buttoning a pale blue cotton blouse up to her throat, she pushed her arms into the sleeves of the jacket and stepped into medium-heeled plain black court shoes. With her light, understated make-up and her long hair coiled neatly into a French pleat, Eleanor was satisfied that she looked every inch the no-nonsense businesswoman. Conscious of an inexplicable nervousness, she went downstairs.

They had arranged to meet in the coffee lounge for afternoon tea. Eleanor spotted him immediately, sitting at a small, circular table in the far corner of the room, where, she realised, he would be able to watch the entrance. He rose as soon as he saw her, a small smile playing around his well-shaped lips as he greeted her, holding his hand out over the table.

'Eleanor?'

Eleanor was aware of a tightening in her chest as she looked at him. He really was rather spectacularly good-looking, far more so than he appeared on the television. She had to force herself to meet his eye and grasp his hand in a firm handshake.

Grant smiled at her and she had the curious feeling that his dark, lambent eyes were seeing right into her, divining the thoughts that she would most like to keep private. What did those eyes see when they looked at her? Could he tell how *empty* she had become? Shifting slightly as she sat in her chair, Eleanor tried to gather her fractured thoughts.

'I have to tell you straight away, Mr Grant—'

'Marcus, please,' he interrupted her smoothly.

'—Marcus . . . that I'm not altogether sure that I'm the best person for this job.'

'Really?' He smiled at her. 'Why not?'

Eleanor's mouth opened, then closed again. She had said the first thing that came into her head without considering that he might expect her to explain herself.

'Um, well, I—'

'Only I know how good you are at what you do,' he interrupted her, sitting back in his seat as the waitress brought their tea and scones to the table. 'I read your book on alternative therapies and thought it excellent. You have such a clear writing style.'

481

'Thank you. If you've read that book you'll appreciate that I like to do a great deal of research before putting pen to paper,' she said.

Marcus raised his shoulders slightly before offering her the plate of scones.

'Of course. The book I propose we write together will need a fair amount of research too.'

Eleanor stared at him as he helped himself to a scone and spread it liberally with butter. Injecting a light-hearted tone into her voice, she said, 'I'm not so sure that I'm keen on that idea!'

Marcus smiled at her, the twinkle in his eye telling her that he had guessed what she was thinking.

'It's not so much of a hands-on approach with my subject,' he assured her. Picking up a buttery half-scone he took a bite.

Eleanor found her eyes drawn to his hands, her gaze lingering on the long, slender fingers. Looking at them, she wasn't so sure that she would want to veto 'hands-on' research after all. To her horror, she felt warm colour suffuse her cheeks. What was the matter with her? She forced her mind back onto the subject of the book.

'May I ask you – why do you want a co-author for this book? As I understand it, you've always worked alone before.'

'I have. However, I feel that I've gone as far as I can, as a man, into the world of feminine sexuality. I've gained a good deal of insight along the way, but with the best will in the world I can't

482

experience the process of sexual awakening from a female point of view.'

Eleanor felt a trickle run along her spine. Dare she suggest that she could act as his guinea pig?

'No,' she said softly, then, holding his eye deliberately she said, 'but I could.'

Several expressions chased across Marcus's face. Shock, surprise and the faint gleam of masculine speculation. Eleanor felt a small thrill that she had been able to provoke such a reaction from him. She wasn't sure how she expected him to react, but she wasn't prepared for his laughter. In spite of her dismay, Eleanor registered that she liked the sound; it was rich and deep and sounded totally genuine.

Catching sight of her expression, he grimaced.

'I'm sorry, Eleanor. You took me by surprise. Look, why don't I give you a copy of the proposal for *Becoming Sexual* so that you can get some idea of what I'm trying to produce? If you could read it this afternoon, perhaps we could then have dinner tonight and discuss it more fully. I take it you are staying in the hotel?'

Eleanor nodded. She needed some time to gather her thoughts. There was nothing in Marcus's direct, brown-eyed gaze that suggested he might be coming on to her and she realised that he had dismissed as absurd her suggestion that she could undertake much of the research in person. Perhaps it was. Of course it was. Then Marcus grinned and his eyes lit up mischievously, making

Eleanor question her own judgement.

'Did you pack an evening dress?' he asked innocently. 'I have a table booked at Two Moons.'

There was no way that Eleanor was going to admit to having nothing suitable to wear to one of the most fashionable restaurants in London, so she summoned up all her reserves of charm and smiled at him.

'Of course. Shall I meet you in the foyer?'

'Make it the lounge bar, then we could have a drink first. Would seven suit you or would that be too early?'

'Seven would be fine.'

'Good.' Now that he had achieved his aim, Marcus was businesslike. 'I'm afraid I'm going to have to rush off – I have another appointment at five. Here,' he reached into a briefcase underneath the table, 'this is the proposal. I'll see you at seven.'

Eleanor returned his smile with every appearance of confidence and watched as he walked away. He had an easy, self-assured stride and heads turned as he past. Seemingly oblivious, he exchanged a few words with the head waiter before disappearing through the doors. To meet a woman, perhaps?

Eleanor frowned as the thought popped into her head. What did it matter who he was meeting? Or, for that matter, whether or not she personally found him attractive? For she did, she realised with a jolt. There was something about

484

the way he looked at her that made her feel warm, but edgy. And she didn't trust him, not at all.

Impatient with the direction her thoughts had taken, Eleanor ordered herself a fresh pot of tea and opened the proposal he had given her. The more she read, the more intriguing she found the subject, especially when she applied it to her own circumstance. According to Marcus, the most unresponsive of women could achieve greater sexual fulfilment by allowing herself to explore her fantasies.

Eleanor raised her eyebrows as she scanned the list of proposed areas for research: massage; pornography; exhibitionism/voyeurism; lesbian experiences; exploring S&M. The final two chapters were to be devoted to the conclusions drawn from the research, discussing, amongst other things, whether the re-enactment of one's fantasies was a valid approach to opening up one's sexual horizons, or whether fantasies should stay safely confined within the mind.

It was an interesting conundrum. Eleanor was intrigued, though reluctantly, by the idea that she might find herself reawakened if she followed the programme Marcus described. If she explored her fantasies . . . Eleanor brought herself up short. What fantasies? Apart from imagining herself with Rhys, which was more wishful thinking than fantasy, she couldn't really say that there were any images she regularly conjured up to arouse herself.

485

She frowned as a picture came into her mind of herself masturbating to a climax as she had the day before with the image of Michael and Duncan flashing into her head. That wasn't a fantasy, for goodness' sake! she told herself angrily. Signalling for the bill, Eleanor slipped the proposal in her own case. Marcus, it seemed had left instructions for the bill to be added to her account, so she went to grab her bag before heading for the shops.

Later, as she changed into the understated black dress she had found in one of the late-opening department stores Eleanor decided that she looked good. Elegant, but not overtly sexy.

He was waiting for her in the lounge bar. Greeting her with a friendly smile, he ordered her a glass of dry white wine and turned to look at her. He had the kind of eyes that made Eleanor feel that all his attention was on her. She felt his scrutiny of her dress, though she couldn't gauge his reaction from the expression in his eyes.

'What did you think of the proposal?' he asked her after a few minutes.

'I thought it was very . . . interesting,' she replied carefully.

'Interesting enough to work on it with me?'

Eleanor grinned.

'Don't rush me!' she said, feeling a warm glow as he returned her smile.

The Two Moons restaurant was lit by gently

flickering hurricane lamps set into innumerable iron sconces placed around the walls. The table to which they were shown with the minimum of fuss was spread with a pristine white cloth and set with gleaming silver cutlery. Looking around her as the waiter went to fetch a menu, Eleanor saw that all the tables were the same, mostly set for two with the odd larger one set for four. There was a generous distance between them so that there was a sense of privacy, yet the overall atmosphere contrived to be cosy and intimate.

Eleanor chose seafood for her main course while Marcus opted for a steak, cooked rare.

'I like my daily helping of red meat,' he commented, his eyes twinkling in the dim lighting as Eleanor grimaced.

'I prefer chicken and fish. I suppose you'd read something significant into that – something to do with the difference in our sexual drives?'

Marcus raised his eyebrows at her across the table and Eleanor felt her stomach somersault. She had meant the comment to be a light-hearted one, and only now did she realise how it could be interpreted.

'What do you know about my drives, Eleanor, sexual or otherwise?' he asked her, his voice low.

Eleanor strove for insouciance as she shrugged. 'I'm only making the kind of assumptions that you make about women all the time.'

'Oh? And what conclusions have you drawn about me?'

Eleanor considered trying to change the subject, but his eyes challenged her and she was seized by a kind of recklessness that was totally alien to her.

'I would say that, with your professional interest in women and their sexuality, you like your sex frequent and varied. I wouldn't imagine that fidelity is very high on your list, nor even tenderness, for that matter. Your interest is too heavily geared to the mechanical, so the more cerebral side of sexual attraction doesn't appear to interest you at all.'

Marcus stared at her across the table as she paused. His eyes seemed opaque, his expression unreadable and Eleanor wondered if she had offended him. Certainly she had managed to surprise him.

'I'm sorry if you feel I've been too personal,' she said stiffly when he still did not respond.

To her surprise, he suddenly tipped back his head and laughed. From the corner of her eye, Eleanor saw that they were attracting the attention of the other diners and she felt uncomfortable.

'Have I amused you?' she asked icily.

Marcus stopped laughing and smiled at her.

'A little. Have another glass of wine, Eleanor, and then you can ask me all the questions I can see you are dying to ask.'

'You're mistaken if you think I'm the least bit curious about you,' she said.

Marcus smiled again.

'I meant about the book,' he said gently.

Eleanor felt the colour seep into her cheeks. Was this evening really going to be nothing more than a series of blunders on her part?

'Of course you did,' she murmured, casting around frantically in her brain for an intelligent question she could put to him. 'Actually, I wanted to ask you about Jennifer.'

'Jennifer?' He looked perplexed.

'In *Women's Secret Lives*. The woman who went dancing with her husband and ended up joining the floor show.'

'Ah yes. Jennifer. What about her?'

Eleanor felt uncomfortable, half wishing she hadn't opened the subject.

'It's just that . . . I can't understand why she would want to do such a thing.'

'But she didn't.'

'Pardon?'

'She didn't. Eleanor, you're confusing fact with fantasy. Jennifer was describing what goes on inside her head when she masturbates, or when she's making love with her husband.'

Hoping he hadn't noticed her discomfort at his casual references to such intimate acts, Eleanor forced herself to look him in the eye.

'You mean, that scene never happened? It wasn't even something that she'd done once and therefore kept remembering?'

'I don't think so. I don't imagine so. Remember the way she describes herself and the clothes she wears?'

Eleanor nodded.

'Well, the real Jennifer is about five foot two and sixteen stone with a penchant for brightly patterned tent dresses – which suit her very well, I might add.'

'But—'

'Part of Jennifer's fantasy is that she's tall and lithe, the kind of woman who could carry off the clothes she described. That doesn't mean that she's unhappy with what she's got, just that her everyday life is enriched by a little creative fantasy.'

'I see,' Eleanor said.

Their meal had arrived and she picked at it thoughtfully. Marcus's next question took her off-guard.

'What do you fantasise about, Eleanor?'

A brief flash of Duncan and Michael pierced her thoughts and she pushed it away angrily.

'I don't,' she snapped.

Unperturbed, Marcus pressed her.

'Everyone has fantasies, Eleanor – though not everybody recognises them.'

'With all respect, Marcus, that's rubbish.'

The faintest of smiles flickered across his handsome features.

'All right,' he said, leaning forward and steepling his fingers under his chin, 'I'll demonstrate to you. What made you buy that dress?'

Taken by surprise, Eleanor replied with the truth.

'The fact that you told me we were eating here and that I had nothing suitable in my overnight case.'

'Ah!' Marcus chuckled. 'I'm very flattered, but that isn't actually what I meant. Think about what you wanted that dress to say to me when we met tonight.'

Eleanor shrugged.

'That I had the right clothes for the occasion?'

'Too literal. Try again.'

Eleanor shook her head.

'I don't know what you're driving at.'

'Okay, I'll tell you my interpretation, and you tell me if I'm right. You chose black, because it'll take you anywhere and it won't draw attention to you.' He paused, smiling slightly when Eleanor refused to answer. 'The buttons up to the neck say "Hands off – I'm off-limits". So does the tightly coiled hair. That also tells me you want me to think you're in control. What you probably didn't realise when you dressed, was the way the fabric skims your figure as you walk. You've also forgotten the fact that concealment is a powerful aphrodisiac.'

Eleanor stared at him. Indignation warred with a slow, churning arousal that made her push her half eaten meal away, her appetite gone.

'Are you trying to tell me that you desire me, Mr Grant?' she said, angry with the way her voice shook betrayingly. She didn't want him to know that he affected her.

Marcus sat back in his seat and smiled infuriatingly at her.

'What do you think, Eleanor?'

'Me? I think that you are one of the most arrogant, conceited men I have ever met,' she said coolly.

Marcus laughed.

'You see? I knew you were crazy about me!'

'What?'

He waved a hand at her.

'Such careful attention to detail, such contrived signals of unavailability – they could only mean the opposite.'

'Why you – ah!'

Eleanor brought her hand up to shield her eyes as a flashbulb went off right in her face.

'Mrs Dawes – will you comment on Michael Dawes's latest allegations against you?' the reporter said quickly as a bevy of waiters bore down on him. 'Mrs Dawes . . .'

Eleanor waited until the man had been bundled out onto the street before daring to glance at Marcus. He was gazing at her with open curiosity and she smiled a small, bitter smile.

'There you have it, Marcus – the main reason why I couldn't possibly help you with your research. I'd be recognised and that would defeat the object. Your work would be announced in every scandal sheet in Britain and my husband would walk away with everything that we once called ours. I have to go. I'm sorry to have wasted your time.'

Eleanor leapt up and, brushing aside the effusive apologies of the maître d', she rushed straight out of the door and flagged down a cab.

Marcus caught up with her in the street.

'Hey – wait up a minute!' He put his hand on her arm, stopping her from jumping straight into the black cab which had drawn up to the kerb.

'Please, Marcus, I'm embarrassed enough as it is,' Eleanor pleaded, well aware that she was perilously close to tears.

Marcus seemed to be aware of it too, for, peeling off a bank note from a roll that he pulled from his trouser pocket, he tipped the cab driver and turned Eleanor away with unexpected gentleness.

'Let's walk away,' he suggested, nodding in the direction of the Embankment. 'It's okay – he's gone.'

Eleanor smiled faintly and forced herself to stop looking over her shoulder for the photographer who had broken up their evening. Walking alongside Marcus, she was grateful for his silence; it enabled her to get a grip on her feelings, so that she could speak to him without the annoyingly obvious tremor in her voice.

'I'm sorry about that,' she said quietly. 'I was going to explain the position . . .'

'What position is that?'

Eleanor glanced sideways at him and saw that he was watching her intently. Realising that she owed him some explanation, if only for the ruined

493

meal if not for the rest, she wrapped her arms around herself and sighed deeply. It was a beautiful night, warm and balmy. A gentle breeze played across her face, cooling her warm cheeks. The noise of the city created a continuous background hum, yet it was still possible to hear the ebb and flow of the inky waters of the Thames.

'My marriage ended six months ago,' she said, making the words as flat and expressionless as she could in the hope of disguising the hurt she still felt at the events she described. 'These things happen every day, of course. Unfortunately my marriage broke down very publicly. My husband was a Member of Parliament, you see. He had to resign his seat—'

'Because your marriage broke up?' Marcus interrupted.

'No. He had to resign his seat, and I had to resign from our marriage, for the same reason.'

'Can I ask why?'

Eleanor bit her lip, her steps slowing as she tried to find the words to describe what she had seen. 'I found my husband *in flagrante*, as they say, with his secretary. They were on the leather chaise longue which I bought Michael for a "now you've really arrived" present.'

Eleanor could feel Marcus's puzzlement and she was not surprised when he said,

'Sure, that's real sad for you, but why did it ruin your husband's career?'

Eleanor smiled bitterly at him.

'Because his secretary happened to be male. And because I had a friend with me who, as luck would have it, is a freelance photographer.'

'Ah!'

'Ah indeed! Aileen never goes anywhere without a camera strung around her neck. She sold the photographs to a tabloid. Since then Michael and Duncan have been trying to bully me into signing the house over to Michael, hence the smear campaign in the gossip columns. I imagine that was what the photographer was referring to tonight.'

They strolled in silence for a few more minutes, though this time it was a more companionable one. Eleanor sensed a sympathy in the man walking beside her that made her want to reach out and touch him. Restraining herself, she waited for him to speak again.

'It seems to me,' he said after a while, 'that you've had a raw deal lately.'

Eleanor chuckled.

'You could say that,' she admitted.

Marcus smiled at her in the darkness.

'That's the first time I've heard you laugh. You should do it more often – it suits you.'

Eleanor, not knowing how to respond, stayed silent.

'What you need is a change of scene, something to take your mind off your troubles. A new challenge, perhaps.'

'Haven't you been listening to me? Writing is

one thing – that's behind the scenes, fairly anonymous stuff. I would sabotage the whole operation if I helped with the *research* for your book.'

Marcus stopped walking and turned to grin at her.

'Not if we move our base outside London.'

Eleanor stared at him.

'There are journalists everywhere – even in the sticks,' she pointed out calmly.

'People rarely see what they don't expect. To make doubly sure, you could cut your hair—' He laughed as Eleanor's hand immediately flew protectively to her neat French pleat. 'You always keep it hidden anyway,' he said.

Something about the way he said this last made Eleanor's pulse quicken. He was looking at her as if seeing her for the very first time, and when he reached out to touch a tendril of long, dark hair which had escaped from its pleat she shivered.

'How do you bear it, having your hair pulled so tightly back, defying gravity . . .?' His voice was low and seductive and Eleanor found herself leaning against the stone parapet overhanging the river as he reached behind her head and deftly pulled the pins out of her hair, one by one. Each made a tiny tinkling sound as it dropped to the ground, yet Eleanor found she hadn't the energy to protest. As Marcus fluffed her newly liberated hair in a dark cloud around her face, all she could summon was a small 'oh' of distress.

'That's better,' he murmured.

He was standing so close she felt trapped, pinned against the parapet even though no part of him was touching her. His chin-length, wavy black hair fell forward, casting shadows over his face. For a moment Eleanor was sure that he would kiss her and she was aware that she wanted him to, more than anything. The blood was pulsing in her veins, warming her, making her lose her sense of reason. Barely realising what she was doing, she swayed slightly towards him, her lips half parted, her eyelids closing slightly.

'Well, Eleanor? What do you think? Shall we do it?'

His voice, still low and evocative, slowly penetrated the fog of sensuality which had enveloped her. She frowned, not able to make sense of his words.

'Shall we do what?' she asked, her voice thick and unrecognisable even to her own ears.

A shadow of a smile passed across Marcus's face. His gaze moved with deliberate slowness over her face and down to her still parted lips. Without taking his eyes off them, he murmured, 'Shall we write the book together?'

It was as if she had been slapped in the face with a cold flannel. Eleanor flinched, her shoulders straightening, her lips pressing together. The book. What else could he have meant, for God's sake? And she had thought . . . dear Lord, what must he think of her? Summoning a bright smile from somewhere, Eleanor nodded.

'Yes,' she said, 'let's do it.' She saw that her answer had surprised him and she looked him squarely in the eye. 'But I want to do it my way.'

'Your way?' he echoed, clearly at a loss.

Eleanor smiled slightly, guessing that he was not used to being caught lost for words.

'Yes. You are convinced that your theories work, that it's possible for any woman to "become sexual", right?'

'Yes, but—'

'Then I want to be a case study. You can prove your theories through me. You can educate me, if you like. That's the deal. I'll get my agent to contact you when you've had time to think it over.'

Before he could reply, Eleanor began to walk briskly back the way she had come, shaking out her hair so that it swept across her shoulders like a glossy brown curtain. She felt his eyes on her, though he made no attempt to follow and she felt suddenly, inexplicably light-hearted.

Now she had taken the decision to sign the contract Eleanor was looking forward to starting work. More importantly, she was looking forward to exploring the feelings which had been growing within her all day. She had felt something when Marcus touched her just now, something thrilling that she had never thought herself capable of experiencing.

Most of her doubts about the man and his work seemed to have been swept aside by her

498

burgeoning belief that he could help her to . . . what? Find herself, she supposed. And if she could unlock the passionate woman she suspected was trapped within her, Eleanor had a feeling that happiness could be just around the corner.

Chapter Three

'WYNN-JONES.'

'Rhys? It's me.'

'Eleanor! How are you?' His voice softened as he recognised her voice on the other end of the telephone.

Eleanor smiled; his obvious pleasure at her call both warmed and encouraged her.

'I'm fine, Rhys. I was just phoning to let you know that I'm going away for a few weeks.'

'You decided to take that job then?'

'Yes, I got the contract through today. How are you?'

'I'm fine.'

Eleanor winced at the stiffness that had crept back into his tone.

'Rhys?'

'Yes?'

She paused, the words on the tip of her tongue.

Don't give up on me yet. . . Instead she said, 'Nothing. Perhaps we can meet up when I get back?'

'If you like. You'll call me?'

'Yes. Goodbye, Rhys.'

'Goodbye, Eleanor.'

The line went dead, leaving Eleanor to replace the receiver at her end with a gentle click. *Wait for me, Rhys, just a little bit longer*, she said to herself.

Reaching up, she went to smooth her hair back from her face, frowning as her fingers encountered bare skin. Her new, cropped hairstyle still felt strange and she often found herself, as now, reaching up to brush a non-existent lock of hair off her forehead.

It was time to go. With one last look around the safe, comfortable interior of the small cottage, Eleanor picked up her case and went out to the car. Leaving her key with a neighbour so that she could feed the cats and water her houseplants, Eleanor set off for the large Midlands town where Marcus had already set up his office.

He greeted her on the steps of the elegant Georgian terrace.

'Eleanor!' He took both her hands in his and ran his eyes over her. 'I love the hair.'

Eleanor grimaced, unconvinced. She knew, though, that she looked different. Younger, somehow, and more carefree. Marcus showed her into the small, high-ceilinged study where she was to work for the next six weeks. There was a desk under the picturesque sash window with a word processor plugged in ready for her to start. A small floral sofa was crammed against one wall while against the other a filing cabinet, two shelves and a photocopier vied for space. A telephone-come-fax machine was perched precariously on one shelf.

'Well, will it do?' Marcus asked her.

'I should think so.' Eleanor smiled at him. 'If I could put my case in my room I'd like to freshen up.'

'Of course. Dinner will be ready in half an hour.'

He showed her up the stairs into a comfortably furnished bedroom with a small bathroom attached. Eleanor glanced around at the warm peach and terracotta tones of the room and knew she would be comfortable there.

'I'll see you downstairs when you're ready,' he told her, leaving her alone.

Eleanor pressed the 'play' button on the CD player in the corner of the room, curious to see what had been loaded into it for her. Immediately, the sound of running water filled the room, interspersed by a gentle piano melody which was clearly designed to soothe and relax her. She smiled to herself as she unpacked her case and went into the bathroom. Everything had been provided for her comfort, from an ample supply of fluffy, soft towels to an array of bath oils and cosmetics in the bathroom cabinet.

As she prepared to join Marcus downstairs, she wondered if he had given much thought to the condition she had attached to her working with him. He broached the subject over the first course.

'How serious were you about making yourself a case study for the book?' he asked her as he put down his soup spoon.

Eleanor smiled serenely at him across the polished mahogany table.

'Very,' she replied. 'Did you think I might not be?'

'It crossed my mind that you might be calling my bluff, yes.'

'Why on earth would I want to do that?'

Marcus shrugged, not quite meeting her eye.

'I'm not so sure it's such a good idea,' he admitted after a few minutes.

Eleanor raised an eyebrow at him.

'Oh? Is that because you don't have the courage of your convictions, Mr Grant?'

Marcus looked directly at her and Eleanor saw that the challenge had hit home.

'Of course not. I wonder, though, what you think you've let yourself in for?'

Eleanor placed her spoon carefully in her empty bowl.

'Well, let me see. As I recall, your book proposal sets things down quite clearly. You submit that by exploring every facet of human sexuality a woman can get in touch with her own needs and desires. How are you going to prove that your theory works, Marcus, if not in a controlled experiment?'

Marcus looked uncomfortable, but he was prevented from replying by the appearance of the housekeeper with their main course. He introduced the smart looking middle-aged woman to Eleanor.

'This is Maggie Soames, who'll be looking after us while we're working here,' he said.

'Pleased to meet you, Mrs Soames,' Eleanor said, holding out her hand.

The other woman wiped her hand on the pristine white apron which was tied around her waist and shook Eleanor's hand.

'Call me Maggie, please,' she said with a smile. 'I hope everything is to your liking – do let me know if there's anything I can get you.'

'Thank you, I will.'

Maggie smiled politely and left them to their meal.

'There are other ways of awakening your sexuality, Eleanor,' Marcus said when she had gone.

Eleanor smiled cynically. 'Such as?'

'Perhaps a more personal approach?'

Eleanor laughed. To think she had imagined she would be so in awe of him. He might be a modern-day guru on all matters sexual, but when it came to his own needs and desires he was as transparent as the next man.

'Such as sleeping with you, I suppose?' she challenged him.

Marcus held her eye steadily, his expression speculative.

'Would that be such a repulsive alternative?'

'No,' Eleanor replied honestly, recognising that his nearness, and the turn the conversation had taken were affecting her. 'But I like my research to be both thorough and objective. Though putting myself in your undoubtedly experienced hands might well be pleasant, it's hardly scientific.'

Marcus was silent for a while and Eleanor was afraid that he had taken her rejection badly. She was relieved when he spoke.

'Why do you want to do this, Eleanor? A beautiful, sensual woman like yourself – why would you want to put yourself through this kind of experience?'

Eleanor decided that, if she was to enlist his help, she would have to be honest with him.

'Because my husband convinced me that I was frigid and I believe that he was wrong. I need to prove he was wrong, or I can't move on. Please, Marcus – help me.'

Their eyes met and held across the table. Marcus still looked troubled, but Eleanor sensed that he would agree.

'Unless, of course, you're afraid that I'll prove your theories wrong,' she pushed him gently.

'You won't,' he replied bluntly. 'Very well, Eleanor, if you insist that this is what you want.

We'll begin tomorrow on the first chapter –
massage. Perhaps you would like to telephone
this number now and make an appointment for
the masseur to visit?'

Eleanor took the folded newspaper from him.
There, ringed in red biro, was an advertisement.

'SENSUAL MASSAGE FOR DISCERNING LADIES BY
YOUNG, MUSCULAR MASSEUR. DISCRETION
ASSURED.'

The advert was one of several in the personal
columns of the newspaper and Eleanor glanced
quizzically at Marcus across the table. He was
watching her closely and she realised at once that
he was expecting her to baulk at the idea of
replying to the ad. Though her mouth had grown
inexplicably dry and she was having serious
second thoughts, she was determined not to fall
at the first hurdle.

Marcus handed her a mobile phone and
watched as she dialled. The telephone was
answered by a woman.

'Hello?'

'Um . . . hello. Is that the number of the
massage service?'

'Yes – how may I help you?'

'I'd like to book a masseur for tomorrow . . .
evening.'

'Certainly. May I take your details and ring you
back?'

'Ring me back?'

'We have to be sure of our clients, madam – I'm

sure you understand. It won't be more than five minutes.'

Eleanor put down the phone and stared at Marcus.

'Will you stay in the house?' she asked him.

'Of course. It's only a massage, Eleanor. You're the one who's in control.'

Eleanor jumped as the phone rang again. Confirming that she would be free at nine-thirty, she again put the telephone down. Marcus was regarding her across the table, his expression unreadable. She smiled and carried on eating, well aware that he could see through her bravado, but grateful that he kept his own counsel.

At nine the following evening, Eleanor was a nervous wreck. She had soaked in the bath until the water had cooled around her and was waiting in her room dressed in nothing but a thick towelling robe. Sitting at the pretty dressing table in the corner of the room, she stared at her reflection.

In the soft glow of the bedside lamps she had switched on, her skin looked pale and smooth. Her eyes were wide and over bright and her mouth trembled slightly as she stared at it.

'Come on, girl,' she said aloud, 'this is your first step on the Marcus Grant path to discovering your sexuality. You're supposed to be enjoying every minute!'

Earlier, they had discussed how she would plot

her progress in the form of a journal, leaving Marcus to write the more scholarly material for the book. Given the intimate nature of her contribution, her name would not appear on the cover and she was to devise a pseudonym for herself. She had spent the day writing a draft copy of her introductory pages and had found her tension growing steadily as the day wore on. Now, despite the restful music and the leisurely soak in the bath, she felt so tense that she was sure she could snap clean in half.

The doorbell rang, making her jump. Her heart began to pound with a dull insistence and her mouth ran dry. She heard Marcus come out of his study and walk across the tiled floor to open the front door and caught the low murmur of male voices as he showed the masseur up to her room.

'Eleanor?' He opened her door a crack and poked his head round. 'Are you ready?'

'I can't do this,' she blurted, her eyes meeting his in the dressing-table mirror.

Marcus turned and said a few words to the masseur before stepping into the room, closing the door quietly behind him.

'What's the problem?'

Eleanor turned towards him, folding her hands anxiously in her lap.

'Supposing he makes a pass at me?' she said anxiously.

Marcus shrugged. 'I guess you'll either go with it, or politely decline, whichever way it takes you.'

Eleanor stared at him. 'Are you serious?'

Marcus regarded her for a moment, his head on one side.

'It's not too late to call it off, Eleanor, if that's what you want?'

She almost did, but even as she opened her mouth to ask Marcus to tell the masseur to go away, something stopped her. A kind of calm settled over her and she shook her head.

'No, I'm all right now.'

'Are you sure?'

'Yes.'

'Okay. I won't be far away – just call if you need me, all right?'

Eleanor nodded and he turned away. As the masseur walked in she felt her stomach turn a small somersault. He was wearing black trousers and a white cotton singlet with cutaway shoulders which showed off his physique to the best advantage.

He had a body that was worth showing off. Broad, muscular shoulders topped a pleasingly sculpted chest which tapered to a neat waist. His blond hair was cropped and he had piercing blue eyes which crinkled at the corners as he smiled.

'Hi – I'm Oliver,' he said, moving forward to shake her hand.

Eleanor smiled faintly, liking the feeling of his cool palm against hers.

'Yes. Um . . . I've never done this before . . . How does it work?'

Oliver's eyes swept briskly over her as he took a step back. 'Well, if you'd like to lie on the bed?'

He spread a towel over the duvet and Eleanor lay down rather self-consciously on her stomach.

'Er . . . do you think you could take the robe off?' Oliver said. 'I have a towel here to protect your modesty.'

Eleanor's cheeks flamed as she wriggled out of the dressing-gown and lay down again. Oliver laid what felt like a minuscule towel over her tightly clenched buttocks and knelt down beside her.

'Now,' he explained, his tone low and soothing, 'I want you to relax and close your eyes. There's nothing to be worried about. I'm going to massage a medley of aromatherapy oils into your skin. First I'm going to put some music on. Relax.'

Eleanor lay still, wondering how anyone could relax in such a situation. She felt exposed and vulnerable, every muscle tensed ready to leap up and flee if she didn't like what he did to her. So far, she thought grimly to herself, this experience was nothing like the gateway to sensual awakening that Marcus had said it would be.

At the flick of a switch, music floated through the room, curiously tuneless and yet soothing, waves against a shoreline, washing over her senses.

Eleanor gasped at the first touch of Oliver's warm hands at the base of her neck. Slippery with a heavy, lavender-scented oil, they slipped across her skin, smoothing down her back to her waist.

510

'Your husband said you were tense – he wasn't kidding!' Oliver murmured as he began to work on her rigid muscles.

Her husband! The idea of Marcus being described in such a way almost made Eleanor laugh out loud. How had she got herself into this? She had to admit, though, Oliver's skilful hands and fingers were beginning to work magic on the tightly bunched muscles in her back. In spite of herself, she could feel her tension gradually unfurling, little tentacles of pleasure working their way through her body. She sighed and allowed herself to sink into the mattress.

'That's better,' Oliver murmured in his low, restful voice. 'Close your eyes.'

Eleanor did as she was told. By denying herself one source of sensory experience, she found the others were magnified. The music seemed to flow over and through her, vibrating in her limbs. She was acutely aware of the sensitivity of Oliver's fingertips as he sought out every tense muscle. Kneading and squeezing until the tension flowed away, he then turned his attention to stroking and smoothing her skin until Eleanor felt she would purr.

When he was satisfied that she had relaxed, Oliver turned his attention to the backs of her legs, working his way down to her feet. Eleanor braced herself for a ticklish sensation as he cupped one foot in his hand and began to work on the sole, but his touch was firm and precise. As he manipulated each pressure point on her foot, she felt as though the effects rippled up her legs and flowed through the rest of her body. By the time he had afforded the other foot the same treatment, Eleanor felt as if she would float away.

'Would you like to roll over now?' Oliver's voice, soft in her ear, made her stir.

'Roll over?' she repeated sleepily. She frowned as she recognised what he meant. 'Well—'

'I have another towel ready.'

She could sense the smile in his voice as he guessed the reason for her reluctance. To some Eleanor knew she might seem prudish, but she simply wasn't used to displaying her naked body to complete strangers and she wasn't comfortable with nudity. Michael's unhidden distaste for her body had reinforced her natural modesty so that it was not until Oliver handed her the second towel and discreetly turned his back while he selected another bottle of oil did she roll over, draping the towels hastily over herself before he turned back.

Oliver smiled at her and gently pulled the towels straight before warming the oil between his palms. He really was rather attractive and Eleanor found her body responding to the appreciative gleam she detected in his eyes as he ran them swiftly from her head to her toes.

Enjoying a back massage with her eyes closed and her head turned away from the masseur was one thing, but having to actually face him as he went to work on her body was rather too intimate for Eleanor's comfort. Whereas before she had finally been able to relax and enjoy the experience, now she could feel herself tensing again, the adrenalin beginning to pump through her veins once more.

Oliver noticed it too and he glanced at her assessingly as he worked on the fronts of her legs.

'Relax,' he repeated lightly. 'This isn't going to hurt!'

Eleanor forced a smile. 'I know . . . I just feel a bit . . . odd, that's all. Don't your other clients feel inhibited about having you in their bedrooms?'

'Is that how you feel, Eleanor? Inhibited?'

'It is a little *intimate*,' she said, hoping she didn't sound as panicky as she felt.

Oliver smiled enigmatically. 'That's what most of my clients enjoy most about my visits,' he said, moving round so that he was kneeling by her head. 'Don't talk any more,' he said. 'I want you to concentrate on nothing but sound and touch. Close your eyes, please.'

Eleanor obeyed him and his hands splayed across her chest, his fingertips playing across the small bones in a way that made her feel as if she would sink into the bed. Her capacity for rational thought slipped away with alarming speed.

His body was too close for comfort; she could feel the long muscles of his thigh pressing against her shoulder. As he leaned over her to massage her shoulders and her chest, she could smell the clean, male scent of him, an intoxicating perfume that, combined with the tuneless beat of the music, made her feel oddly disorientated, as if her head had somehow been disconnected in some way from her body.

Opening her eyes slightly, she watched the play of muscles in his arms and chest as he concentrated on giving her pleasure. The sight of his youthful, well-toned body and the thought of him using it solely for her pleasure made Eleanor feel warm and heavy-limbed. Recognising the feeling as desire, she tried to rouse herself sufficiently to call a halt while she still had her wits about her.

She opened her mouth to speak, but at that moment, Oliver transferred his attention to her stomach. Eleanor sucked in her breath, conscious of the little ripples of pleasure travelling in ever decreasing circles from her hips to her navel. Oliver pressed gently with the heel of his hand and manipulated her soft flesh in a circular movement which made Eleanor want to sigh with delight.

Beneath the towel, which barely covered her breasts, she felt her nipples gather into aching little peaks. The flesh of her breasts felt heavy and swollen. Though she kept her thighs pressed tightly together, she was aware that the sensitive folds of flesh at their apex had unfurled, moistening in response to Oliver's rhythmic caresses.

Through half-closed eyes Eleanor watched Oliver's face. His whole concentration was focused on what he was doing and a part of her mind, the writerly part, filed the realisation away that one of the most powerful aphrodisiacs was to be the sole object of an attractive man's attention.

Eleanor felt as though she were melting into the mattress, her arms and legs weightless, and there was an ache, low down in her womb. It seemed like the most natural thing in the world when his fingertips edged up her ribcage so that they brushed against the lower curve of her breasts.

Her nipples reacted to the innocuous caress by hardening, pressing against the towel. Eleanor murmured restlessly as Oliver removed it, sighing with pleasure as his warm palms covered her breasts.

'You have beautiful breasts,' he told her, his fingers performing their magic over the sensitive flesh.

Eleanor told herself she would stop him, but she was enjoying it too much. Just a few minutes more . . .

Oliver dipped his head and pressed his lips against the tip of one aching nipple. If she didn't stop him now she knew he would open his mouth and draw it in and then she would be lost. She knew then with blinding certainty that she wasn't ready to take things further yet.

'No,' she said quietly, her voice emerging as a croak.

Oliver straightened instantly, offering her his hand as she stood up and pushed her arms into the sleeves of her robe.

'I'd like you to go now,' she said shakily, avoiding his eye.

'Of course. Please do ring again it you need me.'

Eleanor glanced at him and saw that he seemed unoffended, perfectly businesslike as he packed away his oils and towels and removed the CD from the player.

'Thank you, I will,' she assured him.

He flashed her a friendly smile as he left and any embarrassment she had begun to feel was swept away, leaving her with nothing but the slow-burning arousal he had invoked with his clever fingers.

Turning towards the full-length mirror which stood by the dressing table, Eleanor allowed the robe to slip off her shoulders. It fell to the floor in a soft heap, unregarded. Her breasts looked full and heavy, the nipples still standing out like two hard little cones. The oil which had been worked into her body made her skin glow in the half-light of the bedroom. She still felt warm, her sex pulsing gently as it remembered the touch of Oliver's fingers on her breasts.

Shivering slightly, Eleanor wrapped her arms around her body and closed her eyes. Her skin felt silky soft, and her fingers moved as if of their own volition down her sides and across the gentle swell of her belly. Leaning her head over to one side, she ran one hand up her neck, caressing the straining tendons before sweeping her hand down again, brushing across the crested tips of her breasts.

It was a featherlight caress, but the effect was electrifying. She began to tremble, her arms and legs shaking as if gripped with fever, a fine film of perspiration pushing through her pores, mixing with the oil.

'Eleanor?'

Her eyes flew open as she heard Marcus's voice, low and resonant from the doorway. She hadn't heard the door open and, turning her head, she opened her mouth to protest at his invasion of her privacy. One look at his face silenced her. He was staring at her, his pupils dilated, his expression swiftly turning from surprise to desire. A slow pulse began to beat steadily between her legs and she turned slowly towards him, her eyelids drooping heavily and her breathing fast and shallow.

'Marcus!'

It emerged as a whisper, the tone redolent of her unspoken, barely acknowledged need and he responded to it at once. He strode purposefully across the room and his larger hand replaced hers at the side of her neck. Eleanor leaned into his palm and sighed.

'Eleanor . . .' he breathed her name, his warm, wine-scented breath brushing her cheek.

Holding herself in readiness, Eleanor silently willed him to relieve the aching desire which gnawed at her belly. There was no time for thought, for reasoning, for the making of choices. There was only the urgent physical need which had to be assuaged at all costs.

Marcus's arm came about her, supporting her as he lowered her slightly, so that her breasts were tipped up to his heated gaze. With his free hand he stroked the swell of her breasts, sweeping the tip of one finger along the cleft between them. Eleanor shivered and sighed, her arms coming up to cling to him as his hand stroked lower, setting her stomach on fire and causing a potent, liquid heat to seep between the folds of her hidden flesh.

The heel of his hand brushed against the soft fleece of hair on her mons and Eleanor moaned softly. Behind her closed eyelids she was aware of nothing but sensation. Her legs parted slightly so that the cooler air of the room touched the petal-soft flesh between them. She sucked in her breath as Marcus's fingers curled gently into the molten heat of her sex.

'Oh-h!' she sighed, her pelvis tipped upward, pressing against his hand.

'Ssh!' he whispered against her hair, his lips brushing the top of her ear, causing little shivers to run down her neck. 'Hush now.'

He began to move his fingers, playing her like a precious musical instrument, anticipating exactly the moment when she wanted the tempo to change. Her clitoris was swollen, straining towards his fingers so that, when he pressed the pad of his finger against it and moved the small bundle of nerve endings beneath the covering of silken flesh, she felt as if an electric shock had passed from his fingertips through to the very heart of her womb.

Her legs felt weak, incapable of supporting her and she leaned more heavily on Marcus as he moved the small bud round and round with ever increasing rhythm. Gradually, Eleanor felt the sensation gathering at the base of her clitoris, building, layer upon layer, until there was no turning back.

And yet, when her climax broke, it still took her by surprise. Wave after wave of the most exquisite pleasure richocheted through her. Eleanor cried out with the shock of it, and her legs buckled beneath her.

Marcus supported her, his fingers pressing against the vibrating bud of her clitoris, drawing out her climax until she was gasping with the pleasure of it.

'Oh – no more ... no more ...!' she whimpered, pressing her pelvis against his hand in a way that made a nonsense of her protest.

Vaguely she was aware of being lifted, of Marcus's arms behind her neck and her knees. The bed dipped as he laid her down on it and, for a brief instant, his strong, warm body was covering hers. Then he rose and she shivered at the sudden chill which swept over her.

'Marcus . . .?'

'Ssh,' he said softly.

Eleanor tried to open her eyes, but they felt as if they had been nailed shut. She sighed as the duvet wafted across her naked body, moving her head so that her cheek rested against the cool cotton of the pillow. She heard the quiet click of the bedroom door as he left, but was too weary to realise its significance. Within minutes she was asleep.

Chapter Four

BY TACIT AGREEMENT, they did not discuss the events of the previous evening over breakfast the next morning. Marcus acted as though nothing had happened between them and Eleanor, had she not woken with the pleasant afterglow of orgasm enfolding her, might have thought, from his demeanour, that she had imagined it.

Sitting at the word processor later, Eleanor poured out her thoughts and feelings, searching for catharsis.

At first, there was nothing overtly sexual about Oliver's touch. He was strictly professional, working on each muscle group meticulously until he had induced in me a state of pure relaxation the like of which I have never known before. That feeling of well-being enabled me to shed some of the inhibitions I had about my

521

body and I felt my initial self-consciousness gradually slip away.

It was as if the massage had unlocked my hitherto unacknowledged, deep-seated need for physical contact, something I had denied myself for so long. Stroking is, after all, a basic human need which is fundamental to the development of a woman's sensuality. If nothing else, the massage helped me to become conscious of my own body in a way that I hadn't considered before. The concentrated attention lavished upon it made me yearn for more intimate caresses . . .

And I got them, she concluded silently. If she closed her eyes, she imagined she could still feel the imprint of Marcus's hands manipulating her most intimate flesh. He had only to turn her in his arms and she would have opened herself to him readily, would have welcomed the thrust of him into her body.

Why hadn't he? Eleanor remembered the brief moment when his body had covered hers and she shivered. She was sure that he had wanted to take things further between them. Recalling the tenderness of his gesture as he tucked the duvet around her, she was aware of a yearning, a sense of a need unfulfilled. And for the first time she began to appreciate the very real danger into which she had put herself – that in awakening her sexuality, she could, like a psychiatrist's grateful patient, quite easily become sexually dependent on Marcus himself.

Already her body ached for him and she found herself listening for his footsteps as he moved around the house. Yet when he came into her study at midday, she almost jumped out of her skin.

'I didn't mean to startle you,' he said. 'Lunch is ready in the living room. I thought you might be ready for a break.'

Eleanor smiled.

'Yes. I've almost finished the first section already. How are you doing?'

A shutter seemed to close down over Marcus's eyes, hiding something from her.

'Fine,' he said. 'I'd like to discuss the next chapter with you over lunch.'

'Okay. I'll be with you in a few minutes.'

She waited until he had left before concluding the first part of her journal.

Massage is a pampering device which every woman deserves. Getting in touch with one's own body, learning about its responses, its likes and dislikes, is a useful first step to unlocking the desire within.

After my massage with Oliver, I not only felt relaxed and cared-for, I felt sexually primed. If only Oliver had been a partner rather than a professional, I would have undoubtedly wanted things to progress further.

Perhaps, then, a course in mutual massage would be a good starting point for any couple who wish to improve the intimate side of their relationship.

Eleanor re-read her concluding sentence and frowned. If she was to keep to the point and chart her sexual awakening, the sentence would not be relevant. Deciding she would leave it for now and edit the entire journal when it was completed, she exited from the program and went to join Marcus in the living room.

Maggie had left them a large green salad and a selection of seafood. At the sight of the food, Eleanor felt hungry and she piled up her plate before sitting down in an armchair opposite Marcus.

'I've got a selection of books and magazines here, Eleanor,' he said, indicating the coffee table.

Glancing at them, she saw the lurid titles of some of the magazines and felt her cheeks grow warm. Noticing, Marcus chuckled softly.

'Some of them are pretty hard core – don't expect to relate to all of them. It's important to keep detailed notes of both the content and your response to it. I'm going away for a few days to conduct the interviews I set up before we came, so you have the house to yourself. There are videos too – I'll leave those in your study so that Maggie doesn't come across them when she's dusting.'

Eleanor pushed away her disappointment that

he was going away and smiled faintly at him.

'I . . . suppose I'd better reserve the evenings for the actual reading and watching,' she said.

'It might be wise. You'll be on your own then, so you can have a free run of the house.' He smiled at her, a smile that seemed, to Eleanor, to not quite reach his eyes. 'I'm leaving straight after lunch. You can reach me on the mobile if you need anything. Any questions?'

Eleanor shook her head.

'It seems straightforward enough. You're off interviewing, and I'm going to spend the next few days reading and watching pornography.'

Marcus returned her smile and this time his eyes crinkled at the corners with genuine warmth.

'It's a hard life, isn't it?'

Eleanor waited until she had eaten dinner, making sure that Maggie had gone home before she picked up the first of the magazines. She had seen this type of top-shelf men's magazine before and knew that looking at acres of exposed female flesh was not likely to turn her on.

It struck her, though, as she flicked idly through the glossy pages that, from a purely instructive point of view, this was the only time she was likely to see another woman's vulva in such graphic detail. The differences in something that was fundamentally the same in all women were fascinating. Not only did pubic hair seem to run the whole range of colour, texture and quantity, there seemed to be just as many diverse types of labia. Some were thin, some plump and moist-looking; some protruded below the outer labia whilst others were so neat and symmetrical they hardly looked real. Though none could be described as pretty, there was a certain beauty about those displayed. For the first time, Eleanor began to appreciate the male obsession with female genitalia.

Marcus had included a selection of magazines aimed at women and Eleanor spent an hour gazing at page after page of anonymous, semi-erect penises. Concluding that it wasn't the sight of a male member that was designed to turn her on, but the intention of the man to whom it belonged, she soon cast the magazines aside. She would go back to those later.

There were books, ranging from the vaguely raunchy to the downright obscene. She selected a couple, both purporting to be written by women, for women, in the hope that these might be able to touch a nerve. She had three days, after all, to plough through the pile of magazines and books. Before she went to bed tonight, she would watch one of the dozen or so videotapes.

The one she fed into the VCR was short on dialogue, as if the producer had decided to do without a script and so have his actors say as little as possible. There was a soundtrack which ebbed and flowed according to the drama of what was going on.

The plotline, such as it was, was absurd, but as the protagonists began to strip off their clothes and get down to the real business of the film, Eleanor found herself irresistibly drawn to the images on the screen.

The main female character, a stunning redhead with large, silicone-assisted breasts and long, slender legs, performed a striptease for two men who were sitting on a sofa in what looked like a high-rise office block. The woman stood with her back to the partially closed Venetian blinds and swayed to the pulsing beat of the music which filled the office.

She was wearing a red, figure-hugging top and black lycra mini-skirt over minuscule thong briefs and a push-up bra. Eleanor could sense the tension of the two men watching as she peeled off the last of her clothes and stood, gloriously naked except for her ridiculously high, spike-heeled mules, in front of them.

Apart from the artificially pumped-up breasts, the woman had a stunning figure; firm and slender, the skin smooth and pale. One of the men stood up and walked around her, his eyes raking her body with undisguised lust.

Eleanor felt uncomfortable to be witnessing the scene, but she made herself watch, trying to keep a part of her mind objective so that she could record her responses later.

The men were dressed in smart city suits and their impeccable tailoring provided an erotic counterpoint to the woman's nakedness. The man who had risen stood behind the woman's shoulder, so close that she would have been able to feel his breath against her naked shoulder as he leaned over her.

'Walk for us,' he said, his voice low and silky.

Without a word, the woman turned and obeyed him, walking slowly from one end of the room to the other, her hips rolling provocatively as she teetered on the impossibly high heels. The camera switched briefly to the faces of the two men, recording their anticipation as they watched the woman parading in front of them.

The man on the sofa was stroking himself through the fabric of his trousers. The material tented slightly at the front, and he beckoned the woman over. Bizarrely, the next shot showed her covering her full lips with bright, glossy red lipstick before she sank to her knees in front of the man who stood up in front of her.

As he unfastened his trousers, his cock sprang free, fully erect and eager, brushing against the woman's cheek. The camera focused lovingly on the sight of the woman's mouth, garishly bright, opening to admit the bulbous head of his penis.

Eleanor watched, mesmerised, as the woman's cheeks bulged to admit the man's cock into her mouth. She had never seen anything this explicit before and she was dismayed to realise that a dull heaviness had settled between her thighs, a precursor to arousal.

It wasn't as if she found the scenario being played out before her particularly affecting, it was simply the close proximity of intimacy that provoked a reaction from her. Appalled and fascinated in equal measure, Eleanor watched as the man pushed the woman away. His cock was glistening, rearing up from his groin like a baton.

The other man moved forward now and the woman turned, watching as he took off his clothes. Eleanor found herself empathising with the woman's obvious tension as the man peeled off his tight-fitting boxer shorts. She gasped aloud as she saw his cock. It was huge, bigger than anything she had ever imagined. Pointing upwards, the bulb was level with his navel. Not only was it long, it was thick, so much so that when the woman reached for him, her middle finger and thumb did not meet as she circled it.

Miming her delight at its size, the woman stroked and kissed it while the two men looked on. The camera panned down to her buttocks which the first man began to stroke and caress. Slowly, he parted her bottom cheeks to reveal the shadowed crease between and the heavy purse of her sex below.

The woman's sex glistened as the camera lingered lovingly on the intricate folds of flesh. Eleanor's eyes widened as she watched the man open her with his thumbs, exposing the entrance to her body to the steady eye of the camera.

In one of the swift, senseless changes in

camera-shot which seemed to punctuate the action, the woman was now crouching over the well-endowed man, who was lying on his back on the floor. Reaching between her legs, she opened her labia and positioned herself so that the man's massive cock was poised at her entrance.

Eleanor moaned in unison with the woman as she fed the man's cock into her vagina. The camera showed her sex stretching and bulging around it, before panning to the woman's face. Her expression was a cross between ecstasy and pain, a combination which was strangely erotic.

As soon as she had eased the man inside her, the other man stepped forward so that his feet were positioned on either side of the first man's torso. While the first man pumped his hips in time with the woman, the second man gathered up her generous breasts in his hands, forming a channel for his cock.

Eleanor watched as the trio moved with choreographed precision towards the inevitable climax. The woman's mouth stretched wide, the tendons standing out on her neck and her eyes glazing over as she strained towards orgasm. Her neck and breasts were spattered by the semen pumping from the cock which had been moving between her breasts. Seconds later, her hips bucked as the man beneath her came.

When it was over, Eleanor switched off the television set and made her way upstairs in a daze. After so many months of self-imposed celibacy, the past two days had given her sensory overload. When she had first read Marcus's proposal she had genuinely believed that his programme might work for her. Now she was certain it could, and with a speed that had taken her breath away.

She had never dreamt that looking at pictures and watching other people copulate would arouse her as it had, and she wasn't sure whether she liked the revelation. It made her feel slightly dirty, ashamed of the base nature of her response. After all, the people on the screen had been like two-dimensional images, there purely as objects of sexual gratification. There was something rather cold and clinical about the whole affair that Eleanor found vaguely distasteful.

Nevertheless, there was no getting away from the fact that her entire body felt as if it had been stroked all over by a wire brush – her skin tingled and the blood pumped richly through her veins. Glancing down at her bare arms, she was almost surprised to see that they were as pale as ever – the way she felt, she had almost expected them to glow.

Eleanor paused as she walked into the bedroom, for there on the bed was a small, square box, wrapped in red tissue paper. There was a card attached, written in Marcus's large, confident handwriting.

Sorry I can't be with you this evening – the gift inside may help.

Intrigued, Eleanor unwrapped the tissue paper and lifted the lid off the box.

531

'Oh!'

She had seen dildos before, but never one like this. Made of flesh-toned latex, it warmed in her hand as she picked it up gingerly. It was moulded to look like a circumcised penis, the exposed glans smooth and bulbous, the long, life-like shaft below lovingly crafted with veins and a scrotal sac. Twisting the dial in the base of the balls, Eleanor almost dropped it as it began to vibrate gently in her hand.

As she watched, the stem began to rotate slightly, as if searching for entry, and she turned it off quickly. Did Marcus really think she would use such a thing? It was . . . *obscene*. Masturbation wasn't like scratching an itch!

Shoving the offending object back in its box, Eleanor opened the drawer on the bedside table and pushed it inside. Marcus's gift, however well intended, had taken the edge off her arousal, so she showered quickly and slipped into bed.

It was very quiet in the house and there was barely any traffic noise from the street outside. As she lay awake, staring at the shadows on the ceiling cast by the streetlamp outside, Eleanor was suddenly struck by a feeling of over-whelming loneliness. For a moment her resolve wavered and she wondered what on earth she thought she was doing, so far from home. Then she thought of Rhys, and the relationship they might be able to have in the future, and she banished her doubts.

There were other advantages to this assignment. After the debacle in the restaurant when she had been accosted by a press photographer, Eleanor had not heard any more from Michael and the public interest in her and her reactions seemed to have waned. It was a relief to have the time and space to be out of the limelight.

She was tired. Closing her eyes, she rolled onto her side and allowed herself to drift into sleep.

She was standing on a wide sweep of marble steps leading up to an imposing, multi-storeyed mansion. The sounds of people laughing, the clink of glasses, the dull thud of dance music drifted down to her, as if beckoning her. Her dream-self hesitated, torn between wanting to walk up to the imposing double oak doors which stood open at the top of the steps and wanting to turn away.

As if standing outside herself, Eleanor could see every detail of her own appearance. She was wearing a white dress. It was sleeveless with a neat bodice and a full skirt, cinched at the waist with a narrow, white patent belt. It looked like something out of a Fifties film, very Grace Kelly with the neat white courts and white gloves.

Her hair was pulled back so tightly from her face Eleanor could feel the pressure on the roots. It made her head ache, yet she found the tightness of the bun curiously reassuring, as though it anchored her.

She needed anchoring. Her stomach was churning and she was aware of holding herself so rigidly that her limbs trembled as she walked up the steps. A part of her didn't want to join the party and she didn't know why. It sounded like fun, the merriment growing louder as she drew close.

A large, black woman in a full-length red dress greeted her at the door. The dress was several sizes too small, so that it gaped open across the bust and stomach, revealing rolls of smooth black flesh. Eleanor felt the corners of her mouth lifting in a smile.

'Hello, Jennifer,' she said.

The woman smiled, but didn't say a word. Instead, she pointed along the corridor. Eleanor walked the way she had indicated. It was a long corridor with a slippery parquet floor. There were pillars spaced intermittently along it, giving the appearance of a Greek temple. As she rounded the corner, she heard the unmistakable sounds of love-making coming from one of the shadowed alcoves between the pillars.

Curiosity spurred her on. Drawing closer, she saw that there was a stone bench running the length of the alcove. Over the bench, facing away from her, a naked man was draped over the cold stone. There was another man with him, stroking his naked buttocks languidly, displaying little interest in them as he read the *Financial Times*.

'Michael?' Eleanor said, recognising him.

He looked up at the sound of his name and, seeing it was her, he smiled at her. The other man raised his head, and Eleanor saw that it was Duncan.

'What are you doing in my dream?' she asked, feeling more indignant than upset.

Both men stared back at her with expressions of mild surprise, as if her question had been singularly stupid. Then Michael leaned over and gathered Duncan into his arms from behind. As they turned as one, Eleanor stepped back, stifling a cry of shock with her hand as her eyes focused on Duncan's chest. He had breasts – *her* breasts – the pink areolae visible through Michael's splayed fingers.

Backing away, Eleanor bumped into a hard male body. Turning, she was relieved to find it was Rhys.

'Oh Rhys! I'm so glad you're here!' she breathed. 'I—'

'I can't wait forever,' he said, interrupting her, impatience striping his tone.

'But you won't have to! Just a few more weeks, Rhys . . . Rhys!'

Eleanor clutched at thin air as Rhys turned towards another woman in the crowd that had mysteriously gathered around them. Eyes frantically scanning faces for someone she knew, Eleanor was relieved when Marcus stepped forward. He was dressed all in black, his long hair loose and falling around his face.

'Show us how far you've come, Eleanor,' he said, reaching out to circle her wrist with his fingers.

Eleanor resisted for a moment as he drew her towards him, but it was useless to struggle. It seemed to Eleanor that the crowd moved back, leaving a space around them. She had the impression that dozens of eyes were watching her, feeding on every nuance of her behaviour, intruding on her every thought.

'Those pins again!' Marcus said, shaking his head sadly at her.

For a moment, Eleanor didn't understand what he meant. Then he began to take the pins out of her hair and she remembered how he had loosened it on the banks of the Thames.

'No . . .!' she whispered. She could see by the expression in his eyes that he had heard her, but he did not respond. Instead, he pulled out the last of the pins, sending her hair cascading down over her shoulders.

To Eleanor, the gesture made her feel as vulnerable, as exposed as she would have felt if he had stripped her naked. Symbolically, by letting down her hair, she felt that he had signalled to all those watching that she was a fraud. The neat, calm exterior she liked to project to the world was a sham, hiding the passionate, shameful core of her.

Not any more. Now she could feel the lust in the eyes of those watching affecting her, making her feel wanton and abandoned.

'You see?' Marcus said, his lips against her hair. 'They can all see what you are. There's no hiding any more.'

He began to undo the buttons at the front of her dress, peeling back the sides to reveal her naked, unfettered breasts to an appreciative audience.

'Beautiful,' a male voice said. 'Show us more.'

Eleanor's feet felt as though they had been nailed to the floor as she allowed him to strip her dress away completely. Now she was standing in front of them wearing nothing but the neat, lady-like white gloves, a suspender belt and white stockings, and her shoes.

Her skin blushed under the scrutiny of so many eyes, her nipples rising and cresting as warm breath skimmed them, fingertips, butterfly light, brushing casually across the peaks. Eleanor's breath hurt in her chest and she found it difficult to breathe. A blossoming, moist heaviness settled between her legs, her labia aching as they suffused with blood.

Oliver, the masseur, suddenly materialised beside her.

'Discretion assured,' he said earnestly. 'Open your legs.'

Eleanor obeyed, sliding her feet apart so that he could touch her. His fingers were smooth and professional as they massaged the swollen folds of flesh, working the skin back and forth over her burgeoning clitoris.

'She's very wet,' he told the room at large, 'hot

too. It won't take her long to come.'

'No!' Eleanor's cry was anguished, pointless in the face of her escalating fever.

'No!'

Eleanor sat bolt upright in bed, clutching the duvet around her trembling breasts. Disorientated for a moment, she rubbed her hand over her cropped hair, reassuring herself that she could not possibly be that woman standing in the middle of a room, being publically masturbated to a climax.

One thing that was real, though, was the dull, insistent pulse beating between her thighs. Agitated, she pulled the vibrator Marcus had left her out of the bedside drawer.

It felt heavy in her hand, the latex taking the heat from her palm, becoming almost human as she held it. Swallowing hard, Eleanor switched it on and sank back against the pillows. The mock penis slipped easily between the slippery folds of her sex, finding her clitoris with unerring accuracy. As it began to rotate and vibrate, Eleanor closed her eyes and allowed her thoughts free rein.

Images from her dream, of Michael and Duncan and Marcus and Jennifer, mixed with pictures from the video she had watched. Nothing made sense, any more than the dream had done, and she allowed her mind to wander, to travel along paths that bore little relation to reality, where sensation was all.

She saw herself bending over the stone bench,

as Duncan had done. Oliver gathered up her buttocks in his hands and kneaded and squeezed the flesh, indirectly stimulating the sensitive area directly below.

Looking over her shoulder, Eleanor watched as he unfastened his jeans. His cock sprang free, enormous and straight, like the actor's in the film. Incongruously, he winked at her as he positioned himself at the entrance to her body. She gasped as he pushed his way in. His cock filled her, stretching her delicate passage until she could take no more.

The vibrating latex pulsed against the silky, cleated walls of her vagina, burrowing deeper, drawing the pleasure from it, making her clitoris twitch with frustration.

'Yes,' she whispered into the lonely darkness, 'oh yes . . .'

She came then, wave after wave of searing pleasure travelling along her limbs, consuming her, setting her on fire. And she knew that it was not enough, that she wanted . . . no, *needed*, the extra dimension of a man's body, thrusting into her, sharing her pleasure.

Chapter Five

THE WORD PROCESSOR glared impatiently at Eleanor as she stared out of the window. Conscious of its constant belligerent gaze, she dragged her attention back to her work, re-reading what she had just written.

In conclusion, in my experience it is possible to reach a state of constant readiness, where an awareness of the sexuality inherent in the world around us is uppermost in the mind. By the frequent reading and watching of pornographic material the mind can be programmed to respond to the most subtle of stimuli in day-to-day life, stimuli which would previously have gone unnoticed, or otherwise ignored.

After three days and nights submerged in the material Marcus had left for her, Eleanor felt quite out of touch with reality. She had done nothing but read, watch, sleep and eat, and only then when food was put in front of her by Maggie. She had never dreamed that so many variations on a theme could exist.

Before her marriage to Michael, Eleanor's few sexual encounters had, in retrospect, been quite frighteningly mundane. With Michael sex was always a perfunctory event, with him taking her from behind, usually under cover of darkness. She had never dreamt that such a world of sensual pleasures could exist for her as that described in the books she read.

The latex-covered penis had become a well-used friend as she sought to relieve herself time and time again after observing the many varied acts acted and described. Now she was desperate now for Marcus to return so that she could discuss some of her conclusions with him.

She jumped as the telephone rang, the shrill sound breaking into the cloistered atmosphere of her study.

'Hello?' she answered cautiously, half expecting to hear Michael's petulant tones on the other end. Her heart lifted as she recognised Marcus's voice.

'How are you getting on?' he asked her.

Eleanor hoped that he would not be able to tell from her tone just how well she was getting on.

'Fine. I've asked Maggie to cook something nice for us tonight so that we can compare notes.'

'Ah. That would have been swell, Eleanor, but that's what I was ringing you about.'

'You're not coming back tonight after all?' Eleanor battened down her disappointment and tried to concentrate on what he was saying.

'There's something I want to follow up on here in London – I shouldn't be more than a couple of days.'

Eleanor gripped the receiver as the soft sound of feminine laughter sounded in the background and she realised exactly what he meant.

'I see. I'll just carry on then, shall I?' she asked as calmly as she could manage.

'Can you cope?'

'Of course!'

'Did you like the present I left you?'

His voice had dropped an octave, as if he wanted only her to hear what he was saying. Eleanor resolutely ignored the dark thrill that ran through her and answered him with a briskness that she did not feel.

'It was very interesting,' she said.

Marcus chuckled wickedly, making Eleanor's skin prickle with reluctant awareness.

'I've organised a surprise for you this evening.'

'A surprise? What do you mean?'

For some reason, Eleanor felt alarmed. What did he mean, a *surprise*?

'It wouldn't be a surprise if I told you, would it? Get ready as if for going out; all will be revealed at eight-thirty. I'll look forward to reading an account of the evening in manuscript form when I get back!'

'But—!' Eleanor bit her lip as she realised that he had hung up.

The rest of the day passed in a daze of anticipation. At lunchtime, she took herself off for a short walk around the shops to try to take her mind off the evening ahead. Instead, she found herself dwelling on it, buying herself a new perfume and, in a fit of extravagance, an exquisite silk and lace nightdress in a deep ruby red which she promised herself she would wear the first night she slept with Rhys.

Returning to the house, she ate the light tea Maggie had left her, then went to bathe and change. *Dress as if for an evening out*, Marcus had said, whatever that meant. An evening out *where*? With whom?

Trying to cover all eventualities, Eleanor settled for the black dress she had bought in London the day she met Marcus. Her short hairstyle made it look more chic, somehow, and she was pleased with the finished effect as she applied her make-up and stood back to appraise herself in the full-length mirror.

The doorbell rang at eight-thirty precisely. Burning with curiosity, Eleanor went down to answer it. Her jaw dropped as she encountered a man on the doorstep, a huge bouquet of deep pink roses interspersed with gypsophila in one hand.

'Eleanor?' he asked, glancing at the tag on the bouquet.

'Yes?' she replied, her voice faint.

'I am Lars. I am to give you this.'

Eleanor slit open the envelope he gave her and pulled out the plain square of card inside.

Yours until morning, she read, recognising Marcus's handwriting at once, *enjoy!*

She gaped at the man who was waiting patiently to be allowed in.

'What the hell is he playing at?' she gasped.

'Excuse me?' The man's forehead creased in bewilderment. 'I am sorry, my English is not so good.'

'Oh. Well, you ... you'd better come in,' Eleanor told him, taking the roses and watching as he strode through to the living room.

Under cover of arranging the flowers in a vase, Eleanor studied the man who, at her suggestion, was pouring them both a drink. He was young, probably in his early twenties, with chin-length, layered blond hair which fell across his face as he leaned forward. Shown to advantage in the suave black dinner suit, his body looked firm and broad, his hands large and capable. They were a workman's hands, square-tipped with flat, neat nails, but too smooth and clean for those of a labourer.

As he passed Eleanor her glass his fingers brushed lightly against hers. They were warm, sending a small thrill along her arm at the brief contact. His eyes smiled at her, the expression in their cool blue depths courteous and appreciative.

'I suppose you're what they call an "escort", are you?' she said as she sipped her drink.

'An escort – yes,' he replied.

Eleanor realised that she found his accent very sexy and she relaxed a little.

'It's good work, is it?' she asked, genuinely interested.

'Yes.'

'What do you like about it?'

The expression in his eyes told her that he was puzzled by her questions, but he smiled as he answered.

'I like to meet such beautiful ladies,' he said.

His voice had a pleasant, sing-song cadence to it that made Eleanor smile. He seemed to be showing a genuine interest in her. Then it struck her that she did not need to worry in the least about the impression she might, or might not, be making on him – his opinion of her was irrelevant. As Marcus had said in his note, Lars was hers for the evening, fully paid for. She could do anything she liked with him. He was hers to enjoy.

The idea grew in appeal as she studied him, less covertly now that she had acknowledged his function.

'You don't mind being treated as a sex object?' she asked him curiously.

His forehead puckered in a frown.

'A . . . sex object . . .?'

545

'Your English really isn't very good, is it?' Eleanor said, her smile taking the sting out of her words. 'Still, we don't need to talk much, do we? Why don't you take off your jacket, make yourself more comfortable?'

She watched as he shrugged off the jacket and draped it over the back of the armchair. As he moved, the play of his muscles was visible beneath the fabric of his snowy white shirt. What could she do with him?

After her initial shock, the idea of being able to command this young stranger in any way that took her fancy had a definite appeal. Eleanor moistened her lips with the tip of her tongue. Making a decision, she put down her glass and beckoned to him.

'Let's go straight upstairs, Lars,' she said.

Taking her outstretched hand, Lars allowed her to lead him up to her room.

Inside, Eleanor switched on the CD player for a little background music. She had left the bedside lamps on and they cast a warm, womblike glow across the room. Lars stood by the side of the bed and watched her as she took off her earrings and watch and laid them on the dressing table.

The tension in the room was almost palpable, as if an invisible fog of sensuality had enveloped them both, drawing them together. Lars looked quizzically at her, waiting for her to make the next move. Eleanor felt an unaccustomed surge of power run through her veins and she smiled.

Holding his eye, she stepped forward and began to unfasten his tie. She was at eye level with the knot and, as he lifted his chin to make it easier for her, she gave in to the urge to press her lips experimentally against the bulge of his Adam's apple. It moved under her lips as he swallowed and she snaked out her tongue to taste his skin. It was warm and salty and Eleanor felt the adrenalin rushing through her.

She could feel the heat of his potent male body through the thin cotton fabric of his shirt and she wrestled with his buttons, impatience making her clumsy, as she stripped him. His pectorals were like two solid slabs of muscle, the golden skin covering them lightly furred with a blanket of blond chest hair. He shivered involuntarily as she ran her palms over his chest and the flat brown discs of his nipples hardened instantly.

'You have a very attractive body,' she told him.

It was curiously liberating to feel free to make such remarks. Before, she had always been too shy to admit verbally that she had even noticed a man's body, never mind found it appealing. Lars smiled down at her, unthreatening but virile, and Eleanor shivered in anticipation.

'Thank you,' he said. 'Would you like that I undress you?'

Eleanor considered for a moment.

'No,' she said, 'I think I would prefer to have you naked first.'

She could see the query in Lars's eyes, but he

didn't say anything as he unfastened his belt and slowly pulled it through the loops of his trousers. Eleanor watched his face, relishing the tension coupled with a slight apprehension that she could read there. Was this what men felt like when a woman stripped for them? Powerful, in control . . . so many images chased through Eleanor's head as she watched him, replays of the pornographic films and books and magazines which had been her constant diet this week.

Lars was wearing plain grey, jersey boxer shorts. The outline of his semi-erect penis was clearly visible beneath them as he bent to remove his socks. Straightening, he held himself tense as he watched her. Eleanor smiled.

'And the shorts, please.'

His pubic hair was as blond and fine as the hair on the rest of his body. Rising up from it, his cock looked very white, the exposed glans smooth and pink. His balls were full and heavy, the skin pulled tight across the scrotal sac.

He stood very still as Eleanor moved towards him and put her arms around his neck. She could feel the heat and shape of his body through the thin fabric of her dress and relished the sense of control it gave her to be fully clothed while he was as naked as the day he was born.

She turned her head away as he tried to kiss her.

'No – let me explore you.'

'An undiscovered country?'

Eleanor laughed.

'Yes. Do you mind?'

Lars shrugged, but Eleanor sensed that he was excited by the way she had demanded passivity from him.

'I am . . . for you,' he said, his voice low and husky. 'I am happy to bring you pleasure.'

'Good,' Eleanor breathed, 'because you do. Lie down.'

She moved with him to lie on the bed, her body covering his for a moment until she eased herself to one side. Propping her head on one elbow, she ran her fingertips lightly from his throat to his navel. Lars watched her almost indulgently, swallowing hard as the palm of her hand brushed against the swollen shaft of his penis.

Virtually ignoring him as a person, Eleanor explored his body with her hands, marvelling at the essential differences between his body and her own. Where she was soft and pliable, he was hard and unyielding, where her skin was smooth and hairless, his was rough beneath her fingers. Even his feet were different, strong and broad with no suggestion of delicacy.

After a few minutes of touching and feeling, Eleanor bent her head and kissed him. His lips were firm and warm, the inside of his mouth sweet against her tongue. He moaned deep in his throat and Eleanor felt the sound vibrate against her own lips.

'You're hot,' she murmured as she pulled away, her fingers roaming the sweat-slick skin of his chest.

549

'It is the . . . uh . . . *strain*,' he explained with a rueful smile.

'I admire your control,' she told him, smiling, 'but I haven't finished with you yet.'

Lars groaned as she followed the path her fingers had taken earlier with her mouth. Carefully avoiding his cock, which was fully erect now, she explored every satin-coated inch of him, acquainting herself with the taste and texture of his skin.

She could feel the slow burn of arousal growing in her belly and she knew that the time had come to remove her own clothes. Holding Lars's gaze, she stood at the side of the bed and slowly took them off. His eyes darkened from pale blue to periwinkle, growing opaque as Eleanor's body was revealed. The tip of his tongue moved between his closed lips as she raised her arms and turned around slowly, possessed by a streak of mischief that made her want to tease and torment him to breaking point.

'Let me touch you,' he said, his voice gruff and thick with passion.

'Yes – but only as I direct you.'

His eyes registered confusion as she moved towards him.

'My neck,' she said softly, 'I want you to kiss my neck.'

Sitting on the edge of the bed with her back to him, Eleanor closed her eyes in bliss. Lars's lips were gentle as they moved across the sensitive sweep of her neck, planting small, ticklish kisses on the delicate skin. As he moved around to the nape of her neck, Eleanor shivered and bent her head forward. Her breasts were swollen, the nipples gathering into little peaks of desire as he concentrated solely on the area she had specified, patiently working his way across every square centimetre of skin.

How wonderful it was to be able to dictate the pace like this instead of allowing the man to control her! This way Eleanor felt she could ensure she was fully ready for him to move on – or call a halt if she so wished. The freedom to call the shots was liberating, unlocking the deep well of sensuality that, so far, had only been released when she was alone. Eleanor felt her excitement grow.

'Now my back,' she said huskily, determined to make the suspense last for as long as possible.

'You have a beautiful back,' Lars murmured, his warm breath brushing across her shoulderblades, 'so smooth . . .'

His tongue traced the outline of each of her vertebrae while his fingers pressed gently on the tail of her spine, sending a jolt of pleasure through her which resolved itself into an ache.

'My breasts . . .' she whispered, aware as she did so that her entire body had become suffused with heat, her limbs trembling in anticipation of his touch.

Lars seemed to have picked up on her

551

yearning, for when he reached around her body to caress her breasts, his touch was exactly as she needed it to be; soft and delicate, stroking and coaxing the response from her rather than trying to force the pace.

It can't have been easy for him; she could feel his erection pressing into her back as he moved closer to her, so hard and potent she was sure he was ready to come. To his credit, the only indication of the effort it took him to control himself was in the slight shaking of his hands as he kneaded her breasts, and the quiet shallowness of his breathing.

Eleanor allowed her head to fall back against his shoulder and he immediately pressed his lips against her neck again. His fingers squeezed gently at her nipples, sending spirals of pleasure through her breasts and down to her womb. She could feel the secret folds of flesh between her legs moisten and swell in response to his caresses and she murmured incoherently.

'Let me take over now,' he whispered against her hair. 'I know what it is you are wanting. Trust me.'

Floating on a sea of sensation, Eleanor could only murmur her assent. She *did* trust him; he had allowed her to show, rather than tell, him exactly what she required and not once had he tried to use his male strength to impose his own will on her.

She gasped at the first touch of his fingers

against her mons. The backs of his knuckles brushed against the soft fleece, his fingertips gently tracing the crease between her labia. Eleanor felt her legs part of their own accord and Lars slipped his middle finger into the soft, slippery channels of flesh.

It felt divine, the slow, rhythmic caress of his finger against the uppermost point of her labia, coaxing the small bundle of nerve endings at the apex to slip from its protective hood and quiver against his fingertip. Little trickles of ice water seemed to run through her legs as, with his other hand on her inner thigh, he eased them farther apart, giving him easier access to the trembling flesh within.

Slowly, Lars eased her onto her back and half covered her body with his. His cock pressed against the soft flesh of her belly, but he made no move towards self-gratification as he kept up the rhythmic stroking of her clitoris and its surrounds, apparently enjoying the pleasure it was giving her.

Eleanor reached down and caressed the velvety tip of his glans with her thumb. Lars shuddered, his rhythm faltering for a second as she wiped the thin fluid leaking from the tip around the soft-skinned plum. Curling her fingers around the shaft, Eleanor drew her hand up and down, moving the satiny flesh over the hard core of his cock.

With a muttered oath in his own tongue, Lars covered her hand with his.

'Wait,' he whispered, 'please . . . let me pleasure you first.'

He waited for her agreement to show in her eyes, then he dipped his head and dabbed the tip of his tongue against the hard bud of her clitoris.

Eleanor had not expected this, and her hands curled against the sheets as he began to lick and nibble at her burning flesh. Looking down, she could see his golden head moving against the dark fleece of her mons, his tongue pink and coated with the dew of her arousal, moving in and out of her.

The sight tipped her over the edge. Having taught herself to come at will with the dildo Marcus had given her, it was easy to let herself go against his warm, living tongue.

'Oh!' she cried out as her climax broke, meshing her fingers into his hair and holding his face against her convulsing flesh. 'Sweet Heaven . . .!' To her surprise, tears gathered in her eyes and spilled down her cheeks in warm, salty rivulets.

When, at last, it was over, he raised his head and smiled at her. Eleanor could see her own secretions glistening on his chin and she drew his face to hers so that she could kiss it away. Her musk tasted oddly sweet, like thick honey, coating her tongue. Lars kissed her deeply, his tongue exploring her mouth as it had her sex, probing and caressing the insides of her cheeks. With his thumbs he wiped her tears away, gently, making no comment on them. Eleanor was glad she did not have to explain.

'Will you come inside me now?' she whispered as they broke apart.

He smiled and, swinging his feet onto the floor, reached for his trousers. Pulling a condom from the pocket, he unrolled it swiftly over his cock.

'Come,' he said, reaching for her.

Half lifting her off the bed, Lars positioned Eleanor so that she was sitting on his lap, facing him. His thighs were rough against her open sex and she moved her hips slightly, enjoying the rasp of his body hair against her recently sated flesh.

He kissed her again, as if enjoying the anticipation of the moment when he would be inside her. Eleanor looked deep into his eyes and saw the healthy, uncomplicated desire he had for her reflected in their depths. Her sex-flesh stirred again, ready for more indulgence at the thought of him desiring her.

Their eyes held as he lifted her hips and found the entrance to her body with the tip of his cock. Nudging gently, he opened her, then let her sink onto him.

It was like nothing Eleanor had ever experienced before. He came into her so deeply, stretching the walls of her vagina and pressing against the neck of her womb with a pressure which bordered on the uncomfortable, but stopped just short of pain.

For several moments, he held her still, as if giving her time to get used to the feeling. Then he began to lift and lower her on the straining rod, the tendons in his neck standing out at the effort the precise movements cost him. Eleanor held onto his shoulders tightly, steadying herself. Her mouth had grown dry and she tried to moisten her lips with her tongue, to no avail. Sweat pushed through her pores, making her skin shiny and slick under his hands.

Lars was breathing heavily and, although he still looked directly at her, Eleanor could tell that he no longer saw her. Locked in a world of sensation, he increased his rhythm, moving his hips now so that he could deepen each thrust.

Eleanor found herself gasping at each inward movement, her fingers clutching convulsively at his shoulders. She was aware of an unfamiliar sensation gathering momentum deep inside her vagina, a kind of mounting tension that demanded release. She found herself grinding her pelvis against his, grunting as his cock knocked against her cervix, sending a vibration through to her womb.

'Oh, God,' she said, her voice no more than a cracked whisper, 'oh . . . yes!'

It was as if a dam had burst inside her, sensation, raw and red hot, ripping through the channel of her sex and coiling like a tension-spring in her womb. She felt the walls of her vagina spasm around Lars's marauding cock,

556

massaging its surface until he too cried out, brought to the brink by her convulsing sex.

She felt him come, felt the hot sperm pulse out of him as they clung together, as one, joined in ecstasy, their bodies stuck together with perspiration. Lars's eyes cleared as he looked at her, and Eleanor realised that he had found the experience just as moving as she.

'It was good, wasn't it?' she found herself asking him.

'Yes – it was good,' he told her, his face splitting into a grin. 'We rest a little and do it again, yes?'

Eleanor laughed.

'Perhaps,' she said, pressing her lips against his forehead in a spontaneous gesture of affection. 'After all – we have all night, don't we?'

'All night,' he confirmed, his eyes smiling at her. 'And I am free for overtime too . . .?'

Eleanor laughed again and they fell back onto the bed, still joined together. Rolling so that she was underneath him, Eleanor stared up into his eyes.

'You knew exactly what to do . . . how I needed you to touch me. How did you do that?'

Lars stroked her temple with the side of his crooked forefinger and stared deeply into her eyes.

'You must know,' he said.

Eleanor frowned, not satisfied with his answer.

'Please, Lars – it's important to me. No one has ever sensed my needs . . . like this, in bed. You don't know me at all, and yet you knew at once how to arouse me. I know I directed you at first, but when you told me to trust you . . . you were absolutely sure . . .'

'It is not so difficult with a woman as sensual as you. Your body . . . it . . . uh . . .' He glanced away from her for a moment, as if searching for the right word. 'It *vibrates*, yes, that is the word. I can feel the vibration of your pleasure and it tells me how to make it more.'

He bent to kiss her before withdrawing slowly from her. Eleanor watched him through half-closed eyes as he padded to the bathroom and back again, unselfconscious in his nakedness, perfectly at ease with her.

She thought about what he had said and gradually allowed herself to believe him. She had never thought of herself as a sensual woman before. Inhibited, unresponsive, cold, even, but never the opposite of these. Yet Lars had no reason to lie to her, nor even flatter her unduly. He could have walked in, made love with her, and left, the entire transaction over within the hour. Yet here he was, climbing into bed beside her, his beautiful, virile body already stirring in anticipation of the hours to come.

Eleanor saw herself through his eyes and felt her own body respond to his perception of her. Because he knew nothing whatsoever about her, he had no preconceptions about what she would be like in bed, just as she had none about him.

They had come together purely for sex; neither expected any more from the other than this one night.

It was a liberating concept. Lars thought she was a sexy, sensual woman, so that was what she was. Moving into his waiting embrace, Eleanor revelled in this newly discovered facet of her personality and prepared to explore it to the full.

Chapter Six

BY THE TIME Lars had left the next morning, Eleanor was exhausted, both physically and emotionally. They had made love four times more during the night and for the first time in her life, Eleanor had experienced the type of multiple orgasms she had only ever read about before. Time after time under the diligent attention of Lars's fingers, lips and tongue, her clitoris had throbbed, her vagina convulsing around the sure thrust of his cock as he came into her, setting off ripples of sensation that seemed to consume her from head to toe.

Once inhibition had been thrown to the wind, Eleanor found herself sinking ever further into a physical plane where nothing mattered but the pursuit of sensual pleasure. Lars was an enthusiastic partner, joining her in a tireless quest for pleasure that took them through the long, cloistered night.

As her confidence increased, he was acquiescent as she explored his body once more with her lips and tongue, running the tip along the tumescent shaft of his penis and enclosing the bulbous tip between her lips. She loved the way he moaned as she took the length of him into her mouth, loved the taste and texture of his cock as she sucked and licked and kissed the velvety skin.

By dawn she was exhausted, her body stiff and sore, but pleasurably so. Finally, as the birds serenaded them enthusiastically from a branch outside her window, they slept, coiled together contentedly beneath the duvet.

As he kissed her goodbye at the door, Lars looked as drained as Eleanor felt.

'I will see you again, yes?' he said, his voice still smoky with spent passion.

Eleanor knew that was unlikely, but she kept her own counsel. He had been so good to her, so willing to let her bend and shape him to her every whim, and despite the fact that his time had been bought by Marcus, she didn't want him to go away feeling used.

'Perhaps,' she told him, running her fingertips down the side of his face.

Lars caught her hand in his and pressed a small kiss into the centre of her palm. Eleanor shivered, her body stirring with remembered pleasure.

'Thank you,' she said.

'Thank you?' he repeated, his forehead screwing up in puzzlement.

'Never mind,' Eleanor told him, leaning forward for one last, lingering kiss.

Alone again, she went back to bed. The sheets smelled of Lars; of fresh sweat and sex, and she snuggled into them, feeling warm and satisfied. He had been so gentle, so sensitive to her needs and she knew that, no matter how their night together had come about, she would always be grateful to him.

And to Marcus. If he hadn't hired Lars for her pleasure, she would never have taken such a giant step forward in her 'education'. Sighing contentedly, Eleanor closed her eyes and allowed herself to drift into a heavy sleep.

In her dreams, she found herself dancing with Rhys. His strong arms held her loosely, but close enough for her to feel the heat of him. She sensed that her nearness was as arousing to him as his was to her and she felt happy, light-hearted in a way she had not felt for a long time.

After a few moments, she leaned towards him and whispered in his ear.

'Let's go back to the hotel,' she said, her voice reverberating with desire.

Rhys's arms tightened reflexively around her and she felt the sudden tension invade his limbs.

'Yes,' he said, 'we could—'

Eleanor sat up with a start, wrenched from the

pleasant little dream by the discordant shrill of the telephone. Fumbling for it, she pressed the receiver against her ear.

'Hello?'

'Eleanor? Is that you? You sound half asleep!'

For a moment as she registered Rhys's voice, Eleanor felt disorientated, unsure whether she was awake, or still dreaming.

'Rhys?'

'Yes. Are you all right? You sound a little odd, *cariad*.'

Eleanor smiled, the note of concern in his voice warming her.

'I'm fine, Rhys. It's lovely to hear from you – I . . . I was just thinking about you.'

'Were you?' He sounded pleased. 'We must be in tune, then, if we think of each other at the same time. I was phoning to tell you that I have to go to a meeting in Birmingham tomorrow. I'm staying overnight and I wondered if you could meet me for dinner? If you can get away from your project, of course,' he added hastily, as if afraid that she might make some excuse not to see him.

'For you, of course I can!' she assured him. 'Just let me grab a pen and I'll jot down the details.'

After she had put the phone down, Eleanor felt light-hearted. The thought of seeing Rhys now, when she had discovered that she might, after all, have something to offer him, was so exciting and she looked forward to it with a passion. Would he notice the difference in her? And, if he did, would that encourage him to wait?

Hugging her hopes to her, Eleanor sank back onto the pillows with a sigh.

He was waiting for her in the foyer of the hotel. For a moment, as she lingered in the doorway, she was able to observe him before he saw her. Eleanor's heart turned over in her chest as she saw how handsome he looked, as at home in the dark grey business suit he was wearing as in the rugby shirts and trackpants he favoured off-duty.

His handsome face lit up in a smile as he saw her and she walked quickly towards him, eager to feel the warmth of his skin against hers as he took both her hands in his.

'Rhys! It's lovely to see you!' she said at once.

He was looking at her intently, his perceptive, light-blue eyes scanning her features minutely.

'What is it?' she said after a moment, unnerved by his scrutiny. 'What's wrong?'

He smiled and shook his head.

'I'm sorry – you look . . . different somehow. Happier, certainly.'

Realising at once that he was probably thinking there might be some other cause to her happiness than seeing him, Eleanor sought to reassure him.

'It's done me good to get away, Rhys. I don't think I'd realised quite how badly Michael's harassment was bringing me down.'

He touched her hand in a small gesture of sympathy.

'That reminds me – I have a message for you from Amy on that front. She'll be writing to you, of course, but she thought you might like to know in the meantime. She's issued the injunction you talked about before you left and is currently talking to Michael's lawyer with a view to reaching an amicable settlement.'

'Thank goodness! You don't know how much that takes off my mind,' she told him.

She was glad now that she had given into pressure to get nasty with Michael – it seemed that at the first sign of her being willing to fight back with a lawyer of her own, he had rolled over and admitted defeat.

'Please thank Amy for me.'

'You can thank her yourself, when you come home.'

There was a question in his eyes as he said this, a question that Eleanor was not ready to answer just yet. Ignoring it entirely, she smiled at him.

'Duncan will be furious!' she said mischievously.

To her relief, Rhys laughed and the mood between them lightened.

'Good. Let's not talk about that any more. Tell me about your work.'

Eleanor sipped the dry martini he ordered for her in the hotel bar and regarded him steadily. She didn't want there to be any secrets between them, but she knew he would never understand the path she had taken with her research. He must never find out that she was the pseudonymous woman who was writing a journal in a book called *Becoming Sexual*!

'It's going well,' she said cautiously, 'and I'm enjoying it, but that's mainly because I've also been embarking on what you might call a journey of self-discovery.'

'Oh? Explain, *cariad* – I'm not sure I understand.'

Seeing the wariness in his face, Eleanor leaned forward and kissed him gently on the lips.

'It's nothing to worry about, darling,' she said softly. 'It can only benefit us.'

Clearly taken aback by her sudden, uncharacteristic display of affection, Rhys traced the outline of her lips with his forefinger.

'Is there an "us", Eleanor?' he asked softly.

'I hope so. You've been so patient, I couldn't have asked for more understanding from you. Just another three weeks, Rhys – can you give me that long?'

'As long as it takes,' he replied, his voice catching with emotion. Then he grinned. 'Do you think we could eat in the meantime? – I'm famished!'

Laughing, Eleanor took his arm and they walked out of the bar together, in perfect accord.

' "With the pressure of having to compete, to *perform* removed, I felt free to explore my own desires. A man paid to do one's bidding has sold his right to expectations of his own, and although Lars was undoubtedly satisfied with his assignment for his own sake, his enjoyment was no more than a side issue, a by-product of my own." '

Marcus stopped reading aloud from her journal and regarded Eleanor from across the room. His eyes sparkled at her knowingly, his lips curving into a smile.

'So, Eleanor,' he said, leaning back in his seat and stretching his long legs out in front of him, 'what do you think of the programme so far?'

Eleanor picked up her wine glass and sipped at the champagne he had brought back with him.

'You want me to admit that I was wrong, don't you?' she said, half smiling at him. Marcus feigned shock.

'Would I be so petty?'

'Absolutely! I'll reserve judgement, anyway, until the end of the book. You'll know how I feel when you read the last chapter.'

'Fair enough. Going back to Lars – your account is fairly comprehensive, but you don't explore why you think you responded to him so readily.'

Eleanor smiled faintly.

'I think you already know the answer to that question, Marcus.'

'I do? Refresh my memory.'

'You'd primed me. First with the massage and . . . what came after . . .' It was the first time either of them had referred, even obliquely, to Marcus's appearance in her room that evening and Eleanor hurried on, dropping her eyes from his. 'Then this past week, having me closet myself away with tapes and books and magazines with only a vibrator for company.'

Marcus frowned and shook his head.

'Are you saying that it was merely that you were desperate? That any man would do?'

Eleanor considered for a moment.

'In a way, yes, any man would have served the purpose.' She blushed as she said this, aware of how cold it sounded. 'I was fortunate in that Lars was a very attractive young man. Maybe if he hadn't appealed to me, I would have sent him away again. Who knows? The liberating thing was realising that I wasn't under any obligation to sleep with him whatsoever.'

Marcus was silent for a moment and Eleanor could see that his inquisitive therapist's mind was dissecting what she had said.

'Is that how you feel about sex?' he asked her eventually. '*Obliged* to take part?'

Eleanor grimaced, aware of how that sounded.

'In a way, yes. So many men contrive to make you feel like that. They take you out and buy a meal . . . maybe they don't always realise it, but there's *pressure* applied, very often, every step of the way. They've only just met you, and they expect a response.'

'Don't you ever feel like sleeping with a man you've only just met?'

'But that's what I was trying to explain in that chapter – when the pressure was removed, yes, I *did* want to sleep with Lars. Without that sense of obligation, I felt free to follow my own inclination. Now I simply have to transfer that sense of freedom to my everyday life – escorts are all very well, but they are an expensive form of self-gratification!'

Marcus smiled slightly.

'I hope it *will* be simple, Eleanor,' was all he said.

'It won't be, but at least now I know that I have the capacity for spontaneous sexual arousal.'

'Yes. Time to move on, I think, to the next stage.'

'Which is?'

Marcus smiled at her enigmatically.

'You'll see tomorrow night.'

Eleanor paused at the entrance to the club and Marcus glanced quizzically at her.

'Okay?' he asked her.

She hesitated for only a moment more before nodding and preceding him inside. She should have guessed when he presented her with this outfit to wear that this would be no ordinary club. Dressed in a black, rubberised shorts suit which, though surprisingly light to wear, moulded her every curve, she would have looked out of place in an ordinary nightclub.

Eleanor saw herself now as they descended a

staircase which was made entirely of mirrors. She looked good in the outlandish outfit, her legs long and sleek in opaque black tights, shown to their best advantage in a pair of high-heeled sandals. The suit zipped up at the front and the elaborate silver ring-pull at her throat served as her only jewellery.

She barely recognised herself hiding behind the sophisticated make-up she had felt went with the outfit. Full, moist-looking lips were emphasised in deep red lipstick while her eyes, heavily ringed with kohl and mascara, appeared overly bright, lit from within by a potent mixture of apprehension and excitement.

At the bottom of the stairs, their tickets were checked again before they were shown into a dark, windowless room, filled with some twenty or so single pedestal, glass-topped tables which were arranged around a small, circular stage. No one paid much attention to their arrival, but as they made their way through the tables to the one allocated to them, Eleanor was aware of several pairs of eyes appraising her.

For the first time in her life such attention did not embarrass her. She knew she looked good and she was proud of the visual impact her looks clearly had on those around her. Lifting her chin, she swept the room with a bold glance, a small smile playing around her lips.

'Champagne?' Marcus asked her as she took the seat to his left, facing the stage.

'That would be lovely,' she replied, holding his eye and smiling at him as he gazed at her.

'You're looking perfectly edible tonight,' he told her after a few minutes.

Eleanor smiled.

'I know,' she said with a wicked smile. 'Did you see the other men looking at me?'

'Not just the men,' Marcus said.

Eleanor's smile turned to a frown.

'Don't be ridiculous!' she snapped, uncomfortable with the way his eyes were scrutinising her, missing nothing.

There was a small band situated on a podium at the opposite end of the room to the stage, playing jazz. A thick pall of smoke hung in a dense cloud just above the occupants' heads. Eleanor's eyes smarted at the tobacco fumes, her nose detecting the sweeter, fainter scent of marijuana in the air.

Glancing around the room, she saw that most of the clientele were in pairs, various combinations of men and women. All were fully engrossed with their partners, glancing up only every now and again to assess a newcomer, as they had her, or to signal to a waiter that glasses needed replenishing. There was a curiously intent atmosphere in the room, a sense of expectancy that had Eleanor intrigued.

'What *is* this place?' she asked Marcus.

He watched her for a moment, as if deciding how much to tell her.

'It's a branch of a very exclusive, international

club,' he said at last.

'A club? Are you a member?'

'An honorary one, on account of my research. I wouldn't want to pay to belong.'

'Oh? Why?'

Marcus glanced around them.

'An evening here, or at any of the other venues, can be very diverting, but it is possible to over-salt the egg!'

'What do you mean?'

He shrugged.

'Same faces, same champagne, same entertainment.' He grinned suddenly. 'Don't take any notice of me – you'll enjoy the show. If I sound jaded, it's because I am. Don't allow my mood to affect yours.'

'I won't,' Eleanor assured him, her attention distracted by the arrival of a stunning-looking woman, dressed from head to toe in scarlet feathers. Marcus turned his head to follow her gaze and, to Eleanor's surprise, his face split into a smile.

'Jeanette!'

He rose, his arms opening wide as the exotic-looking creature rushed up to them, her red-stained lips stretching across her teeth in a surprised grin.

'Marcus! Baby – what are you doing here?'

'Another book. And you?'

The woman shrugged and grimaced.

'Just hanging around. You know me!'

Eleanor watched the exchange with a definite sense of having been forgotten. She had never seen Marcus display such open warmth and affection and she was ashamed to realise that watching him lavish it on another woman gave her a pang that could only be identified as jealousy. The couple made no move to draw apart, staring deeply into each other's eyes as they spoke in soft tones, words which she couldn't quite catch. Then the woman glanced in her direction, and Eleanor realised that they were talking about her.

Just as she was beginning to resent Marcus's casual attitude towards her, she was suddenly drawn into the conversation.

'Eleanor, this is Jeanette, an erstwhile colleague of mine.'

Jeanette made a face at that and leaned across the table to offer Eleanor a languid hand.

'Don't listen to a word he says – I never do!'

She smiled at Eleanor with a genuine warmth and Eleanor found herself drawn to her in spite of herself.

'Won't you join us for the show?' Marcus said, signalling for the waiter to bring another chair.

Jeanette's eyes met Eleanor's across the table and she smiled.

'I should be meeting someone . . . but until they arrive, it'll be a pleasure!'

No sooner had she sat down than the mood of the music being played seemed to changed, slowing and altering in such a way that a new alertness travelled around the room. People shuffled in their seats, their eyes never far from the small stage which was now lit softly.

Eleanor had heard of live sex shows, and guessed that this was what was about to take place. She felt apprehensive, never having seen a man and a woman making love in the flesh before, yet she was also aware of a growing excitement. Perhaps it was the atmosphere of the room, catching her up in the sense of expectation, making her part of the proceedings.

After a few minutes, a man appeared and began to dance. He was young, in his early twenties, with a well-honed body and sleek, shiny brown skin. Wearing loose trousers and a singlet, he danced as if his heart would break, his body at one with the music which filled the room.

Soon he was joined by another dancer. This one was slightly built, but wiry and he kept pace with the first man, mirroring his movements as closely as if he was a shadow.

Eleanor was struck by the beauty of the two men. The first was blond, with a strong, square-jawed profile and a powerful physique. The second was dark, with an almost ethereal quality to his face that put him beyond mere attractiveness. As she watched them dance, Eleanor found herself growing more and more uneasy. There was something about the way they were moving together that made her feel uncomfortable, though she could not have put her finger on the cause.

'What do you think?' Marcus whispered.

Eleanor glanced at him, frowning as she saw the expression in his eyes. He looked . . . excited – that was the only word she could think of.

'They're very good,' she replied politely.

Jeanette smiled at her and leaned across the table.

'Luke is my brother,' she said, pointing at the dark-haired man.

Eleanor nodded and turned her attention back to the stage. The two men were sweating profusely now, both from their efforts and from the heat of the stage-lights which illuminated them. They circled each other like combatants, reminding Eleanor of ancient gladiators in a ring, yet still her unease remained. Suddenly, the first man reached forward and, putting his hand at the back of the other man's neck, pulled him forward, crushing his mouth against his and kissing him deeply.

At once, the image of Michael pounding into Duncan's body in his office came back to fill Eleanor's mind. As always, anguish was tempered by a swift, shameful flare of arousal and Eleanor made a small sound of distress in the back of her throat, attracting Marcus's attention.

'Why have you brought me here?' she hissed furiously, her hands curling into fists in her lap.

Marcus regarded her steadily.

'To face your fear,' he said simply.

'What's that supposed to mean? Get me out of here!'

Marcus put his hand on her arm before she could stand up. On the stage, the two men were slowly undressing each other, and a couch had been wheeled centre-stage.

'Sit still. Watch – think of it as research. Remember you're supposed to be recording your responses.'

'I only have one response, as well you know – disgust!'

'Don't lie to yourself, Eleanor. Allow whatever feelings occur to come through. Sodomy is no more than another aspect of sexuality.'

Eleanor was about to respond, when she heard Jeanette say, 'Oh, isn't he beautiful!'

Her eyes switching automatically back to the stage, Eleanor saw that Jeanette's brother was dancing now dressed only in his jersey boxer shorts. They clung lovingly to the outline of his cock which was already erect, forming a proud ridge against the fabric.

'I can't watch this,' she murmured, half to herself.

'You can. You must. Trust me on this, Eleanor – I haven't been wrong so far, have I?'

Eleanor pulled her hand away from his and folded it tightly with the other one in her lap. She didn't want to watch this, didn't want to reawaken the way she had felt on that dreadful day when her marriage had finally died. She *wouldn't* watch, no matter what Marcus said. He was wrong to have forced this on her without warning. She would wait until it was over, and then she would get up and leave, if necessary on her own.

The music changed its mood once more, dropping the volume, making the audience feel more involved in what was taking place before them. Reluctantly at first, Eleanor raised her eyes to the stage.

Her heart began to beat a little faster, and her mouth ran dry. The blond man was rubbing a heavy, sweet-smelling oil between the darker man's buttocks as he lay over the arm of the couch. From where she was sitting, Eleanor could not see the prone man's face; he was completely de-personalised to her.

To her horror, she realised that her sex-flesh had moistened in sympathy with him, that she too quivered in anticipation as the blond man positioned his condom-encased penis. All her nerve-endings jumped as he sank into the willing young body beneath him.

'Oh God!' she whispered, her fingers flying to her lips as she was unable to drag her eyes away from the scene.

Marcus put his arm around her shoulders and drew her close. Though she was still angry with him, Eleanor welcomed the support he offered her and leaned into him. She didn't think she was capable of sitting upright on her own, for her body trembled with suppressed emotion, a pulse beating steadily between her thighs, sending little shock waves through her system.

The tempo of the music began to climb, spiralling to a crescendo in perfect accord with the activity on the stage. As the participants writhed in the throes of ecstasy, Eleanor closed her eyes and allowed Marcus to take her full weight.

She didn't quite know how she got out of that room. Afterwards she had a vague memory of saying goodbye to Jeanette, and of Marcus leading her out into the cool night air, but she did everything in a daze, past and present jostling in her head until they seemed to merge and become one. In the taxi Marcus summoned, she leaned forward and put her head in her hands, trying to contain the memory of shock and anguish.

Marcus didn't try to talk to her until they were inside the house. Shepherding her into the living room, he poured her a stiff drink and sat close to her on the sofa.

'Why did you put me through that?' she asked after a few minutes.

'How do you feel?'

Eleanor felt anger surge along her veins and she glared at him.

'Stop bloody analysing me! My feelings aren't just an interesting phenomenon for you to dissect and disseminate all the time! I'm a human being, Marcus, and human beings have a habit of not fitting neatly into proscribed behaviour modules.'

578

Marcus made no response to her tirade, but merely watched her intently, making her feel like an insect on a pin under his microscope. Finally, Eleanor could stand it no longer.

'Answer me, damn you!' she said, leaning forward aggressively.

Marcus put his drink aside and held her eyes. 'Why are you so angry?'

His tone was so reasonable, so professionally soothing, that Eleanor felt her temper snap.

'Because you used me, you bastard!' she shouted, accompanying her words with a light blow to his upper arm.

Marcus caught her arm as she would have struck him again and pulled her bodily against him. Eleanor fought against the constriction, outraged that he was holding her in what, in any other circumstances, would have been an embrace.

'Let go of me!'

'Calm down, Eleanor—'

'Don't tell me to calm down! You knew what happened tonight would upset me! You knew and you still let me go through it. I don't understand you!'

'Be still and I'll explain.' He waited until she stopped struggling, though he made no move to release her. 'You asked me once about fact and fantasy. Seeing your husband with another man was fact – cold, hard fact. Your physical response to that memory has more to do with fantasy – you

579

never wanted to see Michael making love to a man, but the idea of it, whether you were aware of it or not, turned you on.'

'No.'

'Yes. Only now your fantasy is spoiled by feelings of shame and emotional anguish. I thought that seeing two other men acting out a fantasy scenario might help you to divorce the one thing from the other.'

'Of all the stupid, arrogant, wrong-headed—'

Her angry words were smothered by Marcus's mouth descending on hers. There was no gentleness in the kiss, only a desire to silence her, and Eleanor fought against it, gritting her teeth against the onslaught of his tongue and holding her body rigid in his arms.

Gradually, the kiss changed, became more yearning and less angry, and Eleanor began to relax into his embrace. A part of her was determined to hang onto her anger, to fight him, but the greater part of her wanted the slow burning desire triggered by the scene she had witnessed to be assuaged.

Pressing herself against him, she felt the heavy thud of his heart, felt the warmth of his skin through his clothes and her own body began to clamour for release.

'Marcus,' she murmured, her lips moving against his mouth, 'please . . .'

She wasn't sure what she was pleading for, she only knew that she wanted him, suddenly, with a ferocity which took them both by surprise. He did not resist her as she fumbled for the belt of his trousers and pulled the end through the guide. She could feel his erection growing in response to her sudden, unexpected assault and she worked feverishly at the fastening to his trousers.

Meanwhile, Marcus's hands were everywhere; at her waist, her breasts, the curve of her bottom as he searched for a way into the tight-fitting rubber suit. Eleanor freed his penis, then reached down between her legs to unsnap the press-studs at her crotch.

She was naked underneath it. The heat of her sex was shocking as she caressed herself briefly. Taking Marcus's hand, she covered his fingers with her own and pressed them into the hot, wet well of her sex.

'Fuck me, Marcus,' she murmured in a voice she didn't recognise as her own.

'Eleanor—'

'Now, Marcus – come inside me.'

She was desperate, not daring to think that he might refuse her. She couldn't bear it if he did, if he should reject her now when she needed nothing more than a hot, hard cock thrusting into the softness of her body. Lying back on the sofa, she opened her legs slowly, displaying herself to him as he gazed at her.

Beads of sweat stood out on his forehead and upper lip and his cock reared up from his open fly, indisputable evidence that he was as aroused as she. He seemed to come to a decision. Holding her down by the shoulders, he covered her body with his and, without preamble, thrust into her with one sure, firm stroke.

Eleanor squealed as he pumped his hips back and forth, each time making his penetration deeper, harder, closer to what she really needed for him. His hands on her shoulders were not gentle, yet somehow the sensation of being held down added to the desperate need that was clawing at her insides, compelling her to meet him thrust for thrust.

Holding his gaze, she was aware that it was a battle of wills, that he no more wanted to be the first to come than she did. Then suddenly she was past caring and she welcomed the deep, powerful convulsions that spasmed around his penis, drawing his own climax from him seconds later.

Marcus groaned and shuddered, his head dipping so that his lips were pressed against her rubber-clad shoulder. As soon as their combined flesh stopped pulsing, Eleanor pushed him away and struggled to get up. Re-fastening the press studs over her burning sex, she stood up and regarded him coldly.

'Now analyse *that*,' she snapped, making no concessions to his momentary exhaustion.

Marcus looked at her, his dark eyes only slowly clearing as he realised that she was still angry, still hurt, that what had happened between them was her revenge on him for abusing her.

'Eleanor . . . we have to talk about this—'

'Talk to yourself, Marcus. If you really want to know what I think about tonight, and about you, then I suggest you read the next chapter of the book, hot off the printer tomorrow. Until then, you'll have to speculate, won't you? And believe me, I can guarantee that this time, you'll have got it one hundred per cent *wrong*.' With that she spun on her heel and stalked out of the door.

Chapter Seven

IN CONCLUSION, I have discovered that, when the urge is strong, it is perfectly possible for a woman to have sex with a man simply because he is available, without the restriction of needing to know or even like him. When aroused, her sexuality heightened by an evening of stimulation, like a long, drawn-out foreplay of the mind, a woman can use the nearest available man to bring herself relief.

Given the virtual knee-jerk sexual response of the male of the species, it is not hard to find a willing partner.'

Eleanor printed out the final pages of her journal, aware that she would probably rewrite it at a later date. Right now, she was driven by a desire to put Marcus in his place, to shake him out of the smug complacency which seemed to characterise his attitude to female sexuality.

As for what had happened between them – contrary to expectation, she found she had no feelings towards him whatsoever. That part of her narrative, at least, was absolutely true – Marcus had merely been an available cock to satisfy her.

Eleanor grimaced at the crudity of the thought. She never used to think in such terms. Leaving her manuscript pages on Marcus's desk, she took herself off for a long walk in the fresh air.

When she returned at one o'clock, her mind was clearer and she felt physically refreshed. Going up to her room, she showered and changed into fresh clothes before going down to join Marcus for lunch.

She could tell from the expression on his face that he had read her latest contribution to the book, but he made no reference to it whatsoever. He was distant, though, and Eleanor sensed she had angered him. Too bad! she thought to herself. She was still angry at the way he had manipulated her last night, and she was glad that she had been able to redress the balance a little.

'I think I'm ready now to go on to "dominance and submission",' she told him when they were eating dessert.

Marcus looked startled, as if he thought she meant here and now.

'The next chapter?' she reminded him. 'I'm ready to move on.'

His eyes narrowed as he regarded her.

'Yes, I think you're probably right,' he said at last with an edge to his voice. 'In fact, I was discussing the next chapter with Jeanette.'

'Oh?' Remembering the girl in the feathers, Eleanor was cool.

'Yes. She has a friend who supplies dominant services – for a fee. If you're agreeable, she might be willing to take you on as an assistant for a day.'

If Marcus was expecting her to be offended at his suggestion that she turn prostitute for the day, he was sorely disappointed, for Eleanor merely raised her eyebrows at him.

'I see. Have you organised anything yet?'

'As a matter of fact, Cara is calling by this afternoon to meet you.'

Eleanor smiled coolly.

'Good. I'd like to move on as quickly as possible.'

Pushing away her empty plate, she rose.

'Eleanor?'

She glanced at Marcus expectantly, sensing that, for once, he was having difficulty finding the right words to express himself.

'About last night—'

'I think that's a case of least said, soonest mended, don't you?' she interrupted him firmly. 'It's not as if it's likely to happen again.'

Marcus raised an eyebrow at her.

'Are you so sure?'

Eleanor gazed at him, unwilling to acknowledge, even to herself, that he was right – there probably would be a next time.

'Are you?' she countered briskly. 'Now, if you'll excuse me, I want to do a little background reading before I meet this Cara.' She left the room, conscious of Marcus's eyes following her, sensing his frustration.

It wasn't that she'd stopped wanting him, she mused as she went up to her room. Though last night she had used him, it had been good between them. However, over the past few weeks as she had expanded her experience, her confidence had grown. She no longer feared that she could become dependent on him and she was aware that, with a man like Marcus, it was crucial to remain on top of the situation if she was to retain her sanity.

In her room, Eleanor browsed through the magazine she had found on sado-masochism. It was largely concerned with corporal punishment and carried endless photographs of overblown young women in ill-fitting school uniforms and long, repetitive accounts of spankings which were remarkable only for their obsessive attention to detail.

There was another magazine, this time taken up with shots of leather-clad, stony-featured women with a penchant for strutting around in spike-heeled boots. Was this what domination was all about? Eleanor had a feeling that this was going to be the least appealing part of her research to date.

Cara, when she arrived, was a surprise. After flicking through the second magazine, Eleanor had half expected a beefy-looking blonde, probably with a music-hall Germanic accent, dressed in a storm trooper's outfit. Cara, however, although blonde, was petite and slim, her unmade-up face attractively freckled and her slender body dressed in jeans and a fresh-looking white shirt with double cuffs.

'Hello,' she said, holding out her hand.

Eleanor felt the strength in her grip and immediately revised her first impression that the girl was probably as fragile as she looked.

'Pleased to meet you, Cara. It's very kind of you to offer to, er, show me the ropes!'

Cara laughed, a light, natural sound that made Eleanor warm to her.

'I'm sure we'll have a lot of fun together. The only thing I have to ask you is that you be absolutely discreet. You'd be surprised at the identities of some of my regulars!'

'I have a feeling I'll be surprised by more than that!' Eleanor commented ruefully. 'Did Marcus explain that I'm a bit . . . inexperienced in these things?'

Cara smiled, her eyes running quickly over Eleanor, as if weighing up her potential.

'All you have to do is follow my lead – you'll get the idea in no time. Now, do you have time to come into town with me? We'll have to get you kitted out.'

'Sure – I'm entirely in your hands, Cara. You lead and I'll follow!'

Cara gave her a quick look, the meaning of which Eleanor simply couldn't fathom. Then she grinned and picked up her bag and the odd expression was gone.

'Time to shop!'

Cara's idea of shopping was quite different to Eleanor's, though what she had expected she couldn't really say. What she hadn't anticipated was that they would spend the afternoon cocooned in the slightly surreal world of a sex shop.

Pandora's Box was tucked away along a side street just outside the main shopping centre. From the outside, its painted windows and discreet sign made it look like just another respectable Victorian terrace, no different from those on either side. Once through the door, though, it was like entering another world.

Sapphire-blue, satin curtains were draped across the top of a steep flight of stairs leading downwards. The stairs were so small that Eleanor had to concentrate on walking down them, clinging onto the rickety bannister as she followed Cara into what seemed like the bowels of the earth.

Only she would not have expected the bowels of the earth to be decorated like the room she reached at the bottom. Swathes of jewel-bright fabrics lined the walls and ceiling like the interior of an emperor's tent, dazzling the eye and creating an intimate, womblike effect in the small space. Along every wall were rack upon rack of clothes, interspersed by shelves displaying every conceivable kind of sex toy and marital aid.

'Cara – good to see you, darling!'

Eleanor turned to see a small, middle-aged woman dressed in a bright purple kaftan, her dark, slightly greying hair pulled back into an untidy bun. As she embraced Cara her bright, dark eyes surveyed Eleanor over her shoulder. After a moment's perusal, her face broke into a beaming smile.

'Introduce me to your lovely friend,' she demanded.

'This is Eleanor. Eleanor – Pandora Green.'

Eleanor stepped forward and offered her hand. The older woman enclosed it in both of hers.

'Welcome to Pandora's Box, my dear!'

Eleanor smiled, responding to the mischievous sparkle in Pandora's eyes.

'Now – what can I help you with?'

Glancing at Cara, Eleanor grimaced.

'To be honest, I'm not too sure.'

'Eleanor is going to *assist* me,' Cara said with a definite smile in her voice. 'She'll need to look the part . . . How about this?'

She picked up a black PVC catsuit with a shiny, wet-look finish.

'Er . . . no, I don't think so,' Eleanor said, eyeing

590

the outfit with distaste. 'I think I'd suffer from claustrophobia in that!'

Pandora laughed and, running her eyes professionally over Eleanor's body, she picked a selection of clothes for her to try.

'Now, take my advice and get dressed with your back to the mirror. If you watch yourself transforming, bit by bit, it'll put you off. Don't look until you're fully kitted out – then see what you think!'

Pandora handed Eleanor a small pile of clothes and she and Cara went to catch up on news while Eleanor changed.

In the small cubicle, Eleanor stripped off her clothes and looked through the garments Pandora had given her. Everything was made of leather, PVC or rubber, none of which she normally wore. Discarding a red leather dress and an electric blue pair of shiny PVC trousers, Eleanor opted for black.

The skirt she chose was rubberised, lined with white silk that clung to her hips like a second skin. Though it was short, barely reaching mid-thigh, it was too tight for briefs to be a viable proposition, so she opted for sleek black tights instead. It wasn't until she pulled them up that she realised that there was a split at the crotch, strategically placed to leave her sex exposed.

With a small shrug of resignation, Eleanor pushed her feet into the spiky-heeled ankle boots trimmed with maribou feathers and turned her attention to the top half of her. Deciding that chainmail simply wasn't her, and that she couldn't quite bring herself to wear silver lurex, she was left with a supple leather waistcoat which, when she fastened it, gave her an impressive cleavage.

Only now, slowly, did she turn to meet her reflection in the cubicle's full-length mirror.

'Oh my God!' she said aloud.

'Let's see.' Cara pulled back the curtain and Eleanor turned to face them. 'Wow! You look terrific!'

'I look like a tart.'

'As Cara said – you look terrific,' Pandora said, smiling. 'Look again.'

Eleanor turned reluctantly towards the mirror and surveyed her reflection. She had to admit, she looked like the stereotypical view of every man's dream woman, oozing sexuality with a hint of knowingness.

'I do look . . . different,' she said cautiously.

'More powerful,' Cara added.

'I suppose so, yes,' Eleanor said, surprised to realise the adjective was exactly right. 'More powerful. Dressed like this, I could drive a man wild!'

Cara laughed, delighted by Eleanor's response.

'And you will, Eleanor, I promise you. This Friday, ten o'clock. I'll take your gear back with me, then you can change at my place.'

Eleanor nodded, aware that she was beginning

to look forward to this next stage in her research. For if she could feel like this merely by dressing up in these outlandish clothes, what would she feel like when she was given power over a real, living, breathing man?

Cara lived in a spacious Victorian terrace decorated in Laura Ashley prints and sparsely, though tastefully, furnished with antiques sympathetic to the period of the house. It was not what Eleanor had expected from a woman who earned her crust as a dominatrix.

As before, Cara herself was wearing jeans and a shirt, her pretty face bare of make-up and her blonde hair pulled back into a ponytail.

'Hi – I'm glad you're on time. That means we've got time for a coffee.'

She showed Eleanor through to a large high-ceilinged kitchen-come-dining room which was filled with sunlight streaming through the large, uncurtained windows.

'Now, I imagine you've got a few questions,' she said when they had settled at the scrubbed pine table with their coffee. 'Fire away!'

Eleanor took a sip of her coffee and smiled.

'To tell you the truth, Cara, I've come with a completely open mind. I might have questions later, but for now I'd rather learn "on the job".'

Cara nodded approvingly.

'Good. In that case, all I have to tell you is to keep quiet and follow my lead. You'll soon get the idea – but don't, whatever you do, break into my clients' fantasies. You'll see what I mean,' she added cryptically.

The doorbell rang then and Cara glanced at her watch.

'That'll be George – he's early!'

'But we haven't even changed yet!' Eleanor said, panicking.

Cara smiled. 'No need for this one. You sit there and enjoy your coffee. Take your time.'

The doorbell rang again and Cara frowned. 'He's impatient today.'

Going over to a long cupboard by the door, she reached in and brought out a riding crop. Laying it where it couldn't be missed on the table, she gave Eleanor a wink before leaving the room.

Eleanor listened as Cara opened the door, hearing, with some surprise, how her voice changed. Gone was the easy-going, musical cadence, replaced by a strong, almost strident tone that didn't sound like her at all.

'What do you mean by ringing the doorbell twice?' she heard her say. 'You're early – how dare you try to rush me!'

'I'm most sorry, Madam,' Eleanor heard a clipped, fawning male voice say, 'I was just so eager to see you . . .'

They walked into the kitchen. Eleanor saw a grey-haired gentleman in late middle age, wearing a smart city suit, carrying a carefully furled black umbrella in one hand and a capacious-looking briefcase in the other. When the man saw Eleanor sitting calmly at the kitchen table, he looked alarmed, his gaze switching to Cara almost fearfully.

'This is Madam Eleanor,' Cara told him. 'Mind your manners now, and go and change.'

She waited until the bemused man had hurried into what Eleanor had assumed was the kitchen pantry before sitting down again and picking up her coffee cup.

'Don't take any notice of George – he's here to clean the kitchen.'

'He's *what*?' Eleanor spluttered.

'Here to clean. Have you never had a slave, Eleanor? I'd recommend it – they're generally very thorough, and free, of course. All it costs me is the occasional thwack across the rump with this.' She picked up the riding crop and swished it through the air. It made a faint whistling sound and Eleanor winced as she imagined it coming down onto bare flesh.

Cara laughed softly at Eleanor's expression.

'Try not to let him see you're shocked. Contempt and ridicule are fine, but shock would make him feel defensive. Ah, here he is now. Do hurry up, George – I want you out of here within the hour.'

'Yes, Madam, of course. I'll start with the surfaces, shall I?'

'Whatever – just snap to it!'

Eleanor gazed at George, who had stripped off

his clothes and was now wearing nothing but his shoes and socks, a plastic apron which did nothing to conceal his nakedness and a headscarf tied around his head like a Forties housewife. It was all Eleanor could do not to burst out laughing, but Cara shot her a warning look and so she concentrated on pouring herself more coffee.

From the corner of her eye, she could see George clearing the kitchen work surface before arming himself with a scouring pad and a cream cleanser. No wonder Cara's kitchen sparkled! she thought to herself, watching him scour the work tops.

As soon as he'd finished, he filled a bucket with soapy water and went down on his hands and knees to scrub the floor. His skinny buttocks waggled furiously as he scrubbed. Cara got up and, with a wicked look at Eleanor, gave him a half-hearted *thwack* across the bottom.

'Put some effort into it, George,' she said. 'Madam Eleanor and I are going downstairs to get changed.'

'But Madam, I thought—'

'Quiet!' she silenced him with a word, ignoring the disappointment written clearly across his face. 'Let yourself out, George, when you've finished, but see to it that you do a good job! If you do, you may come back on Tuesday at ten, and I'll allow you to clean downstairs as well.'

'Oh, thank you, Madam!' George said, his features transformed with joy as he bent his head and pressed his lips against the top of Cara's foot.

Cara bent down and patted him on the top of his head absently, as she might have patted an obedient dog.

'Come on, Eleanor – it's time for us to get changed.'

Eleanor followed Cara out of the kitchen, still bemused by the sight of George, his headscarf slightly awry, scrubbing the kitchen tiles.

'But what pleasure could he possibly get out of that?' she asked.

Cara shrugged. 'I've never really thought about it. I've had George for two years now, before that he was Pandora's.'

'You mean, she passed him on?'

'Something like that.' Cara flashed her a grin. 'George is getting a bit long in the tooth now – Pandora has a guy in his late twenties who isn't averse to straight sex when she fancies it. I can see you're shocked, but it's an ideal arrangement for a single woman. No housework to worry about and sex on tap.'

'I'm sure it is,' Eleanor said faintly.

Cara laughed. 'Wait until you see my dungeon!'

Eleanor realised that the steps down which they were walking lead to the cellar, but she was totally unprepared for the sight which met her eyes as Cara opened the door and stood aside to let her pass.

'What do you think?' she asked, an unmistakable note of pride in her voice.

Eleanor walked in and looked around her. She

was standing in the middle of a large, square room which was painted entirely in black. Black walls, black ceiling, black tiles on the floor. On one wall there was a rack holding a neat array of whips, canes, crops and various manacles. Along one of the longer walls was an arrangement of metal rings embedded into the brickwork.

There was a small handbasin in one corner, the sanitary ware looking incongruously white against the black background. Looking up, Eleanor saw that there was a contraption attached to the ceiling which looked like a pulley. At the end of the room there was a couch, much like those found in hospital examination rooms. Beside the couch was a trolley set with disposable gloves, a jug, a bowl and various lengths of rubber hosing. Eleanor glanced at Cara questioningly.

'Don't worry, I've made sure that today's clients are all fairly straightforward – I thought that too many bodily fluids might put you off.'

'Yes. Um . . . what do I do now?'

Eleanor was aware that she sounded nervous and she took several deep, calming breaths. Walking over to her, Cara gave her shoulder a reassuring squeeze.

'Now we get changed. Don't worry – this is going to be fun! I promise.'

Passing her an uncertain smile, Eleanor followed her into the small changing room concealed behind a door beside the wash basin.

Once they were dressed, Cara passed her a leather eye mask.

'Marcus explained that you wanted to guard your privacy – this will disguise you, and add to the fun for my clients!'

'Who have you got coming?' Eleanor asked as she eased the mask over her eyes. It was surprisingly comfortable, fitting neatly over the bridge of her nose.

'The first one is a Mr Porter. He's a regular, comes for straightforward CP once a month.'

'CP?'

'Corporal punishment. Pretty tired stuff.' Cara smiled wickedly and crammed her hair up into a mortarboard.

She was wearing a tight rubber mini-dress which outlined every curve of her perfectly proportioned figure. Her legs were encased in black fishnet tights and rubberised boots which reached to mid thigh. While they were talking, she quickly made up her face, so that by the time they were both ready, she was virtually unrecognisable as the fresh-faced young girl who had greeted Eleanor at the door.

'Are you ready?' Cara asked her.

'As ready as I'll ever be!' Eleanor admitted.

'You'll be fine. You look good anyway,' Cara added, holding her head on one side as she ran her eyes over Eleanor from top to toe. 'Good enough to eat!' she added.

Once again, Eleanor felt a small *frisson* of

excitement, tinged with alarm. There was no time to dwell on it though, for as Cara opened the cellar door, they heard George let himself out, just before the doorbell rang.

'Wait here,' Cara said as she went slowly up the stairs to let her client in.

Eleanor didn't quite know what to do with herself. In the end, she opted to lurk in the shadows in the corner of the room, wanting to see and weigh up Cara's client before he saw her. Mr Porter, when he appeared, was a small, nervous-looking man with a smooth, boyish face which went uneasily with his elderly body.

'Madam Eleanor!'

Eleanor snapped to attention as Cara called her and she stepped out into the pool of light shed by the single, unshaded lightbulb.

'Y-yes, Madam Cara?' Aware that she sounded unacceptably timid, she cleared her throat and repeated herself more firmly. Cara nodded at her approvingly.

'I found this . . . pipsqueak,' she said, nudging the man with the tip of her forefinger contemptuously, 'skulking outside on the doorstep. What did you think you were doing, Porter?' she barked.

The man cowered away from her, but Eleanor noticed that his eyes were bright, watching Cara's face avidly. There was a thin covering of sweat on his upper lip and he was breathing rapidly, through his mouth.

'I'm sorry, Miss,' he said fawningly.

'Sorry isn't good enough,' Cara sneered. 'What do you think, Madam Eleanor – six of the best?'

'Oh . . . at least!' Eleanor replied gamely.

'You hear that, Porter? My colleague thinks you deserve more than six!'

The man paled slightly, though he nodded his head.

'Oh yes,' he said eagerly, 'if Miss thinks so!'

'Go and chose a cane then, you miserable boy.'

Mr Porter scurried over to the rack and took his time selecting a long, bamboo cane. Eleanor watched in bemusement as he picked up a long, springy example and touched it almost reverently to his lips before passing it to Cara.

'Right. Trousers down and over the chair.'

As she spoke, Cara drew out an old-fashioned wooden chair and positioned it in the middle of the room. Eleanor felt like a spare part, until Cara directed her to stand beside the hapless Mr Porter, so that she would have a grandstand view of the proceedings.

Waiting until he was lying across the chair, his trousers and underpants pooled around his knees, Cara swished the cane through the air theatrically. Mr Porter trembled, his buttocks, very white under the glare of the bulb, shivering with either cold or anticipation.

Eleanor stared at Cara, who gave her an exaggerated wink. The cane sang through the air and landed across the lower part of his buttocks, neatly striping the point where his thighs and buttocks met. Eleanor's sharp intake of breath matched Mr Porter's. Cara raised her arm again and brought the cane about an inch above the original site.

'The trick,' she told Eleanor as she waited for Mr Porter to regain his breath, 'is to make sure that the cane never touches the same line twice. We're aiming for a series of neat, thin red lines, no broken skin. Isn't that right, Porter?'

'Oh yes, Miss,' he gasped, clenching his buttocks as he sensed that she was about to administer another blow.

Eleanor winced as the third was swiftly followed by two more.

'What have we got to, Madam Eleanor?' Cara asked.

'Er . . . five,' she answered.

'One more should suffice for today I think.'

Cara was perspiring and Eleanor noticed she was slightly out of breath as she striped Mr Porter's buttocks just below the tail of his spine. This was clearly hard physical work, which accounted for Cara's strength.

'Could you apply the salve?' she asked Eleanor, nodding towards a large pot of cream on the shelf.

Eleanor said nothing, but she brought down the jar and opened it. Mr Porter was still lying prone across the chair, his buttocks no longer white but a flaming red. Could she bear to touch him? Fighting down her instinctive distaste,

Eleanor scooped out a generous amount of the cooling cream and slathered it across the wretched man's buttocks.

His skin felt hot, burning against her palm as she smoothed the cream across his flesh. Mr Porter moaned, though it seemed to Eleanor that it was more with pleasure than with pain.

When she had finished, she turned to Cara, who had been watching her closely. She smiled.

'Good. Wash your hands while I see Mr Porter out.'

Mr Porter was already dressing, gathering his dignity as he fastened his clothes. Though he walked a little stiffly, there was little trace of the excited, cringing individual who had walked in. Cara treated him accordingly, fussing over him and taking his money at the door.

'Well?' she said as she came back downstairs and began washing her hands. 'What did you think?'

'I'm totally perplexed!' Eleanor admitted. 'What on earth was that all about? I mean, he didn't even have an erection, never mind ejaculate – what on earth did he get out of it?'

'It's a common misconception that men who like to be beaten tie their obsession in with a climax. There are many like Mr Porter, who get their kicks through physical pain – it doesn't have to have much to do with sex. The atmosphere, the direction of a Mistress and the actual punishment itself is enough.'

'How can you bear it? I mean – it's enough to put you off men for life!'

Cara gave her an odd look. 'I've never been that keen anyway. There are an awful lot of submissive men out there, Eleanor, far more than most people realise. We've got time for a quick coffee before the next caning.'

Over coffee, Eleanor questioned Cara more.

'You did very well, by the way,' Cara told her. 'If you'd like to get gradually more involved with each client, I've booked in someone rather special for our last appointment – someone we can have a bit of fun with!'

Intrigued, Eleanor asked her to elaborate, but Cara would not be drawn, merely smiling enigmatically whenever Eleanor mentioned their final appointment. Over the following hours, they saw three more men, on whom Eleanor practised her fledgling whipping skills.

The first time she picked up a cane and brought it down across bare flesh, she did it with little conviction, wincing as she imagined herself administering pain. Gradually, though, she realised that her enthusiasm for her task was part of the unspoken contract between herself and the client and she tried harder.

There was something rather satisfying about the precision required when striping white skin with bands of pink. It was made easy by the fact that the men were mere faceless ciphers to her, a pair of buttocks waiting to be warmed or, in the

604

case of one man, a body to be wrapped in Sellotape which was then slowly peeled off.

By the time the final client was due, Eleanor was tired and hot and almost as blasé as Cara. Then the client walked into the room and, suddenly, all her weariness disappeared.

He was gorgeous – six feet two, early thirties, slim and healthy-looking. His hair was short and a glossy brown, his jaw square with an attractive cleft in the centre. Eleanor would never have taken him for a submissive, but for the way he looked at her, shyly from beneath his long, dark eyelashes.

'This is Tod,' Cara told her, caressing his arm lazily through the thin shirt he wore. 'He's less of a client, more of a friend, so we can take our time. Enjoy ourselves, maybe. Goodness knows, we deserve it!' she said, rolling her eyes at Eleanor. 'Meet Eleanor, Tod.'

Tod smiled, showing perfectly straight, white teeth, and enclosed her hand in his. His grip was strong and confident, and Eleanor found herself responding to him.

'Pleased to meet you, Tod,' she said, aware that he was looking deeply into her eyes, which were partially obscured by the eye mask. 'Um . . . why are you here?'

He laughed and shrugged.

'I like playing games,' he explained. 'When I'm between girlfriends I come to Cara.'

'Okay, that's enough talk,' Cara said briskly. 'Strip off your clothes, Tod, and lie on the bed.'

Eleanor watched in amazement as with a quick, almost shy smile in her direction, Tod immediately removed all his clothes and lay down as instructed on the couch. He had a well-moulded, smooth body, evenly tanned. His cock was straight and strong-looking, lying semi-erect against his belly.

Cara smiled at him and picked up a blindfold.

'Close your eyes, darling,' she cooed as she tied it around his head.

Glancing across at Eleanor, she indicated that she should pick a selection of manacles from the rack. Then she secured each of his wrists and ankles in turn, so that he was lying spread-eagled on the examination couch.

Eleanor was aware that she found the sight of him, naked, bound and helpless, rather arousing. He had a beautiful body, it was true, but she knew that it was not that which was moving her, but his vulnerability. Tied and blindfolded, he was completely at their mercy.

Cara caught her eye at the very moment when she acknowledged her own growing excitement. She smiled at her, beckoning her over with a crooked finger and offering her a bottle of oil. Touching a finger to her lip to indicate that silence should be maintained, she mimed that Eleanor should massage the oil over Tod's upper body.

Eleanor took the bottle, but did not act immediately. Instead, she stood at his head, looking down at his body, and waited, watching how he tensed, all his senses alert as he wondered what was going on. Gradually, his muscles tautened to the point where Eleanor knew he was ready to fight or take flight, and she could sense the rush of adrenalin through his veins. Only then, when she had eked out the tension for as long as possible, did she lift the bottle high and trickle the thick, oily fluid over his chest and belly.

Tod jumped at the first contact of the cold oil against his skin, his breath emerging on a small hiss of surprise. Putting the bottle aside, Eleanor flexed her fingers and, leaning over him, began to massage the oil into his chest.

Cara nodded at her and, picking up the oil, went to massage his feet. The two women worked in silence, oiling him carefully all over. Eleanor could feel the rubbery points of his nipples brushing against her palms as she worked over the steady thud of his heartbeat. His skin felt smooth and warm, responding to the tactile pleasure by rising up in small goosebumps.

Eleanor felt as she had when Lars had been presented to her – totally in control. It was a powerful feeling, arousing her in a way that was deep and satisfying. The young man bound to the couch trembled beneath her touch as she stroked his skin, mirroring Cara's movements at the other end of the couch.

'How do you feel, darling?' Cara said after a while.

'Wonderful,' Tod admitted, 'but won't you take off the blindfold? I'd love to be able to look at you both.'

'All in good time,' Cara replied mildly. 'First I want to warm you up a little.'

He shuddered with anticipation as Cara fetched two small many-fronded whips from the rack. Passing one to Eleanor, she showed her how to fasten it onto her wrist with a loop, so that the main body of the handle was held at the base of her palm.

Tod gasped as Cara flicked the leather tendrils across his thighs in a sweeping motion. Eleanor followed suit, working her way across his chest and down to his belly with small, flicking motions. It wasn't hard enough to be significantly painful, but it was bracing enough to bring the blood to the surface of his skin, turning it pink.

She noticed that his cock had risen in response to the intense stimulation, and she couldn't resist trailing the ends of the fronds along it, noticing how he squirmed with anticipation. Cara shook her head.

'Use this,' she said.

'This' was an odd-looking contraption, like a harness, made of leather, which Eleanor soon realised was designed to slip over the penis, flattening it down as the strap was buckled around his waist.

'You're too cruel, Cara,' Tod moaned, clearly loving every minute.

'*Now* I think we'll take off the blindfold,' she said, ignoring him.

It wasn't until Tod's eyes were following them slavishly as they walked together round the bed that Eleanor realised quite how exquisite a 'punishment' Cara was meting out. Strapped to the bed, his cock subdued by the leather harness, Tod could only look, not touch.

Smiling at her, Cara reached towards Eleanor and unfastened the top button of her leather waistcoat.

'Mmm . . . Give Tod a peek at these, darling,' she said, running the tip of her finger lightly along the line of her cleavage.

Feeling out of her depth suddenly, Eleanor went obediently to lean over Tod so that he could look down the front of her waistcoat at her bare breasts.

'Aren't they lovely, Tod?' Cara was saying, making Eleanor supremely self-conscious. She looked round in surprise as the dungeon door opened and Jeanette stepped inside.

Cara went over to her and the two women embraced. Then, to Eleanor's intense discomfort, they kissed deeply, their bodies entwining as naturally as any lovers of long standing.

'You've met Jeanette, haven't you?' Cara asked when they finally broke apart.

'Of course,' Eleanor replied, at a loss to know what to do. 'It was at the club.'

Jeanette smiled at her and, striding across the room, kissed her on both cheeks.

'We didn't get time to talk in the club, Eleanor, which is why I've gatecrashed today – I'd love to get to know you better!'

Eleanor was aware that she was very conscious of the light scent of Jeanette's perfume and of the softness of her skin as she pressed her cheek against hers. She'd never noticed another woman in that way before, and the unexpected awareness confused her.

'Pretty,' Jeanette commented, turning her attention to Tod. 'Is it nice and tight?' she flicked the cock harness negligently with one long fingernail, making Tod groan.

'Yes,' he replied through gritted teeth as his nerve endings protested.

'Good. You can relax for a while now,' she told him, slowly peeling off her coat to reveal that she was naked underneath it. 'Cara and I want to play with Eleanor for a while. If you turn your head to one side, you're welcome to watch. Eleanor's going to try a little mild S & M herself – isn't that right, Eleanor?'

Eleanor gaped at her. At once the cellar seemed claustrophobic, the black walls and ceiling closing in on her, making it difficult to breathe.

'What?' she whispered.

Cara came up behind her and slipped her arms around her waist.

'It's a little surprise – we thought you might welcome a new experience.'

'But . . . no thank you, I wouldn't like it! It

doesn't appeal to me at all.'

Even as she said the words, Eleanor knew she was lying. The idea of these two beautiful women tying her up and tormenting her as she had so recently been tormenting Tod sent an unmistakeable *frisson* zinging through her veins.

Jeanette was watching her closely. 'I think you *would* like it, darling. I promise we won't really hurt you, just tease you a little. If at any time you want us to stop, you only have to say so.'

'Do say yes, Eleanor,' Cara said softly. 'It would be such fun!' As she spoke, her long fingers were gently circling her nipples encased in the leather waistcoat.

Swallowing, Eleanor opened her mouth and heard her own voice emerging, as if from far away.

'All right,' it said, and she knew that she was lost.

Chapter Eight

THEY TIED HER with silk scarves so that her arms were pulled apart at shoulder level, bent upwards at the elbow and secured at the wrists to the rings embedded in the ceiling. Eleanor was conscious that the gentle restraint was not unpleasant, that there was something almost liberating about being placed in position like this. She felt as if she was abdicating all responsibility for her own body, handing over to them the burden of care.

She protested slightly when Cara knelt at her feet and fastened a thin metal bar between her ankles which forced her legs apart.

'I don't think—'

'Ssh! Trust me,' Cara said, her voice resonating with suppressed desire. 'It will be better this way.'

Eleanor realised that there was something

dangerously thrilling about having her legs forced apart like this and held in position, but the logical side of her brain still protested.

'Please, I'm not happy with—' Jeanette silenced her, most effectively, by kissing her.

Eleanor had never been kissed by another woman before, and at first she instinctively resisted the pressure applied, and the instant rush of pleasure that followed. She gritted her teeth and held her lips rigid, rejecting the teasing probe of the other woman's questing tongue.

It was useless. Jeanette's lips were soft and sweet-tasting, coaxing her own apart. Eleanor responded with a small sound of distress as her mouth opened under the gently insistent pressure of the other woman's and admitted her tongue.

Jeanette probed softly, putting her arms around Eleanor and pressing her against the firm, curvaceous contours of her own body.

'Relax,' she murmured as she broke away. 'Allow yourself to enjoy.'

Eleanor stared at her, wide-eyed. Though the kiss had been pleasurable, though every muscle and sinew now trembled with anticipation, her inherent discomfort with anything non-heterosexual held her back.

'I've never done this before. I'm not a lesbian,' she protested feebly as Cara began to unfasten her waistcoat.

Jeanette smiled at her as if understanding her dilemma.

'You don't have to be a lesbian to enjoy yourself with other women. You're safe here – forget yourself for a while, Eleanor.'

'Go with the flow!' Cara interjected softly.

'That's right. And afterwards we'll send you back to the man in your life with a new dimension, so you'll have even more to give . . .'

The man in her life? Eleanor thought of Rhys and what he would make of this. Would he understand? *Does it matter?* A small voice in her head asked her. After all, though she hoped he would benefit in the long run, this was primarily for her and her alone.

'This is for you,' Jeanette murmured in her ear, unwittingly echoing her tangled thoughts.

Eleanor shivered as Cara bent down and enclosed one tumid nipple in her hot mouth. Gathering up the whole breast in one hand, she flicked the centre with her tongue, sending tremors of delight through Eleanor's entire body. Her mouth was so soft, her teeth grazing lightly over the sensitised flesh of her areolae, making her gasp.

As Cara worked on her breasts, her mouth at one while she caressed the other with her fingers, Jeanette moved behind her and traced the outline of her bottom in the tight, rubberised skirt with her hands. Eleanor was aware of her body responding, blossoming like a flower under the women's combined caresses.

Glancing across at Tod, still spread-eagled on

614

the bed, she saw that he was watching her. Their eyes met and held and Eleanor recognised her own need reflected in his. Both were at the mercy of these two women, both craved release and had reached the stage where they would do anything to get it.

'Oh!' Eleanor gasped as Jeanette eased her skirt up over her waist and traced her fingertips round the seam of the open-crotch tights.

Curling her fingers round the edge, she eased them apart so that her entire vulva was exposed. As if at a hidden signal, Cara stopped kissing and sucking at her breasts and stood up. Eleanor saw that her features seemed blurred by her own pleasure and she strained forward, wanting to give in to the sudden urge to kiss the other girl on the mouth.

Cara allowed her to touch her lips in a kiss all too brief, then she moved away. She smiled as she produced a blindfold and advanced. Eleanor panicked.

'I don't want you to whip or beat me,' she said emphatically.

'Of course not, darling,' Jeanette said from behind her.

Reaching round to stroke her breasts for a moment, she slipped the waistcoat off her shoulders before taking the blindfold from Cara.

'There's more than one way to play this game,' she whispered enigmatically.

Eleanor closed her eyes as the blindfold

blocked out the light. She felt almost frighteningly exposed, vulnerable in a way she had never felt before. Imagining how she looked, naked from the waist up with just a rucked-up skirt around her middle and the ruins of her tights around her knees, she felt doubly exposed. It was worse, somehow, than being completely naked. More shameful.

'All right?' Cara murmured and, despite her reservations, Eleanor nodded.

Having worked with Cara all afternoon, she knew she was in the hands of an expert, even though it seemed now that it was Jeanette who was calling all the shots.

It was Jeanette who reached round her now and covered her breasts with her warm, oil-covered hands. In much the same way as Eleanor had worked in tandem with Cara, now Cara and Jeanette worked together to oil and prepare Eleanor's body for – what? Eleanor shivered, not so much with fear, though she was afraid, but with excitement.

The sweet, almond-scented perfume of the oil hung heavily in the air, making her feel quite dizzy. Something in it made her skin tingle and grow warm, until eventually she felt as if she was glowing all over. The warmth reached into her, so that she could imagine the source of the glow was within, radiating outward.

Would they go against her wishes and whip her? Eleanor shuddered at the thought, instinctively aware that she would not enjoy any kind of physical pain. As both women stood back for a moment, she tensed, half expecting a blow. The soft brush against her skin took her by surprise.

'What is that?' she said.

'Ssh.'

The object stroked down from her collarbones, between her breasts, and swirled around her navel. It felt like – like a feather. The most exquisite sensations trickled through her as Jeanette began to stroke her from behind with another feather. Her body felt light, almost weightless as they stroked her in a choreographed pattern, so softly she wondered if she was going to be able to bear it. Not quite a tickle, but close enough to it for Eleanor to virtually hold her breath in anticipation.

Her breasts hardened, her nipples cresting into two aching little peaks as the tip of one feather was swirled around them. She heard Tod groan and imagined his cock rising against the cruel restraint of the harness, aching to be free.

'Let me untie you, Tod,' she heard Cara say. 'Do you have any objection, Eleanor?'

Eleanor thought of the contrast of the firm, masculine body against the softness of the two women and shook her head. She felt as if she was on fire, the entire surface area of her skin sensitised beyond endurance by the feathers they had used to stroke and tease her.

She moaned softly as Jeanette's fingers moved

delicately over her labia, knowing that they were swollen and moist. As Jeanette stroked them, they opened, welcoming her fingers in, and Eleanor gave a small sob of submission as she entered her with two fingers.

'Beautiful,' Jeanette murmured against her hair, 'so warm and lovely. I'd like to lick you, Eleanor, I'd like to press my tongue in here and taste the sweetness of you.'

'Oh! No . . . I . . .'

'But I know you'd prefer it to be a male tongue. Pity. Luckily though we've got a willing male right here. On your knees, Tod darling.'

Eleanor tensed as she sensed Tod kneeling in front of her. She could feel his warm breath against her thighs, could hear the way he tried to control his ragged breathing.

'No hands now, Tod,' Cara commanded him, 'just your lips and tongue.'

Eleanor heard the soft whistle of a whip through the air followed by Tod's sharp intake of breath as it landed across his back. He leaned forward and touched the apex of her labia oh-so delicately with the tip of his tongue.

'That's good, Tod,' Cara purred, her long fingers stroking idly down the slope of Eleanor's breast. 'Nice and slow . . .'

'How does it feel, Eleanor?' Jeanette asked, her voice caressing her, adding to the building tension.

'Good,' Eleanor admitted as Tod's tongue slid

along the swollen folds of flesh towards the entrance to her body.

The leg-spreader held her legs apart at a set distance, thwarting her desire to edge her feet outward. Instead, she wriggled her hips, tilting up her pelvis to give him access to the silky passageway, which ached and wept with need.

Gone was the reluctance, the denial – in their place was a raging, all-consuming desire that swept away every inhibition in its path. At that moment, Eleanor knew, it did not matter if the tongue that pleasured her belonged to a man or a woman, it only mattered that it should not stop.

Tod's tongue was stiff and insistent, sliding into her, bringing his nose against the burning promontory of her clitoris. Eleanor's breath began to hurt in her chest as her heart raced in time with the pulse beating between her legs. Perspiration ran between her breasts and down her sides, mixing with the oil that was still to be absorbed by her skin.

'I'm going to remove the blindfold now.'

Eleanor barely registered Jeanette's words; she had withdrawn into a deeper sensual realm, beginning the inexorable journey towards orgasm. She blinked as the darkness eased, taking some time to refocus her eyes.

Jeanette went to take Cara into her arms and, with a seductive smile in Eleanor's direction, began to kiss her. Jeanette held Eleanor's eye as she plundered the other girl's mouth, their expression challenging her not to find the sight arousing.

Eleanor could not deny that it was. Cara, slender and fair, her deceptively fragile-looking body bent over Jeanette's arm, was a perfect foil for the darker, sturdier Jeanette. No less beautiful, but more statuesque, she held Cara almost protectively, capitalising on the aura of control that surrounded her.

Aesthetically speaking, the sight of the two women kissing so passionately was quite lovely, providing a pleasant spur to Eleanor's race to climax. But it was the man on his knees in front of her who provided the focus to her passion.

Tod was working tirelessly at the sensitive folds between her thighs, his expression rapt as he licked and nipped and sucked at her quivering flesh. His cock, still bound cruelly at his belly, had swollen to the point where Eleanor knew that the constriction must be causing him pain, for the criss-crossed leather thongs that made up the harness were biting into the flesh of his shaft.

Cara must have realised this too, for she broke away from Jeanette and released him before resuming their embrace. Eleanor felt Tod's gasp of relief as his penis sprang free and she bore down against his lips.

The scenes being enacted around her: the two women kissing and caressing each other with growing passion; the man kneeling at her feet, pleasuring her with his mouth whilst moving the skin back and forth over his penis with his own hand; the thought of herself bound and oiled, helpless in the face of such relentless seduction – all these things took on a surreal quality, making her feel as though she was an actor in some weird and structureless play.

Yet, in another way, it made perfect sense. Her body certainly thought the situation ideal. Rushing headlong towards climax, Eleanor cried out, bucking her hips and mashing her pelvis against Tod's face. The black-painted dungeon seemed to disintegrate before her eyes into a swirling kaleidoscope of colour.

As if from far away, Eleanor heard Tod gasp as he reached his own crisis and she sagged against the silk scarves that bound her, mind and body closing down as she sought to contain the maelstrom of sensation that rioted through her.

Then all grew silent, save the sound of her own breathing, intermingling with the laboured panting coming from Tod, and the sighs and gasps of the two women as they sank together onto the cellar floor.

Eleanor felt vaguely dissatisfied as she walked back to the house. After they had released her, Cara, Jeanette and Tod had been so unnervingly matter-of-fact about the whole affair that Eleanor felt quite disorientated. Obviously, such encounters were commonplace to each of them, but to her the experience had been a one-off, an aid to her self-education that, though she had enjoyed it at the time, she didn't think she would want to repeat.

It all seemed so cold, somehow. The fact that she had been able to react at all was testament to how far she had come using the 'retraining' techniques Marcus was exploring. She acknowledged that she was able to enjoy the sensual experience, but felt curiously bereft without the involvement of her heart and mind.

That was what was missing. Sex was all very well, but one had to feel *involved*. Eager to discuss this with Marcus, Eleanor quickened her pace.

As soon as she let herself into the house, Eleanor sensed that all was not as it should be. It was quiet, for a start, which was unusual at this time of the day when Marcus was normally finishing work for the day and Maggie was preparing dinner.

She knew he was in, because his hire car was parked in its usual spot outside. Perhaps he was changing before dinner? Deciding to let him know she was back, Eleanor ran lightly up the stairs. Dropping her bag and jacket into her own room, she then continued along the landing to Marcus's.

Her steps faltered as she approached and she heard an unmistakable sound through the half-opened door. A woman's sigh, low and redolent with passion. Eleanor considered turning back to her own room, but curiosity got the better of her, keeping her where she was. Who on earth could Marcus have in there with him?

Edging towards the door, Eleanor found she could see almost the entire room reflected in the dressing-table mirror which was angled in such a way that she could see it from the door. Marcus was standing at the end of the bed, his eyes half closed, his head thrown back. From his expression and the fine film of perspiration on his forehead, Eleanor guessed that he was near to coming – and no wonder, for, kneeling at his feet with his cock in her mouth, was the housekeeper, Maggie.

Suppressing the initial dart of shock, Eleanor found herself taking in every small detail of the scene. Maggie was naked, her dark hair loose, flowing over her shoulders to cover her breasts. It fell forward to conceal her expression, but she gave every appearance of enjoying fellating him, her body undulating in time with the movement of her head.

Eleanor could see the fine sculpture of her spine from the nape of her neck to her tail. Her body was slim and pale, the skin almost translucent in the daylight, peppered with freckles.

Marcus too was naked. It was the first time Eleanor had seen him without his clothes and she liked what she could see. His chest was broad and nicely defined, lightly furred with dark, silky-looking hair. He looked stronger than he did when his body was covered; his biceps bulging as he tensed in the throes of orgasm.

He opened his mouth on a shuddering sigh as he came. Eleanor felt her own sex-flesh stir in empathy as she gazed at the expression on his face. It was one of pure bliss, transforming his features from ordinary handsomeness to true beauty.

Maggie reached up to hold him by the buttocks as she swallowed his emission, her eyes closed, as if receiving a benediction.

Then, as Eleanor watched, Marcus opened his eyes and looked straight at her in the mirror. Their eyes met and held, his dark and smouldering, hers wide and excited. There was no need for words, they communicated by look alone.

Later, his eyes said to her. *Yes*, she signalled back, and by unspoken consent, she withdrew before Maggie saw her. She walked back to her room on shaking legs, stunned by what she had witnessed. It was like an echo of the scene she had stumbled across in Michael's office – someone she cared about making love with someone else. Obviously her feelings for Marcus did not compare with those she had held for her husband, but the principle was the same. Now, as then, she was beset by conflicting emotions. A sense of shock, betrayal, emotional pain, but most of all, a churning excitement.

It was that feeling that she hung onto as she went back to her room to wait for him. That, and a quiet confidence that, this time, she knew exactly what she wanted from him.

Chapter Nine

HE DIDN'T MAKE her wait for long. Eleanor heard Maggie go downstairs, presumably to start the dinner. She wondered, briefly, how long this had been part of the general routine – and how was it that she hadn't noticed? Then she realised that she didn't really care. Marcus was her mentor, her guide through the hitherto unfamiliar territory of sexual experience. She had no claims on him, nor did she want any. But, at that moment at least, she did want him.

'Eleanor,' he began as he walked through her door half an hour later, but she held up her hand to silence him. He looked at her questioningly and she stood up slowly. Holding his eye, she took a step towards him.

'Fuck me, Marcus,' she said.

He looked at her for a long moment.

'Just like that?' he said.

Eleanor smiled faintly. 'What's the matter, Marcus? Are you worried you might have created a monster? We should retitle your book: *From Celibacy To Nymphomania The Marcus Grant Way – How To Learn To Love It.* Or is it just that you're afraid that you can't control the result of your experiments?'

His eyes darkened and she realised that she had angered him. So much the better – she was determined that this time she would elicit some real emotion from him. Even a negative emotion like anger was better than the clinical indifference he normally contrived to display.

'That's not very fair,' he said with infuriating calm.

Eleanor ignored him. She felt hot and restless, her skin prickled and a dull pulse beat an insistent tattoo between her thighs.

'I want you to use all your expertise, all your experience to enable me to put into practice the lessons I've learned over the past few weeks. You said that any woman could "retrain" her sexual responses. Well, here's your chance to test your theory for real.'

'What do you mean?'

'I mean that I've changed, probably beyond recognition. The woman you met at your hotel in London would have run a mile if you'd tried to make a pass at her. Now I'm asking you to fuck me. Thoroughly. Now.'

Marcus advanced into the room. As he came

627

closer, Eleanor saw that, far from being unaffected by her blunt admission that she wanted him, he was having difficulty controlling his breathing and the fabric of his trousers was stretched tight. The image of him standing in front of Maggie as she fellated him flashed into Eleanor's mind, fuelling her desire. Her innate love of voyeurism no longer worried her; she had lost the sense of shame that had spoiled her enjoyment before. Now she used the images she had seen to stoke the fire of her passion.

She stood up and, holding Marcus's gaze, began to undress. Between her legs, her vulva, already sated by Tod in Cara's dungeon, felt heavy and moist. Her breasts also felt full and heavy, her nipples hardening in anticipation of his touch.

The one time they had come together it had been brief and savage, with no time to linger, or relish the giving and receiving of pleasure. This time she wanted it to last, to wring every last vestige of sensation out of him.

Marcus undressed too, in silence, the tension stretching between them, lengthening in the fading light of dusk. There was no tenderness in the way they looked at each other, no real feeling, just the swift, inexorable climb towards sexual frenzy. Eleanor didn't want tenderness. With a clear-mindedness that astounded her, she knew exactly what she wanted from him – passion.

To this end, she evaded him as he reached for

her, enclosing his erect cock in her hand instead and caressing it skilfully.

'Do you want me, Marcus?' she asked him, her voice low and husky.

'Isn't that obvious?'

'I want to hear you say it.'

She flicked her fingertips across the sensitive spot where his cock and scrotal sac met and his eyes momentarily closed.

'Yes, I want you, Eleanor,' he admitted through clenched teeth.

Eleanor leaned forward so that he could feel her warm breath brush his face.

'How much?' she whispered.

Marcus made a deep, primaeval sound, deep in his throat and his hand shot out to catch her at the back of her neck. Though she resisted for a moment, Eleanor knew at once that she was no match for his superior strength and she gave in gladly, lifting her face to his as he crushed her against him.

Letting go of his cock, she brought her arms up, around his neck as he kissed her, hard, grinding her lips against her teeth with a savagery which sent the adrenalin surging through her veins. Aware that what they were doing was closer to fighting than making love, Eleanor revelled in her new-found power to arouse.

Marcus's hands were hard as they moved urgently across her skin. His lips, as they moved from her mouth to her neck, were not gentle, nipping and sucking at her skin so that she shivered with growing excitement.

She felt so hot, as if she was glowing in the dusk, incandescent with desire. She let the feelings flow through her, no thought now of trying to control herself, or of suppressing her deepest, darkest desires. Following her instincts, she began to caress Marcus as he was her, pressing her lips against the tender place behind his ear before biting gently on the fleshy lobe.

As his fingers kneaded the softness of her breasts, so she raked her nails down his back, scoring the skin in her enthusiasm and making him suck in his breath.

'Jesus, Eleanor!' he gasped.

Clasping her head between his palms, he kissed her again, more urgently now, smothering her face with kisses as he manoeuvred her so that her back was against the cold plaster of the wall. Eleanor was barely aware of this small discomfort, she was swept along by the tide of his desire, completely caught up in the battle being enacted between them.

And it *was* a battle. Locked in an exclusive duel, neither wanting to concede to the other, they became steadily more frenzied. With Marcus's hard, lean body pressing her against the wall, Eleanor felt as if she couldn't breathe. Yet she revelled in the wholly masculine strength of him, welcoming the sensation of being overwhelmed, willing, in her mind at least, to submit to him.

Their eyes clashed and held, his dark and stormy, reflecting the tumult of emotion in hers. He didn't touch the melting place between her legs, merely lifting her with his hands at her waist and bringing her down on the strong shaft of his cock.

Eleanor moaned and brought her legs around his waist. Looking deep into her eyes, Marcus pressed her back against the wall and thrust into her, his fingers digging into the soft flesh of her waist. In response, Eleanor gripped him with her internal muscles, moving her hips so that after every savage thrust, she held onto him for a second longer than he wanted her to.

She could see from the look in his eyes that he was determined to maintain his formidable control, that he intended to triumph over her by making her come first. To this end, he shifted position slightly so that her pelvis was tipped forward. This meant that with every inward stroke, her clitoris was stroked by the slippery shaft of his penis, sending electric thrills of delight through to her womb.

Determined that he would not better her, Eleanor concentrated on milking him, squeezing rhythmically with her pelvic floor muscles until his breathing became rapid and his eyes began to glaze.

'How do you like what you've made of me, Marcus?' she whispered as the sweat broke out on the surface of his skin. 'How do you like a real, live, "retrained" woman enclosing you?'

'Eleanor . . .'

'You're going to come, Marcus. You're going to show me how much you appreciate the fruits of your research.'

'No . . .'

'Yes . . . oh yes!' She laughed softly as she saw his control slip away. 'Let it go, Marcus,' she murmured throatily.

Surreptitiously, she reached between them and pressed the pads of her fingers against the most sensitive spot at the base of his scrotum. Marcus's eyes opened wide and he regarded her with surprise as he was tipped over the edge.

'Yes . . . Eleanor . . . ahh!'

Eleanor wrapped herself around him as his orgasm broke, grinding her clitoris against his pubic bone to precipitate her own climax. Marcus sagged against her, and they slid down the wall together, still connected, still shuddering with the after-shocks of pleasure.

It was a few minutes before Marcus recovered. When he raised his head to look at her, there was a quiet fury in his eyes that sent a dark thrill along Eleanor's spine. He withdrew from her and they both lay on the floor, regarding each other warily.

'That felt more like anger than desire,' he said after a few minutes.

Eleanor flushed.

'Perhaps it was,' she admitted.

'Why?'

'Maybe I felt you needed teaching a lesson.'

'Teaching a lesson?'

'For your arrogance.'

Marcus shook his head.

'You're something else, you know that?' he said. 'It was your idea to use yourself as a test model – remember?'

'I remember.'

'Then don't turn on me because you regret it.'

'Regret it?' Eleanor laughed. 'I don't regret it, Marcus. But I'm not made of stone. I know what you've been doing.'

'Then perhaps you'd care to enlighten me?'

'As if you need enlightening!' Eleanor retorted, suppressed anger fuelling her words. 'You've teased and tested me until I didn't know whether I was on my head or my heels! Setting up my "research opportunities" whilst all the time pretending that you were nothing more than a scientist conducting an experiment!'

Marcus looked uncomfortable.

'I had to try to stay objective!' he said defensively.

'But you didn't, did you?' she taunted him. 'You wanted me, right from the start. But instead of being honest about it, you set me up so that you could watch and enjoy my responses without ever having to get involved yourself. It must have given you a shock that night when I pounced on you! How did it feel, Marcus, to be used as part of an experiment? Did you feel dehumanised? *Used*?

633

Did you, Marcus?'

'What's this really about, Eleanor?' he asked her quietly after a few minutes.

Eleanor stared at him, then, to her horror, she burst into tears. Marcus reached out to comfort her, but she turned her face away.

'No, damn you, I don't want your tenderness! Don't you understand? You've "trained" me to want sex, not affection. Goddammit, Marcus, I want you to make love to me!'

He waited until she had wiped her eyes on a tissue he passed her from the box on her bedside table.

'Make love to you?' he said.

'Yes. If it's not too much trouble!'

He smiled faintly.

'As opposed to fucking you?'

'That's right.'

'Okay. You only had to ask – we didn't have to go through that charade.'

Eleanor opened her mouth to protest that, had he wanted to make love to her, he wouldn't have waited for her to ask him, but she closed it again as she caught the look in his eye. Already, he was hardening again and she moved towards him.

'Shall we get up onto the bed?' he suggested. 'We'll be more comfortable there.'

He helped her up, then lowered her gently onto the covers. Eleanor felt herself relaxing, the restless, prickly feeling that had overcome her the first time conspicuous by its absence. Marcus kissed her, gently at first, then with more urgency. His hands were gentle on her body this time, stroking and caressing her, his fingers curling slowly into the hot, wet folds of her sex, seeking out her most sensitive places.

Cradling her head against his shoulder, he played her like a fine musical instrument, drawing out the pleasure until she felt like sobbing with the exquisite tension. When she came this time, it was with a rippling ecstasy, suffusing her with heat and making her want to stretch, like a cat, from head to toe.

Marcus lay back on the covers, watching her through half-closed eyes. Eleanor watched him in turn, knowing that, good though her climax had felt, there was something missing.

She reached for him, feeling him harden under her palm. The skin of his penis was smooth and velvety over the rigid core. Eleanor played her fingers up and down its length, watching his face for his reaction. A small pulse beat in his jaw as she cupped his balls with her hand and squeezed gently, brushing her fingernails across his perineum.

Seized by the same restlessness she had experienced earlier, she knelt up and straddled him, guiding the tip of his penis to the entrance to her body. Marcus looked at her expectantly, reaching up to caress her breasts as she sank down on him.

He filled her, his rigid shaft stretching the walls

of her vagina, knocking against her womb. Leaning back from the waist, she intensified the penetration, little shards of pain slicing through her, making her lean towards him again. Slowly, she began to ride him, lifting herself up to the point where it felt as though he would slip out of her before sinking back down again, enclosing him.

Beads of perspiration filmed his upper lip and Eleanor dipped her head to dab at them with her tongue. Marcus held her close, rising up so that they were sitting facing each other, joined at the centre. They rocked back and forth, he barely moving at all inside her, yet setting up a vibration that seemed to travel through her, even along her limbs.

They kissed, urgently, deeply, and Eleanor felt his climax pulse along his cock before he shuddered convulsively, and came. Gazing into his eyes, she saw that he was sated, satisfied with their encounter. And at that moment Eleanor knew, with utmost certainty, that she was not. Passionate though it had been, though his technique was, technically, as close to perfection as she guessed it was possible to get, there was still something missing. And whatever that elusive something was, it was central to her happiness.

'What are you doing?'

Eleanor turned to find Marcus watching her from the doorway of her study. His expression was wary and she sighed inwardly. How could she explain something that she didn't understand herself?

'I'm going home,' she told him.

'Before the end of the project? Isn't this a bit sudden?'

She shrugged.

'Perhaps, in one way. I'm not reneging on my part of the deal, Marcus, I just feel that it would be better if I write the concluding chapters away from here. I need to distance myself from you, and your side of the project.'

'Why?'

'Call it an intuitive whim.'

Marcus stepped inside the room, his expression thoughtful.

'I thought last night was . . . good,' he said, a note of caution apparent in his voice.

'It *was* good, Marcus. But I need to get away.'

'All right. But so soon? Won't you stay another night at least, talk it over?'

Eleanor shook her head.

'No, my mind is made up. I've learned all I needed to learn. The research is over, my education complete. Last night was my graduation, if you like. Now I need space to draw my conclusions.'

She thought, for a moment, that he would continue to try to dissuade her from the course she had chosen, but he lifted his hands in a small gesture of helplessness.

'Okay. I guess I can telephone and fax you in the

637

Valleys?'

'Of course.'

He nodded, flashing her a small smile.

'I fly back to the States on the thirtieth.'

'I'll send you the manuscript in good time.'

'Nothing I can say will persuade you to stay?'

Eleanor thought of the peace of her home and shook her head.

'Then I wish you a safe journey, until we meet again.'

'Thank you, Marcus.'

Eleanor kissed him impulsively on the cheek then, overcome by a sudden, urgent desire to be on her way, she picked up her bags and walked quickly out of the door. She could sense his all-seeing, all-knowing gaze on her even after the door swung closed behind her. But she did not look back, not once.

Chapter Ten

LOOKING OUT OF the window of the train taking her home, Eleanor marvelled at how everything looked the same. Such momentous changes had occured within her over the few short weeks of her absence, she almost expected the lush, green fields to be sparkling with diamond-bright dew, for rainbows to criss-cross the sky.

She smiled to herself at the fancy. In truth, she did see things differently, though in more subtle ways. Colours seemed to be sharper, flavours more defined, she was more attuned to everything around her. It was as if she had spent her life with her head inside a paper bag, never really noticing what went on around her. A period of looking inward, of being deliberately self-obsessed, seemed to have sharpened her perceptions generally.

Rhys was waiting for her at the station. He was

wearing old jeans and a faded rugby shirt and his hair was tousled by the wind blowing along the platform. Eleanor thought she had never seen him look more handsome and she felt her spirits lift, her heart turning a little somersault as she caught sight of him, and she hurried to get out of the train.

'I didn't expect to see you!' she said.

Moving into his arms seemed like the most natural thing in the world. He looked a little taken aback by the unrestrained warmth of her greeting, but his arms came about her without hesitation and he kissed her upturned face with unconcealed affection.

'Welcome home, *cariad*,' he said gruffly.

Eleanor gazed up at him and realised, with a jolt, that 'home' was here, in his arms. She hadn't realised quite how much she had been looking forward to seeing him, how much she had hoped that her 'casual' mention on the phone that she would be arriving on this train would prompt him to meet her.

'Are you free for the rest of the day?' she asked him as he picked up her bags and walked with her along the concourse.

'I'm on leave until Tuesday next,' he told her, 'so I can drive you all the way home, if that's what you were thinking.'

Eleanor laughed softly.

'Actually, I was wondering if you might be able to stay. If you'd like to, that is,' she added hastily, struck by a sudden, inconvenient shyness.

Rhys stopped walking and turned to look at her.

'Do you mean what I think you mean, Eleanor?' he asked her, his eyes scanning her features as if hoping to find the answers to all his questions in her face.

Eleanor reached up to trace the rugged outline of his cheek with her fingertips. She knew that she was looking at him with love in her eyes, and that he would know how she felt.

'Yes,' she answered, 'I'm ready now.'

Rhys didn't say a word, though his pupils dilated and his jaw tightened as he took her by the hand and they began walking again.

There was a tension between them in the car, but it did not cause an unpleasant atmosphere. Emboldened by her own feelings, Eleanor leaned her head lightly on his shoulder as he drove, confident that she would soon be able to express the way she felt about him in a way that would convince him once and for all.

Poor Rhys – he had had to wait for so long! Yet she knew now that there had been a purpose to his long vigil, that she had needed to find herself before she was ready to share her life with him. She had to learn to love herself before she could be ready to allow someone else to love her.

At the cottage, Dylan and Thomas greeted her with typical feline disdain and stalked past her without so much as a glance. The house felt unlived in and they went around throwing all the windows open wide to allow the fragrant sea air to waft through.

They met on the landing, each of them stopping on either side of the stairwell as if caught unawares by the presence of the other. Eleanor sensed the tension in him as he waited for her to speak and knew that what happened now would affect her always.

She smiled, stepping forward out of the shadows to take him by the hand.

'Love me, Rhys,' she said softly.

'Always,' he murmured in response, walking with her into the small, oak-beamed bedroom.

He dwarfed the room by his presence, having to dip his head as she led him over to the ancient bed beneath the sloping roof. Eleanor turned and smiled at him, aware of an inward trembling that had nothing to do with desire and everything to do with the fear that it wouldn't live up to her expectations. Having conditioned herself to climb the sexual heights, what would she do if making love with Rhys was dull? Or – oh Lord, don't let it happen – if he rejected her now?

She needn't have worried. Such thoughts flew from her mind as he reached out and traced the outline of her cheek with his forefinger, before cupping her face with his hand. Eleanor turned her head and kissed the warm, dry creases of his palm and he responded by brushing his thumbpad across her lips.

All his attention seemed to be focused on her

642

mouth as he caressed the soft, fleshy inner surface of her bottom lip. Eleanor could sense the tension building in him, and knew instinctively that he was as nervous of beginning this as she was. They had both waited so long that they were afraid that the reality might not live up to the expectation.

There was only one way to find out. Trembling, Eleanor touched his face, brushing her fingertips lightly over his lips and closing the small gap which was still between them. Rhys sighed, a yearning, ragged sound, then he put his arms around her and touched his lips against hers.

It was like setting light to touchpaper. Desire rose up between them like a flame, rapidly turning into a conflagration as the kiss deepened and they clung together. Eleanor barely noticed that they had moved until she felt the edge of the bed behind her knees, then Rhys was lowering her slowly onto it, his firm, hard body covering her, imprinting its shape onto the softness of hers.

She was conscious of the unique scent of his skin as she pressed her face against his neck as he removed his weight from her. It was a fresh, woody smell, wholly masculine, and she breathed it in deeply. Then the sensations of sight, sound, smell and taste merged into a blur, subjugated to the pressing need to touch and be touched.

Rhys helped her out of her clothes, pausing every few seconds to kiss and touch the warm flesh he had uncovered. Though she was conscious of a sense of urgency, Rhys was clearly in no hurry, wanting instead to savour every moment of this long-awaited first time together.

He smiled at her when she finally lay naked on the covers and there was such a tenderness in that smile that Eleanor felt unexpected tears brim in her eyes.

'What is it, *cariad*?' he asked, his eyes darkening with concern.

'Nothing,' she whispered. 'Only that . . . I never thought this would happen between us.'

'If you're having second thoughts—'

'I'm not,' she interrupted him, pressing the tips of her fingers against his lips to silence him.

'Good. Because after tonight, Eleanor, we will belong together you and I, just as we always have, but bound by something far more sacred.'

Eleanor gazed at him, awed by the solemnity of his expression and the feeling behind his words. He was looking at her expectantly, as if holding back until she had given him some sign of commitment. She felt herself smiling, wanting to express the joy she felt.

'I know. Make love to me, Rhys.'

He smiled again, only this time there was something about the way he looked at her that sent a shiver along her spine. There was an intensity in the depths of his eyes that set a small pulse beating at the centre of her.

Rhys held up his hand and Eleanor touched his

spread fingertips with hers. The warmth of his skin seemed to spread through her fingers, into her hand and down her arms. Slowly, their fingers entwined, their hands meshing as if one hand, and Rhys held it against his heart. He didn't need to say anything, she could feel his heart thudding in his chest, strong and regular, but a little faster than normal, and she knew that he felt the same way as she did, that he wanted her just as much as she wanted him.

He lowered his head, so slowly, to place a kiss on the tip of one breast. The nipple responded instantly to the tiny caress, hardening and drawing into a small peak of need. Eleanor moaned softly as Rhys teased it with his tongue before, taking pity on her, he drew the aching nub into the warm, wet cavity of his mouth.

Eleanor tangled her fingers in his hair, holding his head against her breast as he pulled it deeper into his mouth. Her womb cramped with longing as he sucked, the sensitive folds of flesh between her thighs swelling and moistening in direct response.

'Oh, Rhys,' she whispered, her voice shuddering.

His hands were at her waist, smoothing the skin, sending little ripples of delight along her nerve endings. She moaned in protest when he levered himself away from her, until she realised that it was only to enable him to remove his clothes.

Eleanor watched through narrowed eyes as he undressed, taking a voyeuristic pleasure in looking at him. His shoulders were broad, the muscles of his upper arms bulging as he pulled his shirt over his head. There was a fine smattering of blond hair on his chest, but his skin was smooth and velvety over the steel of his pecs, his nipples pale and flat.

'You look like you work out,' she commented, reaching out a hand to trace the definition of his stomach muscles. They contracted under her palm as she inched her hand lower to the fastening of his jeans and she smiled wickedly at him. 'Let me take these off.'

Rhys said nothing, but Eleanor could tell by the way he held himself, so still, as if afraid of breaking the moment, that he wanted her to undress him. Standing at the side of the bed, he held himself rigid as Eleanor slipped the buttons through the buttonholes on his fly front and eased the stiff denim smoothly over his hips.

Underneath, he was wearing plain white jersey boxer shorts which clung to the outline of his erection, delineating it lovingly. Eleanor pressed her cheek gently against the length of him, making him tremble, before peeling the briefs down, over his taut buttocks and down his thighs.

His cock was strong and straight, the circumcised tip smooth and pink. As she watched, a tear of fluid streaked the neat slit and she dabbed at it with her tongue, absorbing Rhys's deep sigh of pleasure.

'Eleanor—' he began, whatever he was about to say cut off by the shock of having her lips enclosing the bulbous head of his penis.

She drew him deeply into her mouth, relishing the taste and texture of him, wanting to show him how much she loved him. Rhys stood very still, careful not to give in to the instinct to thrust his hips forward and force himself further inside her mouth. Eleanor was aware that his breathing had grown shallow. His fingers caressed her hair and he murmured ragged endearments as she flicked her tongue along the underside of his cock.

Reaching beneath him, Eleanor stroked the taut, hair-roughened sacs at the base of his penis, pressing gently against the seam.

'Eleanor – wait!' Rhys cupped her jaw with his hands as he withdrew from her.

Eleanor looked up at him quizzically, through her lashes.

'Not yet,' he said softly. 'We've got all night . . . let me look at you.'

He pushed her gently onto her back, one hand reaching beneath her to cup her buttocks, his fingers pressing softly into the crease between them. Eleanor bent her legs at the knees as he tipped her pelvis up, exposing her most intimate flesh to his loving gaze.

Eleanor knew that she was swollen and moist, that the plump, slippery folds of flesh would be a dark rose pink, suffused with blood. There would be no mistaking the extent of her arousal, no doubt how much she wanted him now. She was proud that her body had responded so readily to him.

'So beautiful, *cariad*,' Rhys breathed, his fingers stroking lovingly along the open channels of flesh.

Eleanor shivered and reached for him, wanting to feel his mouth against hers as he pleasured her. They kissed, deeply, tongues caressing, lips nipping and sucking, drawing the sweetness from each other. Eleanor drew away, arching her neck and closing her eyes as the first shards of sensation pierced her. Rhys moved her clitoris, instinctively knowing how much pressure to apply and how fast to move his fingers. He leaned over her, watching her face as she came.

As she opened her eyes, she found herself staring straight into his eyes. He held her gaze as he eased her legs apart and touched his cock against the stretched membranes of her vulva. There was a question in his eyes which she answered gladly by reaching round to place her palms on the taut planes of his buttocks.

He eased into her, inch by inch, so that she was aware of her vaginal walls stretching to accommodate him, her muscles contracting to draw him in further. Rhys's eyes glazed over as he began to move inside her, and Eleanor knew that, this time, it would not take long for him to come.

She was right. He gasped her name as his seed surged along his shaft and Eleanor clung to him, revelling in the way he had given himself to her, wholeheartedly, without holding any part of him back.

'Oh Eleanor,' he whispered when, at last, it was over.

She smiled at him and laid her head against the tender cup of his shoulder. Five minutes, she decided. That's how long she would give him to recover . . .

This time, with the first urgent need assuaged, Eleanor was happy to take her time, to discover as much about him as she could. Rhys lay back and let her explore his body with her fingertips, lips and tongue, until she felt she knew every part of him, and he was hard again, his cock rearing up from his groin like a sentinel, as potent as ever.

Eleanor felt no need for foreplay, she merely straddled him and sank down on his cock. Once he was inside her, she sat very still, enjoying for the moment the simple sensation of him filling her. Their eyes met and held and Eleanor surprised an expression in his that she couldn't quite interpret.

'What?' she said, 'What is it?'

Smiling, Rhys reached up to hold her at the waist.

'I was thinking how magnificent you look, sitting there like that. I always thought you were the woman for me, Eleanor – now I know it. Without the slightest doubt, I know it.'

Before she realised his intention, Rhys flipped her over so that he was on top of her, then, to her dismay, he withdrew.

'Roll over,' he said.

Eleanor responded to the gruff note of command in his voice with a thrill of delight. Only briefly did she recall that this was how Michael had always taken her. Aware that Rhys had breached her final taboo, Eleanor sighed as he sank into her, raising her hips to ease his path.

Folding his body over hers, Rhys held her, one hand balancing his own weight, the other splaying across her pubis, the middle finger finding her clitoris. Eleanor felt it reawaken under his touch, a small pulse throbbing deep inside her.

Turning her head, she found his mouth and kissed him. She came, seconds before he did, the convulsions of her inner sex triggering his own climax. Collapsing in a tangle of sweaty limbs, they curled together under the covers, laughing as they stuck together. Rhys cradled Eleanor in his arms and she pressed her lips against the thud of his heartbeat. Within minutes, they both fell asleep.

The path to *Becoming Sexual* will be a different one for each and every woman, a personal odyssey that only the woman herself can prescribe. Each of us must find our own way to shangri-la. To do so we have to learn to trust our own instincts, to know that we are the best judge of what is right for us.

There is only so much that can be learned from books and videos and the sex gurus of our times. There is no real substitute for personal experience. The main use of a book such as this is to spread the word that it *is* possible to 'retrain' ones learned sexual response, that the ability to unlock our true sexual potential is there in each and every one of us.

As women, we owe it to ourselves to discover the extent of our propensity for pleasure. It doesn't matter how long it has been locked away, it *can* be released, but only *you* can set it free.

Equally, only you can decide what to do with it once it is found. Sex is a wonderful thing, the sharing of pleasures a profound and enduring delight. Yet I have come to realise in the course of my research for this book that sex, in itself, is not enough.

Eleanor paused, aware that this was the message she needed to get across to Marcus, that if she could make him understand this, he would understand, finally, everything that had happened during the writing of the book.

She wanted him to understand, and perhaps to look inside his own heart and realise what she felt was missing in his life. Willing the right words to come, Eleanor sat, fingers poised above the keyboard.

Love is the key. Without love the physical act is meaningless, a soul-less transaction between strangers. Yes, it is possible to 'become sexual' in the ways described in this book, it is possible to 'train' the mind and body to recognise certain stimuli and to react accordingly. But only when there is love between the two people involved can the physical act of sex transcend the mechanical and transport the participants to a plane of pure bliss.

Once on that plane, it is possible to realise that the true joy of becoming sexual is not for its own sake, but for the deepening of a loving relationship. The search for love will always be the nobler pursuit, for without it, there will always be something missing.

'Eleanor?'

She turned to see Rhys was awake, gazing at her through sleep-glazed eyes as if surprised to see her there.

'What are you doing?'

Eleanor smiled at him.

'Just finishing my part of the book. Don't worry – go back to sleep.'

'Alone?' he said, smiling wolfishly at her.

Eleanor shook her head with mock exasperation.

'Rhys Wynn-Jones, you are insatiable!'

He watched her as she stood and unfastened her robe, letting it fall to the ground. Holding his eyes, she slipped beneath the covers and slid luxuriously into the warmth of his embrace, knowing that it could only bring her joy.

Epilogue

RHYS NEVER DID find out the part Eleanor played in the writing of *Becoming Sexual*. Even when the book caused a stir and media speculation was rife about the female guinea-pig described, he never seemed to connect the character with Eleanor. Or so she thought.

Eighteen months later she received a Jiffy bag from the States containing a copy of the American version of Marcus's next book. Opening it, she raised her eyebrows at the title.

In Search of Love.

Flicking through the pages, she realised that, this time, Marcus had used himself as his research tool, acting on the conclusions that Eleanor had drawn at the end of their joint project. Turning to the flyleaf, Eleanor saw that there was a printed dedication there.

To Eleanor, she read, *without whom this book*

would never have been conceived.

Underneath it, Marcus had written in his bold, neat handwriting, *You were right, and I was wrong — thank you!*

There was an envelope tucked into the pages addressed to Mr and Mrs R. Wynn-Jones. Curious, Eleanor slit it open and drew out the single white card inside. It was a wedding invitation.

'So he listened to you, then?'

Eleanor jumped as Rhys came up behind her silently and slipped his arms around her waist. His hands rested comfortably on the growing bulge at her waistline and Eleanor leaned into him automatically.

'You knew?' she said, the significance of what he had said only just hitting her.

'Of course.' There was a smile in his voice which dissipated some of the nervousness that had seized her when she realised that he had known all along about the part she had played in Marcus's last book.

'But you never said . . .'

'You'd have told me, if you wanted me to know.'

He kissed her hair and Eleanor closed her eyes for a moment, breathing in the dear, familiar scent of him.

'And you don't mind?'

Rhys turned her in his arms and she saw that his expression was serious.

'Eleanor,' he said, 'whatever it took – all that matters to me is that it brought you back home to me.'

Eleanor gazed at him, her heart filling with love as it did every time she looked at him. To be so well loved still amazed and overwhelmed her. She hoped that she never lost the wonder of it.

'Marcus has invited us to his wedding,' she told him.

'So he found love.'

'Apparently.'

Rhys scanned her face.

'What do you think of when you think of him?'

Eleanor could feel a blush stealing into her cheeks. Aware that Rhys was watching her closely, she knew that nothing but total honesty would do.

'I feel . . . warmly towards him, I suppose. I'm glad he's found someone. And no, before you ask, I would never have wanted it to be me.'

Rhys smiled and his face seemed to clear.

'When is the wedding?' he asked her.

Glancing at the invitation, Eleanor saw that it was scheduled to take place in California, in June.

'It'll be too close,' she said, laying a hand protectively on their unborn child.

'Perhaps it's just as well.'

'Oh?'

Rhys shrugged, a small, self-deprecating gesture that tugged at her heartstrings.

'I do understand, honestly, *cariad*. But I'm only flesh and blood – I don't really want to meet him.'

Eleanor smiled and moved into his arms.

'I'll write,' she said, 'to wish them well.'

Rhys nodded and touched his lips against hers.

'If they have half the happiness that we have—'

'I know. I think Marcus has learned as much from me as I did from him.'

'We won't speak of it again, then,' Rhys said, his lips brushing softly against hers.

'No,' she agreed. 'It was only a brief moment in time. You and I have our whole lives to look forward to together.'

'Yes, *cariad* – together,' Rhys echoed as his mouth claimed hers for his own.